THE TR

LIGHT

SYNDROME

BY

ROGER PARKES

ISBN-13: 978-1533508348
ISBN-10: 1533508348

To "My Little Man" Josh.

CONTENTS

INTRODUCTION

A sinister plot by Russia to infiltrate the British government, while taking over key positions in the trade union movement. The story revolves around the upsurge in communist activities and their effects on the country's ability to move on from the ravages of war.

Polly Spencer and Daniel Bottomley get caught up in the conspiracy, as their special relationship continues.

Following on from ***The Secrets Container***, ***The Traffic Light Syndrome*** is the second book in the trilogy.

CHAPTER 1

It is early March 1952, and the nation is still mourning the death of their King. He was much loved by everyone, and will be missed very much.

"Well I thought it was very good, Daniel, but I like the circus anyway," says Polly, as she arrives back with Daniel to his apartment after a visit to the local picture house. They had been to see 'The Greatest Show on Earth', a story about a circus. Daniel opens the door to the apartment to find an envelope on the mat addressed to him.

"Not really my kind of film, Polly. Next time can we go and see a western, or even a war film?" he asks, as he opens the letter, and reads the contents with interest.

"If you are interested to know the involvement of the Communist Party membership with the current newspaper strike and active plans to extend the strike further into Fleet Street, call this number." The letter has no name or address, just a telephone number. The newspaper dispute, involving London newspapers, was already two weeks old with no signs of a settlement. Daniel rings the number from the letter.

"Hello?"

"This is Daniel Bottomley."

"Mr Bottomley, thank you for getting back to me, I may have some information that could be of use to you."

"Who are you and what can I do for you?"

"My name is Peter Hennessey, and I am an official in the Print Union. I am concerned by what is happening with my union and proposals to escalate the strike into Fleet Street. Perhaps we could meet?"

"Most certainly, Mr Hennessey. Do you know the cafe in Kensington High Street? We could meet there tomorrow," Daniel suggests.

"Very well, shall we say about midday?"

"That's ok with me, I will see you around midday, bye for now."

"What did he say, Daniel?" asks Polly, curious.

"He wants to meet me, he says he has some information about communist interference in the strike by print workers."

"The communists seem hell-bent on wrecking our survival, Daniel. Are they as big a threat as is being suggested? I hear things in the office which are very frightening."

Polly is working in the Civil Service, as a junior in the Home Office, so may hear conversations relating to communist agitators every day. The Home Office has a responsibility for policing and monitoring insurgents who would plot against the government for political ends, so communist agitators figure high on their list of priorities.

"The threat seems to grow each day, Polly, so I am interested in what this man has to say. It would be very useful for me to have a man on the inside I could trust."

Daniel and Polly go off to their work the next morning, after spending some time talking over the contents of the letter. Polly says she will keep her ears open for any information that may help Daniel. Whilst appreciating her help, he insists that she does not put herself in any danger. Meanwhile, at midday, Daniel walks into the cafe on the High Street to meet with Peter Hennessey. There is just one person sitting alone, so Daniel walks toward him.

"Mr Hennessey, I'm Daniel Bottomley."

"Hello Mr Bottomley, thank you for coming. I will get straight to the point, and tell you a bit about myself. I am ex-army, and knew of you from the raid five years ago on the tunnels at New Haven; I was with Major Baxter. You and your colleagues became quite famous over your exploits, so it was not too difficult to locate you. Now, I am a branch official of the Electrical Trades Union, based in Hammersmith. We have a very active branch and are fully committed to the strike action against the London press. Part of my job is to attend regional and national trade union meetings for the E.T.U. which lately has been dominated by political activists with no allegiance to the E.T.U. or any other union for that matter. They are well educated and good at putting forward their argument, which is to bring down the Tory government. They want a national strike and to promote civil disobedience by the public," Peter Hennessey concludes.

"What you are saying is very serious, do you have any proof of what is being planned, and more relevant, do you have any names that we can investigate?"

"I can give you names and details of meetings, but we need to meet somewhere less conspicuous please," Peter Hennessey comments.

"We can meet at my apartment, you already know my address. Perhaps you can telephone this number when you are ready to meet again. It cannot be traced, and will simply record anything you say," says Daniel, handing him his address details and the number.

"Thank you Mr Bottomley, now I have to go. Goodbye."

Daniel returns to his offices and tells Conrad of his conversation with Peter Hennessey.

"This could be the break we have been looking for, Daniel. A union official ready to help our investigations, sounds almost too good to be true," says Conrad with some scepticism.

"I agree, Conrad, but we have to listen to what he has to say and take it from there." They both agree that a weekend meeting would be preferable, since Peter Hennessey would have more freedom to go anywhere at that time, rather than a weekday. And Polly is going home this weekend, so that will present an ideal opportunity to meet in her absence.

"I don't want her to be around when Hennessy calls. We know nothing about him so we need to proceed with caution, Conrad. So now we wait for him to call."

They don't have to wait long, Hennessey leaves a message on Thursday saying he will meet Daniel in his apartment, at two o'clock on Saturday. Daniel arranges to have some recording equipment sent to his address so that he can record their conversations for his superiors to study. On Friday afternoon, he goes with Polly to Euston and sees her safely onto the train to take her home for the weekend.

"Enjoy your weekend, Polly. I will be here for you on Sunday around five o'clock," says Daniel as he waves her goodbye. He will miss her not being with him, but knows how important her visits home are, and in this case he does not want her around when Hennessey calls. He does not want her exposed to anything that may be a danger to her now or in the future. Meantime, Daniel and Conrad meet up to discuss tomorrow's meeting with Peter Hennessey.

Peter Hennessey arrives at Daniel's apartment promptly at two o'clock and settles down in an easy chair. Daniel introduces him to Conrad, and tells him that he intends to record their conversation, although he will remain anonymous.

"That's ok Daniel, so long as my name is not mentioned," he says as he drinks the tea that Daniel has offered him.

"I have written down some of the details, since I did not know you would be recording our conversation."

"Before we hear what you have to say, why especially are you offering this information?" asks Conrad, still sceptical about Hennessey and what his intentions are.

"I have been a trade union member all my working life, and passionately believe in the trade union movement. It is important in a democratic society that the workers have a voice strong enough for the establishment to appreciate. I do not want to see my union or any union taken over by extremists with their own agenda, and with no interest in serving their members. I believe this is what is happening at the moment, and that is why I am here."

"And you have evidence that this is happening?" Daniel asks.

"Yes I do. I have four names for you to look at, Michael Doyle, Bill Hornsby, Jim Baxter, and Jack Makepeace. All four men are active at branch and national levels. They do not appear to have jobs, yet have active roles within the union movement. Doyle is a very good speaker who constantly advocates public disorder to achieve the best results. He does not seem interested in local union activity, his only interest is in marshalling the membership to agree to a national strike. Bill Hornsby has no background that I have been able to find. I have talked generally with his members in Lambeth, but no one knows where he came from. He has a strong Liverpool accent which gives a clue, but how he got into the print unions in London is a mystery. He constantly advocates the communist ideal of a classless society governed by workers' cooperatives. I firmly believe he has contacts within the Communist Party who fund his activities. Colin Brodie and Jack Makepeace are both hard-nosed activists, who can best be described as troublemakers. They are both ex-army and enjoy being involved in violence, wherever it may take them. They have spent time in Liverpool recently, meeting with dockers, trying to persuade them to withdraw their labour. They are both big men and can be very convincing with any argument. I do not want to see the trade union movement bullied into making undemocratic decisions to satisfy the communists' doctrine. Unless we stop men like this, the union movement will become simply a tool to destabilise our society and everyone in it. You have the contacts, I am sure, Mr Bottomley, to stop this happening."

"Well sir, you have certainly given us plenty to discuss with our colleagues, and we thank you for that. Your revelations are serious by their very nature, although we were not entirely ignorant over what is happening. We would welcome any more information that you are able to offer. Please leave it, as before, by telephone message. Is there anywhere we might leave a message for you should we wish to make contact?" asks Daniel.

Hennessey leaves them a number where he can be contacted in the evening, and leaves the two men to their thoughts on what has been said.

"Well Daniel, he certainly has given us plenty to think about, hasn't he?"

"I think we should arrange a meeting with Fitz first thing Monday morning about this, Conrad. We have to decide what we are going to do with the information Hennessey has given us. If what he says is correct then you and I are going to be busy. If we can find out what the main players intend, then we can pass on the information to those concerned who can be prepared to take whatever action may be needed," Daniel concludes.

'These men sicken me with their doctrines. They convince the workers they are on their side, whilst their true agenda is the breakdown of all that we regard as priceless, a democratic way of life where we all get the chance to make decisions for ourselves," replies Conrad with anger and frustration.

"You're absolutely right, Conrad, but for now we shall put it to one side and enjoy the weekend. Are you ready for something to eat?"

The two men go off to have some lunch and a beer, talking at length about how they can use the information from Hennessey. Their work remit is clearly defined, to find out what the communist agitators are doing, and how they are being influenced by the politics of the party itself. Are they simply troublemakers with no real agenda, or is there an underlying threat to the nation from their actions?

Both Daniel and Conrad have the expertise, dating back to WW2, and were considered ideal to head up a department with special reference to the communist threat and its consequences. Whist their work would normally have come under the umbrella of MI5, they are in fact attached to the Home Office. It was felt that they would be able to operate with more flexibility from here, since they did not know who or what they were up against. If there was 'an enemy within' they would be better equipped to deal with it from outside of MI5.

After lunch together and enjoying a beer, Daniel and Conrad go their separate ways, ready to take up their conversation again on Monday morning. Daniel has a leisurely Saturday and Sunday and arrives at Euston in plenty of time to meet Polly's train due at five o'clock. He is always glad when Polly returns, since he misses her when she is not around him.

"Polly, over here," he calls as he spots her getting off the train. Polly dashes up to him and they both hug each other.

"Daniel, it's good to be back, I have missed you even though it has only been a couple of days!" she says, holding on to his arm as they walk from the station.

Their relationship has blossomed over the last five years. From staying with Daniel over weekends, when she was still at school, to eventually moving in with Daniel, Polly's feelings for him have matured with her. The same can be said of Daniel. They are two people very much at ease in each other's company and their feelings for each other are obvious for all to see. Daniel has enormous respect for Polly, and has been careful not to allow their feelings for each other to spoil their long friendship. Eventually their relationship will grow into a physical one, when the time is right for both of them. For now, they will continue to enjoy being together very happy in each other's company. Daniel tells Polly about Hennessey coming to the flat and his revelations to Conrad and himself. She is surprised that he would want to confide so much information to Daniel at their first meeting.

"I think this man is scared by what is happening around him, Polly. He is frustrated at seeing his union, for which he is passionate, being used in the way that the communists and the agitators are using it for their own ends. I believe he is very sincere and wants us to help."

"Then you must do whatever it takes to destroy these evil people. You remember how those terrible men that Daddy brought down tried to ruin the country, well these men are doing the same thing. You must stop them, Daniel."

"We will do whatever we can, Polly, and you can keep your ears open for me, but be careful, do not put yourself in any danger. You must promise me," says Daniel firmly.

"Perhaps I should speak with Beatrice Carrington, she may be able to help," Polly replies.

"It may be best not to involve Beatrice at this stage. I know you get on well with her, but I do not wish to compromise her very special position and I am sure that Ben still makes contact with her from time to time."

"Ok Daniel, it was just a thought."

"Good, now shall we go and get something to eat?"

On Monday morning Daniel meets with Conrad and they proceed to the office of their head of department.

"Are you free at all, Fitz?" Daniel asks.

"I am. Please come in, both of you." William Fitzroy Jones is a former captain in the S.A.S. with service in Palestine and Cyprus. A tall man in his forties, he was in the army for ten years, before resigning his commission to take on a special role for MI5 involving the investigation of the British Communist Party. This involved finding out what they were up to within the organised labour market, the trade unions, and taking steps to undermine their activities. Whilst he enjoyed some success, he wanted to operate away from MI5, since he believed there was too much internal politics within the organisation, and he was restricted in his investigations concerning Civil Servants. Protocols and red tape made any progress painfully slow and he asked to be moved from MI5 control. He must have put forward a sound argument, because he now has his own team, headed by Daniel and Conrad, working from the Home Office. His remit still concerns the monitoring of communist activity in the organised labour market, and within the Civil Service. However, he now has more latitude for his operations, and reports directly to the office of the Department for National Security.

"What can I do for you two? Do you have some information for me from your recordings?" he asks with enthusiasm in his voice.

"We think we may have found inside help from a trade union official. He approached me, as I mentioned to you last week, and what he has to say you should find most interesting," says Daniel, as he sets up the recording for 'Fitz' to listen. As he listens, it is obvious that he is becoming more and more interested in the contents. It appears they have found a genuine contact inside the trade union movement.

"This is good, Daniel, this is very good. When are you seeing Hennessey again?"

"I will call him this evening, I wanted to put you in the picture to date before making any decisions. I would like to offer him the opportunity to work for us, supplying information, but wanted to run that past you for your comments."

"To have a man on the inside of the E.T.U. would be very beneficial. Do you think he will oblige us, your Mr Hennessey?"

"The man is completely disillusioned by what is happening to his union and I have some sympathy for him in that regard. He is genuine in his wanting to better the living standards of his members. But he does not have a political agenda, and believes the communists are manipulating the membership to further their own ends."

"They call it a workers' revolution, but we know that life under a communist regime is controlled for the benefit of the few at the top, not the workers."

"You should be able to get him on our side, Daniel, if what you say is true. Convince him that we are a better option, democracy and a free vote, than what these people are proposing. I need you to get into one of their meetings to see what goes on. Ideally, I would like to have a listening device planted where they regularly meet, speak with Phil Chandler about that, will you?"

"Ok Fitz, I will go and see Phil now and see what he can fix for me, and I'll contact Hennessey this evening."

He spends the rest of the day checking the names of activists known to them, communist affiliated, but not necessarily operating under the Soviets' instructions. The four names put forward by Hennessey are prevalent in the party in the London area, and one of them, Michael Doyle, is an E.T.U. executive member. The other three, namely Jim Baxter, Colin Brodie, and Jack Makepeace, are active in the union, stirring up trouble whenever they can, but he can find no record of them being in the Communist Party, although that does not mean that they are not members, just that they hide their membership. Daniel goes home that evening and finds Polly busy cooking a meal.

"Hello Daniel, how was your day?"

"Busy, Polly," he replies, and relates to her the discussions he has had about Hennessey.

"Do you think he will work for you, Daniel? Are you going to offer him money for his trouble?"

"I think he can be persuaded, Polly, but I will not offer him money, I want to test his belief in wanting to rid the union of the agitators. Once he is on board, I will then offer to compensate him for his troubles."

"I have been busy too, Daniel, and made some discreet enquiries about communists in the Civil Service. You would be amazed how many employees have communist sympathies."

"You must be careful who you talk with, Polly. We don't want you getting into any trouble asking questions," Daniel replies, a little concerned at Polly asking questions to casual acquaintances in her offices.

"I have only mentioned the printers' strike, that's all, but was really surprised how some people responded quite strongly, saying they should be supported and the government should step in and tell the employers to give them what they want. People are still angry about the continued rationing of things like meat, butter, cheese, and sugar, and the fact that a lot of cities still have bomb damage so long after the war has ended," says Polly.

"As I said, be careful what you ask these people, Polly. Someone may think you are being too curious."

Daniel meanwhile, phones Hennessey and arranges to meet him as soon as possible. He suggests the Science Museum, not too far from Daniel's apartment and usually where there are lots of tourists milling about. He arranges to meet with him the following afternoon around two o'clock. Polly has decided to heed Daniel's advice and does not pursue any more enquiries at her workplace. She is concerned that Daniel may become compromised in some way, so takes precautions by travelling different routes to and from Whitehall. Her suspicions are further aroused when she notices a man and a woman outside of their apartment block.

She is sure that they both work in the Home Office and mentions this to Daniel when he arrives home from his office.

"Are you quite sure these people are from the Home Office, Polly?"

"Positive Daniel, I have seen the woman several times, and the man is on the same floor as I am. What are they after do you think?" she asks nervously.

"I really don't know, I will start using the side entrance from now on. They obviously know you live here so you continue using the main entrance."

Polly's suspicions are further confirmed when she is approached on her way from work.

"Hello Polly, my name is Sally Nugent, I work in the Home Office. You have been asking a lot of questions about the union. Let me give you some advice, stop being nosy and mind your own business. Do you understand?" Sally Nugent tells Polly firmly.

"I only wanted to know how I could become a member, that is all I was asking."

"You don't qualify since you are still under review for a permanent position. Don't let me have to tell you again, Polly," she replies menacingly, and moves on with the crowd. Polly hurries home and tells Daniel what has happened.

"You have obviously upset someone, Polly. As I mentioned, leave things as they are for a while, I do not want you putting yourself in any danger."

"But Daniel, I want to help, really I do," she replies, giving him a hug.

"I know and I'm sure you will be a help as time goes on, but for now leave things as they are, will you do that for me?"

"Yes, ok Daniel, now what would you like to eat?"

The following morning, Polly is further reminded of being watched and targeted. When she gets into work, she opens her desk drawer to be confronted by a dead rat! Everyone thinks it very funny, so Polly shrugs it off as a joke, knowing it most definitely isn't a joke, but a warning. Daniel meanwhile walks to the Science Museum in Exhibition Road, arriving just before two o'clock.

"Hello Hennessey, thank you for coming. I thought this would be a good place to meet, plenty of people about and so on."

"This is ok, Daniel, so what did you want to see me about?"

"Well, I'll get straight to the point, Peter. I want to go to one of your meetings, ideally when Michael Doyle is due to appear."

"Well Doyle is coming to our branch headquarters next week, but getting you into a meeting might be difficult, every member's cards are checked at the door."

"What about the press, do you allow members of the press into meetings?"

"Not usually, but we could use some publicity. If you can get official documentation from one of the national newspapers, then you would probably be admitted."

"Good, I can arrange that, now how do you feel about keeping in regular contact, Peter?"

"What do you mean, Daniel? Are you asking me to keep you informed of union activities?"

"Only those activities which you believe are not beneficial to the members and are being voiced as part of a political agenda by members of the Communist Party. I am not interested in interfering in any way with the democratic process of your movement, but I am concerned about communist interference with union practices."

"I will have to think over what you are asking and let you know. As far as next week's meeting is concerned, can I call you and leave a message to confirm?"

"That will be ideal, and meantime I will arrange to get a pass as a reporter and hope that it will be enough to get me inside." And with that, Daniel leaves him to go back to work and report to Fitz on his meeting.

"I can arrange for your journalist credentials, Daniel. What are your thoughts about Hennessey passing you information?"

"I think he will, Fitz. He is disillusioned and I have assured him my only interest is in Communist Party activity within the union, nothing else."

"Ok, now any more news on Polly being followed?" Fitz asks.

Daniel relates what has happened to Polly, including the dead rat in her desk.

"You must tell her to be careful, Daniel, she could compromise your position. We need to be sure that Polly is the person they are watching and not you."

"We are taking precautions, Fitz. We do not travel together, and I enter and leave my building by a side entrance. I have also asked the porter to look out for any strangers loitering around the building. I don't believe we can do much more, just be careful."

"The point is, we do need someone who can get some information on the communists inside the Civil Service, but do not have anyone that I know of that we can trust. I propose that you invite me to dinner so that I may meet this young woman that is so special to you. What do you say?"

"I do not want Polly to be put in any danger, Fitz, and there must be some sort of contingency plan if she is compromised in any way. You are right in thinking she is very special to me and I cannot have her put at risk, whatever the rewards," Daniel replies firmly.

CHAPTER 2

Daniel goes back to his office to digest what has been said by Fitz regarding Polly. He has only just insisted that she stop any activity at work which may put her in danger, and now she is about to be asked to get involved in Daniel's activities, by Daniel's boss no less! Whilst he is reluctant for Polly to become actively involved with his activities, she is very well placed to secure information on any communist activities within her department. And if it can be arranged that she gets more responsibility in her job, allowing her to move around other departments freely, then she could be a real asset. Perhaps Beatrice Carrington could help with this and secure her position within the department. Daniel decides he will speak with Polly this evening, before their meeting with Fitz.

He leaves early and looks out at the front of the building to see if anyone is following Polly when she arrives. Thankfully, no one is either watching the building or following Polly, so it would seem that threat has been removed. As usual, Polly enters the apartment and rushes toward Daniel, giving him a hug.

"Daniel, have you had a good day?" she asks, looking up at him.

"Yes I have, would you like some tea?"

After making the tea, Daniel relates to Polly the conversation of this morning with Fitz, regarding her activities on his behalf. Polly is surprised, but also delighted.

"Does this mean I will be helping you root out the communists in the service, Daniel? I know they are there, everyone knows but says nothing. I would very much like to find out who they are and help have them removed," Polly says, as she sits down beside him.

"Before you do anything, Polly, we are to meet with Fitz to lay down some ground rules. You will be given guidelines to work to so that you know precisely what to look for and how best to secure information. All this will be explained to you by Fitz tomorrow evening."

"Ok Daniel, now I am going to make us some dinner and have a glass of wine to celebrate," she replies, obviously excited at the prospect of being able to work with Daniel.

"Are we still going to Daddy's this weekend? I can't wait to tell him about the request for me to help," Polly goes on.

They enjoy their meal, and Polly chats enthusiastically about what she is about to embark on. Daniel is still apprehensive, but if she wants to do it then the information she could acquire from the department would be invaluable. She goes off to her room early and Daniel sits for a while contemplating the changes that are about to take place regarding his activities, and how Polly's involvement might influence his position.

The following day passes, and Fitz agrees to meet them for dinner at one of the restaurants in the High Street.

"My dear Polly, how very nice to meet you," says Fitz, as Daniel and Polly arrive at the table.

"Hello Fitz, Daniel has told me a lot about you and I am very pleased to meet you."

"Daniel didn't tell me what a beautiful young lady he had staying in his apartment," says Fitz, smiling, causing Polly to blush, slightly embarrassed.

"Thank you for the compliment, Fitz."

"Not at all, my dear. Now we will order, and I will tell you what we are proposing regarding your activities on behalf of my department," says Fitz, as he attracts the attention of the waiter.

"What has been proposed, is that you listen to what is being said around you, become actively involved in any conversations relating to workers' solidarity, unions to you and me, and see what the mood is in the department."

"Unfortunately Fitz, my movements are restricted because I am only a probationer."

"We are hoping we can do something about that, Polly. I am going to talk with Beatrice Carrington tomorrow. I will ask Beatrice if you can be given some sort of liaison role so that you may be able to move freely between departments without creating suspicion. Once your new position has been established, Daniel and I will draw up a plan of action as to how you may be able to secure information and give you a list of personnel that we have an interest in."

"Thank you Fitz, I appreciate your confidence in my ability and assure you I will not let you and Daniel down."

"I am sure you won't, Polly. Now let's enjoy the rest of the evening, shall we?" says Fitz, as the waiter brings along their meals.

After saying their goodbyes, Polly and Daniel take a taxi for the short journey back to his apartment. Polly is very excited by what she has heard, and cannot wait to get started. Daniel is still apprehensive about what has been suggested, but has no wish to dampen her enthusiasm. On entering the apartment, Polly gives Daniel a big hug.

"Thank you so much for letting me be involved, Daniel. I think I will call it a night," she says, as she plants a kiss on his cheek.

"Goodnight Polly."

*

The following morning, Daniel speaks with Fitz before making contact with Beatrice Carrington.

"What a wonderful girl Polly is, Daniel. You must be very proud of how she has developed into a fine young woman."

"Yes, she certainly has, Fitz, and I care for her very much and must say I still have doubts about recruiting her for the department."

"Of course you do and I would not have expected anything less from you. She is obviously very special to you and I give you my word that she will not be exposed to any danger working for us. I will personally guarantee that."

"Thank you for that, Fitz. I appreciate your assurance very much," Daniel replies. "Now I must speak with Beatrice Carrington."

"Hello, Beatrice Carrington speaking."

"Miss Carrington, it's Daniel Bottomley. I am a close friend of Polly Spencer."

"Daniel, hello, yes I believe we met about five years ago at Ben Spencer's home. Call me Beatrice, by the way. You were responsible for saving Polly on more than one occasion as I recall, and Ben holds you in very high esteem. Without your expertise, Ben was sure they would have lost Polly. I understand she now lives with you in Kensington, is that correct?"

"Yes she does, and it's about Polly that I want to talk with you, if I may."

"Of course, how can I help?"

Daniel tells Beatrice of the hope that Polly can help with his department's work in investigating communist infiltration into the Civil Service, and the dangers such moves pose for our government. He needs someone within the Home Office departments who can be his eyes and ears as to what is happening at the 'coalface'. Polly would be ideally situated to do this, once she served her probation.

"Yes, I understand what you are saying, Daniel, and I can arrange a position for her which would allow her to move freely between Home Office departments and have some access to other ministerial buildings as well."

"That sounds wonderful, Beatrice. Can I ask how long such arrangements would take?"

"Ideally, she would officially start her new position at the beginning of the financial year, in about three weeks' time. However, once the paperwork has been drawn up she could begin her duties immediately and her salary adjustment made at the start of the financial year. She will be known as a Corporate Liaison Officer in the Home Office. She will be moved to the ground floor office block and report to a senior Civil Servant in the immigrations, passport control, and border control department. The office also has some responsibilities relating to the police service. From this office, Polly will have licence to move around freely within the whole building, and should be able to find excuses for entering other buildings in Whitehall if required. Her department head will be Peggy Wright, a long-serving Civil Servant and very reliable. I have known Peggy for many years, and she will take good care of her."

"Thank you for your help, Beatrice. We are going up to Polly's parents' this weekend and they will be delighted to hear how you have been able to assist with securing a position for her."

"I am pleased to be able to be of help, Daniel. I can tell you that there is a document circulating among senior Civil Servants referred to as 'The Traffic Light Syndrome' which highlights how the communist threat has developed since the end of the war.

In 1945, when there was a free Europe with east and west celebrating the downfall of Nazi Germany, it was Green for go. Throughout the forties, however, the annexation of Germany created cracks in relationships with the Soviets and their intentions, calling for (Amber) caution. Now, as time has progressed, the Cold War has developed, as Mr Churchill said, and the communist infiltration into our way of life has become very acute. The Soviets are as hell-bent on domination as the Nazis were, so Red for danger is now in place."

"Thank you for sharing that, Beatrice. I will pass it on to my boss, and thank you again for what you are proposing for Polly, I know she will want me to thank you on her behalf."

"You are very welcome, and I am sure that Polly will not let you down. Look after her, Daniel. Goodbye for now."

So Polly will be just one floor above Daniel's special operations department situated in the basements of the Home Office. The position that Beatrice Carrington has created, will give Polly freedom to move between departments as part of her job description. This will begin as soon as her paperwork authorisation is confirmed, probably sometime next week.

Polly and Daniel finish early on Friday to get ready for the weekend at Polly's home. They catch the train for Carswell at five o'clock, and Polly is bubbling with excitement at what Daniel has told her.

"I will really be able to help Daniel when I am in my new position," she says, hugging him.

"This time next week, you will have a very responsible position, giving you access to so many departments, but we shall have to arrange some way for you to pass on information. If you are moving between departments, you do not want to be carrying sensitive details of personnel, and you don't want to have to remember everything. I will speak with our gadget man, he may have some idea on how you might be able to transmit details via the telephone network. Your new office manager is an acquaintance of Beatrice Carrington, so you will be in good hands."

"I believe we will be a brilliant team, Daniel. You are my best friend forever, and I love you so much. We shall get rid of these wicked communists, who are trying to ruin our country, once and for always. When I am with you anything is possible, can you understand that?"

"Perfectly, Polly. We have been together a long time now, and I believe we will be together for a while yet."

After an uneventful journey, where Polly never seems to stop talking about her new job, they arrive at Carswell around 7.30pm, call a taxi, and arrive at Polly's house just before eight o'clock. She is mobbed by Maisy, Daisy, and George and there are also lots of hugs from Ben and Margaret.

"Polly, Daniel, it's good to see you. Let's go into the parlour and have some tea."

"Mummy, Daddy, I have some marvellous news. I am going to help Daniel with his work at the Home Office, aren't I Daniel?" says Polly enthusiastically.

"I certainly hope so."

"What's this, Daniel? Is it true?" asks Ben with some concern.

The family sit down and have some tea while Polly and Daniel tell them about the new position Polly is due to be given in the Home Office.

Ben is obviously concerned that there may be some danger attached to a position where Polly will be wandering between departments being nosy on Daniel's behalf. Although it is some five years since the terrible events that occurred to the family, over Ben's pursuit of black market racketeers, it is still a painful memory to them.

"I hope Polly will not be put in any danger in her new position, Daniel."

"Ben, Margaret, Polly will have a clearly defined position which will mean that she will be expected to liaise with all departments within the Home Office. Should she be required by her superiors to visit departments outside of the Home Office, then that will be a bonus. The point to remember is that she has full authorisation to go into these departments as part of her job, so there will be no danger attached to her movements. We are hoping that she becomes part of the furniture in the Home Office, and will be known by everyone, giving her a unique opportunity to listen to the conversations and the gossip of members in all of the departments. We will watch over her very carefully, Margaret, and have a contingency plan lined up for any eventualities. I must confess I was a little reluctant with the idea at first, but am happy that her position will be official, well documented, and above any suspicion."

"You see Mummy, Daniel will be taking good care of me as usual."

"Thank you for that, Daniel. If you are satisfied that Polly will be safe, then I am happy for her in her new position, now come along and help me with supper, Polly."

The children sit in the parlour, while Ben asks Daniel for a word in the study.

"You are quite sure about this, Daniel? I really do wonder if Polly is ready for such responsibility, she is only eighteen, after all."

"You know how much I care about her, Ben. I would never allow her to be put in a position of any danger. But Polly has matured considerably over the past few months, the little girl I first met here five years ago has now become a young woman with an ambition to help rid us of the communist menace in our country."

"I had no idea that she had become so concerned in the politics of working in Whitehall. My daughter has the makings of a politician it would seem, Daniel."

"Polly is capable of becoming whatever she wants, Ben. She is very determined, as you know." And with that, Ben and Daniel go back into the parlour and enjoy supper with all the family.

After supper, they sit talking until nearly midnight before Polly goes up to her room, closely followed by Daniel. He taps on her door and goes inside. Polly is still taking things from her case.

"I think your Mummy and Daddy are satisfied by my explanations of your new job, Polly, but they were very concerned about any danger it may present."

"As long as I have you, Daniel, I know I will be fine," says Polly, hugging him affectionately as Margaret enters the room.

"I have put towels for both of you in the bathroom, see you in the morning," she says, a little embarrassed seeing Daniel and Polly together in each other's arms.

"Thanks Mummy, goodnight."

Saturday shopping has been arranged by Margaret for herself and Polly, leaving Daniel to entertain the children, especially George. They have all grown up rapidly over the last five years, and look upon Daniel as their big brother, someone to answer all their questions. Maisy, who is now fourteen, is very much like her big sister, very determined and asking lots of questions.

"You love my sister very much, don't you Daniel?" she asks as she walks in the garden with Daniel.

"Yes Maisy, we have become very close, partly because of what happened when I was living with you. I cannot imagine not being with her and I believe she feels the same way about me."

"But are you her boyfriend, Daniel? Do you want to marry her? That's what I mean."

"You ask too many questions, Maisy. For now Polly and I are very close friends who care for each other very much, so let's leave it there, ok?" Daniel replies with a smile and a frown.

"Ok Daniel, I know you will take care of Polly, I know you will," she replies, as she goes back into the house, leaving Daniel to ponder over what she has said.

The weekend is over all too quickly, and after saying their goodbyes, Polly and Daniel are driven to the station by Ben to catch the four o'clock train for London. The journey back to London is quiet, since both Polly and Daniel have much to think about. Polly will be starting a new job very soon, which will change her life and bring her even closer to Daniel. As for Daniel, he ponders over what Maisy said about his relationship with Polly.

Monday morning sees Daniel in Fitz's office with Phil Chandler discussing how Polly might communicate with them using the internal telephone system. They do not want her writing any details down for fear of discovery. Being able to pick up the telephone and record information would be an ideal solution.

"I will go along to her office – I understand that she will be allocated her own office, Daniel – and fix her phone so that it will respond to a dialling code. When that code is dialled, Polly will simply recite whatever she likes and put the phone down when she has finished. The information will come through to me, and I will record it. No record of any calls that she makes, using the code, will be stored anywhere other than my office."

"That sounds foolproof, Phil, and it gives Polly every opportunity to pass information at any time without having to remember any of it," says Fitz.

"Thanks Phil, not having to remember or write down details will be a great help and reduce any risk of any person discovering her position."

"Ok, now Daniel, what about this union meeting? Phil will need to supply you with some sort of listening device."

"Yes, and what about my journalist pass? Can you fix that, Fitz?"

"Yes. I will have all the details for you tomorrow, and Phil will have a device ready for you to plant inside the union offices."

Daniel arrives at the E.T.U. meeting at seven o'clock on Wednesday, but is not allowed inside.

"Sorry mate, no press, union members only," a rough-looking character tells him.

"I am a union member, and I would like to put your case through my national paper. It can only be good for you, getting the public on your side," says Daniel, annoyed that this man may stop him before he has started!

"Listen mate, I don't care who..."

Just then, a man emerges from inside the building.

"What's going on, and who are you?"

Daniel explains his position, and shows his journalist pass, hoping that this will be enough.

"Let him in, we can do with the publicity. I'm Michael Doyle, by the way."

"Daniel Bottomley, pleased to meet you Mr Doyle," says Daniel, shaking his hand.

The meeting place is a room above a pub, ideal since most members like a drink afterwards. This room is rented by the union on a semi-permanent basis, so an ideal place for Daniel to place his listening device. The device is about the size of a penny and is magnetic. Fortunately, the tables have metal supports, and Daniel secures his device almost as soon as he sits down, ironically next to Michael Doyle. Doyle is a very good speaker, preaching his communist ideals to a captive audience. Daniel is permitted to take notes, he is supposed to be a journalist after all, and records all relevant comments for discussion. The meeting lasts for about an hour, after which the members all go down into the pub.

"So what did you think of our meeting, Mr Bottomley? Do you believe that the worker has a case to be heard?"

"Yes I do – call me Daniel, by the way – and I hope my editor agrees. Do you have any meetings with the management planned at all?" Daniel asks, hoping to show interest.

"Nothing Daniel, my plan is seek to escalate the strike. Unofficially, and this is not for publication, I am meeting with some officials of the dock workers. If we can get the dockers out we will strangle the country into giving in to our demands. Mr Churchill must realise that the workers run this country, not the politicians. People are still suffering with rationing, and the average wage is not enough to live on. I intend to lead my union into a full-blown attack on this government, and get the workers what they deserve."

"You certainly know what you want for your men, and I will do what I can through my paper, Mr Doyle. I must go now, thank you for the drink by the way."

"Thank you Daniel, and I look forward to reading your article," Doyle replies as Daniel makes his way through the crowd and out into the London air. He catches the first bus that comes along to make sure that he is not being followed. Then after taking a second bus, he gets himself a taxi back to his apartment.

"Daniel, how was your meeting?"

"I have placed the listening device, Polly, so we will wait and see. Now I am ready for some supper," he says as he sits down.

On Thursday morning, Daniel reports on his meeting to Fitz, who confirms that the device is working. They will have to wait for the next meeting to see just how useful it is.

"We may need to bring in Paul Horsley, Daniel, with a view to looking in the Communist Party Offices. If you and Conrad could get inside you might be able to have a nose around."

Paul Horsley is the go-to man when preparing any operations. He will supply whatever is needed to successfully complete any mission, wherever it may be.

"Your notes give an insight into what the communists are trying to do, and I find it disturbing, Daniel. We must do everything we can to stop them," says Fitz.

"Ok, well let's arrange a meeting with Paul tomorrow with myself and Conrad. We can hopefully look at the communists' offices sometime next week."

When Daniel gets home that evening, Polly tells him that she has been told about her promotion.

"It's happening, Daniel, it really is happening," she says, giving him a hug.

"That is brilliant, Polly. Let's go out and celebrate this evening."

They both agree that it is worth celebrating and go out for a meal, returning around ten o'clock.

"Thank you for that, Daniel. I really enjoyed this evening."

"When exactly have you been told you will be starting this new job, Polly?"

"I will move into my own office on Monday, on the ground floor. My new supervisor, Mrs Peggy Wright, will tell me what my duties are and I expect she will show me round some of the other departments so that I do not get lost! So I expect I will be settled in by Tuesday or Wednesday."

"Well the very best of luck, Polly. You deserve it," says Daniel, giving her a hug.

"Thank you Daniel," Polly replies, kissing him on his cheek.

CHAPTER 3

Daniel's apartment is a basic rectangular design comprising a hallway with utility room, bedroom, bathroom, and second bedroom off the hallway. At the end of the hallway is the lounge diner, with the kitchen off to the right. Both bedrooms are doubles, Daniel has the one nearest the front door. He is a light sleeper, and listens for what he thought was a footfall in the hallway. He listens intently as he climbs out of his bed, slips on his dressing gown, and grabs his baseball bat. As he approaches the door he hears Polly scream. He opens his door, switches on the hall light and dashes towards Polly's room. One man is on top of Polly, tugging at her pyjama jacket and hitting her across her face, the other man is trying to remove her pyjama bottoms. Daniel hits him hard on the head, causing him to release his hold on Polly, and he falls to the floor.

The man on top of Polly, meanwhile, has half torn off her pyjama jacket, threatening her with a knife. As Daniel tries to pull him from Polly, he turns round and stabs him in the shoulder. Daniel grabs at his shoulder in pain, but still manages to kick out at the man, hitting him in the groin. By this time Polly is hysterical and screaming.

"Daniel, Daniel you've been stabbed."

Daniel hits the man with the knife three or four times with the bat as both the intruders dash for the door. Daniel follows to make sure they have gone, then turns to Polly. Her pyjama jacket is almost torn off and she has scratches on her chest. She also has two red marks on her face where she has been hit. She holds on to Daniel, sobbing.

"Daniel, God I thought he was going to kill me!" she cries, as she holds on to what's left of her pyjamas. Daniel does his best to comfort her, then realises that he is bleeding.

"You're bleeding, Daniel," she says, ignoring her own state. She removes Daniel's pyjama jacket and uses it to stem the flow of blood from his wound.

"You will have to have this looked at," she says, then realising that she is half naked, reaches for her gown.

"I need to call the police, Polly, and an ambulance. You get dressed in the meantime."

Polly gets dressed while Daniel phones to report a burglary and assault, asking the police to call in the morning as he has to go to hospital. The police agree, as Polly goes with him to the hospital. His stab wound is quite deep, and requires a number of stitches since the skin was torn in the attack. The doctor appears surprised by the number of scars on Daniel's body.

"You seem to have been in the wars a lot, Mr Bottomley."

"From the war years mostly, Doctor, and my work since."

"Well you will have to rest for a while with this injury. The cut is deep and any exertion will open it again. We will have another look at it Tuesday, to see how it is healing, meantime keep the dressing in place please."

"I will see that he rests, Doctor, and we will see you again on Tuesday," Polly replies.

"Thank you, Doctor. Goodnight," says Daniel, as he leaves with Polly and gets a taxi back to his apartment.

They return to the apartment, and as they walk into the lounge, Polly grabs hold of Daniel and bursts into tears.

"Daniel, I was so frightened, those men seemed determined to hurt me. I have to admit it brought back unhappy memories."

Daniel looks at her and realises that he too was fearful of what the men intended. He holds Polly to him and kisses her on her forehead.

"You are safe now, Polly. Now shall we have some tea before going back to bed?"

Daniel eventually goes back to his bed around 4.30am. He has much to think about regarding the break-in, but also how it has affected his feelings toward Polly. She has become so much more than a dear friend that he cares for very much. Should he hide these feelings or should he tell Polly and risk damaging their special relationship? He falls into a fitful sleep before waking around eight o'clock. Polly is up and about, and has made some breakfast.

"Good morning Daniel, how do you feel this morning?

Daniel smiles to himself before answering.

"I'm ok, Polly. The wound hasn't opened at all so hopefully it will heal quickly. You'll stay until the police arrive?"

"Yes, I will call the office and tell them I will be in late. You will have to do the same, Daniel."

"I am trying to figure out who was behind the break-in. Were they just opportunists, or was there something more sinister about them? Best just to presume they were opportunists for the benefit of the police. I do not want them asking me questions about my position."

Polly decides she has time for a bath, and had just finishing dressing when the doorbell rings. Daniel answers the door to three police officers who identify themselves as D.I. Jack Manners, D.C. Jonathan Moorcroft, and W.P.C. Becky Peters.

"Good morning Mr Bottomley, how's the wound?" The D.I. asks as they step inside.

"It's fine thank you, Detective Inspector. Can we get you some tea? This is Polly, by the way, she is staying with me for the moment," replies Daniel, as Polly goes to make them tea.

"Did they take anything at all, Mr Bottomley?" the D.I. asks.

"Nothing at all, their sole purpose was to assault Polly. They must have thought she was here on her own. They were very rough with her and threatened her with a knife."

"Polly, did you recognise these men at all?"

"I'm afraid not, I am just so relieved that Daniel was here, it was very frightening."

"What exactly did they do to you, Polly?" the D.I. asks.

"They slapped my face twice and tore my pyjamas, trying to get them off. The one on top of me threatened me with a knife before Daniel came to my rescue."

"It must have been very frightening for you," the W.P.C. replies.

"Your intervention certainly prevented a serious physical assault on Polly, Daniel. We need to find these men quickly before they try again elsewhere," the D.I. comments.

Polly and Daniel give descriptions of the men as best they can before the police depart.

"Thank you both for your details, we will let you know when we have anything relevant. Goodbye," the D.I. concludes as they leave the apartment.

Daniel and Polly sit with each other in silence for a moment, both absorbed in their own thoughts, Polly holding his hand as if to seek assurance.

"Everything is ok now, Polly. You have your new job to think about, so off you go to work."

"Yes I know, I would just like to stay with you today and forget about everything else," Polly replies with a sigh as she gets up from the settee and goes to get her coat ready for work. Daniel, too, would like to have spent the day with Polly, but he also must move on. He arrives at his office around eleven o'clock and recounts the night's events to Fitz.

"What do you think, Daniel, just a break in or something more sinister?"

"I think it was just a couple of opportunists who thought a young female was on her own. They must have watched Polly go into the front door and followed her to see which apartment she was in. They would not have seen me, because I always use a side entrance."

"Ok, so for now we will assume that it is not work related in any way."

"I hope not, Fitz, especially as we will now have Polly in a position to help us. I will keep an open mind until there is definite evidence of who these men are. They could have been sent by someone, we really don't know. Now, regarding Conrad and me having a look around the communists' offices, I will have to put that off for a few days, until this stab wound heals. Meantime, I will contact Hennessey again for any news. I think he could be very useful to us, and I will continue to appeal to his beliefs regarding his fellow workers."

"Ok Daniel, now I suggest you go home early and I will see you Monday. Enjoy your weekend." Daniel goes off to lunch with Conrad to tell him of the night's events and also to have a word with his close friend about Polly.

"You recall, when we were staying at Ben Spencer's house, your comments about Polly growing up and how it would impact on our relationship, Conrad?"

"I do, Daniel, and now you are about to tell me that your feelings toward each other are changing, am I right?

"I am at a loss as to how to deal with this, Conrad. I want our special relationship to continue, but I do not want to spoil anything that we have developed for each other over the years."

"But don't you see, Daniel? You have spent your life with this girl for more than five years. You have shared highs and lows that most people can only imagine. Your influence over her life means that Polly could never contemplate being with anyone other than you, of that I am sure. But what about you, can you imagine moving on without her?"

"No I cannot, but I do not want anything to happen between us that will spoil that special relationship," Daniel replies apparently struggling for explanations.

"I have known you for a number of years, Daniel, and you are a decent, honourable, man. I know you will do what is best for you and Polly. You don't need to worry about what may or may not happen, because when the time comes it will happen anyway!"

Daniel arrives back at his apartment early, and contemplates on what was said between himself and Conrad. His friend was right, when the time comes it will happen anyway.

Polly arrives around 3.30pm, having finished early.

"Daniel, I am to start my new job on Monday. I will be on the ground floor, and have to report to a Mrs Peggy Wright," says Polly, full of excitement as she hugs him.

"I am so pleased for you, Polly. You have earned this opportunity and I know you will be an outstanding success. You and I will talk more about this over the next week or so as you settle into your new position."

"So what are we going to do this weekend to celebrate, Daniel? I would like to do some shopping, I want to look my best on Monday, then perhaps we can go out tomorrow evening?"

"You seem to have everything worked out, Polly. Meantime, I will make some tea."

The rest of their evening is spent talking about Polly's new job, and what she must be aware of as she moves around various departments. Daniel also mentions that her phone is going to be specially adapted for her to leave messages. Polly is in raptures about this and hugs Daniel as he continues to explain.

"Daniel, I am so excited by all this, I will get you all the information I can to stop these people."

Daniel is overwhelmed by her enthusiasm and smiles as she continues to hug him. His thoughts begin to drift back to his conversation with Conrad, but he knows he must not let anything spoil the moment for Polly. His feelings, whatever they may be, have to be set aside but he is aware that sooner rather than later, he will have to talk to her. Eventually, Polly stops talking.

"I am off to bed, Daniel, I am exhausted. See you in the morning," she says, as she kisses him on the cheek.

"Goodnight Polly," says Daniel, as he watches her go off to her room. Daniel sits listening to some music, with his thoughts once more about their relationship. He knows all will be well and he does not have to change in any way. He switches off the radio, and decides to look in on Polly before he goes to his room. Since the break-in, Polly has been sleeping with her door ajar, so he can look in without disturbing her.

"Daniel?" she says as he peers round the door.

"I did not mean to disturb you, Polly."

"You did not disturb me, I wasn't asleep, please come in."

Daniel sits by her side, happy to just be with her. Polly is content to see him sitting there.

"Do you remember when you did this most nights, Daniel, when I was little? I couldn't go to sleep unless you were with me."

"I remember very well, Polly, and I remember you giving me a bloody nose one time!"

"It seems a long time ago, Daniel, and we have grown up now, at least I know I have. But do you know what? I still love you being near me and I think I always will. Can you understand that?" she says, holding his hand.

"Yes I do, Polly, now you get some sleep, we have a busy day tomorrow. Goodnight," He replies, kissing her on her forehead.

"Goodnight Daniel."

Polly is up early on Saturday, not having slept very well. She is not sure why, but presumes it's because she has a new job beginning Monday. She makes some tea and takes a cup into Daniel.

"Thanks Polly," says Daniel, half asleep. Polly sits on his bed while he drinks his tea. For some reason Daniel feels a little embarrassed, why, he does not know, since he has spent hours by Polly's bedside in the past.

"Can we go into town to do our shopping, Daniel? I would like a trip for a change."

"Of course we can."

The two of them enjoy a visit to Oxford Street and a walk around the shops. Polly buys some clothes for her new job, some new pyjamas, and also buys Daniel a new shirt. They spend some time in town, arriving back at Daniel's apartment around four o'clock. Polly is exhausted and goes for a bath while Daniel relaxes on the settee. After a long soak, Polly sits with Daniel in her gown, before dressing.

"Where are we going tonight, Daniel? Can we go somewhere special please?" she asks, hugging Daniel. Yet again, Daniel is a little embarrassed by Polly's closeness to him wearing only her gown.

"We shall find somewhere special to celebrate your new job, Polly."

Daniel takes Polly into Chelsea, a very popular area of London, and they find a little restaurant off the King's Road. Again, Polly dominates the conversation, with Daniel quite happy to listen to her enthusiasm about her new position.

"Corporate Liaison Officer. Daniel, does that sound important to you?"

"It sounds important and it is important I am sure, Polly. You will find out more on Monday, but you can be sure that your position was discussed in some detail before any decisions were made. Finding someone reliable and trustworthy enough to be allowed to wander the Home Office unattended must have been quite a task. There must be definite reasons why you were selected, as I'm sure you will find out next week."

"Well whatever the reasons, I will be the most efficient Corporate Liaison Officer the Home Office has ever had," says Polly, as she tucks into her meal. She also enjoys the surroundings, Kings Road being especially busy and very noisy on Saturday night.

They finish their meal and the waiter fetches their coats, accidently knocking Daniel's left shoulder, where he was stabbed. Daniel winces, but no one notices. He is not sure whether he has done any damage so carries on without mentioning it. Polly continues to chatter on the way back in the taxi and Daniel suddenly feels rather tired. It must have been all the walking this afternoon. He looks at his watch as they enter the apartment, and is surprised to notice that it is after eleven.

"I am off to bed, Daniel. I am worn out from this afternoon."

"Me too, Polly. I will be off myself shortly," replies Daniel, who waits for Polly to go into her room before taking off his jacket to look at his stab wound. It is bleeding and his shirt has a large stain.

He leaves his jacket and goes into the bathroom to examine the wound. On removing his shirt he sees that the wound is indeed bleeding, and Daniel decides it will have to be dressed. Polly must have heard him moving about and comes into the bathroom, to be confronted by Daniel bleeding from his stab wound. The stitches have been broken, and the cut has opened. It is obviously deep, hence it has begun to bleed again.

"Daniel, you are bleeding. Let me see. God, you will have to get this stitched again, why didn't you call me?" She takes a closer look and uses Daniel's bloody shirt to clear the blood from his shoulder and chest. Again Polly finds herself with Daniel's blood on her pyjamas. She finds some plaster and cuts it into thin strips, attempting to pinch the cut together.

"Your body looks more like a battlefield each time I see it, you have so many scars," Polly says as she finishes putting a bandage over the plaster strips. She carefully presses on the pad she has placed over the wound, but it seems to be holding since no more blood is evident.

"We shall have to go back to hospital in the morning, but I think I have managed to stop the bleeding for now."

"Thanks Polly."

"Come along now, get yourself off to bed," Polly replies as she puts her arm around him and leads him to his room. "Goodnight Daniel," she says, kissing him on the cheek before leaving his room.

They call at the hospital early on the Sunday morning. Daniel did not sleep too well but Polly's first aid did stop the wound from bleeding too much. The wound does have to be stitched again and the doctor does express some concern about how deep it is.

"It seems that the blade penetrated some two inches or so, Mr Bottomley, damaging your tendon. Tearing around the cut will mean that you will be left with a ridge rather than a scar, but looking at the number of scars you have already, one more isn't going to make a lot of difference. Where on earth have you been?"

"Most are from the war, and the others from a few scrapes in my job with the military," says Daniel, a little embarrassed.

"Like the knife wound, Doctor, some of Daniel's scars are from wounds he received while protecting me when I was younger."

"I see. Anyway, come along again toward the end of the week and I'll see how it is progressing."

Daniel buys a paper on the way back to the apartment, hoping for a relaxing day ahead.

"Ok Daniel, now I am going to look after you today, so go and sit down and I will get you some breakfast."

Daniel smiles and appreciates Polly's attention. He sits down on the sofa and puts his feet up. He must have fallen asleep, for he is woken by Polly kissing him, which startles him at first.

"Come along Daniel, I have made you breakfast," says Polly, oblivious to Daniel's surprise at her actions. Daniel smiles to himself, Polly once again being Polly and wanting to please him.

On Monday morning, Polly turns up for work eager to start her new position at the Home Office. She is shown into Peggy Wright's office, who beckons her to sit. A woman in her late fifties, Peggy Wright has a powerful aura about her, forceful and dominant in her appearance.

"Now, Miss Spencer, Polly, you have been given a new position with us which carries a good deal of responsibility. As Corporate Liaison Officer, you will have unrestricted access to all Home Office Departments, and also some access to the Foreign and Commonwealth Office. You have been specially chosen for this position for a number of reasons, not least the fact that your security clearance has been checked and found satisfactory. Since you are only eighteen years old and have joined us from school, you carry no baggage, which is ideal for this position.

"Within the Home Office, sensitive memos, files, and documents have to be transported to various departments. It makes good sense to have as few people as possible tasked with moving these documents, and it has been decided that you, Polly, are the ideal candidate," says Mrs Wright. "The documents most sensitive will be in sealed envelopes with the government crest across the seal. These are stamped by heads of department, so please be aware of these."

"I will look out for those, Mrs Wright, and I will not let you down."

"Of that we are sure, Polly. Now because of the sensitivity of the papers you will be responsible for, you will have your own office and phone, so that documents can be handed to you or a message left for you. I understand that an engineer will be adapting your phone to take such messages. Here is your special pass that you should wear at all times. It will open all the doors that you need to pass through. All heads of department have been informed of your position. Should you have any problems, with anyone in any department, you will inform me immediately, is that clear?"

“I understand, Mrs Wright.”

“Ok, now here is your documentation outlining the terms of your contract, including your salary details. There are some forms to be signed by you and returned as soon as possible and this is your office, not particularly attractive, but it will serve its purpose. Whenever you leave your office, you will lock it behind you. Any documents that require your attention will be placed into the letterbox and collected for you to deliver accordingly. Only you and I will have a key, so please do not lose yours. Any questions?”

“I was wondering if there was some sort of map outlining where the various departments are, since it will take me some time to find my way,” asks Polly.

“Yes, the various departments, immigration, passport control, border control, and policing, etc., are all detailed in your documents, together with the names of the department heads and their geographical situation. I am sure you will soon find your way round, Polly.”

“Thank you Mrs Wright,” says Polly, as she looks round her rather sparse office. Just as Mrs Wright is about to leave, there is a tap on the door.

“Ah, you must be the engineer, I will leave you with Polly,” says Mrs Wright as she leaves the office closing the door behind her.

“Miss Spencer, Polly, my name is Phil Chandler, I work with Daniel, and I have come along to fix the phone for you.”

“Hello Phil, I am very pleased to meet you. Daniel mentioned that my phone was to be adapted for me to leave messages, is that correct?”

“Yes, that’s correct, we want to make it very easy for you to pass on information to Daniel, Conrad, and Fitz about anyone and anything that may be relevant. All you would need to do is wait for the tone, then insert five numbers which you will need to remember. After you have done that you will be told to ‘leave a message now’ and you will leave your message. When you have finished say ‘end of message’ and replace the receiver. Unless you enter the five numbers then your phone will simply operate as a normal internal phone. Any questions, Polly?” Phil asks.

"My five-digit code, do you need to know what it is?"

"No, only you need know. That is your access to our department, no one else in the building has access to our department. Ok, that is all done and ready for you to use."

"Thank you Phil, bye for now," says Polly as he leaves her office, closing the door behind him.

Polly sits at her desk, taking in her surroundings and decides that her first job is to set herself a dial code. She decides on 81947. This represents the month and the year that she first met Daniel, so will be very easy for her to remember. She reads through the documents for her to sign, and is pleased to note that she has had a rise in her salary. She then browses through the manual detailing the various departments and is surprised and overwhelmed by how many there are. She decides she must study the details of the various departments, so that she can find her way around quickly. She is not expecting any real work for a while since her position will not yet be common knowledge. As she looks through the names of the department heads, she speculates on how many may be involved in communist activity.

"If they are, I will find out," she says to herself.

For the rest of Monday Polly familiarises herself with the geography of the Home Office departments, and actually makes some office drops. She decides she will keep a log of every drop she makes for reference if necessary. At the end of the day, she locks her office and goes home to Daniel's apartment, bursting to tell him what has happened. Once again Daniel is the good listener as Polly goes on about the various departments and how she now has her phone linked for messaging.

"I know I will be able to help you, Daniel, in my new position. I just know I will," she says, as she curls up by his side on the settee. They listen to some music for a while, once Polly has stopped talking, then go off to their rooms around eleven o'clock. Daniel sits up reading since he is not especially sleepy, when after about one hour, Polly goes into Daniel's room.

"I am struggling to get to sleep, Daniel. Can I sit with you for a while?"

"Of course, Polly," Daniel replies, as Polly sits beside him and holds him close. Once again, Daniel feels a little uncomfortable at Polly's closeness to him in his room, but tries to behave as casually as he can.

"I expect you are still thinking about your new job. Why don't you make yourself a warm drink, or would you like me to?"

"No thanks Daniel, I just want to be close to you, that's all. Remember we used to spend a lot of time like this when I was at school?"

"I remember, but you are not a schoolgirl any more, Polly."

"How long have we been together now?" asks Polly, catching Daniel by surprise with her question.

"You came with me after I had stayed at your home over Christmas."

"I want us to be together forever Daniel, I cannot imagine when we are not together. Do you understand what I am trying to say?" says Polly, looking at Daniel with a tear in her eye.

"I will always be here for you, Polly. You know that, so please don't upset yourself on this special day for you. Now off you go back to bed," says Daniel, giving Polly a kiss on the cheek.

Polly's response is to hold Daniel tightly and say, "I love you so much, Daniel. Goodnight."

*

Daniel makes contact with Hennessey on Tuesday to arrange another meeting as soon as possible and they agree tomorrow afternoon at the Science Museum as before. He seeks more information, from Hennessey, about possible unscheduled meetings that have been arranged and finds out that dockers are being pushed hard to come out with the E.T.U. members.

"The communists know that if they close the docks it could cause public unrest, which is exactly what they want."

"I understand what you are saying, Peter, and it is a very worrying development. Do you know any of the dockers at all?"

"I know some of them from way back, and I have met others at union meetings."

"Do you think you could introduce me to any of them, unofficially? Especially if they share your concerns, Peter."

"I will contact a couple that I know well and see what they think, and leave you a message."

"I look forward to hearing from you when you have had chance to speak with them, Peter. Bye for now," replies Daniel, as he leaves for his apartment. It is now past three o'clock so he decides it is not worth going back to the office.

Polly's new position gives her unique opportunities to investigate communist activity in the Civil Service. There is a secret cache of agents within Whitehall taking instructions from Moscow. Known as the Red Hand, they are attempting to influence policy decisions at home and abroad, and seeking to install a senior communist official into the heart of government. This information is known to MI5, but Polly is not made aware of this for obvious reasons. However, she soon begins to pass names to Daniel using the unique telephone link. Daniel follows up on the names, and there are some internal examinations carried out, but they come to nothing.

"It may be best at the moment, Fitz, to let these people carry on with their activities. We know who they are so it will not be difficult to watch them. We need to find the ringleaders, those who are pulling the strings, and the best way to do that, is to leave things as they are."

"Very well Daniel, it is your operation, but do not let Polly become disillusioned about any of this."

Daniel talks with Polly that evening, explaining to her that they must play a waiting game in order to discover who is running the operation within the Home Office. He makes it very clear just how valuable her information has been, and again asks her to be careful.

"I am getting recognised in most departments, Daniel. Most people see me as an office girl delivering internal mail. I just say hello and pass some comment about nothing particular. I know that some staff are suspicious of who I am, but they have no idea what I am doing, so I will just carry on and do what I can to give you names and any information. I do so want to be of help, Daniel, I am sure that I can make a difference."

"You have already made a difference, Polly. Fitz is impressed with what you have found out in the short time you have been reporting to us."

"Really? Did he say that? Then I really must be making a difference."

Polly has been working as Corporate Liaison Officer for three weeks, and the information she has gained has been invaluable. Unfortunately, she has created some suspicions and is approached on her way home. A man and a woman walk either side of her and push her into a side alleyway between some shops.

"You are asking a lot of questions Miss Spencer. What are you up to from your little office on the ground floor?" the man asks.

"I am just doing the work I get paid to do, delivering and collecting mail. What do you want?" Polly asks nervously.

"We want you to mind your own business, what we do has nothing to do with you."

"If you have a complaint about my work, then you should speak with Mrs Wright," replies Polly, trying to appear casual.

"Listen, you know exactly what we are talking about, you are asking too many questions. Do your work and stop meddling, do you understand?" the man concludes, grabbing Polly by her hair and pulling her towards him.

"Let go of me and leave me alone!" shouts Polly, as the man releases her and moves away with his female companion. Polly runs the rest of the way to Daniel's apartment, and is out of breath when she goes inside.

"Daniel, Daniel, I thought they were going to hurt me!" she cries tearfully as she holds on to him.

"Polly, whatever is the matter? What has happened?" asks a very concerned Daniel.

"I was stopped and threatened by a man and a woman on my way home," replies Polly, holding on tightly to Daniel as she recounts her conversation with the man and woman.

"Did you recognise them at all, Polly?"

"No, but they said they knew what I was doing, asking questions. Do you think they know, Daniel?"

"They cannot know what you are doing, Polly, since outside of my office you are the only one that knows. I believe they are being overzealous because of the enquiries that have taken place. And they have targeted you as someone to blame. They cannot have any idea of your agenda with my department," he says, hoping to reassure her.

"Should I tell Mrs Wright what has happened, Daniel, do you think?"

"There is no need to mention it to Mrs Wright, Polly. If these people have a genuine grievance about you then they will make a complaint, but I don't believe that will happen. I suggest that you don't start any conversations with anyone for a while, wait for them to talk to you, that way you cannot be accused of asking questions," replies Daniel. Whilst he is concerned about what has happened, he must reassure Polly that she is not in any danger. Meanwhile, he will talk the incident over with Fitz tomorrow, and see what he says.

"Ok Daniel, I will do my work and not talk so much for the time being. Now shall we have some dinner?" she asks, apparently satisfied with his explanations. They enjoy their meal, and discuss their forthcoming visit to Polly's home for Easter.

"That sounds just what we both need, Polly, and a few days away will be good for you."

Her unpleasant encounter together with the obvious threats have upset Polly, and Daniel has to go to her during the night.

"Daniel, please come," she calls. Daniel looks at his watch, it is 2.00am. He goes into her room to find Polly sitting up in her bed, shaking and sweating heavily.

"My dear Polly, what is the matter?" he asks as he holds her close to him, hoping to reassure her. She is sobbing and soaked in sweat as Daniel tries to console her.

"You must calm down, Polly, everything is ok. Let me get you a towel to wipe away some of the sweat," Daniel says as he gets a towel and wipes her face. She is absolutely bathed in sweat from her bad dream.

"I suggest you go to the bathroom and change out of your pyjamas."

"No, I will change here, Daniel. I do not want you to leave me," she says, as she goes over to her drawer chest and finds a fresh pair of pyjamas. Much to Daniel's embarrassment, she turns away from him before removing her top, dries herself, then does the same with her bottoms.

"Would you like some water, Polly?" asks Daniel struggling for something to say after Polly's seemingly innocent actions in front of him.

"Please, Daniel, I am very dry," she says as Daniel goes to fetch her a drink, with some relief at being able to go away momentarily and so hide any further embarrassment from Polly's spontaneous actions. He takes the drink into Polly, kisses her on the cheek and returns to his room. Hopefully, she will sleep now, and Daniel goes off to sleep.

The next morning, Polly seems none the worse for her bad dream, so Daniel thinks best not to mention it. It's the weekend again, and Polly and Daniel relax for most of the time, having a walk round the local shops in Kensington during Saturday, and in the evening they go to the cinema. Daniel gets his way and they go and see the war film 'Desert Fox, the Story of Rommel'. It holds particular interest to Daniel, since General Rommel was something of a thorn in the side of British Forces in the deserts of North Africa. Polly was not especially interested, but the film was entertaining and its star, James Mason, was a popular British actor. On the Monday of Easter week, Daniel is contacted with a message from Peter Hennessey.

"Daniel, hello. I have arranged for us to meet with two of my colleagues from the dockers' union. Can you meet up tomorrow evening? There is pub called the North Pole in the East End, meet me outside at eight o'clock if that is ok?" asks Hennessey, as the message ends.

Daniel finds his way to the North Pole pub in the East End, and is amazed how derelict it is in the whole East end area. An area where discontent would flourish and communist agitators would have a ready-made audience. Daniel asks the taxi driver to drop him off about 100 yards from the pub, and walks the rest of the way so as not to attract any undue attention. Hennessey is waiting outside and leads Daniel into an old run-down bar which is full of drinkers already. He leads him to a table in the corner where two men are sitting.

"Daniel, this is Liam Cassidy and Jimmy Rush, I have told them about you and my thoughts so we can speak openly here."

"Pleased to meet you both, and thank you for agreeing to see me."

"Peter has told us how he first knew of you, Daniel, and what you are trying to do. Anything that will stop the commies is ok by us. That right, Jimmy?" says Liam.

"We are dedicated trade unionists, Daniel. We got no time for these people who are stirring up trouble. It stops us from getting on with our business, which is improving the working conditions of our members and securing a fair wage for them and their families. That's all we are interested in," Jimmy replies.

"Anything I can do to bring these communists down, I will do, you have my word on that. Now what is the latest news on the dockers?" asks Daniel.

"There's a lot of pressure being used to shut the docks now that the printers' dispute looks to be coming to an end. There are stoppages every day, and most days very little freight is unloaded or loaded because there are not enough men to handle it. There is a mass meeting called for next Tuesday to try and shut down the London docks, at least we reckon that's the reason, since no demands have been put to management. There is a rumour that there will be some top officials there, but no one can find out who they are. We reckon they are commies, if they are then that will prove what we think is happening," says Jimmy.

"Do you think we could meet up again, after Easter, when you have been to your mass meeting? I would be very interested to know what happens, especially if communist agitators are going to be there to stir up trouble."

"Ok Daniel, but it might be best if we meet somewhere else, say up west, strangers are noticed here and that will mean questions," says Liam.

"Peter, find a pub we can meet round Covent Garden, will you? Leave me a message saying where and when," Daniel replies as he prepares to leave.

"We will come with you until you find a taxi, Daniel, just in case," says Liam.

And so the four men leave the pub to escort Daniel to the end of the road where he hails a taxi after shaking hands and saying his goodbyes. He has much to think about regarding what the communists are trying to achieve in docklands. He desperately needs names that he can investigate, and a visit to Communist Party Headquarters now becomes a matter of urgency.

CHAPTER 4

The rest of Easter week passes without incident. Polly goes about her duties without getting into any unnecessary conversations. She is really beginning to enjoy being able to roam around the Home Office building unimpeded whilst picking up information and names for Daniel to look at. Daniel, meantime, mentions to Fitz about Polly being accosted in the street and they both decide that she has probably been a bit too enthusiastic in trying to get information. Providing it does not happen again, they can afford to treat the incident as a one-off. With Easter break fast approaching, Daniel and Polly are both looking forward to spending the long weekend at Polly's home. The weather is set fair so they will be able to spend time outside in the garden and perhaps go for a picnic. They both finish at lunchtime on Good Friday so that they can catch the four o'clock train from Euston to Carswell. They board the train and secure a carriage to themselves as it leaves the station on time.

"I am really looking forward to this weekend, Daniel, it will be so relaxing to spend time with Mummy and Daddy and the family. I do miss them sometimes."

"I'm sure you do, Polly, families are very special and yours is very, very special having suffered more troubles than most."

Suddenly, the door from the corridor bursts open and four men pile into the compartment. Two of them attack Daniel with baseball bats, while other two violently assault Polly, slapping her hard across her face and ripping her clothes.

Daniel sustains a fearful beating about his body and upper arms as he shields his head. It seems an age before he manages to get hold one of the bats and hit one of the men about the head, rendering him unconscious. The other two men, meanwhile, have ripped off Polly's blouse, and broken the zip in her skirt. She has scratches and bruising on her arms and is kicking and screaming as the men continue tugging at her skirt, finally ripping it off her. Her undergarments and stockings are ripped also from the men's efforts to seriously assault her, leaving Polly very vulnerable. They hit her again as she desperately struggles to stop them from carrying out the violent assault on her.

Daniel finally manages to bang the head of the fourth man against the side of the carriage before hitting him in the mouth with the baseball bat, which knocks him out. He then yanks the emergency cord, but before he can grab Polly's attackers, they open the outside door and as the train slows, jump from the carriage and run across the tracks and down the embankment to the road. Meanwhile, the guard rushes into the apartment, responding to the emergency cord being used.

"My god, sir, what has happened to you both? Have you been attacked?" he asks, as Daniel covers Polly with his jacket.

"You need to detain these two for the police, and call an ambulance if you would, please."

"Very good, sir. I'll get one of my colleagues to call for the police and get you an ambulance, we are only just outside Watford, so they will be here shortly," says the guard.

Despite being in pain from his beating, Daniel's first thought is for Polly who is curled up in the seat, hysterical over her ordeal. She has marks on her face and upper body where she has been manhandled and what's left of her clothes are in tatters from the savage attack. Daniel is trying desperately to console her when a second guard enters the carriage.

"The police will be here in just a minute, sir."

The police duly arrive on the scene, listen to Daniel's brief account of what has happened, before suggesting they will call him later to meet at his apartment to take statements. Polly and Daniel are then transported to hospital in the ambulance, Polly weeping uncontrollably over her attack.

"Daniel what is happening to us? I don't understand why these people want to hurt us," she sobs.

"They are desperate and evil, Polly, and will stop at nothing, it seems, to hurt you."

They arrive at hospital, and a doctor examines Daniel's injuries. He has two cracked ribs, a dislocated shoulder and heavy bruising on his upper arm, a badly bruised eye, and his lower body is also badly bruised from the beating.

"You have taken a hell of a beating, Mr Bottomley, but looking at your body it would appear that you are used to this sort of thing?" the doctor comments, looking at Daniel's scars.

Daniel has his ribs strapped, and his shoulder in a sling after it is reset. He then takes a look at Polly, but thankfully she is not badly hurt. She has scratches on her chest and legs, from her attackers' violent efforts to remove her clothing and her face is slightly bruised, but is otherwise she is unharmed. She is, however, in shock from the assault, and the doctor mentions this to Daniel. As soon as the doctors have completed their examinations, they are returned to their apartment in the ambulance.

"I suggest you have a warm bath, Polly. I will phone home and tell them what has happened."

"Yes, ok Daniel, and I am going to throw what's left of my clothes in the bin."

Daniel follows Polly to her room with a glass of brandy to calm her. She has begun to remove her clothes and Daniel notices that she has indeed been subjected to horrific assault. As she removes what is left of her blouse and skirt he notices bruising on her upper arms, where she was held, and scratches across her chest, neck, and legs. He puts the glass down and leaves her room to phone Ben Spencer. On hearing about the attack, Ben is understandably very upset.

"God Daniel, I thought we had left all this behind us five years ago."

"For the moment, Ben, I just want to reassure Margaret and yourself that Polly is safe. She is in the bath at the moment, but I will ask her to call you later."

"Thank you Daniel, and once again, we are in your debt for our daughter's safety. I will talk to you again later no doubt, bye for the moment."

Daniel makes some tea for both of them as Polly enters the lounge. The bath has brought some of her colour back, but in doing so shows up the bruising on her face and neck. She also shows Daniel the marks on her chest and on her thighs which are extensive. Daniel is in no doubt what the men's intentions were and is just relieved that he was able to stop them.

"Daniel you look terrible, let me look," says Polly, as she helps Daniel with his shirt. She gasps at the state of his arms and chest not covered by strapping. He is literally black and blue from the beating he sustained.

"You will need to rest for some time to allow all your injuries to heal. You saved me again, Daniel, but you could have been killed."

"Yes, I do feel a bit sore, Polly. How about you? Are you feeling better for your bath?"

"I am, and I have thrown all of the clothes I was wearing in the bin."

"I have spoken with Ben and told him you will call back later."

Daniel will let Polly decide if she still wants to go home after what has happened, but feels sure that she will want to be near her family. For now they just need to try and relax after their ordeal. Polly, meanwhile, busies herself making a snack of beans on toast, since they have not eaten since lunch. After they have eaten, Polly phones home and speaks to both her parents about their ordeal. She is in tears most of the time, but ends by saying they will be along tomorrow sometime after lunch. She then hands the phone to Daniel, holding his hand while he talks to Ben.

"Take care of her, Daniel. She is obviously very upset by what has happened, and we look forward to seeing you both tomorrow."

Daniel looks at his watch and is surprised to note that some four hours have passed since the attack on the train. It is half past eight.

"What time did the police say they would be here tomorrow, Daniel?"

"They will call first thing, Polly, I hope it is early morning, so that we can get off."

"Why don't we stay a bit longer? You will not be able to work with your injuries and I can look after you."

"We both have important positions that need our attention, Polly. We cannot let these people dictate what we do. If, on Tuesday you feel that you cannot face going back to work, then I will stay with you, but we must be available. For now let's just sit and listen to some music and not think about next week at all."

"You're right Daniel, we are together so everything will be ok, I know it will," says Polly, as she sits next to Daniel holding on to his arm. They sit together, with their own thoughts, and both drift off to sleep. Daniel wakes first, his bruises starting to become uncomfortable, and notices the time is past eleven.

"Come on Polly, bedtime," he says, as he walks with her to her room.

"Please stay with me Daniel," Polly asks him as he turns to leave.

"I will come back and see you when you have got yourself ready for bed."

Daniel returns to his room and spends a painful few moments removing his clothes and putting on pyjamas. He leaves off his top and puts on his robe instead, anticipating that Polly will ask him to stay for a while.

"Come and sit with me, Daniel. Please don't leave me on my own tonight."

Daniel will stay with Polly, hoping that he can return to his room when she has gone off to sleep. Polly, however, has other ideas.

"Daniel, I know you are strapped up and covered in bruises, but I really need you to be with me tonight."

"Ok Polly, but please don't jump on me or move around too much!" he replies, smiling.

He climbs into her, bed putting his right arm around her, his left arm still in the sling. Polly switches off her light and turns to him, placing her arm carefully across his battered and bruised body. Daniel is not very comfortable at all. Firstly, he really needs his own bed and space so that his aches and pains become less acute and secondly, he is sharing Polly's bed albeit in rather unusual circumstances. Since they are both recovering from the traumatic experience of earlier, neither of them are really aware of their situation. Polly goes off to sleep almost immediately, Daniel lays there going over the earlier events and wondering what he is going to say to Ben and Margaret. There will be questions that he will find it difficult to answer, and Polly will want to continue her involvement, of that he is certain. Finally he goes off to sleep, becoming ever conscious of Polly's presence by his side. He wakes after a fitful sleep around 6.00am and slowly slips from Polly's grasp and goes into the kitchen to make himself a drink, leaving Polly to continue her sleep.

Polly awakes about an hour later, and wanders into the kitchen, still half asleep.

"Good morning Daniel, I hope I did not disturb you too much last night?"

"I was ok Polly, did you have a good rest?"

"I did, now I want to have a look at you before the police arrive this morning, come along," she says, leading him to the bathroom. He carefully removes his robe to reveal his battered body to Polly. She notices that his stab wound is showing signs of bleeding again. How it wasn't reopened during the scuffle on the train is something of a miracle.

"Daniel, you are bleeding again from your stab wound, let me have a look," she says, carefully removing the dressing. Thankfully, the stitches have held; there is a little seepage from the wound area but nothing serious, but Daniel's torso, his upper arms, and his face and neck are in a terrible mess. Polly gently feels some of the bruises to make sure nothing else is broken.

"Ouch. Polly, that was painful!" says Daniel, wincing as she touches him round his shoulder and neck areas.

"Sorry Daniel," she replies as she finishes dressing his stab wound. "I think you may have some more damage, some of this bruising looks very bad," Polly continues with concern.

"Yes, ok Polly, let's leave it for a few days and see how it develops. If it is causing me problems, I will go back to hospital," replies Daniel, hoping to reassure her.

Just then the phone rings and D.I. Manners asks Daniel if they may call in about an hour. Daniel confirms that will be satisfactory. The Detective Inspector duly arrives, with W.P.C. Becky Peters, and takes down details of the assault on Daniel and Polly on the train. He is concerned that this is the second attack on Polly in a short time.

"Do you have any ideas on who is behind these attacks, Daniel? Would it have something to do with your work perhaps?"

"Well I work for the government and Polly is at the Home Office, so it may have something to do with our work, but I have no idea why Polly should be targeted in such a way," replies Daniel, hoping that the D.I. is satisfied with his comments.

"I appreciate that your work may be confidential, Daniel, but I do have to ask these questions, you understand? Did you recognise any of these men? For example, were they the same ones that broke into your apartment?"

"I would be able to identify them as I got a close look while they were attacking me, Inspector. Unfortunately, they were the two that got away," says Polly.

"Well that's a start I suppose, thank you Miss Spencer."

Daniel then gives his account to the D.I. while Polly talks with the W.P.C. Afterwards, the police officers leave, thanking them both for their cooperation, and Daniel phones Euston to enquire about train times, to be told there is a train for Carswell at 12 noon.

"That will be ideal, Daniel. I will call Daddy and tell him to expect us sometime in the afternoon." So they both prepare a second time for their journey, and Daniel decides that he will take a weapon with him this time. He has to have Polly's help dressing and with his shoes, since he cannot bend down because of his strapping. Polly helps him with his shirt and fastens his tie for him. They then call a taxi and make their way to Euston Station. Their journey to Carswell is without incident, and they arrive at Polly's home at three o'clock.

"Mummy, Daddy, it's so good to see you. Daniel and I are really glad to be here at last," says Polly, hugging them both.

"My dear Polly, what on earth have you both been up to?" asks Ben. He looks across at Daniel and is shocked to see how he is injured. He can see the bruising on one side of his face and notices his arm in a sling.

"Goodness Daniel, you have certainly been in the wars again."

"Daniel, Polly, we have missed you so much," say Maisy, Daisy, and George, rushing up to give them both a hug. Daniel winces as they grab him, not realising how badly he is injured.

"Children, Daniel has some bruises so please do not hold him too tightly."

"It's ok Margaret, really," says Daniel, who is in some pain from his ribs.

The family all move into the parlour, and have some tea as Polly begins to tell what happened yesterday, but is interrupted by Daniel.

"I think we can talk about yesterday sometime later, Polly. Instead why don't you tell Mummy and Daddy about your new job? Far more interesting, I would think," says Daniel, not wanting to dwell on what happened, so as not to upset anyone.

"Ok Daniel, I didn't want to talk about yesterday anyway," says Polly, and starts to tell her parents about her duties as Corporate Liaison Officer at the Home Office. Daniel, meanwhile, goes off to the bathroom, but just as he reaches the top of the staircase, he collapses onto the landing. The family rush from the parlour to see him slumped at the top of the staircase.

"Daniel, Daniel what's happened?" Polly screams hysterically as she runs up the stairs and cradles him in her arms.

"Go along and call for Doctor Wilson, Margaret, I will help Polly with Daniel," says Ben with a sense of urgency. He rushes up the stairs and helps Polly gently lift Daniel and walk him to the bedroom, carefully laying him down on the bed.

"Margaret has sent for the doctor, Daniel. Polly will stay with you until he arrives," says Ben, looking anxious over what has just happened.

"Daniel, my dear Daniel, what has happened to you? Why didn't you say something? You were obviously in a lot of pain," says Polly, squeezing his hand tightly.

"The battered body seems to be telling me it wants a bit of a rest, Polly, I guess," replies Daniel with a smile, his face now quite pale.

"What would I do if anything happened to you? Have you any idea how much you mean to me? You are my whole life, I cannot imagine not being with you always, Daniel," she says, laying bare her feelings for him.

"I will be fine, Polly, and I am going nowhere without you, I promise."

Meanwhile, Margaret brings his tea and tells him the doctor is on his way.

"You are very precious to all of us, Daniel. Please remember that," Margaret says as she leaves the room while Daniel and Polly wait for the doctor, who arrives after about half an hour.

"I am sorry to have kept you, I was on another call. I understand that you have been in the wars again, so let's get your shirt off and take a look at you," says the doctor.

Polly helps remove Daniel's shirt and Doctor Wilson is visibly shocked by the bruising on Daniel's body.

"God Daniel, I can't imagine what pain you are enduring at the moment. I believe the bruising around your kidneys is the main reason for your discomfort. Not passed any blood at all, have you?" he asks.

"No, Doctor."

"How is he, Doctor? He will be ok, won't he?"

"He will be, Polly, eventually. Your body has closed down after its recent beating, Daniel, and is demanding some rest. You have severe bruising around your kidneys, which was the cause of your collapsing in pain. You must rest; bedrest for at least a day or so, then only a few hours a day out of bed. You must not consider any strenuous work for at least two weeks. Your ribs should also have recovered by then. Believe me, Daniel, you must do as I say, otherwise there will be consequences from these injuries," the doctor replies.

"He will do what you say, Doctor, I promise," says Polly, looking at Daniel as she replies to the doctor's demands.

"Very well, Doctor, I fully understand what you are saying, and I know that Polly will make sure that I do as you instruct," he answers with a smile.

"I will give you some painkillers to help you sleep, and something to rub into your kidney area to make it more supple, and I will call in again in a couple of days."

"Thank you very much, Doctor, I appreciate what you have said."

"I will see you out, Doctor, and thank you so much," says Polly as she leaves the room with Doctor Wilson. She quickly returns holding the painkillers and a tube of ointment.

"You need to get into bed now Daniel, please," says Polly, as she helps him to the side of the bed. She opens his overnight bag to find his pyjamas, noticing the weapon inside.

"I see that you have come prepared, Daniel?" she says with a smile, and fetches him some water while he gets into his pyjamas.

"I will stay with you tonight, Daniel, our roles are reversed this time."

"There really is no need for you to miss your rest, Polly."

"I would sooner not sleep again rather than lose you, Daniel. I want to take care of you while you recover, I am responsible for you. It was me that you were fighting for, don't forget."

"Ok Polly, whatever you say, now I think I might have a nap, with your permission!" he says with a smile.

"Sleep well, Daniel," says Polly, kissing him on the forehead, then goes back downstairs to join her family and relay the doctor's diagnosis.

"How is he, Polly? What did Doctor Wilson say?" Ben asks, looking very concerned.

"Daniel must have complete rest, Daddy. The doctor said his body was beginning to shut down after the beating he took saving me from those men on the train," she replies tearfully. "He has a damaged kidney on top of all his other injuries. The doctor said it was the pain that he was suffering that caused him to collapse. My god, Mummy, his body is a complete wreck; he has kidney damage, cracked ribs, a dislocated shoulder, and he has a stab wound from when we had the break-in. It's amazing that he has survived for so long. I love him so much and really do not know what I would do if anything were to happen to him, I really don't," says Polly, sobbing as she holds on to her mother.

"Now Polly, Daniel will be fine I'm sure, what he needs is rest and care and we know you will see to it that he gets all the care that you can give him," replies Margaret, as she hugs her daughter.

"I do love him so much, Mummy, you know."

"Yes, I know you do my dear, I think you have loved him for far longer than you realise. Now off you go into the garden and tell Daddy about this new position of yours, he is most interested to know all about it."

"Thank you Mummy," Polly replies, and goes out into the garden to find Ben sitting on the bench watching the children playing with the dog.

"My dear Polly, how are you? I had completely forgotten that you, too, had been attacked." Polly tells Ben she was attacked by two men, and how Daniel fought desperately to save her.

"There were four of them Daddy, yet Daniel somehow managed to fight them off, that's why he is so badly injured," replies Polly tearfully.

"He is a very special person and I know you will take care of him for however long is necessary, my dear. Of course, you can stay with us for as long as you wish if it will help."

"Daniel will get better, won't he Polly?" the children chorus.

"He will be fine when he has rested, but he must stay in bed to allow his bruised body to heal."

Margaret makes the evening meal while Polly goes upstairs to Daniel. He is still sleeping so she leaves him to rest. She tells Margaret to leave something for Daniel and she will look on him later. She stays in the kitchen with Margaret, telling her about her new job and how she is helping Daniel. Could this be the reason for the recent assaults? They appear to have been directed towards Polly rather than Daniel. However, for the moment Margaret keeps those thoughts to herself as Polly goes upstairs after dinner to find Daniel is awake.

"How are you feeling, Daniel? Would you like some dinner?"

"I would Polly, thank you."

While he is eating his meal, Polly prepares to spend the night in his room.

"What are you doing, Polly?" asks Daniel, as she brings in blankets and moves the easy chair close to his bed.

"I will be staying with you tonight, Daniel, and each night until we go back to London. My job is to take care of you, which means I have to be close by in case you need me."

"Ok Polly, whatever you say. Will you be able to sleep in the chair?"

"I will manage, Daniel, taking care of you is all that matters, nothing else. I just need to tell Mummy and Daddy that I am staying in here with you," she replies, as she goes back downstairs to return a few minutes later. Although it is still early, Polly wants to be by Daniel's side in case she is needed. After he has finished his meal, she takes his plate down to the kitchen and returns with tea for both of them.

"You really are spoiling me, Polly, and I am enjoying it," he says, with a smile.

"It is my way of repaying you for all the times you have taken care of me, now I want to rub some of this liniment on you that Doctor Wilson prescribed, so let me take your pyjama jacket," she says, carefully removing Daniel's jacket. The bruising appears more acute each time Polly sees it, and the area around Daniel's left kidney is almost black. Polly carefully applies the liniment to the kidney area, as Daniel winces. Whilst the touch of Polly's hands is pleasing to Daniel, the circumstances make it a most painful experience. Margaret calls in to see how Daniel is progressing to find her daughter gently applying the liniment to Daniel's kidneys, and is visibly upset by what she sees.

"God Daniel, you look as if you have been hit by a train."

"I am on the mend, Margaret, thanks to Polly taking care of me."

"Please let us know if there is anything you need," she adds, as she leaves Polly still gently applying the liniment.

"I hope I am not causing you too much pain, Daniel, I am being as gentle as I can be," says Polly, noticing how he is grimacing as she touches him.

"I will survive, Polly. Anyway, I cannot imagine a better way of suffering pain than having you stroking me!" replies Daniel with a smile. Polly blushes as she realises what Daniel has just said. She finishes applying the liniment and helps him on with his pyjama jacket.

Daniel lies back in his bed, now visibly sweating from the pain that he is feeling. Hopefully, this will subside as the liniment takes effect.

"Is there anything I can get for you?" Polly asks, as she returns from the bathroom.

"No thanks Polly, I have everything I need with you here."

Polly sits in the chair next to him, wondering what next will happen to them. Daniel is dozing so Polly is alone with her thoughts for a moment. They will have to be even more diligent when they return to London, since it is obvious that someone is giving instructions to harm them. She has always felt safe with Daniel by her side, but this last attack has frightened her more than ever. Her beloved Daniel has suffered terrible injuries, and they must both make sure that this does not happen again. Polly looks at her watch, it is just after ten o'clock. She goes to say goodnight to Ben and Margaret as Ben asks about Daniel.

"Mummy has been telling me about the terrible injuries to Daniel. This man has laid down his life so many times for you and we must take good care of him. Do you think you could persuade him to rest here for a while?"

"I am sure he will want to return to London as soon as the doctor says he can; his work is so important to him, Daddy, and he is dedicated to seeing an end to the communist menace in our country. I will take good care of him and make sure that he continues to rest to allow his injuries to heal. He is very precious to me, and I will not let anything happen to him, I promise."

"Of that I am sure, Polly, of that I am sure."

"Will you have a talk with him anyway, before we return, Daddy? I know how much he respects you, and will listen to what you have to say."

"Of course I will, Polly. Now off you go and take care of him.

Goodnight, my dear," he replies as he kisses his daughter on her forehead.

"Goodnight Daddy, Mummy," replies Polly, returning to Daniel's room.

She first goes to her own room to change and put on her gown before returning to Daniel, who is now asleep, having taken one of his painkillers. Polly wraps herself in her blankets and settles down in the easy chair. She sits looking at him, now sleeping peacefully, and dwells on how much this man means to her. He has been her life for most of the last five years, and Polly is sure that they will be together for the foreseeable future. They have a special kind of friendship which has grown into so much more. And that is what makes their work so much more hazardous. Each one would lay down their life for the other, indeed Daniel has done so many times for her and she would do the same for him. With these thoughts on her mind, Polly drifts into a fitful sleep, waking as the daylight filters through the curtains. Daniel is still sleeping soundly, so she gets dressed and goes downstairs to make some tea, returning with a cup for Daniel who is now awake.

"Thank you Polly, but first I really must use the bathroom."

"Let me help you, Daniel," says Polly as she carefully holds him and walks with him to the bathroom. Daniel washes and cleans his teeth, then returns to his room. By now, the children have stirred and go to see how Daniel is.

"Are you feeling better, Daniel?" George asks with concern in his voice.

"Yes I am George, much better thanks. Polly has been taking very good care of me."

"We were very frightened for you, weren't we Daisy?" says Maisy to her sister.

"We want you to get well quickly, Daniel," says Daisy.

"Thank you, I am sure I shall," he replies with a smile. He had no idea that the children were so worried about him, and is a little embarrassed by their attention.

"Mummy, Daddy, and the children are off to church later, for the traditional Easter Sunday service, so you and I will have the house to ourselves," says Polly.

Daniel really does feel so much better for the rest and sleep that he has had, and would prefer to be up and about. However, he decides against making any mention of this. When the family return from church, Ben pays Daniel a visit.

CHAPTER 5

"I trust you had a restful night, Daniel?"

"Yes I did, Ben. I am feeling so much better, thank you."

"I wanted to have a word with you about this new position of Polly's. Is it placing her in any danger at all?" Ben asks, voicing his concerns for his daughter.

"The Home Office has a group of communists operating in the building and they are suspicious of any newcomers, it would seem. Polly's new position is allowing her, quite legitimately, to move freely through every department and they must see this as some sort of threat. Every head of department has been made aware of her position, and why it is necessary to have an internal courier trusted to deliver important messages between departments. I am rather puzzled why they see Polly as a threat; they must be overcautious since they can have no possible reason for thinking she is anything other than a courier."

"Is there anything that can be done about these people, Daniel? I am concerned for both of you."

"I intend to start travelling with Polly to and from the Home Office each day. We will travel the short journey by taxi, and I will be armed at all times."

"That is very reassuring, Daniel, but first we need to get you fit and well."

"Polly will need to call Conrad for me on Monday evening. The doctor is coming back to look at me on Tuesday, and I hope that he will clear me to travel back on Wednesday. I shall probably have the rest of the week at home, so will ask Conrad to take Polly to and from the Home Office each day."

"That sounds a good idea. Well, thank you for reassuring me. Margaret and I both know how much you care for Polly and that you will continue to look after her as you always have."

Polly returns soon afterwards, and Daniel tells her about his conversation with Ben concerning her new position.

"Ok Daniel, now I will be having lunch with you up here shortly, would you like anything in the meantime, a cup of tea perhaps?"

"Yes, thank you Polly."

The rest of Easter Sunday passes peacefully; Polly sits with Daniel, talking over her position and how much she wants to help. He listens to her every word, and appreciates just how much she wants to be a part of his work. They enjoy a good lunch and he has another visit from Maisy, Daisy, and George. George asks for details of the attack on them in the train, but Polly says no.

"We really don't want to talk about that now, George, it was very upsetting for both of us."

"Ok Poll, whatever you say. Bye for now, Daniel."

After tea, Polly brings a bowl, towel, and soap so that she can help Daniel wash.

"I am going to look at your stab wound while your jacket is off, Daniel."

She removes the bandage over the stab wound and is pleased to see how it has healed. As she bathes Daniel, she realises just how many injuries he has had. This is the first time she has had the opportunity to look closely at his body. He has a scar on his upper left arm and another one just above his hip, these two sustained in a firefight at Polly's home five years ago. Then he has a number of marks from shrapnel, as well as two further scars from bullet wounds. Polly gently dries his back and shoulders before handing him the towel.

"God, Daniel, you are covered in scars. You must have suffered terribly in the war, as well as the wounds you received in my house."

"Nothing for you to get upset about, Polly, most of the scars are old wounds."

"I know, but you have certainly taken your fair share of punishment. Each time I look at you, I am reminded of what you have done for me. Anyway, at least your stab wound has healed, I don't think we need to put anything on that, now let me rub some liniment onto your bruised kidneys before you put your jacket back on."

Once again Polly gently rubs the liniment on the severe bruising around Daniel's kidneys. She notices how tense he is to her touch, probably because of the sensitivity of the area.

"I hope this is helping, Daniel, you seem rather tense. Is it painful when I touch you?"

"It's absolutely fine my dear Polly, and thank you for your concern."

The liniment must be working and bringing out the bruising, because his kidneys hurt like hell. By the time Polly has finished, the sweat is pouring from him which causes Polly some concern.

"Daniel, you are covered in sweat, are you ok?"

"It must be the liniment working, pass me the towel will you?"

"Let me, Daniel, please," says Polly as she wipes the sweat from his face and back. Daniel lies back, leaving off his jacket as Polly continues to wipe off the sweat from his body.

"How are you getting on, Daniel?" says Margaret, who arrives as Polly is just finishing.

"He is sweating heavily, Mummy, it must be from the liniment. If it persists, I shall have to give him another wash," says Polly with concern.

Margaret once again is shocked by the site of Daniel's body. She notes how her daughter almost caresses him as she finishes drying off the sweat. She is obviously very much in love with this man, and she is sure that he must know it. Still, those thoughts will keep, for now getting Daniel well again is the top priority.

"I will leave you to cool down, I think, I am going to have a bath to get rid of the smell of you and your liniment!" Polly says as she takes out the bowl and goes off to have a bath.

Daniel lies back and once again dwells on the closeness of Polly when she was bathing him and applying the liniment to his battered kidneys. The way she has looked after him these past couple of days has convinced him that he will very soon have to tell her of his feelings for her. He is in very little doubt of Polly's feelings, so when the time is right he must tell her. But for now, he must get well and continue the fight, with Polly's help, against the menace of communism that is trying so hard to destroy their way of life. Polly returns after about half an hour, dressed in her pyjamas and gown.

"You should be spending time with your family, Polly, not just sitting here with me."

"But Daniel, this is all I want to do, don't you understand? And my family know that this is where I want to be so settle down. Do you want something to read?"

"I'm ok just talking, but tomorrow, I want you to promise me that you will spend some time with Maisy, Daisy, and George."

"Yes Daniel, I will, and I will call Conrad for you tomorrow also."

"And providing the doctor gives me the all clear, I need Conrad to take you and collect you from work. Then when I return, that is how we will have to travel, and I will be armed in case anyone ever tries to harm you again."

"It really is getting so serious, Daniel. I had no idea that there would be such a reaction to my new position. I am amazed that the communist agitators have made the connection so soon about me passing you information."

"I don't believe they have made the connection by guesswork, Polly. It may be that they have an informer, possibly from Beatrice Carrington's department, I really don't know. When we get back to London, I will call her and see what she thinks."

The rest of Sunday evening drifts by and Daniel decides to take another painkiller, since he is still having some discomfort from his bruising. He drifts into a deep sleep while Polly sits and reads for a while before going downstairs to say goodnight to her parents.

"How is he, Polly?"

"He is asleep now, Daddy, so I thought I might have a warm drink before I go up."

"Your Mummy and I are very worried about what has happened, we are wondering whether your new position is putting you in danger. The communists would not hesitate to kill both you and Daniel if they thought you were interfering in their business. These are agents of the state, Polly. They do not work to any rules, their only agenda is to infiltrate and destroy our way of life and they will not tolerate any interference."

"Daniel is dedicated in his pursuit of these people, Daddy, and I want to help him. I do not want to see our way of life destroyed by an ideal which we all know is a myth. We have to have leaders and followers, we can't all be the same, it just would not work. These people are not seeking power for the people, they are seeking to take over and rule us their way, no democracy, just a totalitarian state, no better than Nazi Germany."

"My dear Polly, I had no idea you felt so strongly about what you are doing."

"Daniel and I talk about this a lot, Daddy. He too is a passionate believer in our society and will do anything to preserve what we have."

"You and Daniel seem to be on your own private crusade, and Daddy and I are indeed proud of what you are doing. All we ask is that you appreciate the dangers that you are putting yourselves in and be very careful please."

"We will Mummy, Daniel and I will travel to and from the Home Office together in future, and Daniel will be armed at all times. I trust him with my life, as I have done many times before. We complement each other in what we do, and we will win in the end, I am sure," replies Polly, as she leaves the parlour and returns to Daniel's room.

"I believe we have a politician in our midst, Margaret. I had no idea that our daughter was so passionate in her beliefs."

"Our little girl has grown into a mature young woman very quickly, Ben. Not without a degree of influence from Daniel, I am sure."

"Their relationship is truly amazing, how it has grown since she was a little girl and continues to grow. It is truly special, Margaret, and I am sure that it will eventually reach the most obvious conclusion for them."

"And what a lovely couple they will make, Ben!"

On Easter Monday morning, Maisy, Daisy, and George go off with their parents to watch the Easter Parade in Carswell, while Polly stays with Daniel, and suggests that it might be an idea for him to have a bath.

"I will help you if you would like, Daniel," she says with a cheeky smile on her face.

"I will try and manage myself, thank you." He does, however, do as Polly suggests, and feels better for the warm water over his body. He still has his ribs strapped, but manages to avoid wetting the strapping. Polly gets him a pair of Ben's pyjamas to change into, which he welcomes after so much sweating yesterday. He leaves off his jacket for the time being and sits on the side of his bed wearing his gown over his pyjama bottoms. Polly gets him some breakfast and tells him of her conversation last evening with her parents.

"You are right, Polly, about what we have to continue to do. I believe we can make a difference and your enthusiasm is a great help as well as your input."

His stab wound is healing, some of the bruises are improving, but the bruising around his kidneys is as black as ever.

"The bruising around your kidneys still looks awful, Daniel, but there is no swelling anywhere and the area is not hard to the touch. It probably looks worse than it is, we shall see what Doctor Wilson has to say. My poor Daniel, you are indeed in a mess and I can't even give you a hug!" she replies with a smile as he puts on his jacket and gets back into bed.

The family return from watching the Easter Parade, and the children visit Daniel to ask how he is. There has been genuine concern from all of them since he has always been the big brother they never had. George especially is disappointed that he cannot spend some time with him.

"Are you getting better, Daniel? We need you to get better, don't we Maisy?"

"Polly is taking care of me George and I am feeling so much

better, thank you." Somewhat overwhelmed by the concern that they have for him, he is very fond of all the children, and has struck a special bond with George. He can remember vividly what happened when Daniel stayed in their house and always believed him to be invincible, so being struck down and confined to bed has scared him somewhat. The rest of Monday passes quietly and after dinner, Daniel briefs Polly before she makes her call to Conrad.

"Tell him that we will call again tomorrow to confirm when we shall be back in London, hopefully on Wednesday," says Daniel as Polly leaves to make the call.

"Hello, this is Conrad."

"Conrad, it's Polly Spencer."

"Polly, hello. What has happened?" says Conrad with concern.

Polly tells him of the attack on the train last Friday.

"Daniel has been hurt, there were four men trying to hurt me. Daniel managed to stop two of them, but the other two escaped."

"What about Daniel, Polly? How badly is he hurt? It must be serious for you to be making this call."

"Daniel took a fearful beating from the men using baseball bats. He has two cracked ribs and a dislocated shoulder, but his worst injuries are to his kidneys, which are severely bruised. We are in my parents' home now having travelled on Saturday, after Daniel had been patched up at hospital. He seemed fine until we got here but he collapsed and the doctor has said he must have bedrest for a while," Polly continues tearfully. "I thought they were going to kill him, Conrad, and God knows what would have happened to me if he had not been there to stop them."

"He's a tough old bird, Polly, and I know he is in good hands, so how can I help?"

"Well, we are hoping the doctor will let Daniel travel home on Wednesday, he is coming to look at him tomorrow. We know we are going to have to be more careful from now onwards, so Daniel and I will travel to and from the Home Office together, by taxi, and Daniel will be armed at all times."

"That sounds very sensible, Polly. Now, if Daniel is not fit to go back to work meantime, I will be your escort."

"Thank you Conrad, we were going to ask you if you would. I do not expect Daniel to be fit for work until next week, so it will only be a few days."

"For as long as it takes, Polly, you have become an asset to our team and I know how precious you are to Daniel. You give him my best and tell him I will let Fitz know what has happened."

"Thank you Conrad, bye for now." She ponders over what Daniel had said about her to Conrad, delighted that he has expressed his feelings for her to his friend. She also feels quite proud to have been told that she is an important member of the team.

"How was Conrad, Polly? What did he say?"

"He says get better, and he offered his services as my escort before I asked. I told him we will confirm when we are able to travel back to London."

"Now all we are waiting for is the nod from the doctor."

"Talking about the doctor, let me give your kidneys another rub before he sees you tomorrow." Daniel, meanwhile removes his pyjama jacket and Polly begins her massage. Whilst she is careful not to exert too much pressure, he still winces as she applies the liniment.

"I am so sorry if I am hurting you, Daniel, I am trying to be as gentle as I can."

"My dear Polly, it is not your fault, my kidneys are just so very tender, please continue," replies Daniel, holding her hand. Daniel's right kidney, which is slightly lower down than the left, is particularly tender, so Polly is very careful not to make it worse. He tries to help by lying on his side so that she can get to his back easier.

"Do you have any more bruising below your waistline?"

"I'm not sure, Polly, will you have a look for me please?" he says as he lies on his stomach.

Polly gently pulls down his pyjamas to reveal heavy bruising on his buttocks and down his thighs.

"Daniel your bottom and thighs are covered in bruises, didn't Doctor Wilson notice them?"

"I'm sure he did but they weren't mentioned, he was more concerned with my kidneys."

Polly gently presses on Daniel's bruises buttocks and thighs, which causes him to flinch.

"Ouch, I felt that."

"Sorry Daniel, I will massage you with the liniment, hopefully it will ease the tenderness," says Polly, gently applying the liniment to his buttocks and thighs. Daniel finds the treatment very relaxing and goes off to sleep. When she has finished, Polly gently pulls up his pyjamas and covers him with the bedclothes before going downstairs.

"How is he, Polly?"

"He is asleep Mummy, but his bruising is not really improving, and I have discovered more severe bruising on his buttocks and on his thighs. I'm not sure whether Doctor Wilson was aware, but you wouldn't see it unless you pulled down his pyjamas. Anyway, I used the liniment and hope it will ease the obvious discomfort he is in."

"I see," says Margaret, feeling slightly embarrassed by the picture presented of her daughter rubbing liniment on Daniel's bottom and thighs. Her devotion to Daniel seemingly knows no boundaries.

After a good night's sleep, for Daniel at least, Polly is about early to get him ready for the doctor, who duly arrives at nine o'clock.

"Good morning to you Daniel, how are we feeling today?"

"Very much better than when we last met, Doctor, and I hope you will confirm this."

"Well let's have a look at you, if you would stand up and take off your jacket for me please," the doctor asks. Daniel stands in front of the doctor who examines him closely, especially round his kidney area.

"Your kidneys are still badly bruised, Daniel, but there has been an improvement. Have you been using the liniment I gave you?"

"Yes he has, Doctor, I have been applying it every evening."

"Well you have done a good job, Polly, and I see that the stab wound too is healing. How is the shoulder?"

"I have barely given it a thought, Doctor, the pain from the kidneys has tended to take precedent over anything else."

"Doctor, would you have a look at the bruising on Daniel's buttocks and thighs? It is quite severe."

"I didn't realise that you had been injured there Daniel, let me take a look."

Daniel removes his pyjamas and the doctor carefully examine his buttocks and thighs.

"These are quite serious bruises on such tender areas, Daniel. You may have some difficulties sitting for a while," he says, gently pressing round Daniel's buttocks.

"I used some of your liniment, Doctor, I hope that was ok?" says Polly, standing next to him, apparently unaware that he is naked.

"That would have helped, Polly, certainly. Ok Daniel, you can put your pyjamas back on."

Only when the doctor mentions Daniel putting his pyjamas back on does Polly realise that she was standing beside him while he was naked. She moves away, rather embarrassed at what has occurred.

"Now, whilst there have been improvements, and you have obviously been well looked after, you still need some time to heal, Daniel. I see no reason why you cannot travel back to London tomorrow, but promise me you will stay away from work and rest until Monday? I will leave you some more of the liniment together with a note for your own doctor, should you need to visit him. Good luck to you Daniel, and bye for now."

"Goodbye Doctor, and thank you very much for your help. I do appreciate it."

"I will see the doctor out, Daniel, and telephone Mrs Wright. You can get back into bed for the time being."

Daniel smiles at Polly's instruction, but is happy to oblige, knowing that he can begin getting back to normal sometime after tomorrow. He lies there for a moment and suddenly realises that he was standing naked next to Polly while being examined by the doctor! Polly, meanwhile, sees the doctor to the front door, thanking him again, then goes into the study to call Mrs Wright.

"Good morning, Peggy Wright speaking."

"Mrs Wright, it's Polly Spencer."

"Ah Polly, I was wondering where you were. Is anything wrong?"

"I will not be in to work until Thursday, Mrs Wright. My guardian and I were attacked on the train on Friday, and he collapsed with his injuries when we arrived at my parents' house."

"Good heavens, what on earth happened?"

Polly gives her details of the savage beating dished out to Daniel by the four men.

"I was fortunate to get away with a few scratches and bruises, although my clothes were torn off. I shudder to think what would have happened if Daniel had not been with me."

"It must have been very frightening, Polly. This friend Daniel must be a pretty tough sort to fight off four men. Who did you say he was?" asks Mrs Wright intrigued to know more.

"Daniel is like my unofficial guardian. I have lived with him since moving to London. My family have known him since he stayed with us for some time five years ago."

"That would be the time when your father successfully broke up that black market operation, I remember the Old Bailey Trial?"

"Yes, that's correct, Daniel looked after me and saved me several times from gangs of villains who attacked our house."

"And is Daniel badly hurt? Because you may take as long as you like to care for him, he is obviously very special to you, isn't he?"

"Yes he is, Mrs Wright, he has been a big part of my life since we first met when I was a thirteen-year-old schoolgirl."

"Indeed, well let me know what you decide, my dear, and wish your Daniel well for me. Bye for now."

"Everything ok at the office, Polly? What did Mrs Wright say?"

"She was very concerned about you and has asked me to let her know what I decide when we return."

After some lunch, Daniel decides to get up and go downstairs to the garden for some fresh air. It is a warm day and he savours the garden and its surroundings after being laid up in bed for the last three days. Polly sits beside him and the children ask when they are leaving.

"Can't you stay a bit longer, Daniel? We have hardly seen you at all," asks Maisy.

"We will come along and see you all again soon, I promise, but Polly and I have to get back to work as soon as possible."

The children are naturally disappointed by his response, although it was not unexpected.

"I will ask Daddy to check on train times tomorrow, Daniel. We can get away around lunchtime I would think."

"How are you feeling, Daniel? Enjoying the fresh air, I see. You're sure that you have recovered enough to go back tomorrow? You know how much we care for you and the last thing we want is for you to return home too soon."

"I am feeling much better, Margaret, and I shall rest up at home until Monday. Polly will not let me return if she feels I am not ready, I am sure."

"Yes, I am sure you are right about that, Daniel. She will take good care of you and you don't need me to tell you how she feels about you."

"And I care for her very much, Margaret. Your daughter has become a big part of my life over the last five years, and I cannot imagine not being with her. I intend to make my feelings known to her when the time is right, but for now we will continue to be there for each other. Can you understand what I am saying?"

"I do, Daniel, and thank you so much for telling me that."

"And thank you for listening, I don't often get the opportunity to talk about how I feel towards her." He follows Margaret into the parlour and asks Polly if she would like a walk along the lane.

"I need to get my legs working again after lying in bed for so long," says Daniel, as he and Polly set off along the lane.

"Daddy has checked the timetables for us and there is a London train leaving at one o'clock tomorrow."

"That will be ideal, then when we get back I want to contact Beatrice Carrington about my suspicions."

"Do you really believe that someone in her office has informed on my position and what I am doing?"

"There doesn't seem to be any other explanation, Polly. No one knows other than ourselves, my office, and Beatrice. Meanwhile we will make sure that you are always escorted to and from the Home Office, and just be extra careful."

"I know you will take care of me, Daniel. You always have done," says Polly, looking at Daniel and smiling affectionately.

"We take care of each other, Polly, as you have shown me these past few days."

CHAPTER 6

Ben drives Polly and Daniel to the station the next day, and they leave promptly at one o'clock for the journey back to London. After an uneventful journey, they arrive back in Kensington around 4.30pm. Daniel is relieved to be back in his own apartment and he and Polly sit and enjoy a cup of tea, taking in what has happened to them since they finished work last Friday, just six days ago. They are both just sitting on the settee when the phone rings. It's Conrad.

"Hello Daniel, I was hoping you would be back home. How are you, my friend?"

"Much improved, Conrad, after rest and recuperation organised by Polly."

"Yes, I guessed as much when she called me, now we will talk about what happened when you are back in the office, meantime, I just wanted to confirm that I will call for Polly around 8.30am tomorrow, is that ok?"

"That will be fine, Conrad, and thank you again."

"My pleasure, bye for now."

Polly and Daniel settle down to a light meal since there is not much in the apartment, and neither of them want to go out. After their meal, they sit and enjoy each other's company while listening to the wireless.

"You will take it easy over the next few days, Daniel, when I am not here to take care of you?"

"Absolutely, Polly, I will not involve myself with anything more energetic than making a few calls and reading a book, and possibly getting a meal for you."

"Thank you Daniel, now I am going to have a bath."

Daniel dwells on what he will say to Beatrice Carrington tomorrow; he is somewhat concerned that the detail of Polly's position does seem to have leaked from her office. It will be difficult to discover who is responsible and meanwhile he will have to make sure that she is safe at all times. He recalls the assault on her, which was brutal. It was very apparent what they would have done to her if he had not been able to stop them. Polly has not really mentioned what happened, so he decides it may be best to leave it like that for now. If she wants to talk about what happened, then she will do so in her own time. After about half an hour or so, Polly returns in her pyjamas and gown.

"By the way, when are you going back to the hospital to be looked at? You will need to have your ribs and shoulder examined as well as an update on the condition of your kidneys."

"I will call tomorrow and arrange to visit as soon as possible, thank you for reminding me."

"It is my job to look after you, Daniel, and the priority at the moment is for you to recover from your injuries. I do feel responsible, since they were a direct result of you looking after me," she says, with a tear in her eye.

"Please do not upset yourself Polly, it's over now."

"I love you so much and I really do appreciate how you take care of me, Daniel," she replies, holding on tightly to him.

"Ouch. Steady on, Polly. I have enough bruises."

"Sorry Daniel, I just want to be close to you, that's all."

They sit there together, saying nothing, and Polly eventually falls asleep in his arms. Daniel looks at her and recalls what he said to Margaret, about his feelings towards her. He knows he loves her very much and is sure that she knows how much he cares for her. However, for the time being he is content for their relationship to remain the same as it has always been. Polly is very happy, Daniel is very happy, so leaving things as they are seems to be a sensible way forward. He sits with her for a while before deciding she needs to go to her bed.

"Come along Polly, it's time for bed."

"Ok Daniel, I must have dropped to sleep. Goodnight," she says, kissing Daniel on his cheek.

"Sleep well, my dear. I will see you in the morning."

Polly is up early on Thursday morning and looking forward to returning to her work. She makes tea for Daniel and sits beside him.

"I'm looking forward to being back at work, but would have liked also to be with you today."

"You enjoy your day, Polly, just be aware of what has happened. Now off you go while I dress."

Conrad duly arrives at 8.30am.

"Good morning Daniel, how are you feeling?"

"Getting better, Conrad. Will you tell Fitz I will call him in about an hour?"

"Hello Conrad, thank you for being my escort today."

"It is my pleasure Polly, anything for you and Daniel."

Polly kisses Daniel on his cheek before moving towards the door, and Daniel confirms with Conrad that he is carrying his weapon. Conrad has booked the taxi for them which is waiting at the apartment's entrance. After thanking Conrad and arranging to meet him at five o'clock, Polly goes into the ground floor of the Home Office building, and walks towards Mrs Wright's office.

"Come in, Polly. How are you? I hope Daniel is improving?"

"I am very well thank you, Mrs Wright, and Daniel is getting better after his terrible beating."

"It must have been very frightening. Do you have any idea who it might have been that wanted so badly to hurt you both?"

"No I don't, I am just relieved that Daniel was with me, the men made it very obvious what they wanted to do to me, so I will be escorted to and from work from now onwards as a precaution."

"You are fortunate to have someone such as Daniel taking care of you, Polly. I should like very much to meet him someday, meanwhile, you had better get on with it, you have two days' work to catch up with."

Daniel makes his first call of the morning to Fitz.

"My dear chap, Conrad has been briefing me on what happened, how are you feeling?"

"On the mend, Fitz, but I would not like to take that sort of beating too often."

"These people seem hell-bent on getting to Polly. I understand from Conrad that she will now have an armed escort to and from the office?"

"Yes, Conrad will do the honours today and tomorrow, and from Monday it will be my job."

"It's a job which you have carried out with distinction, Daniel. Is Polly ok? She is a very special young lady, I have to say that I was very impressed when we met."

"She has been so busy taking care of me, I'm not sure that she has had time to think about what happened to her, Fitz."

"Indeed, it was obvious when we met that she worships you and I'm sure you are more than just fond of her."

"You are not wrong on that, Fitz."

"Now do you have any leads on who is behind these attacks at all?"

"I don't, but I am going to have a word with Beatrice Carrington later, since I believe that someone in her department must be involved."

"What on earth do you mean by that?" asks Fitz, somewhat concerned at Daniel's inference.

"The two attacks, one at my apartment and the one last Friday on the train, have both occurred since Polly took up her new position. A position which has been made official to all department heads. No one could have determined what she has been doing on our behalf, unless they had first-hand knowledge and that could only have been obtained from Beatrice's office."

"I see, well put like that, you certainly have a point. Now, I must get on, let me know what Beatrice says, will you? Bye for now."

Daniel contacts the hospital and arranges to go to be looked at after lunch. He makes himself some tea before calling Beatrice Carrington.

"Hello, Beatrice Carrington speaking."

"Beatrice, good morning, it's Daniel Bottomley. I wonder if we might have a word?"

"One moment Daniel while I secure the line. Ok, now how may I help you?"

Daniel tells her of the two attacks, which both seem to focus on Polly, and waits for her comment.

"This is not good, Daniel, I recommended Polly for that position, and feel some responsibility for what has happened."

"You believe as I do, that they are linked to her new position?"

"I do indeed and if that is so we both know that the information about her position could only have been leaked from my department."

"That is precisely what I believe, Beatrice, which makes it very worrying."

"It does. You must leave this with me, I need to make some urgent enquiries, I will get back to you as soon as I have any news. Give my best to Polly, will you?"

So with Beatrice confirming his suspicions, Daniel has a sandwich before going off to hospital. The doctor is pleased with the improvements to his injuries, but is still cautious regarding the bruising to his kidneys, especially after hearing of Daniel's collapse. However, his other injuries are progressing very well.

"Your kidneys took a hell of a beating but the liniment prescribed has improved things. I will replace your strapping and suggest that you leave it in place for another week. Providing you feel no more discomfort, you can then remove it. Your stab wound is healing well, how is your shoulder? Is it sore at all?"

"It is fine, Doctor, no discomfort at all."

"Ok Daniel, well that's all for now," says the doctor as Daniel puts his shirt back on and leaves the hospital. He does some shopping on the way back, arriving about 4.30pm, and decides he will call Fitz back and tell him of his conversation with Beatrice Carrington.

"This is indeed more serious than I imagined, Daniel, and Beatrice must be very concerned. I've a mind to contact Quentin Blake at MI5 and ask his advice on this. He may have an idea of any communist infiltration in the Home Office at high levels. He is aware of your work in this, and I have told him I would keep him informed. If Russia has succeeded in planting a mole in the higher echelons of the Home Office, MI5 will need to act."

"What about Polly, Fitz? Is she in any danger?" Daniel asks with obvious concern.

"As long as you and Conrad are accompanying her to and from work, she should be safe, but you must be diligent. Keep your eyes open for any strangers hanging about your apartment block."

"I'll ask the concierge to look out for any strangers, I know him very well and he is a helpful chap. and I will contact the police tomorrow to see if they have made any progress."

"Ok Daniel, I will call you if I have any details relevant to this, bye for now."

Daniel sits reflecting on what has been said and decides for the moment that he will not tell Polly of Fitz's concerns, but he will tell her of his conversation with Beatrice Carrington. He finds himself looking out of the window, waiting for Conrad to arrive with Polly, suddenly feeling quite lonely in his apartment, having become so used to Polly being with him and missing her when she is not around.

Conrad eventually arrives and delivers Polly safely.

"Thanks Conrad, can I offer you anything at all?"

"No thanks, I have asked the cab to wait for me, I will see you both in the morning."

"How was your day, Polly, any distractions?" Daniel asks, hoping Polly does not note the concern in his voice.

"I had a lot of catching up to do. Mrs Wright was very sympathetic and asked about you, she seemed very concerned.

"Did she ask if we had any ideas who might be behind the attack?

"She did ask, Daniel. I just said I had no idea and left it at that."

"Well I have spoken with Beatrice Carrington and she is very concerned. She believes there may be someone in her department that has found out about your position."

"It sounds more serious than I imagined. Did she say she would get back to you?"

"Yes she will, meantime I have spoken with Fitz about this and he wants to speak with his colleague in MI5. If the Home Office has a mole in a position to secure information of a sensitive nature, then MI5 have to be involved."

"We must do what we can to beat these people, Daniel. They must not be allowed to dictate how we run our lives. I will do what I can to help you find out who they are and, if necessary, expel them from our country."

"You must promise me that you do not take any risks, Polly. Do your job and collect what information you can. Do not do anything that will point any fingers at what you are doing, these people are ruthless and would kill you in order to achieve their ends."

"Daniel, please, you are frightening me. It really can't be as bad as you say."

"My dear Polly, I did not mean to frighten you, I just want you to be careful."

He sometimes forgets that Polly is only eighteen years of age and still growing up in the world. He has been with her for so long now, that he looks upon her as being much more mature than her age suggests.

"Now why don't we start preparing some dinner? I collected all the shopping you asked for."

"Ok Daniel, I will make some chips, and we have plenty of eggs."

Daniel makes sure they don't talk any more 'shop' during the evening by asking Polly what she would like to do this coming weekend.

"I would like to see a show of some sort, we haven't been to the theatre for ages."

"I will make some enquiries tomorrow, it will give me something to do on my last day at home, and I want to ask the police if they have any news on the break-in and attack on the train."

The rest of the evening passes quietly and they go off to bed around eleven o'clock.

"Goodnight Polly, sleep well," says Daniel, kissing her forehead.

Daniel is in a deep sleep when he is woken by Polly shaking him in hysterics.

"Daniel, there is someone in the apartment, I can hear them moving about," she says, pulling at him to get out of his bed. Daniel gets up and goes toward the lounge, switching on the lights to reveal an empty room. Polly is clinging to him, obviously in some distress from what must have been a bad dream.

"There is no one here, Polly, you have had a bad dream. Come along, back to bed."

"I am frightened, Daniel, please let me stay with you. I do not want to be alone in my room."

"You really should go back to your room, Polly, it is not acceptable that you sleep in my bed, we have mentioned this before."

"But Daniel, we have shared a bed before. I need to feel safe and want you by my side, please."

Daniel realises that Polly will not rest until she is with him and, with some trepidation, goes back to his room with Polly beside him. He looks at his bedside clock to see the time is just after 3.00am. He knows he will not get much rest with Polly by his side, but hopes that she will soon go off to sleep now that she is with him. However, he does eventually go off to sleep and when he wakes he sees that it is 6.30am. He climbs out of his bed slowly so as not to disturb Polly, who is still sleeping soundly, and goes to make himself some tea. He sits on his settee, musing over another difficult and confusing period, with Polly in his bed. He realises that her trust in him is so strong that she has no hesitation in wanting to share his bed as though he were her brother or some other sibling. For now, Daniel decides he must accept how she feels and behaves, as long as she does not mention it to anyone. He finishes his tea, washes and shaves, and returns to his room to dress. Polly is still sleeping soundly, so he decides to leave her for a little while.

Eventually, about 7.30am, Polly stirs and goes off to the bathroom.

"Daniel, you should have woken me, how long have you been up?" she says, sitting beside him.

"Not long, Polly. I left you since you were sleeping soundly and the extra rest will do you good."

Just after 8.30am, Conrad duly arrives to collect Polly, who kisses Daniel goodbye before going off to her work. After another cup of tea and some toast, Daniel calls the local police station, and asks for D.I. Jack Manners.

"Good morning Detective Inspector, I was wondering if you had made any progress."

"Daniel, good morning, I was going to call you today. Are you free at all?"

Daniel tells him that he is at his apartment and free to see him anytime, so he suggests that he calls around eleven o'clock. Daniel, meantime, busies himself around his apartment waiting for the D.I., who duly arrives just before eleven o'clock.

"Come in, Detective Inspector."

"How are you, Daniel? You have certainly been in the wars looking after young Polly."

"I am very much on the mend. I shall be returning to my work on Monday, Polly returned yesterday." He then gives the D.I. a brief note on what has transpired over the Easter period, and proceeds to ask him if he has any information.

"The three men that attacked you and Polly here in your apartment, were local villains for hire. Billy Swift, Jimmy Jones, and Shaun Devlin are all known to us as hard cases who will hurt anyone for money. All they have told us is they were contacted by some chap in an East End pub. He told them your address and gave them twenty pounds each to give you a beating. They were told to be particularly unpleasant to Polly. I would not have mentioned this if she had been here, but it was obvious that they intended to sexually assault her as well as give her a beating."

"Did they give you a description of the man who hired them?"

"Only that he had a weird accent. Didn't speak English very well, they said."

"And what about the two you arrested from the assault on the train?"

"Now this is where it gets interesting, we are not the only people interested in them. I was visited yesterday by two gentlemen from MI5. They asked to speak with the men I have in custody, namely David Piper and George Reagan. They spoke with them for quite some time, then asked me if I would keep them in custody, while they made some calls. Do you know what this is about?"

"Unofficially, you understand, Detective Inspector, I believe they are Communist Party members, and the two men that escaped were Russians. I cannot be more specific, but should MI5 make contact with my office, I will let you know. What I will say to you is that it is obvious that this was not just an assault on two people on a train."

"Indeed, I don't know what business you and young Polly are involved with, but I do urge you to take care. If I can help you in any way, please let me know."

"Thank you Detective Inspector, we will be in contact again, I am sure. Bye for now."

Daniel returns to the lounge to digest the information given him by D.I. Manners, and realises that events have just changed dramatically. The direct intervention of the communists means that Russia is pulling strings and has orchestrated an attack on two British citizens. Daniel decides to call Fitz immediately.

"Morning Fitz, it's Daniel."

"Daniel, how are you?"

"I'm fine Fitz, will be back in on Monday. Tell me, have you heard anything from MI5 at all?"

"No I haven't, why do you ask?"

Daniel relates the details of his conversation with D.I. Jack Manners.

"My god, this changes everything, Daniel. I will speak with Quentin Blake today and arrange a meeting. You will be back

Monday you say, so I will try and fix a meeting. We shall need some advice on this. We may have to give Polly some additional protection, although I have to say I am at a loss to know what more you can do."

"I can take care of Polly, Fitz, and I want to carry on with my union investigations. Polly will want to continue with her job finding any relevant information. We can beat these people, Fitz, and anyway if we stopped now, it would not prevent them from continuing to intimidate anyone who gets in their way. Let us see what MI5 have to say before making any decisions. I will have to tell Polly what the D.I. has said, but I know for sure that she will be as determined as ever in wanting to continue."

"As you wish, Daniel, which reminds me, you had a message yesterday from your Peter Hennessey; he asked that you make contact."

"Thanks Fitz, and I will see you on Monday morning, enjoy your weekend."

He sits for a moment, contemplating his conversation with Jack Manners and then with Fitz, and realises that the lives of Polly and himself are about to change forever. It is now clear that Polly especially is being targeted by the communists, as well as himself. He must talk with Fitz, on Monday, about how he can improve the security at his apartment to prevent any breaches, and he must talk with Polly about what he must do to ensure her safety. Whilst he is most reluctant to worry her too much, he owes it to her to be open and honest about their position. Meantime, to take his mind of all this he rings round some theatres to book seats for tomorrow Saturday. The musical 'South Pacific' is on at the Theatre Royal, which is only a short distance away, in Drury Lane, so he books tickets for the evening performance. Conrad duly arrives with Polly around 5.30 and confirms that Fitz has mentioned his conversation with Daniel.

"Have a good weekend, you two."

"You too Conrad, and thank you for bringing me home safely."

"How was your day, Polly?"

"Busy, Daniel, I had no idea just how many departments I am looking after. I feel worn out."

"Well we shall have a good day tomorrow, I have booked tickets for 'South Pacific' at the Theatre Royal."

"Thank you Daniel, that's wonderful," she replies, giving Daniel a hug, before going off to the kitchen to make some tea.

Daniel uses the time to contact Peter Hennessey, who tells Daniel that there is to be a mass meeting of dockers next Wednesday. The agenda is to seek a mandate for an all-out strike at London docks.

"Do you think that you and your two colleagues will be able to meet me on Wednesday evening to discuss what happened?"

"Yes I think so, but they won't want to meet in the same place. Can you suggest somewhere?"

"What about the Lamb and Flag in Covent Garden, far enough away from the docks, but not too far to travel?"

"Yeah, that sounds ok Daniel, about eight o'clock?"

"Eight o'clock will be fine, Peter. I will have a young colleague with me from the Home Office. She liaises with my department, and is fully aware of who you are," Daniel replies, realising that he cannot leave Polly alone at any time in the future after today's revelations.

"Ok Daniel, I will see you Wednesday, bye for now."

"Did I hear you say I will be coming with you when you meet your union contacts?"

"Yes Polly, you and I will be together at all times from now on. Sit down a moment, I want to talk to you." He then relates to Polly what the D.I. told him, and how MI5 have become involved.

He then goes on to tell her that he will be talking with Fitz on Monday to discuss how they might improve security at the apartment.

"Are you saying that the Russians ordered those men to hurt me, Daniel? How can I be so important that they want to kill me? They must have agents in the Home Office, and are looking to strengthen their position. I must have caught them off guard, and they are concerned at what I may find out."

"So long as I am here, I will protect you and no harm will come to you, Polly. The last thing I want to happen is for you to become a frightened young girl who is scared of everything and everyone. You and I will still go out and enjoy ourselves wherever and whenever you wish. A long time ago, I made a promise to your parents that I would protect you, and I intend to keep that promise. The situation has changed somewhat since I made that promise, since I now care for you and love you very much. You have become far too precious for me to allow any harm to come to you."

"Thank you Daniel, I love you very much too you know, I think I always have done right from when I was thirteen years old and I always knew you loved me, but it is nice to hear you say so."

"Now, what do we have for supper? I am feeling rather hungry."

"I'll see what we have, Daniel. I'm sure I can make something for you," she replies, going off to the kitchen. After their meal Daniel talks with Polly over the seriousness of the discovery that Moscow may have been behind the attack on the train. He has no wish to frighten her unduly, but does need her to be aware of what they are up against.

"I want you to come along with me on Wednesday, when I meet Peter Hennessey, because I do not want you to be left alone in the apartment. We have to make a few changes to our lifestyle, one being that you do not go anywhere on your own in future. I am going to talk with Fitz on Monday about security here, possibly install some sort of alarm and lighting in the hallway. And I want to teach you how to use a firearm which you will carry in your bag at all times. I know it may seem rather dramatic, Polly, but I am just being cautious."

"I will do whatever you suggest, Daniel."

They sit listening to the wireless for some time before Polly goes off for a bath. Daniel, meantime, goes to his room and checks on the two firearms he possesses to make sure that they are in good working order. He has two handguns which he has used on several occasions during his career within special operations department, and also when he spent time protecting Ben Spencer's family. The Browning M1911 is his weapon of choice, and he also possesses a .38 special revolver. He keeps both weapons in good working order and regularly carries the Browning. He has full authority to carry both weapons at any time. He must now decide what would be a suitable weapon for Polly to have once she has been trained in how to use a firearm.

Hearing Daniel in his room, Polly joins him, after changing into her pyjamas and gown.

"I had no idea you had two guns in your room, Daniel," she says, noticing the weapons on his table with the bullets removed.

"Just checking that they are in good working order, it is important to look after your weapon in case you may have to use it. It could save your life. I want you to learn how to use a firearm, then we shall select one suitable for you."

"Do you really think I should have to carry a gun, Daniel?"

"Yes I do, it is obvious that these people are becoming more desperate in their attempts to harm you, and you being prepared makes good sense. I will take you along to my regiment's firing range as soon as I can arrange for someone to give you instruction."

"Ok Daniel, not sure whether I will enjoy using a gun, but I understand what is happening and will do as you suggest," says Polly with a degree of resignation.

They both arise early on Saturday, Polly being eager to go to the West End again and look in the shops. She adores window shopping, being just the right age to begin wanting to buy clothes and look attractive. Daniel is just pleased to see her enjoying herself without a care in the world, it would seem. In reality it is quite different, but for now she is a typical eighteen-year-old out shopping. After what seems hours to Daniel, they have some lunch before returning to the apartment.

Polly has bought some new clothes which she shows off to Daniel, who is quite impressed by her choice, although he is hardly an expert anyway! Daniel has tickets for the eight o'clock show at the Theatre Royal, so he and Polly go off for some dinner before arriving at Drury Lane. 'South Pacific' is not really Daniel's choice of entertainment, but he knows how much Polly loved musicals so the show is very much for her benefit. She is captivated by the musical, the surroundings, and everything about their evening. No one would have guessed that she was the target of desperate men who would seek to harm or even kill her. Part of Daniel's responsibility toward her was to make sure that she enjoyed her life no matter what she may have to endure. Seeing her this evening, laughing and clapping, the performance was proof enough that he could make her happy no matter what.

Polly is humming the tunes from the show on the way back in the taxi, and is still doing so as they enter Daniel's apartment. They both have some tea before going off to their rooms. Polly sleeps soundly, Daniel not so. He knows that they are now being targeted directly by communist thugs and goes over in his mind how best to combat this, whilst still continuing his work. Hopefully, his contacts in the unions will be helpful, and also Beatrice Carrington will have some news. He reminds himself to speak with her on Monday, eventually goes off to sleep. He is woken by Polly with a morning cup of tea.

"Good morning Daniel, did you sleep well? I did and am ready for breakfast, how about you?"

"I will have whatever you choose," he replies, smiling and delighted that Polly is so bubbly.

After a lazy Sunday morning, they go off to walk around the gardens of Kensington Park. It is a favourite place for Londoners to walk and relax, which is what they do for a couple of hours or more, before returning to the apartment for a Sunday lunch which Polly had prepared earlier. The rest of the day is spent talking, listening to music, and generally enjoying each other's company.

"Thank you for a wonderful weekend, Daniel."

"You are welcome, Polly. We have a busy week next week, so I wanted to be sure that the weekend was relaxing."

Polly sits next to him and is very soon dropping off to sleep. Daniel puts his arm around her and walks her to her room, kissing her goodnight as she climbs into bed. He decides he too will have an early night, and settles down to read for a while. He now sleeps with his .38 pistol under his pillow, and checks that it is fully loaded. He will carry his other weapon at all times in future, which he keeps in a locked drawer. Tomorrow will be an important day for decisions about security at the apartment and how Polly can be kept safe. He considers options, which are limited, since he does not want Polly to feel too restricted in her job. With these thoughts in mind he drifts off to sleep.

On Monday morning, they set off to for the Home Office, both deep in their thoughts. Daniel kisses her on her forehead before she leaves the taxi, and reminds her to wait inside the entrance for him at five o'clock.

"Enjoy your day, Polly, but do take care my dear."

"I will, Daniel," she says as she goes off to join other workers entering the Home Office building.

Daniel tells the taxi driver to move about 100 yards further along Whitehall before he gets out, asking the driver if he would pick him up outside the entrance to the Home Office at five o'clock.

"Good morning Daniel, I trust you are fit and well?"

"Fit and ready Fitz, thanks. I need to talk when you have a moment."

"Of course, dear boy. About half hour ok?" asks Fitz, which suits Daniel since he wants to speak with Conrad first of all.

"I am meeting with my union contacts this week, Conrad, and hope that they have some real information about the communist agitators. We have to consider a visit to their headquarters to get the sort of information that may implicate them. Meantime, I will see what Hennessey and his colleagues have to say."

"Whenever you are ready, Daniel, just give me a shout."

While waiting to meet with Fitz, Daniel decides he will call Beatrice Carrington.

"Good morning Beatrice, it's Daniel Bottomley, I hope you are well?"

"Very well thank you Daniel. More to the point, how are you?"

"I'm very much better now thank you, do you have a moment?"

"One moment Daniel," she asks as she transfers to a secure line. "Now how can I help?"

"I was hoping you may have some news concerning a possible security leak?"

"I do believe we know where it may have occurred, but it would be very difficult to prove. So I have made some changes to my personnel and have moved four of my staff to other departments. I have moved four personnel so that the person concerned does not suspect that we know who she is. She will have no way of accessing any information relative to your office or Polly, and she will be carefully monitored by one of the personnel I have moved with her."

"Well that is good news Beatrice, although I fear it may not stop these people, they seem determined to stop Polly's activities no matter what it takes."

"I have set up a small team of my most trusted colleagues to look hard within the Home Office and the Foreign Office for any subtle policy changes that may suddenly appear. I have spoken with the one of my colleagues in the management department who has the ear of the Permanent Secretary, and asked him to be alert to any sudden promotions or personnel changes, and let me know. Currently, we are aware of who the main players are, and are content to be able to watch them without there being aware, but newcomers could present a problem. To date, we have only dismissed two members of the civil service for communist activities, but we are sure there are many more. As for Polly's safety, Daniel, that has to remain very much your responsibility. Living with you and being in your company will be the best way that you can protect her, and we both know you have had plenty of practice in that regard."

"Yes that's true, Beatrice. Well thank you for the information, and we will keep in touch should circumstances change, bye for now," says Daniel.

"Now then Daniel, what can I do for you?" Fitz asks as Daniel enters his office.

"I was hoping that you could give me some ideas on improving security at my apartment. It is obvious that the communists are hell-bent on getting at Polly, and I am anxious that they cannot get into my apartment again."

"Quite so, Daniel. Let's bring in Phil on this." Phil enters the office and Daniel voices his concerns about a possible further intrusion at his apartment.

"Well we could install a sensor above your door which would warn you of anyone approaching and arrange for the hallway light to come on and alarm be set off at the same time. We could also fit a deadbolt locking device and drawer bolts at the top and bottom of your door. The door itself is pretty strong, so no need to replace that. And since your apartment is on the third floor, entry by a window is most unlikely. That's about all we can do, and since you have a weapon you are ideally positioned to be able to protect Polly."

"That sounds very good, Phil. Can I leave it with you to make the arrangements? Let me know when you will be ready, and I will give you my key."

Phil leaves the office and Daniel relays Beatrice's comments to Fitz, who is very concerned about the obvious communist infiltration into the Home Office.

"You have to get some information to help us get rid of these vermin, for that is what they are, Daniel, trying to corrupt and destroy our way of life with their communist dogma. Let's break up their party any way we can, make life difficult for them, harass and thwart their every move and if necessary, squash them under our feet," says Fitz, his anger apparent for all to see.

"I am meeting with my union contacts on Wednesday, I hope they will have some names for us to work on."

"Let's hope so, Daniel, for all our sakes."

Wednesday evening arrives and Polly is both apprehensive and excited at being involved with Daniel's visit to meet with Hennessey.

"Shall I take a pad and make notes, Daniel?

"Yes, that would be useful, Polly, but only use it after I have asked them if it's ok to take notes."

Polly and Daniel arrive at the Lamb and Flag pub, suitably dressed, at around eight o'clock and meet with Peter Hennessey, Jimmy Rush, and Liam Cassidy. He introduces Polly as an office worker in the hope that there will be some information to record.

"She ain't very old, she looks more like a schoolgirl to me, not a secretary," says Cassidy.

"Is that a compliment, Liam? If so, thank you," quips Polly, as Liam smiles, a little embarrassed at her remarks.

"Ok, so gentlemen what do you have? How was your meeting today?"

They give Daniel details of the moves to bring out the dockers on strike so causing unrest among the public at the additional hardship the shortages will bring. Their mass meeting was chaired by Michael Doyle, who introduced guest speakers who were obviously communists. Daniel must find out who they are, though at the moment, he has no idea how.

Polly makes relevant notes of what is said.

"The speakers, introduced by Doyle, left no one in doubt of their intentions. The only way forward for them was to force a vote only when they know they will win."

"They are calling for unofficial stoppages whenever we feel the management is not listening to our demands. We don't even know what proposals have been put forward. They talk about shorter working hours, guaranteed employment, and longer holidays, but they never say what they are actually asking for."

"They have proposed that we send representatives to Liverpool to get them to come out as well. They asked for volunteers and offered to pay all their expenses for going. So we are being told what to do rather than vote on what we should do," says Jimmy Rush.

"I don't like anybody, union or management, telling me what to do, especially when I don't know why I am being told to do it. It seems to me that the dispute is just for their political benefit; the workers, or their grievances, are not being considered at all," says Cassidy.

"Unfortunately, there are a lot of blokes who are easily convinced about going on strike, even though they don't know why they are doing it!" says Rush.

"Did you manage to get the names of these guests that were urging you to strike?" Daniel asks.

"I heard one of them called Alexei, but that's all I heard, but it was obvious that they weren't British because they didn't speak English too well," Cassidy replies.

"And what is happening next, Liam?" asks Daniel.

"It's rumoured that if the men threaten unofficial stoppages the management will close the docks, which would play right into the hands of these commie agitators."

"And what about the E.T.U. Peter? How do they fit in with all this?"

"I believe that if the management close the docks, there will be a recommendation that a National Strike is called," says Peter.

"Good god, when is this supposed to happen?"

"Well it's not something that they can arrange overnight, I think they will want to see what the dockers' response is if the management do close the docks. Can you do anything, Daniel?"

"I have to try and get some evidence to discredit the communists. I will be working towards that from tomorrow. Meantime, if you can keep me informed, gentlemen, it would be appreciated. And one more thing, and please do not be offended by this, if any of you incur any undue expense while seeking this information, please let me know, is that ok?"

"Thank you Daniel, that will not be necessary," Hennessey replies.

"Well the offer is there for all of you, now if you can keep Peter informed of anything relevant, I would be obliged. Meantime, I will pass this information on to my colleagues and hope we can do something to stop these troublemakers."

The three union colleagues say their goodbyes and leave the pub closely followed by Daniel and Polly. They walk along Garrick Street toward King Street, where they hail a taxi and arrive back at Daniel's apartment at 9.30pm.

"What a weird pub that was, Daniel, I could feel everyone watching me all the while I was there," says Polly as they enter the apartment.

"That was because they rarely, if ever, see a young female in pubs around Covent Garden. It is very much a man's domain, Polly."

"Anyway, I have all the notes of the meeting here, I hope they will prove useful. You must do something to stop these people holding our country to ransom."

Daniel speaks with Fitz and Conrad the following morning, and it is agreed that they will pay a visit to the Communist Party headquarters as soon as possible. Daniel suggests Friday evening since it is reasonable to assume that no one will be about over the weekend. It is agreed that they will break in on Friday around eight o'clock, and will talk more about it on Friday. Daniel, meanwhile, must ask Polly if she can arrange to meet with a colleague for a few hours while he is away. Polly has become friendly with two girls at the Home Office, namely Sam Collingwood and Penny Carstairs, and Penny lives in Kensington.

"Do you think you could go and stay with her for a couple of hours or so on Friday, Polly?"

"I'm sure I can, she is always asking me to call on her so I will take up her invitation this time."

"Thanks Polly, Conrad and I should not be more than a couple of hours. We have to get something that can tie in the communists with the strike action being proposed at the docks."

"Why don't I ask some questions at work and see whether anyone will give me any information?"

"What do you mean, Polly?"

"Well, I know who some of the union activists are, and could imply that I know what they are planning and see how they react."

"Absolutely not, Polly. That would be far too dangerous. These people will not hesitate to remove anyone who gets in their way," he says, concerned that Polly would be putting herself at risk.

"I understand, Daniel, but we have to somehow find out who we are dealing with; a few comments from me in passing might just give you what you want."

Daniel looks at Polly and holds her close to him.

"I know you are determined to do this, Polly, and I cannot stop you, but promise me that you will not say or do anything that will give them reasons to be suspicious of you. They must believe that you are just doing your job and making conversation in passing."

"I promise, Daniel, I will try and introduce conversation that is relevant to the message I am carrying and then casually mention what is happening at the docks. I will only mention what has been written about in the papers."

"Ok Polly, let's leave it like that for now."

Friday morning sees Daniel, Conrad, and Fitz in conversation about the proposed break-in, and what Fitz can do to influence government officials about the actions proposed by the dockers' representatives.

"Is there anyone you know of, Fitz, that could talk unofficially with management at the docks, and stop the threatened closure? Because that will only inflame an already difficult situation. It will play right into the hands of the communist agitators who would have the perfect excuse to incite the dockworkers to take the law into their own hands. Negotiations and reason would be ignored, which is just what these agitators want. Management need to be seen as the side of reason, ready to listen to anything that the dockers have to say."

"Yes, I see where you are coming from, Daniel. They need to publicly hold out the olive branch to the workers, which could thwart any attempt by their representatives to call an unofficial walkout. I have a colleague in the Ministry of Works that may have contacts in dock management. There is talk of developing some area of docklands, so he will have been in contact, I am sure, with the port authorities. It would not be in their best interests to have continuing unrest, and politically, it is damning for Churchill and his government."

"How soon can you make contact with him, Fitz?" asks Conrad.

"I will talk with him today, and I suggest that we meet with him on Monday afternoon after you have briefed me on your 'visit' this evening. Now, is there anything you need?"

"Just torches and mini cameras, I expect that Phil can supply those."

So Daniel and Conrad go off to see Phil Chandler and Paul Horsley to discuss the evening break-in at Communist Party Headquarters. Paul has a layout of the building which will help them to move around in the dark, and Phil duly provides small torches and mini cameras.

"I suggest you come round to my apartment around 7.30pm, Conrad. We will take Polly to her friend's home, then continue to the headquarters near Covent Garden. If we get the taxi to drop us at Covent Garden, we can walk from there to our destination."

"Are we sure there will be no one in the building, Daniel?"

"Not completely sure, Conrad, but Friday is a good choice, because the office workers will have gone home for the weekend. Whether there are any other occupants, we will have to wait and see. It is unlikely there will be anyone in the offices, and that is where we will be looking."

So Daniel and Polly go home to the apartment on Friday, and Polly prepares them a light meal.

"How long do you think you will be inside their offices, Daniel? I am worried that something might happen to you, to both of you."

"We will be in and out in no time at all, Polly, and since there should be no one there, you have nothing to worry about."

"If you say so, Daniel. What time is Conrad calling?"

"Conrad will be here for 7.30pm, we will take you to Penny Carstairs' home, and continue to Covent Garden in the taxi. Tell Penny that I am calling for you around nine o'clock, if she asks."

"You will be careful, Daniel. I don't know what I will do if anything happens to you," says Polly with concern. She is obviously worried by what Daniel and Conrad will be doing. If they are caught the consequences do not bear thinking about. They both sit and have a light meal, then wait to leave.

Conrad arrives prompt at 7.30pm, and they take Polly to Penny Carstairs' home in Kensington before continuing on to Covent Garden and the Communist Party Headquarters.

CHAPTER 7

The offices of the British Communist Party occupy a large old house near Covent Garden. Set back off the road, the house is in need of repair, with decaying windows and crumbling brickwork, and the frontage is overgrown with weeds. Daniel and Conrad go to the back of the property to find a way in. Several of the windows are in urgent need of repair, making it easy to force an opening. The room is damp from condensation, and is full of boxes of files. Both men leave the room, looking for any offices that may be in regular use, hoping to find recent correspondence. They find the main office at the front of the building, and force the door to gain entry. There is a street light outside the building, given them adequate light to glimpse the files. There are memos relating to dockers' meetings and Daniel notices that some files relate to engineering works in the Midlands.

"They are trying to shut down transport, Daniel. Here is a file referring to meetings with the rail unions."

"What we are looking for, Conrad, is files that link Moscow with the activities of their members here in Britain, and details of their intentions."

The two men take pictures of as many pages as possible, hoping that the information will be relevant, and make notes of the names of officials of the party. They force open the desk drawers and find a number of papers referring to recent Russian visitors to the headquarters. In all, there are some twenty pages of references to meetings and dates when it is proposed that strikes take place. There are specific timelines for the strike to be escalated to take in the

Midlands Engineering Plants in Birmingham and Coventry.

They can only glance at the contents as they photograph it, but they know that what they have discovered is exactly what they were looking for, namely direct interference from Moscow. They put everything back in its place, and move upstairs, not sure what they may find in the rooms on the first and second floors. It appears that they are occupied or are used as living quarters. There are clothes for men and women; presumably officials can bring their ladies here. They have plush furnishings and a very full bar. Not the sort of surroundings you would associate with a worker struggling to put food on the family table.

Daniel takes pictures of the splendid decor that the comrades have provided for themselves. Just as they prepare to move on to the top floor, a door opens and two men appear. They have obviously been in there all the time, probably sleeping. Daniel and Conrad run for the stairs as one of the men fires at them. Daniel turns to return the fire as they are rushing down the stairs. The other two men both open fire and Daniel and Conrad are both hit. They dash into King Street and disappear into the crowds, eventually finding their way to the Strand, where they hail a taxi. They examine their wounds and thankfully, they have just broken the surface. Daniel asks the taxi driver to take them back to his apartment, which is only a short journey. Both men go inside to examine their injuries. Conrad has a graze on his shoulder which is soon cleaned and bandaged. Daniel has a deeper, but not serious wound to his forearm, which he cleans and bandages also.

"A reasonably successful night I would say, Conrad. I shall be most interested to see what is in the documents we have photographed."

""I will get those pictures developed over the weekend so that we can examine them on Monday morning, Daniel."

"That would be brilliant, now I suggest you get off and I will go and collect Polly."

"How was it, Daniel? Did you find anything?" asks Polly as soon as she is in the taxi.

"Hold on Polly, wait until we get back to the apartment."

"It was a successful operation; we have retrieved a lot of

information which I hope will tell us just what the Russians are up to," says Daniel, taking off his jacket.

"Daniel, you are bleeding, were you hit?" asks Polly, seeing a blood stain on his shirt.

Daniel looks down at his makeshift bandage to see blood seeping through.

"It's just a nick Polly, really."

"Let me see, did you attempt to apply the bandage?" says Polly, as she removes the bandage to reveal an open wound on Daniel's forearm.

Daniel did not realise how deep the wound was, and it is beginning to throb.

"Go into the bathroom, Daniel, I need to bathe and disinfect the wound. If it is no better tomorrow, you will have to go to hospital."

The wound is torn where the bullet pierced Daniel's forearm, but not too deep. Polly cleans it and pushes the skin into place before placing a plaster over the wound to prevent it opening. She then puts a bandage over the top.

"That's fine, Polly. Thank you. I think I could manage a drink."

They go through to the lounge and Daniel pours himself a small whisky. His adrenalin level has now dropped and he is in some discomfort from his wound.

"Is Conrad ok, Daniel? I forgot to ask, seeing your wound."

"Conrad also has a nick in his arm, but he was ok."

"Well I hope it was worth it, your body is only just recovering from what happened at Easter."

Daniel looks at his watch, and sees the time is just before ten o'clock. He sits back on the sofa and closes his eyes, reflecting on the night's events. Both he and Conrad came perilously close to being seriously injured in the gunfire at Communist H.Q. Hopefully, the documents they photographed will prove to be well worth it.

"Daniel, come along to bed, you need to rest," says Polly, waking him from his sleep.

"I'm sorry for that Polly, what time is it? Goodness, it's eleven o'clock, I must have fallen into a deep sleep. Goodnight Polly," he says, kissing her on the cheek before going into his room. He doesn't get much sleep, because of the wound in his arm, and is eventually woken by Polly with some tea.

"What shall we do today, Polly?" asks Daniel, as she sits on his bed.

"I think the first thing we must do is get you to hospital, Daniel. After that, some shopping."

*

The doctor has to stitch Daniel's wound as it is torn from the bullet.

"In the wars again Daniel, I see? Come and see me towards the end of the week to have the stitches removed. Meantime, see that the wound is kept covered, Polly."

They spend the rest of the morning shopping before having a sandwich in the High Street, then returning to the apartment. The rest of the weekend passes quietly with Daniel and Polly enjoying their time together without interruptions.

On Monday morning, Daniel and Conrad enter Fitz's office at ten o'clock prompt. They had spent the last hour looking through the documents they photographed. The contents are illuminating, giving names and strategy details of plans to escalate the strikes in the docks and bring out the engineering workers in the Midlands. Three names are mentioned several times: Vladimir Barinov, Boris Yankovsky, and Alexei Malakhov. These men have been tasked with closing the docks as soon as possible. They are also instructed to meet with party members in the Midlands, Birmingham especially, with the aim of bringing out the engineering factories. They will use the notion that rationing is starving the workers in favour of the establishment.

They will demand a 25% increase in basic wages and more paid holidays per year. Equally disturbing is the plot to install a Moscow party member into a government position and give him support from party members currently installed in the Civil Service. Also present in Fitz's office are Quentin Blake from MI5 and Jeremiah Winterton from the Ministry of Works.

"My god gentlemen, this is explosive reading. We all have something to work with here, well done.

"It would have been better if you had made us aware, Fitz, in case they were caught," Quentin Blake comments.

"We have a specific remit concerning trade union activity in the docks and the Civil Service, Mr Blake, there was no reason why you needed to be involved," replies Daniel.

"Yes, quite so. Talking of the Civil Service, how is your little girl, Miss Spencer, coming along? I heard you two were attacked on a train, is that correct?" asks Blake.

"Polly is providing a number of leads for us to pursue, and yes we were attacked on the train at Easter."

"And are you recovered, Daniel? I understand you took quite a beating."

"Yes, I am on the mend. Thank you, sir."

"So what happens next, Quentin?" Fitz asks.

"We need you, Jerry, to sound out the management in the docks; they need the public on their side, they need to be appearing sympathetic to the dockers' situation, anything to stall them. What they must not do is lock out the workforce, this will play into the hands of the agitators. I will talk to some of my Russian contacts regarding these names and see what I can find out about them. So there is much to do, gentlemen. I must leave you now, and thank you, Fitz, for your information," Blake concludes as he leaves Fitz's office.

"Now Jerry, how soon can you talk with your friends in dock management?"

"I will make some calls after lunch, Fitz, and get back to you. Bye for now Conrad, Daniel."

"Well gentlemen, I think that was a successful meeting, don't you? Now we need to spend some time looking closely at the information you obtained. There will be other details in there, I am sure."

Phil Chandler calls into the office while Daniel is still there to tell him he has requisitioned the deadlock and the alarm lighting for his apartment. It will be about a week before it arrives, which is quicker than he expected. As soon as he has all the parts he will come along and install them in Daniel's apartment. Daniel and Polly meet at five o'clock for the taxi home and he begins telling Polly of his meeting. When they are inside the apartment, he mentions that Quentin Blake knew who she was and asked how she was progressing.

"Really, Daniel? MI5 were asking about me? How exciting."

"Your information is proving useful in other departments, Polly. You should be very proud of your achievements." His only concern is that if MI5 know of Polly, it is certainly a possibility that the Communist Party do also. And this is the danger that Daniel always feared when Polly began her work in the Home Office as a Liaison Officer. And this is why she has been specifically targeted. Daniel makes no mention of this, but he is most concerned. Every possible precaution will be taken to ensure her safety, and under no circumstances can she be left alone or travel anywhere without his being by her side. Meanwhile, he has arranged for her to go along with him at the weekend to learn how to handle the weapon he has secured for her, a Walther P22 pistol.

Phil Chandler has managed to get the deadlock and the alarm for Daniel's apartment sooner than expected, and installs the deadlock on the door, together with two additional bolts at the top and bottom. He also installs a sensor which will warn of anyone approaching. It will switch on the lights in the hallway and sound an alarm. The alarm is controlled with a passcode just inside the door. The alarm system can only be neutralised by inserting a specific sequence of numbers into the unit within thirty seconds of entry into the apartment. Phil explains the working of the system to Daniel and Polly when they arrive from their work.

"This is just what we needed, Phil. We will both feel much more secure for your efforts, thank you."

"Very happy to have been able to help, Daniel. I'll leave you both to it, bye for now," replies Phil as he collects his tools and moves off down the stairs.

On Thursday morning, Polly goes about her duties as usual, and notices that a number of staff seem to be particularly polite towards her. 'Good morning Polly. How are you, Polly? Are you keeping well, Polly?' These comments seem to be directed towards her by just about everyone she sees. Perhaps they are getting used to her moving around their departments and no longer view her presence as threatening in any way.

The Civil Service is a very secretive organisation; no one trusts anyone, least of all someone who is visiting their departments every day. There has never been a Corporate Liaison Officer, who has the authority to go into any department and approach any member of that department. As time has passed, Polly's position has become more acceptable, hence the pleasantries now being heaped upon her. Polly is delighted that she is at last being accepted, and it will make her job of collecting information so much easier. If members of staff are entering into conversations, then it will only be good manners for Polly to respond. This will be her opportunity to ask questions.

Polly returns to her office after her first round of calls, and begins sifting through the messages, ready to move them on to their destinations. One file has a message for Polly.

"Please meet me in the reception are at 1.00pm, I will be carrying some knitting and some knitting patterns," the message reads. Polly is obviously delighted to have been approached directly with someone who may have useful information. Come lunchtime, she goes down into the reception area, looking around cautiously for the lady with the knitting. The woman is sitting in the open and is easily spotted by Polly.

"Hello Polly, I have bought some of the knitting patterns I promised you," she says, handing Polly two brochures. "My name is Elizabeth Berkley, Polly. Please take the brochures and whilst we appear to be talking about knitting, can you suggest a time and place where we might meet?"

"Thank you for those, Elizabeth. I will meet with you on Saturday at noon at the Science Museum entrance," says Polly, as she takes the brochures and returns to her office. She is intrigued by what has occurred, and looks through the brochures for any more messages, but there is nothing other than the brochure contents for her to look at.

"What do you think she wants to talk about, Daniel?" asks Polly as she tells him of her meeting with Elizabeth Berkley at work this lunchtime.

"She must want to tell you something, but why she thinks you can help, I have no idea. I suggest we ask when we meet her."

"Should we be suspicious, Daniel? We don't know anything about her at all."

"Until we know more, Polly, we have to be suspicious of everyone we don't know. I suggest we arrive about half an hour early and watch from a distance before we make ourselves known."

"I hope she is genuine and has some useful information. It feels as though information has dried up for now, Daniel," says Polly with disappointment in her voice.

"You won't get information easily, Polly. Remember, you have had to put up with some hostility from your workplace, hopefully this has now subsided. You being there for people to be able to approach is important. Your position allows staff to talk with you in your official capacity as a Liaison Officer without anyone seeing your conversations as suspicious. You are just doing your job, and you cannot prevent your fellow workers from approaching you at work," Daniel replies, hoping his words will make her feel better, and show her how important her job is to him and the department.

"Thank you Daniel, you have made me feel so much better," she replies, giving him one of her special hugs. Daniel responds and enjoys having Polly in his arms. They stand there for a moment, each with their own thoughts, Polly encouraged by Daniel's remarks and Daniel just enjoying the moment. As time passes and Daniel and Polly's lives have become more closely intertwined, he realises just how difficult it is becoming to just be Polly's friend. He loves her deeply and so wants to take their relationship to the next level. However, until there is some stability in their lives regarding the dangers surrounding their work, he will continue to love her and care for her from a distance. Polly is especially looking forward to the weekend, as Daniel is taking her to the shooting range. But first they must meet with Elizabeth Berkley and find out what she has for them.

They arrive about half an hour early and watch the entrance to the Science Museum. She arrives on time and looks round anxiously for Polly. She is obviously a little uneasy, but does not appear to have been followed at all. After a few moments and a final look around, Polly and Daniel approach.

"Hello Elizabeth, I hope you haven't been waiting too long?"

"No, I have just arrived," she replies, surprised to see someone with Polly.

"Elizabeth, this is Daniel, my closest friend. I hope you don't mind his being here. He is aware of who you are and wanted to be sure that you were not followed.

"Hello Elizabeth, shall we find somewhere to sit?"

There are numerous seats scattered around the Science Museum and Polly leads them to a table outside, away from the main entrance.

"I have wanted to talk with you for some time, Polly, since I was sure that your position was created so that you could talk to anyone and be approached by anyone without causing suspicion. I have been a Civil Servant for many years and am dismayed at what is happening. There is a secret organisation, operating within the service, that is determined to bring down the government and install a communist leadership in its place. Since the end of the Second World War, the Soviets have slowly eroded away the democracies of Europe and being able to influence policy in this country would be a massive boost for them. It is well known that they have the services of academics, who are sympathetic to communist ideology. And they are moving into the trade union movement at an alarming pace."

"Can I ask you where you have got this information from, assuming that it is true?"

"Because, Daniel, I have been a member of this secret organisation for some time."

Daniel and Polly look at each other in astonishment.

"You are a member of a communist-controlled organisation, operating from inside the Civil Service, seeking to overthrow the British government?"

"I have been a member since my husband died five years ago. He was a lecturer in business and politics, and passionately believed in the communist solution to the right-wing beliefs of fascism. In the beginning, I think many people believed that a government run by the working class was the ideal solution to everything. But, as we all know Moscow has its own agenda. It has no real interest in the needs of the workers, only in forcing its ideology on everyone to service its final goal of removing the democratic process. I have stayed with the organisation for two reasons. Firstly, I do not believe I would be allowed to walk away, and secondly, I have been waiting for an opportunity to pass on information that could finally destroy the communist hold in the Service. When Polly took on the position of Liaison Officer, I presumed that she was a link to members of the security forces, and took the chance of making contact with her direct. And that is why I am here," Elizabeth Berkley concludes.

"That is quite some story, Elizabeth. Now let me tell you what I believe should happen in order for you and I and Polly to maintain any further contact. Firstly, I will make a few enquiries to find out what I can about you and your late husband. When we are sure that you are genuine in your approach, then we will contact you again and arrange another meeting. Polly will get a message to you as soon as our checks have been completed. I would think it will be Wednesday or Thursday of next week, so look out for her on those days."

"Thank you both for listening to me, I hope to hear from you soon. Now that I have spoken with someone, I am anxious to help. Goodbye for now," says Elizabeth, as she looks around nervously before departing towards Exhibition Road.

Daniel and Polly sit watching her walk away before Polly mutters, "Gosh, Daniel, what do you make of all that? Do you believe that Elizabeth is genuine?"

"Well if she is, Polly, we have a very strong ally who can provide us with details of the organisation that is a cancer in our Civil Service and in our country also."

They both return to the apartment for some lunch before collecting the pistol Daniel has selected for Polly, and going off to the shooting range. Polly shows herself to be quite a marksman, and surprises Daniel, quickly learning how to handle the .22 pistol efficiently.

"You are a natural, Polly. You have surprised my colleagues with how quickly you have learned how to use the pistol. We will have another half-hour target practice, then return home."

"Ok Daniel, I must say I did not expect it to be quite so easy to handle something that is capable of actually killing someone."

"Like all weapons, Polly, it is the people that use them that do the killing, not the weapons."

On returning to the apartment, he suggests that Polly keep the pistol in the top drawer of her dresser when in the apartment, and get used to carrying it with her at all times. It is not too big so is not intrusive, and will fit easily into her bag.

"And remember to always lock it in your office drawer at work, Polly."

So Polly accompanies Daniel to her place of work at the Home Office on Monday morning, carrying her pistol for the first time.

Daniel, meantime, meets with Fitz and Conrad to brief them on his meeting with Elizabeth Berkley.

"If she is genuine, Fitz, she will be a hell of an asset to us, someone at the heart of the organisation in the Civil Service."

"I will ask questions about her, Daniel, but I imagine that she has been carefully selected and her details will have been screened already by the Russians," Fitz replies.

"What about Blake at MI5, can he help at all?" asks Conrad.

"I will call him now," says Fitz, picking up the receiver of his phone. He contacts Blake and mentions Elizabeth Berkley and Daniel's meeting with her. Blake agrees to make some calls and meet up with Fitz at two o'clock to update him.

"I believe Quentin knows Mrs Berkley, Daniel, I just got the impression from his wanting to meet again so soon, which is not like him at all."

Polly, meanwhile, goes about her business with a spring in her step. She will continue to listen to what is being said, but now there has been contact, she really believes that she is making a positive contribution to the fight. She talks only to those members of staff that engage her in conversation, but is surprised to find another note inserted into one of her files when she returns to her office. It is a document encouraging her to enlist in the union of Civil Servants. Ironically, the note with the membership form is signed by Sally Nugent, who not long ago warned Polly to keep out of the business of the union! Polly smiles to herself, and decides she will wait and see if she is approached directly by Sally Nugent, to hear what she has to say. If Elizabeth Berkley is genuine in wanting to help the fight against the communists in the Civil Service, there is no real need for Polly to become a union member. However, since she expressed a wish to do so, it might be best to go ahead with the application, eventually, so as not to draw any suspicion from her actions.

At two o'clock Quentin Blake arrives at Fitz's office, nodding at Daniel and Conrad as he sits down.

"Quentin, thank you for your prompt response. What do you have for me?"

"I have to say, that being able to make contact with Mrs Berkley is fortuitous, Fitz. I have made enquiries and she has no agenda outside of the organisation. We know of some of the members, but they are incredibly difficult to identify. Ordinarily we would interrogate them, but they operate in very small cells, so the information they could offer would be limited. But to have a cell member who is willing to give information freely will be very useful to us."

"So you would like us to continue, confident that she is genuine?"

"I would say yes, Daniel, but with caution. Do not let her believe that you are anything but sceptical of what she has to say. We don't want her to feed us information that we already know so as to gain some kind of trust with Miss Spencer. You must impress upon her that this woman has been operating for a long time, and may try to influence her in some way."

"I understand, sir, and will tell Polly to be cautious; she is very sensible and would not do or say anything without first discussing it with me."

"Good show, Daniel, so I suggest the sooner Miss Spencer arranges a second meeting, the sooner we can find out what she has to offer. Now I have to go, Fitz, I have another appointment. Goodbye gentlemen, and good hunting," replies Blake, leaving Fitz's office.

"Well Daniel, that was a bit of a surprise, MI5 being so cooperative. I can only imagine we have something that they want, namely Elizabeth Berkley. I suggest that you ask Polly to arrange another meeting towards the end of the week. Hopefully, we should have got something from Jeremiah at the Ministry of Works by then."

So Daniel and Conrad leave Fitz's office with plenty to think about in the coming week. That evening, Daniel and Polly discuss the day's events and decide what they should do next.

"How soon can you get a message to Mrs Berkley do you think, Polly?"

"I will try from tomorrow, Daniel; it depends whether I have files for her department, and whether I have a reason to pass her desk so that I can get a message to her."

"I believe we should meet here in the apartment, that way we can be sure that we are not seen talking to her."

"Ok Daniel, I will contact as soon as possible, and suggest Thursday evening at seven o'clock."

"Meantime, Polly, we will have to devise a way that she can pass you messages other than using the filing system."

"I will leave you to suggest something, Daniel. Now what about this union application? I think I must go ahead, and it could be useful attending meetings, don't you think?"

"It will give you the perfect excuse to talk with other members, Polly, without them being suspicious, which can only be a good thing for us."

"I really feel that we are making progress now, Daniel," says Polly, curling up beside him on the settee and kissing him on the cheek. Daniel kisses her forehead before replying.

"Just remember to be careful at all times, I do not want anything to happen to you."

"I will be careful, but I have you to look after me so nothing will happen to me, Daniel."

Polly and Daniel sit together, enjoying each other's company, for about half an hour before Polly goes off to have her bath, leaving Daniel to his own thoughts. Events are moving quicker than he could have hoped for and he realises that they are both entering dangerous territory. Polly is very upbeat about her contact, and also the fact that Sally Nugent has given her the form to apply for union membership. Daniel himself, gets a degree of pleasure seeing Polly so happy and positive with her life. His love for her continues to grow each day and he looks forward to being able to make their life together complete at some time in the future, hopefully not too distant! Meantime, Polly enters the lounge and goes off to prepare them a meal. She never stops talking through the meal and Daniel is quite content to listen.

"I shall have to try and contact Elizabeth Berkley without

attracting any attention. Hopefully, I will have files in her office to deliver, so should be able to pass a message to her."

"It might be best if you simply say a time and 'same place', Polly. We can then meet her outside the Science Museum, check that she hasn't been followed, then bring her back here.

"Ok Daniel, I will pass that message on to her as soon as possible. I believe she is in the same department as Sally Nugent, so I will have an excuse to go in there. I will contact her tomorrow, I do not want her to think I am ignoring her now that she has sent me the application forms."

They go off to their rooms and after about half an hour Polly taps on Daniel's door and goes in.

"Daniel, I really am not very sleepy, can I sit with you for a while?"

"Of course, Polly. Come in," Daniel replies. He is not very sleepy himself and will enjoy Polly's company. She climbs onto his bed and sits beside him.

"We spent so much time together in my bedroom at home, it is nice to be able to come and spend time with you, can you understand that, Daniel? And I can remember when we went to Stratford and you told me off for getting into your bed when you were asleep, do you remember?"

"I do most certainly remember, I was horrified in case Ben or Margaret found out."

"But nothing happened, Daniel. I just wanted to be by your side."

"I know nothing happened Polly, but a thirteen-year-old girl should not share a bed with an adult; it is wrong, as I told you at the time," Daniel replies, a little flustered by the conversation.

"Anyway, that was a long time ago, Daniel, and there would be nothing wrong with us sharing a bed now that I am eighteen years old, would there?"

"There wouldn't be anything morally wrong with that, Polly, but for now you should sleep in your own bed," Daniel replies, trying to sound matter-of-fact. Polly really has no idea just how difficult it is for him to respond to her comments about the two of them sharing a bed.

"But I can stay here for a while, can't I? Please?"

"Stay as long as you wish, Polly," Daniel replies. He is reading his book and Polly is looking at her magazine. At last Polly stops talking and Daniel continues with his reading and as he becomes more relaxed, he falls asleep. Polly smiles as she gets up from his bed, switches off his lamp, removes her gown and carefully gets in beside him. Daniel is sound asleep, and Polly follows very quickly, nestling beside him. They lie together, sleeping soundly until Daniel wakes around dawn, suddenly conscious of Polly beside him. He smiles to himself, resigned to the fact that Polly had planned to spend the night with him one way or the other, and he has to admit that having a beautiful young woman beside him wasn't exactly a chore! He goes off to the kitchen to make tea, and returns as Polly is waking.

"Good morning Miss, and who has been sleeping in my bed?"

"Sorry Daniel, I could not resist. I won't do it again, well not for a while anyway," she says, laughing loudly.

Polly and Daniel set off for work after their breakfast, Polly hoping to be able to contact Elizabeth Berkley, Daniel to meet with Fitz, hoping to have heard some news from Jeremiah Winterton.

The Home Office is a large building off Whitehall, responsible for immigration, security and law and order. So it has a wide remit covering police, border controls, and the security of the country generally. The departments are overseen by Permanent Secretaries, non-political who report to State Undersecretaries. Elizabeth Berkley is on the third floor of the building, which handles mostly immigration issues. Sally Nugent also works from this department, giving Polly the opportunity to visit. However, she has files for that floor anyway, so proceeds, looking for an opportunity to pass Elizabeth Berkley's desk. She spots Elizabeth, and whilst appearing to look around, approaches her.

"Excuse me, can you point out Sally Nugent for me please?"

Elizabeth points out Sally Nugent's work station.

"Thank you. Meet at seven o'clock Thursday, same place. Thank you very much," says Polly, quickly moving on to Sally Nugent.

"Good morning Sally, thank you for sending me an application form."

"Well you did ask, Polly, and if I was rather offish toward you, I apologise."

"That's ok, now the form asks for two referees. I was going to ask Mrs Wright to be one, will you be the other, as I do not know too many people that I can ask?"

"Of course, Polly; get the form filed in and I will put my name forward as a referee when you return it."

"Thanks Sally, I will get that back to you later today," says Polly, moving on to continue delivering her files.

Daniel and Conrad, meanwhile, meet with Fitz and Jeremiah Winterton for an update on the threatened shutdown of the London Docks. There are currently no talks planned, and the dockers are becoming frustrated. Unofficial action is taking place on a daily basis, preventing the unloading of vital produce. With rationing still in place, the strikes are taking effect very quickly, creating even more shortages.

"I have told my colleagues in dock management that they must offer to meet with the union officials," Jeremiah Winterton says. "I made it very clear that they cannot allow the union agitators to gain the upper hand here. I also pointed out the bigger picture relating to Moscow's interference, making them aware of government concern and the fears associated with the Traffic Light Syndrome. You are familiar with the reference, Daniel?"

"Yes sir, the expression is used to note how the situation with the Soviets has gone from green through amber for caution into red for danger, since the end of the war years."

"Yes indeed. Now Fitz, can Blake in MI5 do anything about the information you received from the visit to Communist H.Q., I wonder? Perhaps an unofficial word with one of his contacts might persuade them to ease off if he makes threats of expulsions," Winterton continues.

"I can certainly ask, the situation is now very serious and the management need to take the initiative away from the communist agitators."

"Good, well let me leave that with you, Fitz. We must get the dockers back into work no matter what, and Daniel, keep in contact with your union colleagues, it is always useful to know what the workforce is thinking on the ground," Jeremiah Winterton concludes.

"Very well, sir, I will keep you informed of any developments they report to me."

Since Daniel has received no news from Hennessey, he assumes that there is nothing additional to report other than what is common knowledge. The dockers are walking out every day and disrupting all business in the docks, trying to force management to lock them out so that they will have justification for an all-out stoppage. So far, there has been no mention publically of escalating the stoppage to the engineering workers in the Midlands. The communist agitators are probably waiting to move as soon as they get a mandate for an all-out stoppage from the dockers. All these thoughts are going through Daniel's mind as he waits for Polly outside the Home Office entrance.

On Thursday, Polly and Daniel meet with Elizabeth Berkley, and take her back to the apartment. She is rather apprehensive of being asked to go to the apartment, but Daniel assures her that it is safe, and they will see that she is not followed when she leaves. Polly makes tea and she and Daniel sit on the settee; Elizabeth sits in the easy chair.

"So Elizabeth, what more can you tell us about the secret organisation within the Civil Service?"

"Can I first ask if you will protect me should they find out that I have been passing information to the security services? I am very worried that talking with you could put me at risk."

"If your information is useful to us, we can arrange for you to be shadowed by one of my operatives, and we will guarantee that you do not lose your job. This will only be done, Elizabeth, once you have supplied incriminating evidence. We always protect our sources. What we need to do this evening is find a way of you passing information, possibly to Polly, securely without anyone being aware. We do not want to meet at all if it can be avoided."

"Why don't I simply drop messages to Polly through her letterbox on the ground floor? That way I do not need to have any contact."

"Not a good idea, Elizabeth; you are very likely to be seen, and you would be exposing Polly as your contact. Why don't you simply use the post office, and send the information to Polly by letter? I do not expect the information to be sent on a regular basis, and it would seem to be the most secure way of communicating without giving yourself away."

"I think that is an excellent idea, Daniel. Don't you, Elizabeth?"

"The organisation has the name Red Hand. Nothing official, it has just become known as Red Hand over the years. As I mentioned before, the Soviets are committed to placing agents in key posts to influence government policies. The Home Office, with direct responsibilities for security, police, and immigration, is a key department for the activities of Red Hand. The organisation is determined to install an agent into a senior position and we will supply him or her with information that can be used to influence the Minister or someone close to him. We have not been able to penetrate the senior positions, but we have been issued with precise instructions to make this happen as soon as possible."

"Who are the key members that we should be worried about?" Daniel asks.

"That is the problem, I don't know and I do not know anyone who does know. We operate in small groups; I get information passed to me by agent A, and I pass it on together with any information I have, to agent B. Those are the only two that I know of, that's how secretive it is," Elizabeth replies.

"We need to find out who gives information to agent A and who agent B passes the information to. Have you ever tried to find out who they are?"

"No I haven't, Polly, because I have never needed to; I only pass on information to my contact. I don't know how difficult it would be to find out who other members are but I can certainly try."

"And tell me, Elizabeth, how do you receive and pass on your information?" asks Daniel.

"It used to be very hit and miss, in the washrooms as we passed each other on the way into and leaving the building and so on, but now it is so much easier. We are now using the facility provided by Polly's position. We simply pass messages via the internal messaging system!"

"Well that's a stroke of luck, so all Polly has to do is take note of your file and view its contents when she returns to her office. Obviously, this will not affect what you may want to send by post, but you will continue sending on your information to your agent using the internal system," says Daniel.

"Can I ask you, Elizabeth, are you a member of the Civil Service Union?"

"Yes I am, Polly, but I keep a very low profile because of my membership of the organisation. I do not know any details of the members, but I assume that some of them will be in the Red Hand organisation."

"Well, I have become a member and Sally Nugent has sponsored me, so perhaps I may be able to find out details of membership."

"Do be careful what you say to Sally Nugent, Polly. She is a committed party member, and believes in the destruction of the capitalist society, and the introduction of a socialist state. She will try to convince you that the only way the workers can achieve their utopia is to overthrow the elected government and replace it with the communist ideology. She advocates violent protest as a means of breaking down law and order. Then when the anarchists are running riot, and the elected government seems powerless, the communists will appear to come to the rescue to secure the safety of the people. I'm sorry for preaching but Sally Nugent is a very dangerous woman who will go to any lengths for the party."

"You seem very concerned about this, Elizabeth. Can I ask why you are involved with wanting a communist state, feeling the way you do?"

"That is my problem, Daniel, I was never committed in the same way that my husband was. I wanted to support him in whatever he felt was right and did not consider the circumstances. When he died, I realised that I was in too deeply. People looked to me to take a lead following in my husband's footsteps. I have to say I did not have the courage to walk away from it so simply continued to be a member of the organisation. I wanted to walk away so many times, but lacked the courage to do so," Elizabeth Berkley replies with a sigh.

"I appreciate your honesty, Elizabeth. Hopefully you can now make a contribution to bring down the spread of the communist ideology in the Civil Service and elsewhere."

"I hope so Daniel, and I am pleased to be able to be of assistance. Now I think it is time that I left."

Daniel secures a taxi for her and sees her safely off, before returning to his apartment. With Elizabeth Berkley now committed to helping rid the Service of the communists, there is a real opportunity to take the initiative away from them. What he would now like to achieve is some level of success in the docks, but he does not have the influence to be able to do anything other than pass on information. The following morning, he asks Fitz if he has received any news.

"The management has offered an olive branch to the union, Daniel. They have agreed to set up a committee, comprising of elected representatives and management, to discuss their grievances openly. They have asked the union to put forward their nomination to be the impartial chairman of the committee. Once this has been agreed, they will meet at the Ministry of Works. Meanwhile, the unions have agreed to call off all unofficial actions by the dockers. I am confident that this will take the wind out of the sails of the agitators, I certainly hope so. Perhaps you could make contact with your colleague and find out how the rank and file have reacted to the proposals put by the management?"

"I will arrange a meeting as soon as possible, Fitz, now let me tell you about last night's meeting with Elizabeth Berkley."

"Good show, Daniel, and tell young Polly well done also. She really is proving herself to be an asset to us, you must be proud of how she has taken to her new role?"

"Yes I am, Fitz. She has proved herself to be an important member of the team, and I will pass on your compliments."

Daniel makes contact with Hennessey that evening, and arranges to meet him and his colleagues again in the Lamb and Flag pub in Covent Garden on Monday evening.

There is a mass meeting on Monday morning, so there should be plenty to discuss. Daniel really needs to get some definitive information on what is going on with the dockers. Daniel and Polly enjoy a marvellous weekend together; they have a meal in a local restaurant on Friday and visit the cinema on Saturday and see the film '13 East Street'. The plot concerns robberies at the docks, which Daniel finds amusing in the circumstances. It has a good plot and was well worth watching. Polly spends some time on the phone to home on Sunday, and Margaret asks if they will be home for Whitsun weekend.

"I will mention it to Daniel, Mummy, but I am sure it will be ok."

On Monday evening, Daniel arranges to meet with his colleagues in the dockers' union along with Peter Hennessey. As before, Polly will accompany him. The mass meeting decided against an all-out stoppage because of the proposals put forward by management. The meeting was rowdy and there were a number of scuffles between members and troublemakers. However, when a vote was eventually called, the majority agreed to let their representatives sit down with management to see what was on offer.

"There was a lot of members very angry that the strike was not proposed, and some of the representatives were manhandled after the meeting. The mood of some of them was to strike anyway, they obviously don't want a peaceful settlement, it ain't in their interests," says Jimmy Rush.

"So what do you think the men will do now? Will they wait and see what management offers?"

"The communists will keep trying to stir up the troublemakers, and will use bullying tactics against the representatives to get their message across. Our union representatives are meeting with management on Friday, so they have all week to intimidate and threaten them. It'll get ugly, but I just hope that they get the chance to sit down and listen to what management have to say," Liam Cassidy replies.

Daniel and Polly leave the men, asking that they bring him up to date via Hennessey, of any developments. Daniel meets with Fitz on Tuesday morning and briefs him on his meeting with the dock workers. He voices some concerns relating to the violence at the dockers' meeting and hopes that bullying tactics will not influence too much the meeting between the union representatives and management.

"Intimidation is the staple diet of communist agitators, Daniel. It is the weapon favoured by Moscow to settle most arguments. We just have to hope that the rank and file can overcome the small minority trying so hard to bully them into surrender," says Fitz.

Polly, meanwhile, suggests to Daniel that she go to her first Civil Service Union meeting. The meeting is due to be held in the cafeteria in the Home Office, on Wednesday from five o'clock, so that anyone wishing to attend does not have any travelling.

"It will be an ideal opportunity to see who is there, Polly, and to hear what is said."

"I will try and get names if I can, Daniel, then you can check who they are."

And so Polly goes along to the cafeteria when she has completed her last round of collections on Wednesday. She has passed on a message from Elizabeth Berkley today which calls for members to push harder to achieve the goal of a party member to be elevated to a higher position in the Service. Because she is going to a meeting, Daniel will wait in a taxi for her a little way down the road from the Home Office entrance from 5.30pm.

Polly walks into the cafeteria and is immediately approached by Sally Nugent.

"Polly, let me introduce you to some of our members," she says, and introduces Polly to Marion Frobisher, David Boroughs, Robert Denham, and Gordon Hastings. All of the members are wearing name tags, which is convenient.

"Let me introduce you to Polly Spencer, she is a new member and will be most useful to us, I am sure. Polly is the Corporate Liaison Officer I mentioned to you. Her position gives her access to all departments, and that could be useful to us, I believe," says Sally Nugent.

"Anything I can do which will help the members, I will be happy to oblige."

Sally Nugent chairs the meeting, which is also attended by Elizabeth Berkley, and the main topic is to further promote the trade union within the Civil Service, especially among women, and push for more recognition at the highest level.

"I believe that we have a duty to make the government members listen to what we have to say. I believe that we should be able to make a contribution to policy decisions, even have representatives at that level."

Polly is stunned by the directness of her aims; she did not realise that the union and the communists would be quite so bold in their aims and ambitions.

"We have to be prepared to do what is necessary to achieve these aims, and that may include some sort of civil disobedience if the need arises. We are forbidden to go on strike, but there are other ways that we can use to bring our grievances to the notice of the establishment. While you think about what has been said, let me introduce you to our newest member, Polly Spencer," says Sally, beckoning Polly to the front of the meeting.

"You may have seen Polly going about her duties as Corporate Liaison Officer. As I have mentioned to some of you already, her position gives her the authority to go into any department and liaise with any member of that department. So any urgent messages can be taken by Polly to any member at any time."

"Hello everybody, can I just add that my office is on the ground floor. So, if you have a message and I am not around, take it to my office and leave it in my letterbox. I make four, sometimes five rounds of the building each day and any messages left will be delivered on my next round," says Polly. She is making a mental note of as many names as she can from the twenty or so people attending the meeting.

"Is your father a Civil Servant, Miss Spencer?" asks Gordon Hastings.

"My father works in local government in the Midlands and is semi-retired," Polly replies, concerned that they should be asking about her father. The meeting closes with a proposal that they all put pressure on their department heads for more recognition for the union and its representatives.

"Some of us are off to a bar for a drink, Polly. You're very welcome to join us."

"Can I leave it for another time, Sally? I think I must have walked ten miles today, I just want to have a long soak and go off to bed," says Polly, hoping Sally will not push.

"Another time then, and thank you for your input. See you in the morning," Sally replies, as she leads a number of members off to find a bar. Polly waits until they are out of sight before she walks towards the waiting taxi and Daniel. What she doesn't notice is Gordon Hastings, who has followed her out of the cafeteria and noticed her getting into the taxi.

Polly is keen to tell Daniel what was said at the meeting, since she believes that the union are going to use her to deliver messages. This would mean another opportunity for her to talk freely and openly with members without arousing any suspicions.

"Sally Nugent is proving most helpful, Daniel; she introduced me to a number of members personally, and I was given the opportunity to offer my services to them through my position. Only one of them, Gordon Hastings, was rather standoffish toward me."

"I will make some enquiries about any we don't already know, especially Gordon Hastings."

"And I also was able to intercept Elizabeth's mail to her contact today. There is frustration among the agents at the amount of time it is taking to secure a position of influence a member of the organisation. Sally Nugent also mentioned this and talked of more action by the members. Like Elizabeth said, Sally Nugent is a very dangerous person, Daniel."

"Well I think you have had a very successful meeting, Polly, and I know Fitz will be delighted with what you have discovered."

Polly goes off to have her bath while Daniel makes some tea and looks at what they may have to eat. He goes over in his mind what Polly has said, and realises just what an asset she has become. Her enthusiasm knows no bounds, and he knows he must be watchful that she does not take on too much. She does not see the danger in her activities, she just sees it as part of her role, with Daniel, to help rid the country of the menace of the communists. For Daniel, the Traffic Light Syndrome seems to be firmly stuck on red, with all the dangers associated with it, and he must work towards changing that. He is brought back to reality by Polly calling him from the bathroom. He enters to find Polly still in the bath.

"Daniel there is no towel, will you get one for me please?" Daniel returns with the towel to find Polly stepping out of the bath as he enters the bathroom, apparently oblivious to the fact that she is standing there completely naked.

"Thank you Daniel," she says, as she wraps the towel around her and goes off to her room, leaving Daniel somewhat embarrassed. Polly is always surprising him with her actions and once again she has just done that. Daniel smiles to himself, appreciating yet again just how much Polly trusts him and how reassuring it is to know that she is so comfortable in his presence.

Daniel meets with Fitz on the Thursday morning and briefs him on Polly's successes from her first union meeting.

"Now how did young Polly get on with her union meeting?"

"Very well, and it seems that Sally Nugent has taken a bit of a shine to her; she introduced her to the membership and gave her the floor."

"You know, Daniel, that young lady has become a real asset to us. I believe that she is destined for high places."

"Thank you, Fitz. Her enthusiasm knows no bounds, but I do get concerned that she does not appreciate the danger that she may be putting herself in sometimes."

"I think you may, in part, be to blame for that, Daniel. Your history with Polly is unique in every respect. You have known her since she was at school and have protected her from untold dangers. It is because of what you have done to protect her from so many attempts to harm her, that she honestly believes that while you are with her she will always be safe."

"Perhaps you're right, I will just have to watch over her carefully. I do not want her to be over concerned about her own safety. So long as I am with her I shall continue to protect her as I have always done."

"You have just received a message from your union contact Hennessy, Daniel," says Phil Chandler as he enters Fitz's office. The message is just what Daniel did not want to hear.

"Daniel, Liam and Jimmy have been attacked and are badly hurt in what seemed to be a pub brawl. They are in St Thomas's hospital, but I don't have any details. I'm gonna lay low for a while. I suggest that you don't visit Liam and Jimmy, it may be bad for them if you do. Sorry about all this, I will call you when I can." The message ends.

"Damn, I knew things were going too well."

"You and Polly will have to be especially careful now, Daniel, be advised," Fitz replies.

Polly, meanwhile, carries on with her duties, which have been made so much easier now that she can talk with staff without rousing suspicion. She does not talk with Elizabeth, however, thinking it may be better to continue communicating with her by post when required. Sally Nugent always speaks with her when she is in her department. However, she is stopped by Gordon Hastings, who starts asking her questions about Daniel.

"Who was the man in the taxi yesterday, Polly?"

"He is my guardian while I am living in London. Why do you ask, Gordon?"

"And what is his name?" Hastings replies tersely.

"May I ask why you are asking me these questions?"

"No, you may not, now who was that in the taxi with you last night?" Hastings replies threateningly.

"I have nothing more to say to you Gordon, now unless you have something for me, I have work to do," says Polly as she walks away from Hastings to make her next collection. She decides that she will tell Sally Nugent of Hastings' comments toward her and see what she says.

"I really cannot understand Gordon's behaviour, Polly, and apologise for him. Please ignore him, but let me know if he persists."

Polly thinks no more about Gordon Hastings' questions, thinking more of the weekend. She completes her last round of collections, locks away safely in her office, and walks out into reception looking for Daniel's taxi.

"Waiting for someone, Polly? Perhaps I can walk with you?" says Hastings, who seems to have been waiting for her.

"No thank you, Gordon. Please leave me alone or I will report your behaviour to personnel," replies Polly, as she hurries towards Daniel's taxi.

"That is Gordon Hastings, Daniel. He has been bothering me today asking questions about you. I told him you were my guardian while I am in London, but I did not give him your name. Now he has just asked to walk with me. I have mentioned his behaviour to Sally Nugent and told him I will report him to personnel unless he leaves me alone."

"I haven't been able to find out anything about him, Polly, which I find rather puzzling. He is forty-eight years old, lives alone, is not married and has worked for the service for about five years."

"So why is he pestering me, Daniel?"

"Perhaps he just wants to get to know you a bit better," replies Daniel, smiling.

"Well I think it's a bit creepy and hope that he stops asking me questions."

"So why don't we go out for something to eat this evening and forget all about work and Mr Hastings?"

"Yes please, Daniel," replies Polly, giving him a huge hug.

The two of them enjoy a meal together and both discuss the Whitsun weekend.

"I am really looking forward to next weekend, Daniel. It seems a long time since we saw Mummy and Daddy, although it was only Easter."

"I always enjoy going to your home, Polly. It is a bit like my home too."

After a pleasant evening, Polly and Daniel decide to go shopping on Saturday, and leave the apartment around eleven o'clock. They do not pay any attention to the van which stops outside the entrance just as they arrive onto the footpath. Suddenly, they are faced with two armed men who usher them into the back of the van.

"Please do not attempt to escape, Mr Bottomley. If you do we will shoot Polly, do you understand?" one of the men says to Daniel.

"Yes, I understand, please do not hurt her and I will make no attempt to escape from your van."

They are driven to an old enclosed yard from where they enter an unused warehouse. Both are stripped down to their underwear, Polly is tied to an old wooden bench, and Daniel is tied to an overhead beam.

"What do you want from me? Polly cannot tell you anything, why don't you let her go?" says Daniel, hoping to reason with the abductors.

"On the contrary, Mr Bottomley, Polly will be very useful to us. If you do not tell us what we ask, we will use Polly's presence to persuade you, do you understand? So you understand, Mr Bottomley?" a second man with a pronounced accent says menacingly.

"We know that you paid a visit to our headquarters near Covent Garden, and that you looked at some of our confidential papers, is that correct?" a third man asks.

"You really don't expect me to admit to any crime, do you?"

Daniel's comment causes him to be the subject of a ferocious attack by two of the men, hitting him about his body and face.

"Stop it you brutes, for God's sake you will not get anything from him if you kill him!" screams Polly.

The men stop momentarily, before turning to Polly.

"You are in no position to make demands, Polly. We will be dealing with you soon; I am sure what we have in mind for you will help Mr Bottomley to give us the information we want. In my country, you would be an asset, to be used as required by my friends and colleagues," the man says with a grin. Polly shudders at his comments, but tries not to show any fear.

The men continue to question Daniel, who offers them titbits of information, hoping it will keep them from harming Polly. He manages to stall them for a short while before they lose patience.

"This is getting us nowhere, Mr Bottomley; take her next door and do what you have to with her," says the man who appears to be the ringleader.

"Daniel, Daniel, please help me," says Polly, terrified at what may be about to happen to her.

Despite Daniel's protests, two men take Polly from the room, manhandling her as they do so.

They take her to a room further down the corridor, remove the rest of her clothing, and subject her to a nasty indecent assault before hitting her across her body and face.

Daniel, meanwhile, is questioned again before being beaten by the men who finally leave him and Polly, who they have brought back into the room, saying they will return to question them again.

"My dear Polly, what did they do to you? I am so sorry, I will tell them what they want to know as soon as they return," says Daniel, with tears in his eyes.

"Don't tell them anything, Daniel. I don't care what they do, you must not tell them. They did not harm me too much, just manhandled me and threatened worse if you did not tell them what they want to know." However, when the men return they release Daniel from the beam and leave them some bread and cheese and water.

"Perhaps you might want to use this to clean yourselves," the ringleader says, placing a bowl, soap, and towel on the table.

"Thank you," says Polly, as she bathes Daniel's body and face which is covered in dried blood. She also wipes her own face.

"Daniel are you ok? You look terrible. What can we do? We have to try and escape," says Polly, her voice showing how desperate she has become. Unfortunately, the men are just outside the open door, so for the moment escape is impossible. After a short while, the men return, their mood very menacing. They tie Daniel to the beam again before the ringleader speaks directly to him direct.

'Mr Bottomley, let me tell you what will happen to you both if you do not cooperate. You will be tortured by experts who will subject your body to excruciating pain. You will wish you were dead but we will keep you alive until you have told us what we want. You have caused us a great deal of trouble, by putting a number of my men out of action. I have to recruit new agents to replace those you have either shot or had arrested. You will pay for your interference. As for Miss Spencer, I told her that she would be an asset in my country and that is where she will be taken as soon as we can arrange passage. These are not idle threats, Mr Bottomley, we are very good at what we do, and we will carry out our threats when we have to."

"You're insane if you think you can get away with this. Let me tell you, I will hunt you down like a dog and kill you if any harm comes to Polly, so you have a choice, you kill me and get nothing or you let her go and I will give you the information you want."

"You are in no position to make demands, Bottomley," the man says, as he pummels Daniel and strikes him with a cane. He lashes out, apparently out of control, annoyed at Daniel's comments.

"Easy with him, Alexei, we need him to tell us what he knows," one of the other men says.

Daniel is barely conscious, but can hear Polly's screams, and has the satisfaction of knowing that what he said has caused a division among their captors. One of the captors throws some water over Daniel, before they go off together.

"You are very close to being executed where you stand. When we return, you will begin telling us your government's plans for stopping the spread of communism. Believe me, we will break your resolve eventually. If you do not provide us with those details, then we will begin our persuasion tactics and will remove Miss Spencer in preparation for her being shipped to our country," he says as they leave.

Daniel realises that they must escape before these men return. He urges Polly to move the table toward him and stand on it to see if she can free his binding. The binding should be easier to release while wet. Polly pushes the old table over toward Daniel and climbs on it before reaching up to try and free his hands.

After struggling for about five minutes or so, she manages to loosen the ropes which bind him and Daniel quickly helps her down from the table. Their clothes are in a bundle in the corner, and Polly's bag is still there, untouched.

"They did not look inside your bag, Polly, and look what they left behind," says Daniel, smiling as he holds up Polly's .22 pistol. They quickly dress and make their way out of the room, along the corridor, down the stairs towards the yard as the men return. Daniel shoots the first one to enter the stairwell, hitting him in the chest.

As the others run across the yard he fires and hits a second man in the shoulder. The other two men disappear into the street. Daniel and Polly hurry toward the busy street also, and manage to hail a taxi.

"Blimey guv'nor you look a mess. Do you need the hospital?" the taxi driver asks.

"Yes please, if you would," says Daniel, holding Polly close to him as they drive away. It looks as if they are in the Soho district which is very busy on the Saturday evening. Daniel looks at his watch, it is six o'clock.

"My god, Daniel, those men were going to torture you; that was really clever of you to take control the way you did."

"My concern was what they threatened for you, Polly," Daniel replies as they draw up outside the hospital. The doctor is visibly shocked by the sight of Daniel, who has had a severe beating. His eye is closing from being punched, and his lip is torn. There is heavy bruising to his body, and he has a cut on his head. Polly is also examined by the doctor, but fortunately her injuries are not too severe. She has pinch marks on her chest and bruising to her thighs and buttocks where the men assaulted her. Her face is also bruised where she was hit by the men who assaulted her and her lips are bruised from the men crudely kissing her.

"You look as if you are used to this sort of thing," says the doctor, examining Daniel. "I suggest you rest for a few days and give those bruises time to heal, and you too, young lady. The pinch marks will show up as bruises, but won't leave any scars once they heal. Do you wish me to examine you further, Miss? Did these men do anything else I should be aware of?" the doctor asks, concerned that Polly may have been subjected to a more serious assault.

"No, Doctor, they just mauled me and crudely touched me between my legs."

"Very well, if you are sure then I am finished for now."

"Thank you Doctor. I wonder if I might use your phone to call the police?" asks Daniel, who calls D.I. Manners and leaves a message asking him to call at the apartment as soon as he is available. He and Polly then get a taxi and return to the apartment. As soon as they are inside Polly collapses into Daniel's arms, sobbing and shaking uncontrollably.

"Polly, it's all over now and we are safe," he says, holding her close to him. Polly hangs on to him as if her life depended on it and slowly stops her sobbing.

"Are we really, Daniel? Will we ever be safe? Please hold me tight, I cannot bear not being close to you. Those men, what they did to me and what they threatened to do, it was horrible," she sobs.

"You should go and have a long bath, Polly, and try not to upset yourself too much. We are safe now," Daniel replies, trying to move Polly from him as he winces from his beating. Polly goes off to have her bath while Daniel looks in the kitchen for something to eat. After the events of the day, they are ravenous and feel so much better for the meal.

Afterwards they sit together in silence for a while, both deep in their own thoughts. Daniel is sure their abduction was an instruction from the highest level and would have culminated in his being shot and Polly being taken to Moscow. How does he combat this new threat to himself and to Polly? The mention of losing some of their agents as a direct result of Daniel's actions brings a satisfied smile to his face. There will be much to discuss when he goes into work on Monday.

Polly drifts into a deep sleep, relaxing next to Daniel. He carries her to her room and lays her into her bed, still sleeping soundly. Then he calls Conrad to tell him what has happened.

"How are you, Daniel? You have taken another beating by the sound of things."

"I'm a bit battered, Conrad, but I am concerned about Polly. Physically she did not take too much of a beating, but the threats of removing her to Moscow have terrified her."

"She is being used as a pawn against you, and it would seem they are unaware of how she is supplying us with information, thank goodness. If they knew about that the consequences for her would be even worse."

"That is my concern, Conrad. I am beginning to wonder if she should stop all her activities for the time being. What do you think?" asks Daniel to his close friend.

"Well, I understand your concerns for Polly, but would it make any difference to the threats against her if she stopped retrieving information for us? It seems that they are unaware of what she is doing, so she may as well continue. I do not believe it will make any difference to the threats against her, Daniel, I really don't."

"Yes, you may be right, I may be overreacting, but I am concerned for her safety."

"My dear friend, you love this girl very much and need to remember that fact when you are talking about her."

"I do love her very much, Conrad, and believe that my feeling sometimes affect my judgement."

"Caring for her and taking care of her can be achieved without affecting your judgement, Daniel. Enjoy the rest of the weekend, I suggest you both take Monday off, and let's see what happens."

"Ok Conrad, I will call you Sunday evening to confirm whether I will be in Monday, and thank you for your advice, my friend, much appreciated."

Daniel dwells on Conrad's comments and appreciates what a good friend he is. Whilst he wants to protect Polly from any danger, his emotional involvement must not be allowed to cloud any judgements he has to make. A career in the military has made him used to leading an organised and disciplined existence. Some of that discipline has been strained, and having an eighteen-year-old girl living with him, has meant that compromises have had to be made. He must remain focussed on the job in hand, to seek out and eliminate the communist threat. So far the success has been limited, but he must continue to do everything he can to beat the communist threats, whatever it takes. He cannot do this without putting himself and Polly in danger sometimes, but this is how it has to be. Daniel decides that a good night's sleep is in order, and although it is early, goes off to his room. He looks in on Polly who is sound asleep, and he leaves the hall lights on in case she wakes. In no time at all Daniel is asleep, having had a brandy before turning in. He has been asleep for some time when Polly wakes him.

"Daniel, I need to be with you please, I have just woken up and don't want to be alone. Please let me come into your bed."

"Very well, my dear Polly, if it helps you get some rest."

Polly nestles beside him and appears to go back to sleep almost immediately. Daniel lies there with his arm around her, feeling the effects of the beating he received every time Polly stirs, but happy that she at least is able to get some rest! He sleeps fitfully for the remainder of the night and rises around seven o'clock, leaving Polly still asleep. He decides to have a bath and inspect the damage to his battered body. As he lies in the bath he notes the heavy bruising around his chest where the men beat him with their fists. When he gets out of the bath and looks at himself in the mirror, he is surprised at the state of his face. He has a badly bruised black eye and a split lip, together with a cut on his forehead. *You definitely would not win any contests for your looks, Daniel,* he thinks to himself before going back to his room. As he begins to dress, Polly stirs and looks at Daniel's bruised and battered body with horror.

"God, Daniel, you look terrible," she says with tears in her eyes.

"I will recover, Polly, you lie back and relax while I make us some tea," Daniel replies, leaving the room. The rest of Sunday is spent resting and relaxing. Daniel would have liked to go out, but decides that his appearance would attract too much attention. However, Polly does phone home to confirm their visit next weekend, and tell them of what has happened.

"My dear Polly, are you ok? And Daniel, is he hurt again?"

"I am ok Daddy, just a few bruises, but poor Daniel has taken another terrible hiding."

"That man seems capable of withstanding anything that is thrown at him, Polly. Perhaps I should have a word with him.

"Daniel, my dear chap, Polly tells me you have been in the wars again. Thank you for taking care of my daughter."

"A few more bumps and bruises, Ben, but I will survive. I'll tell you more about it at the weekend."

"Ok Daniel, I look forward to seeing both of you on Saturday. Bye for now and look after yourself."

Then, just as he is about to call Conrad the doorbell rings. It's D.I. Jack Manners and W.P.C. Peters.

"Hello Daniel, I don't need to ask what your call was about," he says as he enters the apartment.

"These men were particularly threatening, Inspector; we were very lucky to be able to escape."

"Well Daniel, we may have two of them, they are both Russian nationals. One man was found staggering around Soho with a bullet wound to his chest. He is in hospital at present, I am hoping to talk with him later. The other was spotted by a constable who took him to hospital with a shoulder wound."

"I did shoot one of them in the chest, and managed to hit another one in the shoulder."

"And what about you, Polly, are you ok?" the D.I. asks.

"They were very rough and manhandled me a bit but nothing like what happened to Daniel, they gave him a hell of a beating. I know, I saw them," Polly replies tearfully.

"Well, once I have been able to speak with this man in hospital, I will get you to have a look at him to confirm he is the man you shot."

"Any ideas who they were, or would that be a difficult question for you to answer, Daniel?"

"I'm afraid so Inspector, national security and all that, but I will say that Polly and I will cooperate fully. Being Russian nationals, MI5 will no doubt want a word with them.

"Thank you Daniel, I appreciate that. Well that's all for now. I will be in touch about an identification," the D.I. concludes as he leaves the apartment.

"Hello Conrad, it's Daniel."

"Daniel, how are the bumps and bruises, and is Polly feeling better?"

"We're both better off for our rest, Conrad, although I have to say I do look a bit of a mess. I will take tomorrow off, but need you to do something for me if you would."

"Anything old chap, how can I help?"

"Well I lost my Browning to our captors. Could you requisition me a replacement? Hopefully I can pick it up on Tuesday."

"I'll see to that for you, Daniel. Anything else?"

"No, I will speak to Fitz first thing in the morning and see you Tuesday."

Daniel and Polly decide that she should explain her absence to her work colleagues as an assault in the street by two men trying to steal her handbag. She does not want them to be aware of Daniel, because of his position and Polly's relationship to him. Any hint of Daniel's activities and Polly would be forced to leave the position she is in.

On Monday morning she contacts Mrs Wright, and tells her the story about an attempt to steal her bag.

"My dear Polly, are you alright?"

"I'm fine, Mrs Wright, just a bit shaken up but I will be in to my work tomorrow."

"Well if you're sure, my dear, I will see you then."

Daniel talks with Fitz, who is shocked to hear of the events of Saturday.

"This business is getting out of hand, Daniel. I will speak with Quentin on this and ask him to meet with us. Are you sure you are fit to return tomorrow?"

"Absolutely, Fitz. I may not look too good but I will be fine, thanks," replies Daniel.

"Well ok then, we will see you tomorrow, bye for now."

Daniel is anxious to return to his duties to show the Soviets that he will not be bullied, and hopes that they can take the initiative with the help of MI5. Expelling a few of the Russian communists might just stir up something. So after spending the rest of the day together and enjoying a good night's sleep, Daniel and Polly set off for the Home Office on Tuesday. Daniel checks with Polly that she has her weapon in her bag before she kisses him on his forehead and gets out of the taxi, which moves a further 100 yards or so before Daniel pays the fare and enters the Home Office by the side entrance.

"Good morning Polly, how are you feeling?"

"I'm fine thank you, Mrs Wright, and pleased to be back."

"Well, if you are sure, and you will have some catching up to do."

Polly unlocks her office and finds a number of files for delivery. She places her bag in the drawer, locking it afterwards. She turns to leave her office to find Gordon Hastings standing in the doorway.

"Mr Hastings, you startled me. What do you want?" Polly asks, somewhat annoyed at his presence in her office.

"I missed you yesterday Polly, I was worried about you."

"Well please leave me alone, I have a lot of work to catch up."

"I only want to be friendly with you, Polly. You must know that I am fond of you and I hope we can become good friends."

Polly is shocked and rather concerned with his outburst.

"Mr Hastings you are beginning to annoy me, I have no wish to be your friend and am insulted by your comment about being fond of me. As I said before, if you continue to pester me, I will report you to Mrs Wright," says Polly, her voice raised in anger.

"Very well, but you may regret your actions. I have some powerful friends who could make life difficult for you in the Service."

"My god, are you threatening me? I am going to report you for this," says Polly, as she pushes past him and knocks on Mrs Wright's door.

"Mrs Wright, I am sorry to bother you but I must complain about Gordon Hastings bothering me and behaving in a threatening manner."

"Are you sure, Polly? That is a serious allegation."

"Yes, I am quite sure, the man has become a nuisance."

"Very well Polly, I will speak with personnel, now you had better get on."

Polly starts her deliveries, still angry at Hastings' comments and hopes that Mrs Wright can handle her complaint effectively. The last thing she wants right now is someone entering her life with no reason to be there. Meanwhile, as she enters Sally Nugent's department, Sally is waiting to speak with her. She relates the assault story to her, pointing out the red marks on her face.

"My dear Polly, you could have been seriously hurt. Do they know who they are?"

"Probably a couple of men short of money who took a chance with a woman on her own shopping," says Polly, trying to be matter-of-fact.

"My god, our streets are not safe anymore; you be careful from now on."

Polly thanks Sally for her concern and carries on with her deliveries and collections. She notices a file for collection on Elizabeth Berkley's desk which she collects and discreetly places on the bottom of her pile. She returns to her office, from her first collection, goes in and locks her door to check Elizabeth Berkley's file. There is mention of a Percival Smith as being destined for a significant promotion within the Home Office. The promotion is imminent and the position is one of Undersecretary to the Minister.

"My god Daniel, you look as though you've been in the ring with Jersey Joe. What the hell happened? Is Polly ok, by the way?" Fitz asks as Daniel enters his office.

"Polly is fine, very shaken, some of the threats directed towards her were quite frightening."

"I have asked Quentin to come along, I think he may be able to help us with this. It is unusual for the Soviets to target an individual in this way, you must have really upset someone, Daniel," says Fitz. "Ah, Quentin, I'm glad you could come along."

"Good morning, I see you are in battle mode again, Daniel. Is young Polly ok, by the way?"

"Badly shaken from the experience, sir, but physically she's ok, thank you."

"Now Quentin, why are the Soviets so hell-bent on harming Polly and Daniel? Any thoughts?"

"I believe, from my sources, that they are very angry with the number of their operatives that have been put out of action. They seem to know of his relationship with young Polly and see her as a means of exacting vengeance on him. You have put some of their experienced operatives out of commission, Daniel. It would seem that all of the men sent to get you are experienced agents who have been in the country some time. They have had to change their plans because of you. I can see to it that they are all removed from this country once the trials are concluded.

"Meantime, they are having to find half a dozen new agents to fill the gaps, which can't be easy. My contacts inform me that they are very determined to get to you by any means, so you need to be aware," Quentin replies.

"Are you sure there isn't more to it, Quentin? Revenge doesn't sound a very professional way to carry out their business," Fitz asks.

"I must confess I am a little surprised why they should send so many agents after one person, but that is what they are telling me.

Daniel's actions have disrupted their plans, and that has annoyed them intensely. They are not used to losing the initiative to the opposition. Their planning is meticulous, and Daniel's actions have flung a spanner into the works."

"Well can you keep me informed, Quentin. Daniel, meanwhile, will remain vigilant, won't you?"

"I certainly will. By the way, did Conrad requisition me a new Browning?"

"It's here, Daniel, you just need to sign for it," says Conrad.

Polly makes a note of the information that she needs to pass on to Daniel, before going to the cafeteria for her lunch. She has just sat down when Gordon Hastings appears.

"Do you mind if I join you, Polly?" he asks, sitting down beside her.

"Yes I do mind very much!" replies Polly loudly, as she gets up and moves to another table. Several people look up and see the confrontation between Polly and Hastings, wondering what it can be about. Sally Nugent notices and joins Polly at her table.

"Polly, what was that all about?"

"That man has become a nuisance, Sally. I have reported him to my supervisor but he is still bothering me."

"Would you like me to speak to him for you?"

"No thanks, I will take care of it, but thank you for offering. He is just a sad old man with nothing better to do than bother me."

Daniel, meanwhile, ponders on Quentin's comments and wonders what the communists will try next in their efforts to silence him. For now, he has to focus on the work to be done and wonders how he might contact his friends from the docks, but first, he has to wait on the meeting between the dock management and the unions on Friday to see what happens. Polly, meanwhile, tells Daniel of the message regarding Percival Smith and the attempt to install him as an Undersecretary in the Home Office. This is the information that he had been waiting for and informs Fitz immediately.

"Quentin will be pleased about this, Daniel. MI5 are anxious that he is put in place quickly, so that they can begin monitoring his conversations."

"It would be good if we can confirm the names of other members of the organisation, so that we can keep an eye on them also."

"Well, judging by her success this far, I don't believe it will be too long before Polly gets another name or two, Daniel," Fitz replies with a smile.

"If enthusiasm helps, it will be very soon, Fitz, believe me."

When Polly and Daniel return to their apartment after work, they receive a message from D.I. Manners asking them if they would mind going along to identify the man in hospital. They agree and arrive at the hospital around 6.30pm to be met by the detective inspector.

"Thank you for coming so promptly, it will only take a moment," says the D.I.

Daniel and Polly peer through the window of the room where the man is being kept, and Polly grips Daniel's hand as she recognises the man who made the threats towards them.

"He was their leader, who made threats to kill me and have Polly sent to Russia."

"We thought he might be Russian, but he hasn't asked for anyone from the Embassy yet."

"They may have instructions not to make contact if they are compromised; the Russians would not want to become involved in any bad publicity that might harm their cause."

"Well, for now we have him and here he will remain. Thank you both for your cooperation," says the D.I., showing them to the hospital exit.

"Well that's one of them who won't be doing any more damage to anyone, Polly."

"I am glad that you shot him, Daniel. The man was a beast and deserves everything he gets."

The next morning, Polly is again approached by Hastings as she enters the building.

"I just wanted to apologise, Polly. If I upset you I am sorry."

"You didn't upset me, Mr Hastings, just annoyed me, so can we just forget the whole thing now?"

"I meant you no harm, Polly. I could be a very good friend to you, I do have a lot of influence in the Service, I could help you."

"What do you mean, you have influence and could help me?"

"I am a member of an important group of Civil Servants who could shape the future of the Service in years to come and you could be part of that."

"What possible influence could you have over my career prospects Mr Hastings?"

"There are big changes that will be taking place shortly. I will be part of those changes and could see that you were promoted within my department," Hastings replies, smiling.

"I have to go Mr Hastings, please just leave me alone, goodbye," says Polly, realising what Hastings has implied. She picks up her first round of deliveries and leaves her office, locking the door behind her. As she passes Sally Nugent's desk, Sally asks if she might have a word at lunch time.

"Certainly Sally, I will see you then," says Polly with a smile.

At lunchtime, Polly meets up with Sally and is concerned by the questions she is asked.

"Polly, I just wanted to ask you about your guardian. Who is he?"

"Why Sally, you are asking the identical question that Mr Hastings asked me. I must confess, why so many people want to know who my guardian is puzzles me a little. He is just a family friend who has been kind enough to let me stay in his apartment. Otherwise it would have been difficult for me to take up the position offered me in the Civil Service," Polly replies, somewhat concerned about Sally Nugent's interest in Daniel.

"Is he the man that brings you into work and collects you in the evening?"

"Yes he is. How did you know about that, Sally, have you been following me?" replies Polly, becoming rather annoyed at this questioning.

"We like to know about our members, Polly, that's all. I'm sure you understand."

"I'm afraid I don't understand, Sally. I don't understand at all. First Mr Hastings offers me promotions if he can be my friend, and now you are asking me questions which have nothing to do with my position here. What is going on?"

"We want to be sure of your commitment to the union, that is all, Polly."

"And how does wanting to know who my guardian is help the union?"

"I think we have talked enough now, Polly. Sorry if I appeared to be asking a lot of questions, bye for now."

Polly sits there, puzzled and perplexed at Sally Nugent's questions. She gets up to leave, when Hastings appears at her table. Polly can contain herself no longer.

"Mr Hastings, you are beginning to annoy me, please go away!" she says loudly, as she leaves the cafeteria. She goes back to her office and recites brief details of the last half hour or so in a message to Daniel, telling him she will talk later. She puts the phone down and begins to prepare for her afternoon deliveries, when Mrs Wright knocks her door.

"Is everything ok, Polly? I heard there was some shouting in the cafeteria?"

"Just Mr Hastings making a nuisance of himself again."

"Should I speak with him?" Mrs Wright asks, sounding concerned.

"No thanks, I just want to forget about it, Mrs Wright."

Mrs Wright leaves the office and Polly sets off on her deliveries, relieved that she has no drops on the third floor. She is concerned about the sudden interest in Daniel, especially after what happened over the last weekend. What is the connection between the union activists sudden interests in who Daniel is and his relationship to Polly?

"I should not worry about what has happened, Polly, but think about what you have uncovered," says Daniel as they talk about the afternoon's events that evening. "I believe Mr Hastings, in his haste to impress you, has implied that he is a member of the Red Hand organisation. If that is so then MI5 will be very interested in what he said to you," Daniel tells Polly, hoping his comments will reassure her.

"You really think that is what he said in so many words when trying to impress me?"

"Yes, I most certainly do. As for Sally Nugent's questions, I don't know, she is someone we must be wary of. I can only think that she was backing up Hastings in some way, although she would not necessarily be aware that he is a Red Hand member."

"So Mr Hastings being a nuisance has been useful to you, Daniel. The stupid man's actions have opened another door for us. And Sally has let her guard down also. From now on, I know who they are but they do not know that I know, if you understand what I am trying to say," Polly replies with a smile.

"I think so Polly, they don't know what we know so let's keep it that way, use them for our own ends."

Daniel is hoping to hear some news today, Friday, regarding the union meeting with employers. A positive decision will stop the dockers from an all-out strike and thwart the communists and their troublemakers for the time being at least. Meantime, he talks over the developments regarding Polly's 'suitor' Gordon Hastings and the implications of his comments about being a member of an influential group who could further Polly's career.

"Do you think he has inadvertently let slip that he is a member of Red Hand?"

"I certainly think we can assume that, Fitz, especially as Sally Nugent tried to divert questions about him. Whilst she may not know officially of his membership, she will have an idea, I am sure, and will want to protect him. I am very concerned about that woman; she is totally committed to her cause and will stop at nothing to see it through to its conclusions."

"I think we'll keep an eye on Sally Nugent, Daniel, to see what she does next."

"And I will contact the Ministry of Works to see how the meeting is progressing, Fitz. Let's hope they are in the holiday mood and call off any proposed strike action."

Polly, meanwhile, goes about her duties as usual and is again approached by Gordon Hastings. She has decided that she will continue to remain standoffish whilst challenging him to show his hand regarding what he may be able to offer her.

"Have you thought over what I said to you yesterday, Polly?"

"You do not impress me with your claims of what you can do for my career, Mr Hastings, you are just a lowly Civil Servant trying to be something you are not. Please don't bother me any more with talk of what you can do for me," Polly replies, and moves on. She does not have to wait long for a reaction, as Sally Nugent approaches her again at lunchtime.

"You really should try to be more friendly with Gordon, he might just be in a position to help you."

"Really, Sally? And how can he possibly be of help to my career? Can you tell me, because I am obviously curious?"

"Let's just say that he knows people with influence within the Civil Service. People who can shape policy and make selections of key personnel into important positions."

"It all sounds very much like he is full of his own importance. If he knows so many people of influence why is he still sitting behind a desk on the third floor? Why isn't he in a position of importance himself? I'm sorry Sally, but I don't believe a word of it, the man is a fraud and a pest as far as I'm concerned," Polly replies, leaving the cafeteria. She has thrown down a gauntlet and waits to see what will happen. She does not have to wait long, since both Sally and Hastings approach her outside her office after lunch.

"Polly, might we have a word with you in your office? It is important."

"Really Sally, I do not have the time for all this, I have work to do and you, Mr Hastings, are becoming very annoying," she replies sharply.

"I have a position for you, Polly, to prove how influential I can be to your career."

Polly smiles to herself; it would appear that Mr Hastings is about to show his hand in his eagerness to prove to Polly how important he is.

"You are in no position to offer me anything, Mr Hastings. You know that only too well, so please don't say you are."

"What Gordon is offering, Polly, is a chance for you to meet some of his influential friends in the Service. People who will soon be running all the key positions and be making policy decisions. There are a number of these people who need to be informed of events, without going through normal channels of communication. We need someone that can move messages between them without creating any suspicions from current department heads. And we do not have anyone who can transmit messages direct to the Foreign Office, which I believe you do from time to time."

"Yes, my security pass allows me full access to the Foreign Office, but what on earth are you talking about, Sally?" Polly replies, feigning ignorance.

"Something far greater and important than the union, Polly. We are talking about an organisation with real power to make decisions and alter the way we do things in our country. An organisation poised to take control when the time is right," says Hastings with a smile.

"Well I must say it sounds very exciting, but I don't understand why you have picked me, Mr Hastings, and my feelings toward you still remain the same, whatever I decide."

"We understand, Polly, now here is a list of names with their stations. We want you to visit them every day to see if they have any messages to deliver to their comrades. Their messages will be easy for you to separate as their files will have a red rose circled by a red hand on the front. Under no circumstances must these files be left in your office. They must be delivered as soon as you receive them, do you understand?"

"Very well, Sally, now I really must get on. Perhaps you can talk with me more about this after the holiday?" Polly replies, trying to be as casual as she can.

"Yes of course, Polly. Now you must not mention this to anyone, do you understand? And from now onwards Gordon will not be bothering you," says Sally, as she leaves the office accompanied by Gordon Hastings.

CHAPTER 8

Polly collects her files, her mind racing at what has just been discussed with her. In a few short moments, she has been supplied with a list of names of key players within the communist organisation operating from inside the Home and Foreign Offices. She has been tasked with acting as a courier between agents, which could give her unlimited access to their messages.

Daniel, meanwhile, contacts the Ministry of Works for information about the meeting between Union and Management. If agreement can be reached between the two parties, then an all-out strike of the dockers will be averted.

"The news is not good I'm afraid, Daniel. There has been some trouble outside of the meeting with dockers shouting and trying to get inside," says Jeremiah Winterton.

"It doesn't look like any decisions are going to be agreed before the holiday then, sir?"

"Apparently not but if anything changes, I will let you know."

Polly goes about her collections and deliveries, anxious to pass on the news to Daniel as soon as possible She has left a brief message via the special telephone service she has had installed, and hastens to meet him at the end of the day.

"You have been busy, Polly," he says as she climbs into the taxi.

They reach the apartment, and Polly almost jumps on Daniel with excitement as they enter.

"Daniel, we have found a way into this Red Hand organisation. I didn't do anything, they came to me. Apparently, they have chosen me for a similar reason to why I was chosen as Corporate Liaison Officer. They see me has not being in the service long enough to have established any relationships or formed any opinions."

"They believe they can mould you into one of their members, and meanwhile use your position for their own convenience."

"I will show them just what they have let themselves in for. I am more determined than ever to see this organisation destroyed now that they have tried to take advantage of me."

"And so we shall, Polly, but you must be even more careful now. I will have to give you some sort of cover story about me, but more importantly we must let MI5 know that you have been recruited by them. We want to be sure that you are not compromised in any way by your actions.

"Well we shall have plenty to talk about over the holiday, Daniel. What time are we leaving tomorrow, by the way?"

"There is a train around noon, so we can have a leisurely morning before we go."

They enjoy an evening meal together, listen to some music, then go off for an early night. On Saturday morning, they pack for their break, and pick up some shopping on the way.

The journey home is uneventful and their taxi pulls up outside Polly's home just before three o'clock.

"Mummy, Daddy, we're here, it's so good to be home again," says Polly, dashing toward the parlour, leaving Daniel with the cases!

"My dear Polly and Daniel, it's so good to see you both," says Margaret, hugging her daughter.

"Daniel, my dear chap, it's good to see you again," says Ben, shaking his hand.

"Daniel, Polly, we have been waiting for you. Where have you been?" ask Maisy, Daisy, and George. The children gather round Polly and Daniel, overwhelming them with their welcome. They miss their sister very much, especially Maisy who is growing up fast. It is a warm day so they go out into the garden while Polly joins Margaret to make some tea.

"How are you, dear? I know it was only Easter when we saw you last but it seems a lot longer."

"I am very well, Mummy, and enjoying my job very much, thank you."

"And you and Daniel?" asks Margaret who, as a mother, still remains curious about her daughter's special relationship with Daniel.

"Daniel and I go from strength to strength, Mummy, we both love each other very much, as I am sure you are aware. We will be together forever, I am sure of that."

Her response surprises Margaret a little. Polly's comments about their love for each other was the first time that she had mentioned their true feelings for each other.

"He is a very fine young man, Polly, and you have both spent some wonderful times together I am sure, as well as some harrowing ones."

"I cannot imagine my life without him, Mummy, and I know he feels the same. I am very lucky to have met Daniel, and very grateful to you and Daddy for making it happen, now, let's take them their tea."

The family sit outside for about an hour before Margaret decides that she must start preparing dinner. Polly goes off with her while Daniel and Ben sit outside watching the children amusing themselves with the dog.

"How are you feeling, Daniel? Polly said you took another beating last weekend."

"Recovering, Ben, still a bit sore and as you can see won't be winning any prizes for my looks for a while."

"And how is Polly progressing? She sounded rather upset when we spoke."

"She was frightened more by what was threatened than what actually happened, Ben. However, on a positive note, she is doing very well in her new position. She has fitted in and has been able to secure some valuable information. We are close to being able to pass detailed information to MI5 about the communist organisation operating within the Home Office and the Foreign Office. My boss is really impressed by her, in fact Fitz has taken quite a shine to her I believe."

"She is very determined, Daniel, but with you by her side, she believes she is invincible."

"Yes, and that worries me sometimes. I care very much for Polly, Ben, as I am sure you are aware, and when the time is right, I want to make our relationship more formal. Do you understand what I am trying to say?"

"Yes I think so, Daniel, and I assume the time will be right when you feel the dangers surrounding you both have been removed?"

"That is exactly it, Ben. I love your daughter very much, but have no desire to ruin her future happiness by making premature decisions about our time together. What I will assure you of, Ben, is that we live together as friends, even though we love each other. Can you accept that?"

"I accept it completely, Daniel, and will keep this conversation strictly between us for the time being."

"Come along Daniel, we need to take our cases upstairs and unpack before dinner," says Polly, calling Daniel from the conservatory. They take their cases into their rooms, and Daniel decides to freshen up before dinner. He removes his shirt just as Polly enters.

"Did you tell Daddy about how well I am doing, Daniel?" she says, giving him a hug.

"I certainly did, Polly, and he is very proud of you," Daniel replies, wincing slightly at Polly's grip on him. Margaret enters his room, and notices his grimace as Polly is holding him.

"Daniel, are you ok? I noticed you flinching a little as Polly held on to you."

"Just a few bruises, Margaret," Daniel replies, smiling.

"Daniel, let me see, you should have told me," says Polly, peeling off Daniel's vest.

"God, Daniel, you're covered in bruises, why didn't you say something?"

"Polly's right, Daniel, you are black and blue. I suggest you have a hot bath before dinner. I had no idea you had received such a beating," Margaret replies rather tearfully.

"Do we have any of that ointment left, that Doctor Wilson gave Daniel at Easter, Mummy?"

"Have a look in the bathroom cabinet, it will be in there if there is any left."

Polly looks in the cabinet and finds an unopened tube of the ointment.

"I will massage some of this into your bruises after your bath, Daniel."

As Daniel goes off to have his bath, Margaret speaks with her daughter with some concerns.

"Polly, I had no idea just how badly Daniel had been hurt, and what about you? Have you got bruises too?"

"I was hardly touched at all, Mummy, they just used the threat of harming me to try and get Daniel to give them information."

"Seeing the bruising on Daniel's body, I worry about what permanent damage is being done to him, I really do."

"Please do not worry, Mummy, I will take care of him and his bruises will heal eventually," says Polly, hoping to reassure Margaret.

"The two of you have been through so much, and I know how much you care for each other, I just fear for you both sometimes."

"I love Daniel very much, Mummy, and he loves me very much also. There is nothing and no one that will stop us being together for each other, whatever happens," says Polly, giving Margaret a hug.

"Thank you Polly, I needed that. It was reassuring to hear how you feel towards each other, although Daddy and I were sure that you both care for each other very much. You can see it when you are together and almost sense it when you are apart."

Margaret leaves Polly waiting for Daniel, and goes downstairs to continue with dinner. She is delighted to have heard Polly expressing her feelings and feels sure that their relationship will eventually come to the natural conclusion. Daniel, meanwhile, goes back to his room where Polly is waiting. She gently massages his shoulders, stomach, and back, holding back her tears as she sees just how badly he has been bruised by his beating last weekend.

"You really must allow your body to properly recover from these bruises, Daniel. You will promise me, won't you?"

"Of course, Polly, I have nothing strenuous planned at the moment."

"Please Daniel, I am serious about this, I'm afraid that you may have done permanent damage to your body with the beatings you have suffered over the past few weeks."

"Now please, Polly, no tears. We are here to enjoy the weekend with your family. They do not want to see you upset. Now let me get dressed and we can go down for some dinner."

"Ok Daniel, I will see you downstairs when you are ready," says Polly, leaving the room.

After dinner, Daniel is approached by Maisy, anxious to ask about him and Polly.

"We all know how much you and Polly must care for each other, Daniel, but when are you going to get married?"

"There is plenty of time for that, Maisy, but you are right to say that your sister and I care for each other. Polly is very special to me and we shall continue to enjoy each other's company for many years. Do you remember, Polly was only a year younger than you when we first met?"

"Yes, I remember when you first came to our house. Did you know that Polly was very upset that Peter Forsythe had to leave?"

"I'm sure she was. Peter was a good friend and saved her from those villains on more than one occasion."

"I hope I meet someone like you, Daniel, when I grow up," says Maisy, as she plants a kiss on his cheek before going off to the kitchen. Sunday passes all too quickly, and on Monday morning, Polly goes with Margaret into town where there is a Whit. Monday market. George finally gets his chance to talk with Daniel.

"You look as if you have been fighting, Daniel. Did you get hurt again?"

"Just a few bruises, George, nothing to worry about," Daniel replies with a smile.

"Were you protecting my sister from bad men? Why are they always trying to hurt Polly, Daniel?"

"Sometimes, it just seems that way, George, but I will always be there to look after her for you."

"I don't know what any of us would do if anything happened to you, Daniel. You are my best friend and Maisy and Daisy's best friend as well."

"Thanks for that George, that is very kind of you to say so," Daniel replies. He is taken by surprise by George's comments and really appreciates what he said.

Polly and Margaret return in time for lunch, and Daniel and Polly pack their cases soon after, ready to take the five o'clock train back to London. Polly spends some time with her sisters, and George, while Margaret, Ben, and Daniel sit in the conservatory.

"Polly seems to be settling into her new position, Daniel. Just how important is it to your work?"

"Her contribution is proving invaluable, Margaret."

"And is she in any danger from these people that she is gathering information on?"

"There is always some danger in any business involving security, these are desperate and ruthless people determined to destroy our way of life. What I will say to you is that I have been surprised by Polly's commitment. She may only be eighteen years old, but she believes passionately in preserving our way of life. In fact, her enthusiasm has not gone unnoticed, as I mentioned to Ben. My boss has taken quite a shine to her and is very impressed with what she has been able to give us so far, and I might add that MI5 are also aware of her work."

"Good lord, I had no idea our daughter had become so important," says Margaret, smiling.

"She is very determined, Margaret, and I too am very proud of her for what she has achieved in such a short time. Rest assured, I will take good care of her for you both."

The time for Polly and Daniel to leave comes round too soon for everyone; the goodbyes are all said, with a few tears, before Ben drives them to the station.

"Have a safe journey, both of you," says Ben, as he hugs Polly and shakes Daniel by the hand.

"Bye Daddy, see you again soon," says Polly, waving as the train slowly pulls out of Carswell Station.

They arrive back at the apartment around eight o'clock and settle for eggs on toast for supper. Fortunately, they had a good lunch before leaving Polly's home, so are not especially hungry.

Tuesday morning sees Daniel organise a meeting with Fitz and Conrad for ten o'clock.

"Good morning Daniel, I trust you and Polly had a pleasant weekend in the country?"

"We did, thank you Fitz. It was over far too quickly, but it was enjoyable."

"Now what do you have for me?" asks Fitz.

"I have the names of the key players in the Red Hand organisation, and the means to monitor their communications," Daniel replies with a smile.

"Good grief Daniel, are you serious? And if so, how on earth did you manage that?"

Daniel outlines the series of events leading up to Polly being given the list of members of the Red Hand organisation.

"You have trained young Polly well, this information will prove invaluable to the security services. We can now monitor the organisation and keep abreast of all their activities until we have enough evidence to make the necessary arrests."

"I know you will want to talk with MI5 on this, Fitz, we have to make absolutely sure that she is not implicated in any way by her activities for Red Hand. There is another consideration as well. Sally Nugent has been asking questions about me. Can you arrange some sort of cover for me that can be set up should they start digging into my file?"

"Yes of course, I will get on to Quentin as soon as we have finished, it is very important that you have good cover in order to maintain Polly's innocence in her involvement with this organisation.

You must tell her to be extra careful what she says and does in their presence. These are very dangerous people, totally committed to their cause. Anyone threatening them will be crushed, so look after her Daniel, please."

"I appreciate your concerns for her, Fitz, she is very special to me, as you know, and I will watch over her carefully. She is very determined to make a difference, and I will impress on her the need to be vigilante.

"Meanwhile, here is the list of names that Polly has given me, namely, Marion Fisher, David Boroughs, Roberta Phillips, and Gordon Hastings. I think we can add Sally Nugent to that list as well, and of course, we are aware that Percival Smith is to be their man destined for high office, so we can add him to the list. I will talk with Conrad and other members of the team about how we can go about checking on their movements. Ideally, we want to see who they make contact with outside of the Home Office."

"Very good, Daniel, now where are we with the problems in the docks? I understand the meeting on Friday broke up in disarray?" says Fitz.

"I will have to try and make some sort of direct contact with Michael Doyle. I have lost my two other contacts for the time being; they are both in hospital having been attacked in a pub brawl. Hennessey has gone to ground, worried that he might be in danger himself, so the only way I am going to get any information in the meantime, is to contact Doyle on the pretext of wanting another interview," replies Daniel.

"I will have to check that your cover is still in place, meanwhile, we need pictures of these Red Hand members so that they can be recognised by our chaps. If you can arrange that, Daniel, and get some surveillance set up on these people."

Polly goes about her regular duties, and is soon collecting and delivering messages to members of Red Hand. She is joined at lunch by Sally Nugent and Gordon Hastings.

"You have had a couple of messages to deliver already this morning, Polly?"

"Yes, easy to recognise the files, Sally. I was a bit miffed by Marion Frobisher. She asked me all sorts of silly questions, doesn't she know that you have asked me to deliver messages?"

"She was just being careful, that's all, Polly," says Sally, smiling.

"Well I hope this doesn't happen each time I deliver or collect from your colleagues, otherwise it will stop me from my work. I have to complete my collections by the end of each day so that no files are left unattended," Polly replies, sounding indignant.

"We have told the people concerned who you are, Polly dear, please do not concern yourself about any questions they may ask," Gordon Hastings comments.

"It's not about being concerned, it's about offering to help you and being questioned by those who should be getting on with their work, instead of bothering me."

"Yes, very well, Polly. I will see to it that any questions are directed to me in future," says Sally Nugent, becoming restless at Polly's remarks. Polly leaves the cafeteria after a somewhat fractious lunch break and goes about her afternoon collections, only to be harassed again by another Red Hand member, David Burroughs. Polly goes to pick up the file from his desk, when he grabs her arm.

"What are you doing? This file is confidential, Miss. Please leave it where it is," he demands.

"You don't want it delivered, Mr Burroughs?" replies Polly politely.

"No thank you, Miss Spencer, you have no business in this department. Please leave before I call security."

"Very well, please tell Sally Nugent that I did try to collect your package, won't you?"

"Just a moment, where are you going?" he replies, trying to prevent Polly from moving on.

"Take your hands off me please or I will call security!" Polly shouts at Burroughs. She hurries out of the department, and goes back to her office, locking the door behind her. Polly is unsure how to respond to this incident. She cannot tell Mrs Wright, since she was collecting an 'unofficial document'. After sitting for a few moments to compose herself, she continues with her duties. She has decided that she will not collect any documents from Red Hand members until the situation with David Burroughs has been resolved. If the organisation wish her to carry on helping them with moving messages between their members, then they will have to apologise for the embarrassment that they caused her. After completing her second round of collections, Polly returns to her office, to be met by Sally Nugent and David Burroughs.

"I really don't have time for more meetings, Sally, I have to get on with my work. Mr Burroughs is the second member of your organisation to question me and embarrass me in front of other members of staff. I don't think I can help you with any more collections, I'm sorry."

"We are sorry for the embarrassment, Polly, but we do need you to continue helping us, it is important."

"And what about you, Mr Burroughs? Why did you threaten me with security in front of your colleagues? It was very embarrassing. I'm sure Mrs Wright will hear about it. My job is very important to me and your behaviour could cause me problems."

"My apologies, Polly, I did not realise the position you had been given for our organisation," replies Burroughs rather sheepishly.

"Well I have work to do, but Sally, should Mrs Wright ask about this incident I will have to consider whether I want to carry on helping you," says Polly as she walks past the two of them and goes off to continue her work. She is rather pleased with the outcome of the meeting, since Sally will now have to approach her again about the position and reassure her that she will not be embarrassed further. Thankfully, the rest of her working day passes without incident. However, as she is about to leave the building, she is confronted by David Burroughs.

"Although I was happy to apologise to you, Miss Spencer, I am not happy with the responsibility that Sally has given you. I do not believe you are the most suitable person to collect and deliver such sensitive messages."

"In that case, Mr Burroughs, please tell Sally of your concerns, and that I will not be making any further collections on her behalf," Polly replies firmly, as she walks past him into Whitehall. She is furious about what has happened, but determined that she can use it to her advantage. She recites the events of the day to Daniel, when they are in the apartment.

"I would like to be a fly on the wall when Burroughs passes that message on to Sally Nugent, Polly. She will be furious, of that I am sure," says Daniel with a smile.

"Do you think what I did was the right thing to do, Daniel? I must say I was annoyed by what he said."

"You did what you had to do, Polly, now let me tell you about the cover story that Fitz has prepared for me," says Daniel, as they sit down with tea.

Daniel relates to Polly his proposed cover as a BBC researcher. His work allegedly involves assessing scripts for all types of BBC television programmes to ensure that content is acceptable for public viewing. He is able to do some of his work from his apartment, so able to approach what is required without being compromised by any outside influence.

"That sounds very exciting, Daniel, and television will become popular eventually, I am sure."

"We just want to be sure that no suspicions are aroused as to who I am. This may mean that I will introduce myself to some of your colleagues if the need arises."

"I just hope I have not put off Sally Nugent with what I said to Burroughs, I do so want to be able to help you, Daniel."

"You have been very helpful, Polly, and knowing the names of these people will mean we can monitor their movements as we build up evidence against them. Without your help we wouldn't have had that evidence."

The following morning sees Polly busy with a heavy workload of files to deliver. The morning passes quickly, and Polly decides to avoid the cafeteria and has a sandwich in her office. She is just about to begin her afternoon rounds when she is confronted by Sally Nugent.

"Polly, what's this I hear from David about you not wishing to continue helping us with distribution of our messages?"

"Since Mr Burroughs does not think I am a suitable person to deliver your messages, I cannot see how you would want me to continue."

"I think David was overreacting, Polly, we really would appreciate your help."

"And I do want to be a help, Sally, but I am concerned about my position. If Mrs Wright is told that I am having arguments with members of staff, I could lose my job, do you understand? I am very worried about what she may find out," Polly replies, sounding very concerned.

"I will sort out this misunderstanding, Polly. Let's meet up in the cafe around the corner at five o'clock and have a chat."

"Very well, I will see you just after five o'clock, now I have to go," Polly replies. She manages to finish her deliveries in plenty of time to leave a message for Daniel to collect her from the cafe about 5.30pm.

She enters the cafe, about 100 yards from the Home Office entrance, to be confronted by Gordon Hastings, David Burroughs, Sally Nugent, and another man that she does not recognise.

"Polly, this is Percival Smith. Percival is the unofficial head of our group and wanted to meet with you personally."

"I am very pleased to meet you, Mr Smith, I'm Polly Spencer."

"My dear Polly, I've heard so much about you and wanted to thank you myself for agreeing to help us. We have so much work to be done, and need people in key positions in the Service to help us with our cause, so that we can achieve what we have set out to do."

"Thank you very much, Mr Smith, but I am not sure whether I can be of any use to you since Mr Burroughs does not think me suitable," Polly replies indignantly.

"Nonsense Polly, I am sure David did not mean to say that, did you David?" Percival Smith enquires, looking hard at David Burroughs.

"Well I just thought…"

"Well you were incorrect, David. From what Sally has told me there is no one more suitable than Polly to do this job. We need to be able to move round the Home Office and the Foreign Office unhindered. This young lady does that every day. How could she not be the most suitable person for this important role?" says Percival Smith.

"I must apologise for my comments, Polly, it will not happen again," Burroughs replies, clearly embarrassed by what Percival Smith has said.

"Now, Polly, I shall also be calling on you from time to time with messages. I shall be moving into the permanent secretary's department shortly, and will need a reliable contact who can move my private messages to members in the organisation. Your position, as Liaison Officer, allows you to do move freely throughout all departments, making you the ideal person to do that. Will you do that for me?" Percival Smith asks, looking straight at Polly.

"Certainly, Mr Smith, I will be very pleased to help you whenever I can."

Just at that moment, Daniel enters the cafe, formally dressed in a raincoat and trilby.

"My dear Poll, there you are. We really should be getting on."

Polly introduces Daniel to all those present, especially Percival Smith.

"Mr Smith has asked me to help him when he moves into the permanent secretary's office, Daniel, isn't that exciting?" says Polly, holding on to his arm.

"Delighted to meet you, Daniel. This young lady is proving quite an asset; you must be very proud."

"Indeed I am, sir. Her father gave me guardianship when she acquired her position with the Civil Service, and she seems to be going from strength to strength."

"Tell me Daniel, what is it that you do?" asks Percival Smith with an enquiring tone in his voice.

"I am with the BBC. I look at programmes that are offered for the television service to determine if they are suitable for public viewing. Quite interesting, really," Daniel replies with a confident air.

"I'm sure it must be, Daniel, and worth noting that we have a friend in the BBC," says Percival Smith with a forced smile.

"Indeed. Well, awfully nice to have met with you all, come along now Polly. Bye for now."

"Gosh, Daniel, that was brilliant. Percival Smith was impressed by you, and he has told me personally that he wants me to help the organisation. We should celebrate with a meal tonight," says Polly as they hurry along the Mall to the waiting taxi.

"You have just secured the endorsement of the man heading the organisation within the Home and Foreign Offices, Polly. Your input from now onwards will be even more important, and you have succeeded in ruffling the feathers of some of the organisation's members, which is always worth doing since it can create divisions among them."

In celebration of the events of the last few hours or so, Daniel and Polly enjoy a quiet meal in Kensington. They are both delighted by what has happened, although Daniel knows that there could be additional dangers for Polly. For now, however, they just enjoy the moment and their time together.

"I think Percival Smith has taken a bit of a shine to you, Polly, and we should exploit this whenever we can, without giving anything away. This man is very dangerous, and we want to put him away. To do this we need definite evidence that he is involved directly with the Russians."

"I will do whatever you think is best, Daniel. I can send you a message each time I get called to his office, and keep you informed of all the other messages that I collect and deliver for the organisation."

After their meal, they walk the short distance to the apartment, Polly still chatting away about what has happened.

Over the coming days, Polly continues to ferry data between Red Hand agents during the course of her work as Corporate Liaison Officer. She also makes a number of collections from Percival Smith, some of which she delivers to the Foreign Office. Percival Smith has been duly promoted to the permanent secretary's office. Whilst not an official undersecretary, he has become one of his advisors, giving him access to policy meetings. This will offer opportunities to mould policy decisions at the highest level.

Daniel and his team, meanwhile, continue to monitor the agent's movements outside of their offices and determine that Percival Smith is meeting with a number of people that may be Soviet agents. They take pictures of the meetings and send them to MI5 for analysis.

"What we need to be able to do, Daniel, is take a look at the messages that are being carried by Polly. Whilst it is useful to know who is talking to who, what they are talking about would be even more useful to us," says Fitz.

"The only way would be for us to use duplicate envelopes, but this would involve Polly having to read the messages then replace them in another similar envelope before somehow disposing of the used envelope. That is too much to expect of her, Fitz, and there would be a time element involved. We do not want anyone to become curious about how much time she is spending in her office instead of her deliveries and collections. I will speak with Polly and see if there is another way."

Then, after about a three-week gap, Daniel is contacted by Hennessey. He asks to make contact the following evening in the Lamb and Flag at Covent Garden. Daniel decides that it may be better if Polly does not go with him this time, and suggests she invite Penny Carstairs round for the evening.

"Yes, ok Daniel, I will mention it to her tomorrow. It will be nice to have a gossip with Penny, I have not had chance to speak with her since becoming involved with Sally Nugent and her organisation."

Daniel goes on to mention how it would be beneficial to know what is being said in the messages that she carries. Whilst it is useful to know who is talking to who, actually knowing what they are saying would be even more useful.

"Well the envelopes are unsealed, Daniel, I could always take a look."

"Are you saying that they don't actually seal down the correspondence between each other?" asks Daniel in amazement.

"They don't need to since no one has access to them except me. They pass them to me and I carry them to their destination. They are never left anywhere, and never out of my sight. That's why they need me, Daniel, no one else is able to do what I do, and they see me as just a messenger with no interest in what I may be carrying."

"I'll mention this to Fitz. We had no idea that it was possible to access the files without detection."

They talk through their meal about how Polly might get the

information from the files to Daniel, and the obvious method would seem to be using a camera to photograph the documents. For his part, Daniel is reluctant to put more responsibility and risk, on Polly's shoulders. She knows no limits in her willingness to help him in his work, and is totally committed in helping rid the country of the menace of communism. Daniel's only concern is that her willingness could be her undoing.

He has to impress on her the need for caution whilst not curbing her enthusiasm too much. These points are running through his mind as Polly returns to the lounge from her bath. She sits across Daniel, hugging him tightly.

"Do you think Fitz will let me use a camera, Daniel? I could easily take pictures of the messages from the organisation. It would be easy enough to remove them from their envelope and replace them again afterwards."

"We will have to see what Fitz decides, Polly. I am concerned about the risk you will be taking."

They sit with each other for a moment, Daniel conscious of the closeness of Polly, while she just hugs him tightly as she has done so many times before. Should anything happen to her, it would be too devastating for him to even consider, but Daniel has to consider what might happen should Red Hand find out about her. This is why no move can be made against them until all the evidence is in place to make the arrests.

"I will be ok, Daniel. I promise I will be careful, anyway I will be doing my job for most of the time, no one can be suspicious of me doing what I am paid to do. Please don't worry about me," she says, holding his hand as if to give him assurance. Daniel and Polly sit there, comfortable with each other's company, each with their own thoughts. After a little while Polly goes to sleep in his arms again, as she has done so many times before. He gently lifts her and carries her to her bed, pulling the bedclothes over her before leaving the room.

He has to agree that this latest revelation by Polly means that they may be able to move against Red Hand sooner than they could have hoped. Having access to their correspondence will give Daniel and his team inside knowledge of their activities. Once they can tie in their relationship with the Russians, they will have definitive evidence to move against them. And this action will greatly enhance Daniel's standing within the Service. Moving on from direct field activities will give him the opportunity to have a better life with Polly and begin to plan for their future together. Smiling to himself, he goes off to his bed and is soon fast asleep.

"Daniel, are you awake? I can't sleep thinking about what I have to do with the messages and taking pictures of documents."

"Come along, Polly, but you must get to sleep, we have a busy day tomorrow," he replies as she nestles beside him.

Daniel meets with Fitz the next day and tells him what Polly has said about the unsealed documents she is delivering for the Red Hand organisation.

"Good lord, Daniel, they actually move documents between departments unsealed?"

"Well, there is no reason to seal them since the only person handling them is Polly, and they seem to trust her completely."

"Yes, so it would seem. We must take advantage of this good fortune, Daniel, and take a look at those documents."

"The simplest way would be for Polly to photograph them, but it would be a risky business, Fitz, and I am concerned about that."

"How secure is Polly's office? Would she be able to lock the door and close the blinds so as to be unseen from outside?"

"As far as I know, the office is secure because of the sensitive files that may be in there overnight."

"So Polly would be able to photograph documents unseen and locked inside?"

"I have already mentioned the use of a camera to her and she is naturally keen to help."

"Ok, well we will get you a camera, and ask Phil to give her some instruction. This court case you have, when exactly is it due to start, Daniel?"

Daniel and Polly had received a court date last week for the men accused of breaking into the apartment. It is not expected to last more than a day or so because the evidence is conclusive.

"The 7th July, Fitz. I am going to suggest to Polly that she books the time off as a holiday. We don't want her work colleagues, especially Sally Nugent, asking questions about what happened and why."

"That's a good idea, Daniel. The last thing Polly will want is awkward questions about why she was attacked twice."

Polly has a quiet day, giving her time for her thoughts about how she will further help Daniel by photographing documents that she receives from agents of Red Hand. Her office is secure enough for her to be able to look at the documents without being seen. However, she decides to leave things as they are until Daniel has confirmation that she can begin photographing papers. In the meantime she asks Penny to come round in the evening and spend some time catching up. Penny is delighted, as she has not had the chance to talk with Polly for a while. Polly asks her round for dinner with her and Daniel, so that he can get away in plenty of time for his meeting with Hennessey.

After dinner, Daniel goes off to meet Hennessey, reminding Polly not to answer the door to anyone as she sees him out. This is the first time that Penny has met Daniel, and being Polly's age, is curious about him.

"I had no idea you were living with such a good-looking man, Polly. Who is he exactly?"

"He is my guardian while I am in London. Daddy has known him for many years, and I have known him since I was at school," Polly replies.

"And you live together in this lovely apartment. You are very lucky, Polly, it must be nice living with someone like Daniel being with you," says Penny, obviously curious.

Daniel arrives in good time at the Lamb and Flag and spots Hennessey standing at the bar.

"Daniel, what can I get you?" he asks. Daniel has a pint of beer and settles down with Peter Hennessey at a table in the window.

"You will be glad to hear Jimmy and Liam have recovered, it was their idea that we meet. It's getting worse in the docks, there are constant threats to anyone not backing an all-out strike, and shipments are being sabotaged on a regular basis. Something has to be done, Daniel. The agitators are taking over, there is definitely an organised plot to shut the docks as soon as possible. Can you talk with someone on the management team about this?"

"I will talk with them again, Peter, it seems that the troublemakers are determined to shut the docks by any means. I would like to meet with Michael Doyle again, any ideas?"

"I don't think any meetings are planned, but you might be able to contact him at the union office, I will give you the telephone number."

"Thanks Peter, that will be a start, I have to find out what they are planning. The concern at the moment is that the strike will escalate, to the railways and into the engineering business in the Midlands."

"I will keep my ears open and let you know if I hear any details about that, but I have to go now, Daniel. I still get a bit nervous when I am out in the evening."

"Yes of course, Peter, and thank you for the update," says Daniel as he leaves the Lamb and Flag to return to Kensington.

"Do you go out much with Daniel then, Polly? I mean, is he like a boyfriend to you?"

"Daniel is my very best friend, Penny, and I am fond of him of course, but he is my guardian who is responsible for looking after me. We do go out together and he is good company, but most of the time we are together in the apartment," replies Polly. She realises that she did not mean to say that they were together, it just came out that way.

"Come along Polly, I think Daniel is a bit more than your guardian, I think you care for him," says Penny, pushing Polly for an answer.

"Please Penny, I cannot say any more about Daniel and me. I have to respect Daniel's confidence, I do not want to embarrass him," Polly replies, getting more and more confused with her response.

"Of course, Polly, I did not mean to pry."

"You are my best friend, Penny, and I trust you completely, but you must understand that my relationship with Daniel, whatever it may be, has to remain confidential."

Polly had just finished making them some tea when Daniel

returns. Whatever she had said to Penny about her relationship with Daniel, her response to his return left no doubt as to her feelings towards him.

"Daniel, did you have a good meeting with your friends?" Polly says, dashing towards him as he enters the lounge.

"I did, yes, and what about you two?"

"Oh we had lots to talk about, Daniel, didn't we Polly?"

Polly fetches Penny's coat and Daniel walks her down the stairs to the waiting taxi.

"Polly certainly seems to enjoy being with you, Daniel. I know you will take care of her, she is a very good friend to me," says Penny as she gets into the taxi.

Daniel and Fitz agree that they will wait until after the trial next week, before they ask Polly to start photographing documents. Daniel has talked it over with Polly, and is satisfied that the risks are worth taking. The trial should not take more than a couple of days, so Polly has booked three days as holiday. She tells Mrs Wright that she has some personal business to attend to and apologises for any problems her absence may cause. Mrs Wright is very understanding and assures Polly that they will manage until she returns.

The trial of the three men who broke into Daniel's apartment duly begins on Monday under the stewardship of Judge William Forsythe at the Crown Court.

The accused, Billy Swift, Jimmy Jones, and Shaun Devlin are charged with breaking and entering and attempted burglary. Billy Swift and Jimmy Jones, are further charged with grievous bodily harm, including assault with a weapon to Daniel Bottomley, and grievous bodily harm with gross indecent assault against Polly Spencer.

They are both asked to relate details of the assaults, which is particularly upsetting for Polly.

"Can you tell the court what happened on the night in question Miss Spencer, please?"

"I was woken up to find one man on top of me and another pulling at my pyjamas. He ripped off my jacket, and slapped my face hard while he was on top of me," says Polly, pointing to Billy Swift.

"The other one was trying to remove my pyjama bottoms. Then Daniel arrived and fought with them. That one stabbed Daniel, but he still fought them off before they escaped," Polly continues, pointing out Billy Swift as the man who stabbed Daniel.

"If Daniel had not been there to rescue me, these men... I don't know…" Polly begins to sob as she recalls the details of that night.

"Thank you Miss Spencer. Usher, will you help please?" the judge asks.

Polly dashes over to Daniel, who does his best to console her. The defence counsel declines to ask any questions of Polly.

After a short break Daniel is asked to take the stand. He gives his occupation as a government researcher at the Home Office, and identifies himself as Polly's guardian while she works in London. He too identifies the attackers and points to Billy Swift as the man who stabbed him.

"And when you went into Miss Spencer's room that night, what did you see occurring?" the Crown asks.

"Both men were attempting to remove Polly's pyjamas. One of them was on top of her trying to get her jacket off, while the other was pulling at the bottoms. It was obvious what their intentions were, thank God I was able to stop them," replies Daniel angrily.

"And would it be reasonable to assume that these men probably thought Miss Spencer was alone in the apartment that night, Mr Bottomley?" the Crown asks.

"Yes, they wanted to take advantage of a young woman on her own."

"If the defence has no questions, you are excused, Mr Bottomley. Thank you," says the judge.

Again, the defence counsel decline to ask any questions.

"In that case we shall adjourn until tomorrow when I shall sum up and give my deliberations," the judge concludes as he leaves the courtroom.

Daniel spends Monday evening consoling Polly, who is distressed by the day's events.

"We only have to listen to the verdicts tomorrow, Polly, then we can go off and relax for a day," says Daniel, as Polly curls up beside him. They sit together for about half an hour or so before Polly goes off to have her bath, leaving Daniel to his thoughts. He realises that there will be another trial for them to go through after what happened on the train. That will be far more detailed, because of the injuries sustained by Daniel. And while the apartment break-in can be dismissed as men seeking out a young woman on her own, the attack on the train was obviously planned in detail with the intention of harming Polly, and this could be reflected in the questions asked. However, for now, Daniel has to support her through the delivery of the verdicts so that they can put the events of that night behind them. The following morning, they arrive at Crown Court to listen to the verdicts. After guilty verdicts are reached, the judge begins his summations.

"There is no more offensive act than that of a man who would attempt to force himself on a woman, especially when that woman is young in years. It is indeed obvious that was your intention when you broke into Mr Bottomley's apartment. You must have followed Miss Spencer one time and made the assumption she would be alone on that night.

"Your actions toward her were disgusting and degrading, and the fact that one of you had a weapon shows just what lengths you were prepared to go to, to satisfy your urges. Society has no place for people, like you, who seek to use women to forcibly satisfy their own ends.

"Shaun Devlin, whilst you did not actually take part in the attack on Miss Spencer, you must have known what the intention was, yet did nothing. You will go to prison for three years.

"Billy Swift and Jimmy Jones, I find no words to describe how I feel towards you for your actions towards Miss Spencer. I sentence both of you to eight years in prison, with a further three years for you, Billy Swift, for your knife attack on Mr Bottomley. That sentence will be served consecutively.

"Take them down, officers. Finally, I would just like to thank you, Miss Spencer, for the courage you have shown in giving such unpleasant evidence clearly and concisely. This case is adjourned."

Daniel and Polly return to the apartment to collect their overnight requirements, before boarding the tube for their short stay in Kingston on Thames to relax before getting back to work. They leave Tuesday afternoon and book into the Riverside Hotel for the one night.

"Thank you for bringing me here for the day, Daniel, it is just what I needed after the trial. Having to go over what happened that night was very upsetting," says Polly, as they sit in the lounge over tea.

"My pleasure, Polly. There is so much to do over the next few weeks, so a break will do us good."

After tea, they go up to their rooms to get ready for dinner. Daniel has booked two adjoining rooms for them overlooking the river. Polly has a bath, while Daniel tells her he will wait for her downstairs. It is a warm summer's evening so they enjoy a walk by the river before dinner. The Thames looks especially good this time of year, with all the shrubs in full flower.

"We shall have to try and get a weekend at home while the weather is fine, Daniel. I will check with Mummy when they might be away and see what we can arrange."

"Whatever you decide will be ok with me, Polly, I always look forward to going to your home."

They walk for a while before returning to the hotel to sit down for dinner just after eight o'clock. Polly is on good form over dinner, the events of the trial forgotten, telling Daniel that she can't wait to start her new role for him, taking pictures.

"I am really pleased because it should shorten the time you need to put these people away. When you have done that, you and I will have more time together, won't we?"

"That time cannot come too soon for me, Polly, but we must finish the job first. We cannot make any plans while the efforts to stop the Soviets are unfinished. These people are determined to wreck our country, Polly, and I would not want to live in a country controlled by their ideals."

"But what about the fight against the communists in the unions, Daniel? That will be more difficult to win, won't it?"

"I have to make certain that any of the problems that occur within the trade unions are being sorted by the democratic process, not by the Soviets stirring up trouble. The battle between union members and the bosses will be around for some while yet. That's what democracy is all about, and I have no wish to interfere. Once we have removed the menace of communist agitators, my job will be done."

"Let's hope it will be soon, Daniel," she says, knowing only too well that any future that she and Daniel may have together can't happen while there is any risk to either of them from their activities. So for now she enjoys being with Daniel, especially in moments like this.

"What shall we do tomorrow, Daniel?" asks Polly as they sit relaxing after dinner.

"Well since we are next to the river, I suggest that we take a trip tomorrow."

After spending most of the day on the river and a trip to Hampton Court, they head back to the hotel, arriving around six o'clock.

On Thursday morning, Daniel meets with Fitz and Phil Chandler to discuss Polly's new responsibility, taking photographs of documents, and passing on the film to the department. "Because of its size the camera will only take twelve pictures, so I suggest that Polly keeps a couple of rolls of film locked away in her office," Phil remarks.

"And Polly will bring home the film each day for me to bring into the office for you to develop, Phil."

"Shall I call round this evening with the camera to show Polly?"

"Thank you Phil, that would be ideal."

"Ok Daniel, let's hope that we can now get some real evidence against this organisation working against our government," says Fitz.

Phil calls round to the apartment that evening and shows Polly how best to use the camera. It is quite small, which is ideal for purpose. Phil impresses on her to stand far enough away from any documents to make sure they are in focus. He also shows her how to empty and reload film for processing. She is delighted with the camera, but does ask about the poor lighting in her office and how it may affect the quality of any pictures.

"I have set it to its widest aperture, Polly, which should give reasonable exposure."

"I am going to practise taking pictures this evening, Daniel, and you can get them developed tomorrow so that we are sure the camera is working perfectly."

"That's a good idea, Polly," says Phil, as he picks up his bag before being shown out by Daniel.

"See you tomorrow, Phil, and thanks very much for your help."

Polly spends some time practising with the camera that evening, and Daniel takes her efforts into his office the following morning. The developed photos are very clear, so Polly is ready to begin taking pictures from Monday. Meanwhile, Daniel has a message from Hennessey, saying Michael Doyle will meet with him at the union offices on Monday evening around seven o'clock.

After a quiet weekend, Polly goes into work on Monday, ready to start taking pictures. She must also ask Penny if they might meet that evening.

"Why not come to my house, Polly? We can sit out in the garden if it's sunny."

"That will be nice, Penny, I look forward to that. See you around 6.30."

On Monday afternoon, Polly has two files to deliver to Percival Jarvis. She enters his office just as his secretary leaves.

"Thank you Polly, I was meaning to ask you if you would accompany me to a function in Birmingham later in the week. We would meet some very influential people and have a very enjoyable evening together," he says with a smile as he pulls her towards him, stroking her back and bottom before attempting to kiss her on her lips. Polly is taken by surprise as Jarvis begins to unbutton her blouse and fondle her.

"Mr Jarvis, I have no intention of going anywhere with you!" she replies, hitting him hard across his face, and hurrying from his office. She decides she will tell Sally Nugent about his behaviour.

Sally Nugent however, appears puzzled as to why Polly should be so upset.

"You are fortunate that he has given you this opportunity, Polly," she says firmly.

"In that case Sally, why don't you take my place? And please tell Mr Jarvis that in future I will only deliver documents to his secretary, I will not be entering his office again," she replies, astonished at Sally Nugent's response and determined that Jarvis should pay for his behaviour. Putting the unpleasant incident behind her, Polly quickly returns to her office, since she has two files with the Red Hand logo on them. After checking her route for her next round of deliveries, she locks her door, checks the blinds, and photographs the relevant documents. Her heart is pounding while she is doing this, expecting a knock on her door at any time. But all goes well, and she carefully replaces the documents in their files before setting off on her second round of collections and deliveries. The rest of the day passes without any more Red Hand documents coming into her possession. She sends a message to Daniel asking him to meet her a little earlier at 4.30pm. She can't wait to tell him that she has taken some pictures.

"There are only ten exposures used, Daniel, but you may as well take this roll and I will replace it ready for tomorrow."

Daniel goes off with Polly and drops her at Penny Carstairs' house on his way to meet with Michael Doyle, who tells Daniel that they will force the management to close the docks with their unofficial strikes, giving the members the perfect excuse to vote for an all-out strike. Doyle then goes on to tell Daniel of what they are planning next.

"We have a man inside government that will push for legislation to introduce anti strike laws. This is what our communist colleagues are looking to implicate, giving them an opportunity to come out on the side of the trade unions. What you must tell your readers, Daniel, is how wrong the management are in locking out the members from their place of work, and suggest that anti strike laws may be the answer. We want people to know what we are doing for the workers."

"Do you think that communism is the answer, Michael?"

"I don't agree with some of their ideas, but they do have a strong argument, and I will do my best to put that argument to my members."

"And I will try and get my editor to put your points of view forward in my editorial. I mostly work as a freelance, but I do have some contacts that I can get in touch with."

The two men shake hands and Daniel leaves to return and collect Polly, noticing when he met with Doyle that the table, where he previously planted the listening device, had been replaced. That was the reason why they had not received any information back at the office.

Polly and Penny enjoy looking at some magazines together, before Penny inevitably asks Polly about Daniel.

"You must be the luckiest person I know, Polly, having someone like Daniel to look after you. When did you first meet him, did you say?"

"I've known him since I was thirteen years old, Penny, and we have been through a lot of unpleasantness together. My Daddy was responsible for breaking up a black market operation back in 1947, and those responsible tried to intimidate him by attacking our family. Daddy asked Daniel to stay and protect us. They tried many times to intimidate my family, and Daniel was responsible for saving me from getting hurt many times. They would probably have killed me and Mummy if it hadn't been for him," says Polly with tears in her eyes.

"I'm sorry Polly, I did not mean to upset you, I had no idea what a terrible time you had back then," replies Penny with concern.

"That's ok Penny, but you must not mention this to anyone, do you understand? And Daniel does not like me talking about it at all. It was a difficult time for all of my family, and we have tried to put it behind us."

"I understand Polly, and I will not mention it to anyone, I promise."

Daniel arrives just after nine o'clock and he and Polly return to the apartment. Realising that they had not had any dinner, she opens some soup, which they have with toast and scrambled eggs.

Polly tells Daniel of Percival Smith's advances, and he is furious.

"The idea that he would even attempt to do anything so crude and unprofessional shows that he is not fit to hold any public office, and I will see to it that he is brought down."

"Please don't make a fuss, Daniel. I do not want you to put your work at risk just to see that he is punished."

"Of course not, Polly, I will use his indiscretion against him when the time is right."

By mid-morning the next day, Phil has developed Polly's pictures, and the results are disturbing and far reaching. There is definite mention of conversations between Percival Smith and Communist Party members. He is to strongly recommend that anti-strike laws are to be forwarded as soon as possible. The point is stressed that to get the unions be fully committed to the communists, they must get the anti-strike rules in place so that they, the communists and the unions, are seen to be in agreement.

"The Traffic Lights look to be stuck on red, Daniel. I have asked Quentin to sit in with us on this news and have given him a copy of the information."

"We will have to inform the Permanent Secretary of these developments, and be sure that he has suitable stall tactics in place Fitz. Meantime, the dockers' management must continue talking to the unions," says Quentin Blake.

"Polly has done well, Daniel, but do impress upon her the need to be careful, this business could get messy."

"I will, Fitz. Her enthusiasm knows no limits, but I'm sure she would not take any risks."

On arriving back at the apartment, Daniel mentions the contents of the documents she photographed, and asks her to be extra careful in what she says and does at work.

"Of course, Daniel, I would not take any risks that may cause you any embarrassment."

"It's your safety, not my embarrassment that is most important, Polly. You must remember that."

Meantime, Daniel opens his correspondence which gives details of the Crown Court dates for the trial of the men accused of attacking them on the train on Good Friday.

"God, Daniel, we have only just gone through one trial, and now we must go through it all again."

Daniel appreciates Polly's comments, but realises that these trials have to take place so that those responsible for the attacks on Polly and himself are punished. The trial is due to commence on Monday 21st July. However, there is a setback at the end of this week for both of them which may be significant, given the closeness of the trial.

Daniel and Polly arrive home on Friday evening, looking forward to the weekend. They walk into the lounge to be confronted by four armed men.

"Good evening Mr Bottomley, Miss Spencer. Please do not do anything stupid, if you do you will be shot, do you understand?"

"How on earth did you get into my apartment and what the hell are you doing here?"

"One of my colleagues posed as a gas engineer and was let in by your concierge. Before he left, we were able to get in unseen. Easy really. Now please turn around, Mr Bottomley, while we tie your hands, then sit down on this chair. We have some questions for you about your visit to our H.Q. We also want to talk to you about your discussions with union officials. My two colleagues, meanwhile, will take Polly into her room to see how she might be able to help."

Two of the men leave the lounge with Polly and take her to her bedroom.

"What do you want? I will not tell you anything, do you understand?"

"Shut up, Polly. Remove your outer garments and please listen to what I have to say."

"I will not remove anything, what is it you want from me?"

"Polly, if you do not do as I say, we will remove the garments for you."

Reluctantly, Polly does as she is asked and removes her blouse and skirt.

"We do not wish to harm you, but we need some information and we will get the information we need, one way or the other, do you understand? You must persuade Daniel to stop meddling in our affairs. We have the means to get rid of both of you if necessary. And we have our suspicions about what you do, Polly. Your job gives you a great deal of freedom within the Home Office and the Foreign Office, and we believe you are being used for something else. What exactly is it that you do?" the older man asks.

"You must know what I do, I am Corporate Liaison Officer, I do not understand what you think I am doing, I am sure your colleagues in the department have told you what I do," Polly replies showing signs of being confused.

Suddenly, the man grabs Polly round her throat before pushing her back in the chair.

"Don't pretend you do not know what I am talking about, Miss!" he says as he leans over Polly and squeezes her breasts hard, causing he to scream out.

The other man stands behind Polly, with his hands on her shoulders.

"Talk to us, Polly. What do you do all day at the Home Office?" the man asks as he strikes her hard across her face before forcing her legs apart. Polly gasps as he grabs and squeezes her at the tops of her thighs.

"Tell me what you do at the Home Office!" he shouts, pulling at her pants. Polly kicks out, trying to stop him, and he punches her hard in the stomach several times. Polly gasps and screams in pain and slumps back into the chair, whereupon she is slapped again. This time the man grabs hold of her top, pulls her towards him and rips it off.

"Tell us Polly, we want to know what it is that you are doing at the Home Office. Who are you really working for?" he shouts at her as he again pushes her back into the chair.

"Do you really want me to continue hurting you? We have plenty of time and we have only just begun; we can stay here all night if we have to. Now please tell us what it is you actually do, and what is your actual job?" he asks, moving towards her menacingly. He grabs her hair with one hand and grasps her around her throat with the other. The other man lifts her up and between them they throw her onto her bed.

"Now Polly, tell us what we want to know about you," he says as both men move towards her.

Daniel, meanwhile, is been given a beating. He has bruises on his face mostly, and his captors have used threats against Polly to get him to talk to them.

"You must know what is going to happen to Polly, if we don't get what we want from you? My colleagues are no doubt enjoying her company right at this moment."

"I know that you will do whatever you want no matter what I say, but I tell you this, if you harm her in any way I will kill you!"

The man strikes him hard several times in the face and stomach and shouts at him.

"You cannot do anything about what we do to her, Mr Bottomley, we can do as we wish. I wonder just what they are doing with her now," he says, as he turns away from Daniel, and both men look across towards the door. Daniel sees his chance, and dashes towards the two men, together with the chair, crashing into them and into the wall by the side of the kitchen. Both men end up in a heap on the floor, stunned by the impact of Daniel crashing into them.

Polly, meanwhile is frantically trying to keep the two men off her as they grab at her near-naked body. Suddenly, there is a loud noise from the sitting room, and the two men rush to see what has happened. As they leave the room, Polly sees her opportunity and pulls on her robe before grabbing her pistol from the drawer. There is absolute chaos in the lounge, with both of Daniel's captors on the floor, winded from being hit by Daniel in the chair. The other two men go to grab him when Polly appears at the doorway and shoots at one of them, hitting him in his shoulder.

"Untie him and hand him your firearms!" shouts Polly. One of the men attempts to grab at Daniel and use him as a shield. Polly fires again and hits him twice in his leg. He releases Daniel and grabs hold of his leg, screaming, bleeding from the gunshot wound. The other man quickly releases Daniel, who ties them together.

"Well done, Polly. Can you call the police and an ambulance please?"

Polly goes over to the phone and makes the calls. She wraps her gown tightly around herself, conscious of her nakedness, and goes over to Daniel who has lined up the injured men next to the two that are bound. Polly holds on to him tightly, shaking with anger at what has happened.

"You people disgust me, I will tell the courts what you said and did and you will be sent away to rot in a prison cell!" she sobs, still holding on to Daniel and kicking out at one of the men on the floor, hitting him in his chest.

"It's ok Polly, try not to get too upset," says Daniel, realising that Polly is reacting to her actions in shooting two of the captors.

"Now it is our turn, gentlemen. What are your names and who sent you?" he demands as he strikes one of the men across his face with his weapon.

"Ok, I'll tell you who we are, it won't be difficult to find out anyway," he says as he yelps in pain from the blow across his face. After he has recited their names, Daniel pushes him to tell him who sent them to the apartment.

"We have friends in high places, Mr Bottomley. They will take care of us."

Daniel pushes him for more information as the doorbell rings. Polly opens the door to D.I. Jack Manners, his sergeant, three P.C.s and W.P.C. Becky Peters, closely followed by two ambulance officers.

They are treated to a scene of carnage in the lounge of Daniel's apartment.

Two men have gunshot wounds, and a third, one of the two bound together, has an open cut on his face. Daniel has severe bruising to his face and his left eye is damaged and Polly has red wheals across her face and throat.

"God, Daniel, I see you and Polly have been busy. Are either of you seriously hurt?"

"Perhaps your W.P.C. might go and look at Polly, she needs to get dressed anyway."

The ambulance officers patch up the two injured captors and they go off accompanied by a PC. The other two men are handcuffed and leave with the other two PCs.

Daniel pours himself a large brandy and sits down on the settee.

"This is a bad business, Daniel. I assume we both know that this was not just an attempted burglary?"

"I can tell you, Detective Inspector, these men were sent by people in high places, their words. I believe they were from the Communist Party in collusion with someone within the Civil Service."

"Are you sure about that, Daniel? That is quite an accusation you have made," the D.I. comments.

"I am quite sure, and I will get the evidence to prove it. I cannot be specific, but we have a contact within their organisation that may be able to substantiate what I have said."

Polly returns with the W.P.C. having dressed and washed her face, which shows the marks where she was slapped.

"I think it may be an idea for both of you to get checked. Becky, will you call for an ambulance please? Meanwhile, can you both give me a brief statement of this evening's events?"

Daniel and Polly outline details of the events to the D.I. with W.P.C. Peters taking notes. Polly sits close to Daniel, who has his arm round her for support, while she outlines what happened to her, ending with her shooting of two of the men. She identifies the two men, by their names, who assaulted her in her bedroom, and is now just beginning to realise what she has done. She has shot two men, albeit for very good reason, and is very distressed. Daniel follows up with a brief outline of what happened to him and the mention, by one of the men, of friends in high places.

"I have to warn you, Detective Inspector, that MI5 will want to interview these men, so I suggest, unofficially, that you speak with them as soon as possible. I have their names for you."

The ambulance duly arrives, and Polly and Daniel go off to hospital.

"Many thanks for your comments, Daniel. We shall need a comprehensive statement at some time, but for now we have enough to charge the men we have in custody."

"Give me a call when you need us, Detective Inspector," replies Daniel as they all leave the apartment. Polly clings on to Daniel in the ambulance, probably suffering from some delayed shock over the evening's events. They arrive at hospital and once again Daniel is patched up.

He has a badly bruised eye and cheekbone, and his ribs are strapped from being kicked.

"Come along sometime next week, Daniel, to have the strapping removed," the doctor says.

Polly, meanwhile, has her face looked at. There is some bruising but nothing serious. The doctor examines her to see if there is any bruising on her stomach, but no bruising is showing He also notices the marks on her thighs and breast and he is concerned about her demeanour.

"You're quite sure that the men did not assault you in any other way, Polly?"

"Yes Doctor, you can see the marks where they touched me, but nothing else really."

"She will need to be kept quiet for a day or so, Daniel, she is obviously suffering from her ordeal."

"I will take good care of her, Doctor. Will you want to see her again?"

"I suggest that she visits her GP sometime next week if she feels unwell at all."

Daniel and Polly travel home by taxi, without saying too much, and arrive back at the apartment around seven o'clock. Daniel suggests to Polly that she take a bath while he cleans up the lounge.

There are some blood spots on the carpet, but he manages to remove the small amounts on the wall and chair. The chair is broken anyway, so he takes it into the utility room, ready to discard it. Everything else is clean, thankfully. After about half an hour, Polly joins Daniel in the lounge in her dressing gown.

"I am trying to understand what I did earlier, Daniel. I shot two men didn't I?"

"You only did what you had to do, Polly. You saved me and yourself."

"I just never thought I would have to use my pistol, especially to shoot someone," she says, upset by what she has done. Daniel gets her to have a drop of brandy, hoping it may calm her.

"I need to speak with Daddy, Daniel, and tell him what has happened," she continues, still shaking over her ordeal.

"Polly, I think you should leave the call until tomorrow when you are calmer. You need to rest for now. We'll sit awhile then get an early night. I am sure you will feel better tomorrow. Now let me make you some tea and toast."

He is rather concerned how the shootings have affected Polly, and hopes that a night's rest will help her. He returns to the lounge with some tea to find Polly asleep, so he carefully carries her to her room and places her gently into bed. He notices that she has not put on her pyjamas, but leaves her wrapped in her nightgown. He leaves her room, careful to leave the door ajar. Going back to the lounge, he reflects on just what he has learned from the intrusion and subsequent firefight in the apartment. The attack was almost certainly instigated by the communists, and he is sure that the Red Hand are tied in with it in some way. He must speak with Fitz on Monday to discuss whether Polly's position is now at risk. They have taken all of the precautions that can be taken, there really isn't anything else they can do.

He also decides he must talk with Polly over the weekend about her position and whether they should consider her moving on. In any event, if her position has been compromised, there wouldn't be any real point in moving anywhere else and Polly will make up her own mind. She may only be eighteen years old but she has matured immensely since being with Daniel. He decides he must talk with Jack Manners over the weekend to find out what he can about the intruders before MI5 gets to them. If there is a connection with Red Hand, there must be arrests, and that would help Polly's dilemma. Daniel drinks his tea, and finishes his toast. He looks in on Polly before going off to his room and leaves the light on in the lounge and hallway in case she wakes up. He is sitting up reading when Polly comes into his room.

"Daniel, how long have I been asleep?" she asks, sitting beside him.

"About four hours, Polly. You fell asleep while I was making tea."

Polly does not ask if she can join him, she simply slides in beside him.

"You don't mind, do you Daniel?"

"Whatever makes you comfortable, Polly," says Daniel as he switches off his lamp. He puts his arm around her to give her reassurance and within minutes she is asleep. Daniel however, will take a little longer. He has a restless night being constantly reminded of Polly's presence next to him wearing only her dressing gown. He gets up early Saturday and cooks himself breakfast.

He leaves Polly to rest, and sits listening to the wireless. Her pistol is still on the table by the phone, so he takes it back to her room and puts it back in the top drawer of her dresser. He leaves Polly until about nine o'clock before taking her some tea. She is still sleeping, so Daniel gently taps her on her shoulder.

"Good morning Polly, I trust you slept well?"

Polly stirs, somewhat disorientated, and asks the time as she sits up in bed. She quickly grabs at her dressing gown to cover herself as she realises that she is not wearing pyjamas.

"I slept very well, Daniel. Not sure how I got here without my pyjamas," she replies, a little embarrassed.

"Get yourself dressed, Polly, and have something to eat. Remember we missed dinner last night."

Polly calls her parents around ten o'clock and relates details of what happened. She is very calm and tells them she is ok. They are obviously concerned, but she assures them that Daniel has taken every precaution.

"I have to see this through, Daddy, I must if only for Daniel. I owe it to him to do my very best to help him brings these evil people to justice."

After asking them to pass on love and kisses to George and her sisters, she hands the phone to Daniel.

"A bad business, Daniel, I don't know what to think about what has happened. My daughter shooting two intruders, I wonder what will happen next."

"Well I know MI5 will be all over this incident, Ben, since the intruders admitted that they had help in high places. There will have to be arrests. If they do nothing it will send the wrong message. We still have to play their game, which means we must arrest somebody even if we have to leave the ringleader still in place until we have the conclusive proof about a Soviet conspiracy."

"You will both be careful, won't you? Margaret and I would be devastated if anything stopped you two from fulfilling the happiness together that you both deserve."

"I give you my word on that, Ben. Now, Polly and I have another trial next week, of the attackers from the train. When that is finished, I thought it would be a good time to spend some time at home, we both will be ready for a holiday."

"What a wonderful idea, and I know Margaret will be delighted, Daniel."

Polly, who has been listening, jumps all over Daniel when he puts down the phone.

"That's the best news I have heard for a long time, Daniel. Thank you for suggesting it to Daddy," she says, hugging him.

"Ok Polly, can I have my damaged ribs back now, please!"

"Sorry Daniel, I was just so pleased to hear what you said."

Polly and Daniel spend the rest of the morning giving the lounge a thorough clean. After lunch, they do some shopping and go out to dinner on Saturday evening. Sunday is spent relaxing, with Polly experimenting with makeup to hide her bruises on her face, before the start of a new week.

Daniel's first call on Monday, is to brief Fitz on the events of Friday evening.

"This is disturbing news, Daniel. Let me contact Quentin, we must think carefully about this, and of course you have another trial coming up next week," says Fitz, after arranging for Quentin to join them.

"And you say that there was mention of friends in high places?"

"Those were the words they used, Fitz, but what was more concerning to me was their insistence that they suspected that Polly was involved with something. They kept asking her what she did as if they knew she did something other than collect and deliver messages."

Quentin Blake enters Fitz's office and Daniel recounts to him the events of Friday evening.

"I need to talk with these men as soon as possible. We must establish just what they do know about Miss Spencer. For the moment, she should continue with her good work photographing Red Hand documents. I see no point in making any changes in her routine now, since that may do more harm than good."

Daniel has to agree that any changes made by Polly to her routine may send signals to the organisation operating within the Service. However, once MI5 has spoken with the intruders to Daniel's apartment, it may become clearer just who was responsible for issuing the instructions to break into the apartment. Meanwhile, Daniel makes contact with Beatrice Carrington, and relates the recent events.

"It must have been very frightening for Polly, Daniel. I hope she is ok."

"She was upset by it all, Beatrice, not least the fact that she shot two of the intruders, but she has recovered now and is busy at her work now. That is what I wanted to talk to you about."

He then tells Beatrice of Percival Smith's behaviour towards Polly, and how reprimanding him officially could be beneficial to Daniel's fight with Red Hand influence.

"I had heard that the communists are hoping to influence government policy using the position of their high-ranking official in the Home Office, namely Smith. His input to the Permanent Secretary could influence any decisions regarding possible legislation against the trade unions, Daniel," says Beatrice.

"The communists want to force the government to introduce anti-strike laws and so inflame the workers. What could follow would be very serious for the government and for the country. If you could see to it that Smith gets reprimanded for his behaviour, then it will affect his credibility within the department, and his influence on the Permanent Secretary."

"I will get on to this right away, Daniel. I welcome being able to help you in your fight against the communists, and I despise anyone who abuses their position for their own gratification. Thank you for bringing this to my attention. Percival Smith will regret his actions towards Polly, when he realises that he has jeopardised his career," Beatrice replies.

Polly has a quiet day, although Penny comments on the amount of makeup she is wearing when they have lunch.

"There is a very good reason, Penny, but can we not talk about it now please?"

The last thing Polly wants is for questions to be asked about why she is wearing so much makeup, which she has had to do to hide the marks on her face. Fortunately, Penny thinks no more of it, and Polly does not spend any time close enough to anyone else for them to notice.

Just before the end of the day, Polly knocks on Peggy Wright's door before entering.

"Hello Polly, what can I do for you?"

"I'm sorry to trouble you, Mrs Wright, but it is the trial next week of the men who attacked Daniel and me at Easter. You will remember, we were on the train on our way to my parents' home?"

"Yes I do, Polly, your guardian was badly hurt as I recall. You will have to be available, so take what time is necessary my dear."

"Thank you Mrs Wright, whilst I do not know how long it will last, I will book two weeks off. I would like to go home for a few days once it is all over."

"That sounds very sensible. Let me make a note that you will be off from the 21st July to the 4th August inclusive. I will notify all department heads of your absence, and they will have to make their own arrangements for collection and distribution while you are away. Please call in on Friday afternoon and leave your office key with me."

Now that she has made the arrangements to include time off with Daniel, the thought of the pending trial does not seem so daunting. The sooner it is over, the sooner she can spend time with Daniel and her family. She goes about her work with a certain contentment until on Thursday morning, she is confronted by Sally Nugent.

"Do you realise what you have done, moaning about Percival's behaviour?"

"I didn't do anything, Sally. If you recall, he assaulted me!" Polly replies indignantly.

"You must have friends in high places, Polly. He has been reprimanded for what happened, and his credibility as a future Permanent Secretary, badly damaged, all because of you," Sally responds with a degree of menace in her reply.

"Sally, if Mr Smith goes around making advances to members of staff, he does not deserve to have any position in the Service," says Polly as she walks away from Sally Nugent.

Sally Nugent is obviously furious at what has happened, but knows that Percival Smith has only himself to blame, and will certainly let him know when the time is right. His actions have severely damaged the organisation's hopes for their cause.

Daniel, meanwhile, contacts D.I. Jack Manners who confirms that MI5 have questioned the men. "These men were definitely working under instructions, Daniel. Other than that they didn't say anything to me."

"Thanks anyway, I hope that MI5 have more luck with them. I will let you know of anything relevant to your case, Detective Inspector."

CHAPTER 9

Daniel and Polly spend the weekend together trying not to think too much about the trial. Polly has been rather edgy since her confrontation with Sally Nugent, and Daniel tries to console her. There have not been any messages sent by Red Hand during the last week, which may be because of what has happened to Percival Smith. Polly, however, thinks that it is her fault.

"They must have found out about me, Daniel. That wretched man's actions have spoiled everything," she says tearfully as they sit together after finishing work on the Friday.

"Polly, it is not your fault, what Smith did was inexcusable and he has been reprimanded for that. If he had not been so stupid, he would still have his influence, for now he has lost that and arrests can be made without any suspicion falling on you."

"Ok Daniel, if you think so, I just feel so disappointed that nothing has happened this week, and now we have to go through this beastly trial. I am dreading having to go over what happened to us on that day again. You were seriously hurt saving me and I can never forget that. It seems so unfair that we have to live it all again."

"You should focus on what happens after the trial, Polly. You and I will have a well-deserved break at your home. Try not to think too much about next week, it will be over soon enough."

They go out shopping on the Saturday, but Polly asks that they go back to the apartment soon after they leave.

"I don't feel very well, Daniel. Can we go back to the apartment please?" she asks after they had been out less than half an hour.

"Of course Polly, can you tell me what is wrong? Do you have a headache?' asks Daniel, concerned by Polly's behaviour.

"I just need to lie down for a while," says Polly, as they arrive back at the apartment.

Daniel helps Polly into her room and places a blanket over her, leaving her to rest. Just what is wrong, he is unsure, but his thoughts are broken hearing Polly cry out as she is violently sick.

"Polly, what is it?" says Daniel as he goes into her room. Polly has been sick and is very pale and sweating. Daniel removes her cover and helps Polly to the bathroom. She wipes her face before returning to her room.

"Daniel, I have a terrible pain in my stomach," she says as she removes shirt, skirt, and slip to reveal severe bruising in her lower abdomen.

"My god Polly, how did this happen and why did you not mention it?" asks Daniel, looking at the bruising. Polly lies down on the bed as Daniel examines the bruising low down in her abdomen, extending almost to the groin. It is obviously very tender, Polly yelping as Daniel gently examines the affected area. There is a slight swelling as well, but Daniel thinks that may just be the bruising.

"One of the men that broke in punched me, but I didn't notice any bruising at first."

"We shall have to take you to hospital to find out what has happened Polly," Daniel replies, concerned at what he has seen.

Polly gets dressed as Daniel calls a taxi, and they arrive at the hospital around midday.

The doctor looks at Polly, and asks for an x-ray so that he can see more clearly what has happened.

"You may have ruptured a small blood vessel, Polly, so we need to be sure," says the doctor as he examines Polly's abdomen. With a blow so low down in a female, there is the risk that the damage may be permanent. How long ago did this happen?"

"About a week or so, Doctor. We were attacked by intruders in the apartment," Polly replies as she puts on the hospital gown before going to the x-ray department.

"What is it, Doctor? Is she going to be ok?" asks Daniel, very concerned.

"She may have burst a small blood vessel, causing the bruising to look much worse than it really is. Polly says she was punched by this man who also squeezed her abdomen with his hand. This may have broken a small blood vessel which has slowly leaked blood on the surface of the skin," the doctor replies, as Polly returns from x-ray. She sits down on the bed while the doctor examines the x-ray. He asks Daniel to wait outside as he will want to take another look at Polly.

"It looks as though a small blood vessel has ruptured around this area, Polly," he says, pulling aside her gown and pointing to the lowest part of her abdomen. The slight swelling is just the bruise coming out. I don't think there is anything too serious to worry about," he continues, as she puts her gown back in place. He then calls Daniel back into the consulting area.

"Polly has a severely bruised abdomen; the burst blood vessel will clear fairly quickly. I believe you being sick was your body sending you a message that something was wrong. I will prescribe you some painkillers which will help if the pain becomes a nuisance. I suggest you get plenty of rest, and do as little walking as possible. Take care of her, Daniel, and she will be fine in no time," the doctor concludes as he goes off to his next patient.

Polly gets dressed and goes back to the apartment with Daniel, who insists that she sits down on the settee with her feet up.

"You must do as the doctor said, Polly, and rest as much as possible. Next week should not be too bad as far as you overdoing walking about since we are in court so will be sitting down most of the time, and the following week we shall be going home."

Daniel makes Polly some dinner and suggests a bath might be relaxing for her.

"Ok Daniel, I will go and soak for a while."

After her bath, Polly dresses in her pyjamas and gown and sits on Daniel's lap with her feet up as he suggested.

"The bruises don't look as bad after a bath, Daniel, do they?" says

Polly showing him the bruised area. The bruising is severe, but the discolouration is no worse. Her abdomen is soft to the touch, so nothing else is damaged, as the x-ray suggested.

"I think you were very lucky, Polly," says Daniel as he pulls her gown back in place.

They sit there for a while before Polly goes off to sleep. Daniel leaves her for a while, until around nine o'clock, then he carries her to her room, takes off her gown, and puts her to bed. The discovery of the bruising has shocked him, he had no idea the intruders had treated Polly so badly and she must have been in some pain when she shot two of them. He will keep a very close eye on her progress over the next few days. Should she deteriorate at all, he will have no hesitation in applying for an adjournment of the trial. He sits for another hour or so himself before going off to his room around 10.30pm. Daniel is a light sleeper, and hears the faint movement from the lounge. He looks at his clock which says 3.00am, before climbing quietly from his bed.

He opens his door as quietly as possible and sees Polly's light and the lounge lights on. He goes into the lounge to find Polly sitting on the settee.

"My dear Polly, what on earth are you doing sitting up at this time?" he asks, puzzled that she didn't come to him.

"I cannot sleep, Daniel, thinking about next week. I just don't think I want to face it anymore," she sobs, and curls up into Daniel's arms as he sits beside her.

"Each time I close my eyes, I see men trying to hurt you or me, their eyes full of hate and leering at me when I am tied to a chair, a bench, or a table. I know they will try to kill you to get at me. What they will do to me terrifies me, Daniel. I am so sorry, but I cannot take any more threats or beatings, I have had enough," she says, tears streaming down her face.

"Listen to me, Polly. What you have had to put up with over the past few weeks is more than anyone would want to endure. But this is what we have to do in our position. Someone has to stand up to these people. Your courage has been exemplary, your input of information invaluable. You are admired by Fitz and by MI5 for what you are doing, and I know that your parents are very proud of you.

And not least, I am proud of you. More than anything, I would like to take you away and just live happily ever after. But we both have a job to do first, and I know that you want to see it through just as much as I do. Now I will make us some tea then back to bed."

"Ok Daniel, I will do as you say because I love you very much and do so want to put these people away forever."

They sit drinking tea, both deep in their own thoughts, Daniel about the injuries to Polly, and Polly herself still fretting about the trial. She is firmly convinced that word of the trial to the agents in the Home Office, may cause her problems.

"Daniel what if they find out about the trial at the office? Won't they wonder why you and I were attacked on the train?"

"Polly, the office is already aware of what happened, you told Mrs Wright when you returned to work after Easter."

"But I didn't tell anyone else, won't they think it strange that I did not mention it at all?"

"There is no reason why you should have mentioned it to anyone else, Polly. Please, you must not worry yourself over the trial and what may happen. Come along and stay with me for the rest of the night," Daniel replies, as he walks with Polly to his room and puts her into his bed. "Now off to sleep and no more worries."

His actions work – Polly is asleep within minutes, leaving Daniel alone with his own thoughts as she lays beside him.

The journey to the Crown Court is about five miles, and Daniel and Polly arrive at nine o'clock, to be met by the Crown Barrister.

"Good morning to you both, Richard Brown, I am the prosecution barrister for the Crown, very pleased to meet you both. We have a strong case against these men, so the trial should not be too long."

"I understand that MI5 may give evidence, is that correct?" asks Daniel.

"Yes, they will be giving evidence. The agent will be behind a screen to hide his identity from the public. I'm not sure how much you both know about MI5 involvement, but suffice to say they have questioned two of the men in the dock, the two that ran off after the attack."

"You may like to know that the presiding judge is Walter Donaldson, known for handing out maximum sentences for violent crimes," he continues as they enter the courtroom.

The four accused are already in the dock, closely guarded by police officers. Polly casts a quick glance in their direction, and shudders as she recognises the two that attacked her.

The judge enters the courtroom and makes his introductions.

"This is an unpleasant case for you to hear, because of the nature of the attack on the young woman, Miss Penny Spencer. Violent crimes against women, especially those of indecent assault, are the most despicable. Society has no place for such behaviour, and if found guilty the sentences will be severe for those concerned. You will also hear evidence in closed court from the security services, so introducing a sinister aspect to the attacks.

"Their evidence may not necessarily affect your decisions as to the guilt of the accused, but it does have a relevance, as will become clear. Very well, usher, please read out the details of the accused," the judge concludes.

The usher reads out the accusations against the four men in the dock.

"David Piper, George Reagan, Bill Williams, and Jack Styne, you are all accused of violence against the persons, namely grievous bodily harm with intent to endanger life," the usher begins.

"Bill Williams and Jack Styne, you are further charged with a violent and indecent assault on Miss Polly Spencer. How do you plead?"

All four men plead not guilty to the charges, as the Crown Prosecutor stands to outline the case against the accused.

"The evidence against you four men is both obvious and overwhelming. Whilst the court may be interested to know the reasoning behind the savage attacks on Daniel Bottomley and Miss Polly Spencer, the Crown will offer undisputed evidence as to the guilt of the accused. The ferocity of the attacks, especially the indecent assault on Miss Spencer, may prove upsetting to you and I apologise for that," he says, looking at the jury.

"These men, whatever their motivation, sought to inflict severe harm to both Daniel Bottomley and Miss Spencer, in fact were it not for the efforts of Mr Bottomley, we may well have had a murder trial taking place here today. You will hear the evidence, first-hand from Miss Spencer and Mr Bottomley, together with the police evidence and the medical reports of the injuries inflicted on both persons. You will also hear evidence from the security services, who have had an interest in two of the accused. I will call on Mr Bottomley as my first witness, please.

"Mr Bottomley, can you tell the court what happened to you on the train on the afternoon of Good Friday last?" the Crown representative asks.

"Polly – Miss Spencer – and I were travelling north, by train, to spend the Easter weekend with her parents. Four men entered our carriage, and proceeded to attack me with baseball bats as they made for Miss Spencer. It seemed that they were intent on indecently assaulting her as violently as possible. She was definitely the target of their assaults, the two men being particularly violent towards her. After what seemed an age I managed to get a bat off one of the men, hitting him hard and knocking him out. I grabbed another attacker and hit his head against the side of the carriage and pull the communication cord to stop the train. This gave the two men attacking Polly the chance to escape."

"Please continue, Mr Bottomley."

"My first concern was for Polly, who was very distressed by what had happened. Then the guard entered the carriage, responding to the cord being pulled, I imagine, and I asked him to call the police and an ambulance. The police took away the two men, and Polly and I went off to hospital."

"And are those two men you rendered unconscious in court?"

"Yes they are, it is the two accused sitting on the right," Daniel replies, pointing to David Piper and George Reagan.

"Thank you, Mr Bottomley. Unless the defence barristers have any questions you may step down," the Crown replies as the defence barrister declines to ask any questions.

"The Crown calls Miss Polly Spencer."

"Miss Spencer, if you could give the court your version of the events of Good Friday. Please take your time, and you may stop at any time if you wish."

"As Daniel said, we were travelling to spend time with my parents at Easter, when we were attacked in our carriage by those four men. They beat Daniel with baseball bats and manhandled me, slapping my face. Both of them were ripping at my clothes and hitting me as I was trying to fight them off and screaming for Daniel," says Polly, as she struggles to continue reliving the terrible events of Good Friday.

"Are you ok to continue, Miss Spencer, or would you like a break?" the judge asks.

"I'm ok, thank you, sir."

"Can you please continue with your evidence of what happened, Miss Spencer?"

"One of the men was holding me down as he ripped off my blouse and the other broke the zip on my skirt trying to remove it. I was bruised across my chest from the man trying to remove my blouse and my legs were scratched as they tugged at my skirt and stockings. One of them was straddled across me as he pulled at my skirt which was now almost off and my slip was also torn as he pulled at it. Thankfully, Daniel pulled the cord and as the train slowed they got off me and ran off. They were getting more and more frantic by now and I was terrified of what they would do to me," says Polly, bursting into tears as she looked across at Daniel. He gets up from his seat moving towards her.

"We will have a fifteen-minute adjournment, gentlemen, to allow Miss Spencer to compose herself," says the judge.

Polly dashes over to Daniel, who does his best to comfort her.

"It's ok Polly. It's almost over now."

"I'm so sorry, Daniel, it just came flooding back. Those men, what they were trying to do to me, what they did to you, all of it.'

"What they did was inexcusable, Polly, and they will be punished for it, believe me. They will be found guilty and go to prison for a long time."

After the adjournment, Polly resumes her evidence.

"Are you quite fit to continue, Miss Spencer?" the judge asks.

Polly nods and the Crown barrister continues.

"Miss Spencer, may I ask, did these men say anything to while they were brutally attacking you?"

"No, they just grunted and leered at me as they ripped at my clothes and hit me in my face. I thought they were going to kill me, I really did."

"And are the men who attacked you in the court?"

"Yes, they are the two men on the left."

"Thank you Miss Spencer, thank you for being so detailed. I'm sure it was difficult having to recall what happened that day," concludes the Crown.

After the defence barristers again decline to ask any questions, Polly leaves the witness box. The judge adjourns for lunch as Polly and Daniel leave the courtroom

"Can we go home please, Daniel? I have had enough for today."

"Let me have a word with Mr Brown, Polly, just in case there are any other questions for us. If not, we shall go back to the apartment."

In fact, Polly and Daniel are not required for the afternoon session, the Crown will give details of their injuries, and listen to the police evidence.

"My lord, this is a copy of the injuries sustained by Mr Bottomley and Miss Spencer during the attacks upon them," the Crown says, handing Judge Donaldson a copy of the medical reports.

"Mr Bottomley suffered two broken ribs, a dislocated shoulder, a black eye, and severe damage to his kidneys resulting in his collapse the following day. He was prescribed bedrest for four days and remained away from his work for a further week. This attack was savage and could have resulted in a fatality had Mr Bottomley not fought back so valiantly.

"The attack on Miss Spencer was both savage and sinister. The sole intention of the accused was to indecently assault her by any means possible. Miss Spencer incurred severe bruising to her arms and legs as well as scratches on her chest and thighs. Though her injuries were not deemed medically serious, the intensity of the attack and the obvious intentions of the men towards her, resulted in her being severely traumatised. This type of assault on a young woman for sexual gratification is both despicable and inexcusable and I trust the court will reflect this when considering their verdicts," the Crown barrister concludes.

After hearing the evidence of the police and the train guards, the judge then adjourns the trial for the day. The following morning, Polly and Daniel make themselves available at the court, although it is doubtful that they will be called.

"Good morning to you both, I don't think you will be needed today. It is the judge's intention to put the security service in the dock for questioning, meaning that the court will be closed to all but the officials. However, it is very likely that you will be recalled, Daniel, because of your position. There will be no mention from any quarter as to the security work carried out by you, Miss Spencer. This will serve to protect you from any interference from outside agencies," the Crown barrister says.

"So MI5 will not relate any knowledge of the information supplied by Polly, is that correct?"

"That is correct, Daniel. The information will be referred to as 'information from a reliable source'. There will be no reference to any persons."

"So your identity will be protected, Polly," says Daniel, hoping to reassure her. Daniel suggests that they go and have some tea, and return to the court in about an hour. Since Daniel has been told that he may be recalled, he has to make himself available within the confines of the court, so they will return and remain in the waiting area for his call.

The judge enters the courtroom and begins his comments relating to today's proceedings.

"Some of the evidence to be heard today will be relayed in closed court. The evidence relates to national security issues, and those giving the evidence may need to have their identities protected. Usher, please clear the courtroom of all non-essential personnel," the judge orders.

Once the courtroom has been cleared, a screen is erected to hide the identity of the first witness from the court. The first witness is Quentin Blake of MI5.

"For the purpose of the record the witness will be referred to as Mr X."

"Mr X, can you tell the court your occupation please?"

"I am an agent with the secret service at MI5," Blake replies.

"And will you tell the court your interest in this trial, or should I say the accused?" the Crown ask.

"The government believes that communism is a real and present threat to this country and the Empire. There are fears that they, the communists, are seeking a revolution in this country and national liberation in the colonies that could result in socialist breakaway states. We believe that communists should be treated as enemies, not liberators. We know of their activities within the trade union movement, designed to create unrest and civil disobedience. We have been monitoring them for some time, with the assistance of a special operation working outside of MI5 to protect its identity," Blake says.

"And what precisely is your interest in this case, sir?"

"We believe that two of the accused are members of the Communist Party. We believe that your witness, Mr Bottomley, was their target, and that the young lady was to be used to get information from him," Blake continues.

"And may we ask why you believe that Mr Bottomley was a target for these people?"

"Mr Bottomley is known, by the communists, to have been responsible for the arrests of some of their members. He heads a task force that is looking into the connection between them and their attempts to infiltrate the trade union movement."

"So his efforts are helping to prevent these people from doing their work, whatever it is?" asks the Crown.

"Yes, that's correct. The communists, backed up by the Soviets, are determined to achieve their ends. Living in a democracy, as we do, makes it very difficult to control their actions without introducing draconian legislation, which is what they want us to do. Then they could be seen to liberate the country before applying their own doctrine. We need dedicated brave young men and women prepared to risk their lives to stop these people from achieving their aims and aspirations. Mr Bottomley is one of these people. As a soldier, he put his life on the line for his country during the war; he is now doing the same during the peace," Blake answers.

"Mr X, are you saying that the Soviets are behind these attacks on British citizens in our own country?" the judge asks with concern.

"That is precisely what I am saying, my lord. Mr Bottomley has become something of a thorn in the side of the agents operating in this country. The security services have ongoing investigations at this time, which we believe will inflict still more damage on their operations, as a result of his team's endeavours."

"And you have proof that the men in the dock are communist?"

"Two of the men, Bill Williams and Jack Styne, are active members of the party, and we have details of their membership. Whatever the outcome of this trial, they will ultimately be expelled from Britain. As for the other two men, we have no knowledge that they are communists," Blake replies.

"Mr X, just how close are you to exposing this communist infiltration, which you say is hell-bent on creating a communist state here in this country?"

"Our successes so far has been moderate, Your Honour. I believe the Soviets are testing the water to identify if the British people are vulnerable during these difficult times. There are still shortages from the war years, and the public are restless. The Soviets are hoping to be able to expose the general public's restlessness. We have known of the existence of their influence among the academia for some time.

"The Cambridge connection was exposed when two of its members, Burgess and Maclean, fled to the Soviet Union last year. We have to keep working very hard, with the help of people like Mr Bottomley, to stop them," says Blake.

"Meanwhile, we can expect further attempts on the lives of British citizens like Mr Bottomley, by communist members, Mr X?"

"Yes, I'm afraid that is so."

The Crown barrister sits down and the defence barrister stands.

"Mr X, you say you have proof that my clients, Bill Williams and Jack Styne, are members of the Communist Party. If so, can I ask how it was acquired?"

"Our information was acquired from a reliable source within their group. We cannot divulge the identity of any persons involved, since it would place them in jeopardy. What has happened to Mr Bottomley is clear evidence of what happens to anyone who would seek to prevent them from their goals."

Before Blake leaves the dock, he is addressed by the judge directly.

"Mr X, your evidence to this court has been both enlightening and disturbing. To be told by the security services of this country that there is a plot to force the communist doctrine upon us is indeed disturbing. Let us hope that you are able to prevent such an occurrence without affecting our liberties too much in the process. Thank you. Mr Brown, after lunch, we will hear additional evidence from Mr Bottomley. I think it reasonable that we hear just what he has to say in light of the security services evidence and his own participation in their activities. The court will remain closed to the public whilst he is giving his additional evidence."

"Very good, my lord, I will see to it that he is available," Mr Brown replies.

The Crown barrister confirms with Daniel that he is required to give additional evidence.

"Your colleague from MI5 gave a glowing description of your activities, Daniel, so I need to clarify some points for the jury about you, and the defence barrister has to be given the opportunity to cross examine. The only mention of Polly, was to infer that the attackers were trying to use her to get to you. There was absolutely no mention of any activity relating to her and the security service. All that was said was that the communists were hoping to use the attacks on her as a lever against you. "

Daniel goes back into the witness box and is reminded that he is still under oath.

"Mr Bottomley, can you clarify, for the record, what your occupation is?"

"I work for the government heading a group of agents seeking to prevent the communists from infiltrating the trade union movement for their own ends. My remit is to use whatever is necessary to stop their activities. They have agents from Russia working here to pursue their aims of a British communist state. I have seen documentation outlining how they hope to proceed by infiltrating Her Majesty's government. This is a war and our country is both the battlefield and the prize for the winners."

"And would you say you are winning this war, Mr Bottomley?" the Crown asks.

"I don't believe we can ever completely win, but we must do everything possible to make the lives of the communists as uncomfortable as possible, within the laws of the land, you understand. The prize for the Soviets is control of one of the mightiest nations on Earth, and they are pouring massive resources into their efforts. But they have to get the people on their side.

"We have to make sure that the communists are exposed for what they are. If we do that, they will not win anything. My colleagues and I will fight them with whatever means possible, and with the assistance of the security services. It is a fight we just cannot afford to lose."

"Thank you Mr Bottomley, will you remain there please?" the Crown asks, as the defence barrister rises.

"Mr Bottomley, what do you mean 'by any means possible'?" the defence barrister asks.

"The communists have tried a number of times to seriously injure or even kill me and my colleagues during our endeavours. We will do whatever we have to should they try to stop us."

"And tell me, Mr Bottomley, how did you obtain your information allegedly implicating my clients in this communist plot?"

"From within the headquarters of the Communist Party, and by intercepting messages between their agents."

"In other words, from someone within their party who is spying for you?"

"I did not say that, you are drawing your own conclusions, sir," replies Daniel firmly.

"And just where does the young lady, Miss Spencer, fit in all this? Is she an agent too?" he says sarcastically.

"Miss Spencer works at the Home Office, and I am her elected guardian while she is in London, at the request of her parents. She has no relevance in all this, an innocent bystander that the communists have shamefully attacked to get at me. These are the type of people we are dealing with, sir. Abusing and injuring a young woman, with no thought for her welfare, hoping to influence my efforts. They are cowards and should be treated as such," replies Daniel angrily.

"Are you saying that she has no knowledge of your activities, despite what has happened? I find that hard to believe."

"What I am saying, sir, is that she has a job at the Home Office which in no way is influenced by the security services or myself. She is a member of staff along with many others. What she does has nothing to do with me or the security services. I have not told her any more than is absolutely necessary about my work. Obviously, given what has happened, she is aware that it must be important, but that is all she knows and needs to know."

"Do you have any more questions pertinent to your client's defence counsel?" the judge asks. As the defence counsel declines to ask any more questions, the judge addresses Daniel directly.

"Mr Bottomley, can I take this opportunity to thank you for giving your evidence so comprehensively. You have a difficult and dangerous task on your hands, and this country applauds you for your endeavours. You are excused. We shall adjourn for today. Tomorrow I will sum up and direct the jury in considering their verdicts."

Daniel and Polly hurry from the court, hail a taxi, and head for Kensington and the apartment.

The following morning Judge Donaldson begins his summing up.

"This has been a particularly difficult trial to administer because of the security implications and the very serious threats that have been detailed by the security services. As for your deliberations, you have to concentrate on the evidence relating to the charges against these men today, nothing else. The evidence against the accused in the dock is overwhelming, and it is with this in mind that I ask you to consider your verdicts," the judge concludes.

The jury return from their deliberations around three o'clock and give their verdicts.

All four men are found guilty of grievous bodily harm with intent to endanger life.

Bill Williams and Jack Styne are also found guilty of violent and indecent assault. The judge thanks them for their efforts and continues.

"The accused have been found guilty of the charges and I will pass sentence on you all tomorrow. I warn you now to expect long prison sentences for your actions. The court is now adjourned."

So Polly and Daniel have only to attend court to hear the sentences passed before they can go off for a well-deserved holiday. They arrive at the court to be met by the Crown barrister, Mr Richard Brown.

"Good morning, this is the part of the proceedings that I always enjoy, seeing justice in action," he says as they file into the courtroom to await the judge. He begins his summary before announcing his sentencing tariffs.

"The four accused have been found guilty of all charges and will be sentenced accordingly. Your gratuitous violence against Mr Bottomley and Miss Spencer, a young woman, was unprovoked and inexcusable. The reasoning behind it is something which may be discussed further at some other time. It is my intention that you receive the maximum sentence for your actions.

"David Piper, Bill Williams, George Reagan, and Bill Styne, you will all go to prison for seven years. Bill Williams and Jack Styne, your actions towards a defenceless young woman were degrading and despicable. You obviously intended to force yourselves on her, for your own gratification, and were prepared to go to any lengths to get what you wanted. Society has no place for such behaviour and I sentence you both to a further seven years for your actions, your sentences to run consecutively. Officers, take them down.

"It just remains for me to thank especially Mr Bottomley for his work in seeking to remove the communist threat from our society. We spent six years of war against an enemy seeking world domination, and it must not be allowed to happen again. Whatever it takes must be done to protect our society from such totalitarianism. We must applaud the security services for the dangerous work they undertake to keep us safe. These people, who would seek to destroy our democratic process and impose their will upon us, must be stopped with whatever means at our disposal. And anyone using violence in our society, whatever their cause, will be dealt with by the courts. This case is now adjourned," the judge concludes as he leaves the courtroom.

"I believe that was a good result, Daniel, and I believe we may be seeing you again according to my case list?" Richard Brown comments.

"Yes, I'm afraid so, Richard, but for now we are both relieved that it is over for the time being," Daniel replies as he leaves the court buildings with Polly hanging on to his arm.

"I can't believe that it is all over, Daniel, and we are off on our holiday break."

"We will go and get some lunch on the way home, Polly, and get ready for our journey tomorrow."

They are both pleased that the trial has ended, and do not notice the two men who were in the courtroom to hear the verdicts and who have followed them out into the street. Polly calls home on Thursday evening to confirm they will be arriving in the early afternoon of Friday.

"How was the trial, Polly? Not too distressing, I hope?" her mother asks.

"I am just so glad that it is all over, Mummy. I am looking forward to coming home to see you all."

"So we can expect you just after lunch?"

"We are catching the eleven o'clock from Euston so we should be home about two o'clock, so we'll see you then."

On Friday morning Daniel calls Fitz to give him the news of the verdict.

"I knew Donaldson would dish out a maximum sentence, he is known to come down hard on crimes of violence. Conrad and your colleagues will hold the fort while you are away. We are hoping that the Red Hand mob might be indiscreet and meet with known communists. Anyway, you don't need to concern yourself with any of that for the next few days. Off you go with Polly and enjoy your holiday. Look after that young woman, Daniel, she is very important to us all."

"She is rather important to me as well, Fitz, but thank you for your concern. See you in a week or so, bye for now."

They are both up early on Friday, packing their cases for their week away.

"Do you realise, Daniel, this is the first time we have had a whole week away since I have been with you?"

"I am so looking forward to the time away from our work, Polly. Sometimes you have to take the break and recharge the batteries, and it will be good for you and I to spend some time in the country. I always enjoy the peace and quiet when we are at your home."

"It's your home too, Daniel. It always will be, you know that?"

"Thanks for that, Polly. Now how is your packing coming along? You seem to have packed enough for a month rather than a week."

The taxi is waiting as they arrive at the entrance, and neither of them notice the same two men from the court standing at the end of the street, who hail a taxi and follow them. The train journey is uneventful, but seems to take forever, although they still arrive in Carswell in good time. The taxi takes them to Polly's home where they arrive about 1.30pm. Polly rushes in, leaving Daniel with the cases, calling out as she enters the hallway.

"Mummy, Daddy, we're here. Where are you both?"

"We're here Polly, in the parlour." Polly rushes to hug both of her parents as Daniel drops the cases in the hallway and follows Polly into the parlour.

"Daniel, so good to see you again, my friend. How are you?"

"Hello Ben, Margaret. It's good to be spending some time with you."

They settle down for some tea, before Polly and Daniel take their cases to their rooms to unpack. Daniel looks round the room that was so familiar to him some five years ago and smiles. *How times have changed*, he thinks, as Polly enters his room.

"This is going to be the most memorable visit home, Daniel, I know it is, and we can spend as much time as we wish doing whatever we want," she says, hugging him.

It will certainly prove to be a most memorable visit for all the wrong reasons. The children arrive home from school, almost delirious in their excitement at seeing Polly and Daniel. Polly is surrounded by her sisters and George is delighted to see his friend Daniel again.

"Daniel, I'm so glad that you and Polly have come to stay, we can play some cricket if you like."

"I look forward to that, George," he replies, as they all go into the garden.

Daniel, meanwhile, finds himself with Maisy, anxious for an update on his relationship with Polly.

"Are you any closer to getting married, Daniel? It is so obvious that you and Polly are mad about each other."

"Yes, I'm sure it is, Maisy, but Polly knows that the time is not right to settle down just yet. It would not be a good idea for certain people to know of our relationship; we are just friends to all but a few people. For now it has to stay that way. What I will tell you, is that Polly and I will get married as soon as circumstances allow, you have my word."

"Gosh, Daniel, I had no idea that your work could be dangerous for Polly, but you will protect her, you always have," says Maisy, smiling, and holds on to Daniel's arm as they enter the parlour.

Polly goes off with Margaret to help with dinner, always keen to talk with her mother.

"So how are you and Daniel? You seem to be glowing as usual," says Margaret with a smile.

"We are getting along wonderfully well, Mummy. I think I love him more now than when we last talked, if that is possible. Daniel is my life now, and I know we shall be together forever, and for your information, I also know that we will get married, when the time is absolutely right. I'm sure that is what you wanted to hear, Mummy, wasn't it?" says Polly, giving her mother a hug.

"Yes my dear Polly, that is exactly what I wanted to hear," Margaret replies with a beaming smile.

The evening is soon over after the meal, and Margaret and Polly go up leaving, Daniel with Ben.

"How are your efforts against the communists going, Daniel? Are you making progress?"

"We are making progress, Ben, but it is a huge task, and they are pouring in resources to destabilise the union movement."

"And what about Polly? I do worry about her, she is so determined," says Ben, voicing, yet again, his concerns for his daughter's safety.

"Polly is proving a huge asset and every effort to protect her is being made. It has been dangerous at times, as you know, and I will always keep you abreast of what is happening. But we are dealing with a ruthless group of people desperate to force their communist dogma on the British people. They will stamp on anyone and anything that gets in their way. We shall not let that happen, Ben. We must not let that happen. It is a secret war and a dirty war, but we are holding them for the moment."

"I really had no idea it was so serious. I admire your courage and determination, I really do."

"Anyway, enough gloom and doom, Ben, we have a busy day tomorrow, so I will go up now. Goodnight," says Daniel, leaving the parlour and going up to his room. He had only just entered the room, when he is joined by Polly.

"I wondered where you were, Daniel. Has Daddy been quizzing you about me?"

"Your Daddy worries about you, Polly. I would be worried about you if you were my daughter."

"I know, Daniel, but so long as I have you, I will always be safe," Polly says, hugging him tightly.

"Ok Polly, now off you go. You cannot be in my room tonight, so goodnight my dear," Daniel replies, kissing her on the cheek.

Polly decides to go into town on Saturday with Margaret; she always enjoys a trip into Carswell, and the opportunity to be with her mother. They are very close, having shared a number of bad experiences when she was younger, which brought them even closer together. And now Margaret is waiting for the day when her daughter marries her knight in shining armour, who has been so much a part of her life since she was at school. Sometimes, when Margaret talks with her daughter, she finds it hard to believe that she is only eighteen years old.

"I thought I might get a new jacket for my work, Mummy, and perhaps some shoes. The prices in London are rather steep, and I enjoy shopping here so much."

"There is plenty of choice, Polly, I'm sure you will find something suitable."

After having lunch in Carswell, they return home to find Ben and Daniel entertaining the children, and the dog, in the garden. The garden is in full bloom, thanks mainly to Margaret, and looks an absolute picture.

"I really did wonder if I would ever be able to restore it to its former glory after that terrible day five years ago, Daniel," says Margaret, referring to the explosion which wrecked the garden and rear of the house.

"It looks absolutely wonderful, Margaret. You can be proud of all your efforts."

"Come along, Daniel. Can we go for a walk with Rusty?" asks George.

"Why don't we all go, George? Come along, Maisy and Daisy."

"I am going to help Mummy with the dinner, Daniel, so will see you later."

The walk up the lane leads to open fields, so gives the dog time to enjoy himself. They walk for about half an hour away from the house, George in full voice asking Daniel about his work with Polly. Daniel answers him as best he can without being too detailed.

"I am going to work for the secret service when I grow up, Daniel."

Daniel smiles at George's comments, and watches him run off after the dog. Both Maisy and Daisy are walking each side of Daniel, holding his hands.

"We really enjoy you and Polly visiting us, don't we Maisy?" says Daisy. She doesn't have much to say, but she, too, is very fond of

Daniel. He is the big brother she always hoped for.

"And Polly and I love to be here, Daisy. It is my second home, having spent so much time here when you were small."

Daniel is exhausted by the time they return to the house. Looking at his watch he sees they have been out for almost two hours. Sunday lunch has been booked in the Carswell Hotel. Ben thought it would be a pleasant change, and give Margaret a break from cooking. The meal is enjoyed by everyone, although the choice was limited since many food items are still in short supply. No one pays any attention to the two strangers sitting at the end of the bar, watching the Spencer family closely. On returning home Daniel and Polly go off for a walk. They have not spent too much time alone together, being with the family.

"I have missed not having you to myself, Daniel, but I know that Maisy, Daisy, and especially George want to spend time with you."

"The time will pass quickly enough, Polly, and we shall be back together in the apartment before you know it."

"Can we go out tomorrow, Daniel? Do you know where I would like to visit? Bradgate Park. Do you remember Bradgate Park?"

"I certainly do remember Bradgate Park, and look forward to visiting there again."

Polly and Daniel spend some time together, walking along the lane and through the field before returning back via Milton Road, a walk of some three miles or more.

After tea, the children go up to their rooms and prepare for tomorrow's school. Ben is in his study, while Polly and Daniel spend some time in the garden with Margaret. Eventually, Margaret has to check on the children, so Daniel and Polly go to her room and talk about tomorrow's trip to Bradgate.

"I think I will have a bath now that everyone has finished in the bathroom," she says, stripping down to her underwear, oblivious to Daniel's presence. She puts on her gown and goes off to the bathroom. Daniel smiles to himself, never surprised by Polly's actions around him. He sits in the chair and must have dropped off to sleep to be woken by Polly jumping into his lap.

"Daniel, you can't sleep in my room you know," she says with a cheeky smile as she hugs him, making him very aware that she has nothing on beneath her gown.

"I am exhausted with all the fresh air and walking, Polly, not used to it in London."

They sit together, deep in their own thoughts, relaxed and contented with their own company. Daniel always enjoys having Polly in his arms and Polly usually falls asleep in her contentment. This time is no exception and after a short while, she is asleep. Daniel looks down at her and wonders at just how this young girl has become so much a part of his life, his whole life, in fact. He is sitting there with Polly when Margaret enters the room.

"I have just made some tea, Daniel. I didn't realise you were both asleep."

"It must be all your fresh air, Margaret. We will be down in a moment," Daniel replies as Polly stirs.

Margaret leaves the room and returns to the parlour with a smile on her face.

Next morning, Polly awakens Daniel around 6.30am, having had an early night.

"Come along Daniel, time for you to wake up," she says as she leaps onto his bed.

"Polly, it is only 6.30, I am still asleep!" he says, turning over, whereupon Polly gets into bed beside him, which wakes him up rather quickly.

"Ok Polly," he says, giving her a hug.

"Let's stay here for a while, Daniel. You did say it was early," she replies, laughing. They lie together for about ten minutes before Polly goes off to the bathroom, leaving Daniel with his thoughts. After breakfast, Polly prepares a picnic lunch for their trip to Bradgate Park, Margaret gets the children ready for school. She drives the children to school most days to save time, and returns just after nine o'clock, and Polly and Daniel set off for Bradgate around 10.30 on a gloriously sunny summer day. There are quite a few visitors in the park, so neither of them pays any attention to the two men close by, who look rather overdressed for a day in the country.

"Daniel, can we live in the country when we get married?"

Daniel almost spills his drink with surprise at Polly's question.

"Well, I suppose, I'm not sure. Really Polly, you have caught me off balance," he replies, struggling for an answer to Polly's directness.

"But Daniel, we are going to get married when our work is finished, aren't we?"

"Yes we are, Polly. I want to marry you very much. But we have to wait for both our sakes. I hope it will not be too long before that day comes. For now we have each other. And yes, I would like very much to move to the country, I enjoy the open spaces and the peace and quiet."

"Ok Daniel, sorry if I startled you about us getting married, but I do think about it a lot."

"And so do I, Polly, so do I. Now come along, we ought to be getting back. Margaret will want the car to collect Maisy, Daisy, and George."

They walk back to the car, Polly still elaborating on their house in the country.

"It will have to be large enough for the children, of course."

"Of course, Polly. How many children are we expecting?"

"Oh, about three or four I would expect, Daniel. What do you think?"

"Whatever you say, Polly, will be absolutely fine by me. I don't suppose you have selected their names yet?" he laughs.

"Really Daniel, you cannot begin talking about names, until you are sure you are going to have a baby!"

"Well you seem to have everything worked out, Polly, and I hope we can make arrangements very soon. But please be patient, we do have so much work to do," he says, bringing the conversation back to the present.

"So long as we are together, I don't really mind how long we have to wait, Daniel. I love you so much, and I know you love me, so that really is all that matters for now."

"I agree, Polly. So long as we are together we will be ok," says

Daniel as they turn into Crabtree Lane and park outside the house.

"Did you have a good day, dear?"

"Yes, thank you Mummy. Daniel and I had a lot to talk about and it was so nice to visit Bradgate again."

Margaret goes to collect the children from school, while Polly begins preparing the family dinner, while Daniel calls on Ben in his study.

"Ben, I just wanted to have a word with you about Polly and myself. I am sure you and Margaret know how we both feel about each other. I love your daughter very much and do intend asking you formally, at the earliest possible time, for her hand. However, I have a job to do, as does Polly, and it would be unfair to her to get married for appearances only. We live together, and we love each other very much, but we are not yet man and wife, Ben. I hope you will accept that."

"I trust you completely with my daughter, Daniel, and know you will do what is right and I thank you for being so honest regarding your relationship. Polly is very precious to Margaret and I, and to see her so very happy makes us very happy for both of you."

The children arrive home from school, all talking at once to Daniel about their day at Bradgate.

"Can you take us before you go back to London, Daniel?"

"We'll see if we can arrange something at the weekend, George."

Meanwhile, Polly has been talking with her mother about her relationship with Daniel.

"We all know how much you two love each other, dear Polly, and we will all be happy for you when you can finally tie the knot. In the meantime I know you will take care of each other as you always have."

"Thanks Mummy, I do love him very much, but it is always nice to hear you say so."

After a superb evening meal and a glass or two of wine, the family sit around chatting, until Polly decides to go up to bed around midnight followed, shortly after, by Daniel, Ben, and Margaret. Ben and Margaret will sleep soundly, having had more than a glass of the red wine.

The masked intruders enter the house from the front, silencing the dog with some doped horsemeat.

It is just after 2.00am, and the five men, two of whom are Soviet agents, move silently up the stairs to carry out their instructions. The communists are convinced that they have to silence Daniel once and for all, and the Soviets have previously expressed an interest in Polly. Two of the men attack Polly in her bed and she is stunned by blows to her face. They drag her roughly from her bed, screaming and kicking, and manhandle her whilst trying to get her out of the room. Her pyjama jacket is torn from her as she frantically tries to escape. They slap her again and one of them grabs her by her hair while the other holds on to her legs. Daniel hears the scuffle just as two men enter his room, firing their weapons. Fortunately, he is out of his bed before they enter, and reaching for his pistol he shoots one in the chest; the other is struck on his cheek, shattering his jaw. Daniel is grazed on his arm from one of the shots, but is otherwise unhurt. He dashes from the room to see the two men turning to go down the stairs with Polly, being half dragged, half carried by them.

"Daniel, Daniel!" she screams as she tries desperately to escape.

"Give her a slap and hold on to her legs!" one of the men shouts.

"Hold her round her waist she won't be able to struggle so much, and rip off her pyjamas, she will be easier to carry. You! Stop struggling!" he shouts.

Daniel meanwhile, kicks away the weapons of the two men he has shot, and goes after the others who by now are at the bottom of the stairs.

"Ben, we have intruders, hold the two men in my room!" he shouts, knocking on Ben's bedroom door. As he reaches the stairs, a fifth man fires at him from the hallway, hitting him in the upper chest area. He had no idea there was a fifth man and had been distracted calling out to Ben. Daniel staggers in pain from the wound, but continues down the stairs firing back at the man, hitting him in the stomach and neck. He is struggling to stay on his feet, but is desperate to stop the two men who have Polly. She is kicking and screaming as the men hold on to her near-naked body and move toward the front door.

"Please Daniel, help me!" she screams hysterically, still trying desperately to escape from the men. One of them is holding her by her shoulders, the other has her legs. She is perspiring heavily from her attempts to escape, making it difficult for them to hold on to her.

"Let me go, Daniel please help me!" she screams as the men continue to fight with her, hitting her hard across her chest and legs. Then one of the men tries to carry her himself so that his accomplice can deal with Daniel. Polly scratches him and he grabs the top of her leg, trying to hang on to her. Daniel takes his chance and fires, hitting one of them twice in his thigh. As he falls to the floor, his accomplice lets go of Polly and runs off into the night. She falls on the injured man before running to Daniel, who by this time is feeling the effects of his gunshot wound, which is bleeding heavily.

"Daniel, my god you've been shot!" she screams in panic.

Ben and Margaret cannot believe the scene as they rush down the stairs, past the injured man.

Daniel has by now slipped to the floor, and Polly is trying to determine where exactly he has been shot. She holds on to him, desperately trying to stem the bleeding, covered in his blood over her chest and arms and with her legs also covered in blood from the man shot by Daniel. As Daniel slips into unconsciousness, she screams at Ben to call an ambulance.

"Daddy, Daddy, for God's sake call an ambulance, Daniel is seriously hurt. Hurry, please. Mummy, please help me with Daniel, we have to stop the bleeding."

"Polly, you are covered in blood, and virtually naked, put this on," Margaret says as she hands her dressing gown to her daughter who did not realise the state she was in herself, her thoughts only for Daniel. Ben Spencer calls the police and two ambulances. He has also brought the two men downstairs from Daniel's room and sat them down in the hallway, together with the other two injured men, and removed their balaclavas.

"Daniel, please talk to me, the ambulance is on its way," says Polly tearfully.

"I seem to have made a bit of a mess, Polly. Are you ok?" he asks, wincing in pain from his wound. By now he is very pale and barely conscious.

"I am ok, Daniel. You saved me again, but you have a serious wound to your chest. Please stay with me, don't you dare leave me," she sobs as she holds on to him, fearing she may lose him.

The doorbell rings and D.I. Wishart, Sergeant Parsons, and W.P.C. Becky Garrett are shown in by Ben Spencer.

"Good lord Mr Spencer, what on earth has been going on here? Is that Daniel?" he asks with concern.

"It's the bad old days again, Detective Inspector, these men tried to kill Daniel and take Polly."

Margaret tells Polly to go and get dressed so that she can accompany Daniel to hospital.

Polly dashes upstairs and returns a few moments later, as the ambulances arrive. The officers stabilise Daniel before moving him.

"The bullet is still embedded in his chest, but I can stabilise him before we move him, Miss. He has lost a lot of blood, but he should be ok."

"Please take care of him, he saved my life and I care about him very much," Polly replies tearfully, as she follows the stretcher to the ambulance.

"I will call you as soon as I know something, Daddy."

The D.I. phones the station to request more officers to accompany the wounded intruders.

"I will have to visit the hospital to talk with Daniel and Polly, Mr Spencer. Is there anything you can tell me about what happened?"

"I came down when it was all over, Inspector. As far as I can tell, Daniel shot the two men that entered his room, intending to kill him. Then as he chased after the men who had Polly, one of them must have hit him. He must have somehow returned fire, hitting two of them, before collapsing in the hallway.

"The man is indestructible, Mr Spencer. His actions tonight are nothing short of amazing."

"His work at the moment is dangerous to the extreme, Detective Inspector. He has been involved in a number of attempts to harm Polly and himself, in fact they were in court only last week."

Four more police officers arrive and remove the four injured men, instructed by the D.I. to stay with them until they can escort them to the police station.

Polly holds on to Daniel's hand for the journey to hospital, talking to him as the ambulance workers attend to his wound. He is still bleeding from his wound and barely conscious.

"You are going to be ok, Daniel, really you are, and I will look after you. And I will stay with you all the time you are in the hospital."

"Thanks Polly. Did the police catch the fifth intruder? You need to tell them about him."

"Never mind him now, Daniel," says Polly, as the ambulance arrives at the hospital and Daniel is taken through to the emergency department.

The doctor examines him carefully and tells the nurses to prepare him for immediate surgery.

"He will be ok, Doctor, won't he?" asks Polly nervously.

"We will know more, Miss, when we have operated, but he should be ok. The wound is clean, we just have to see if it has done any internal damage."

Polly paces up and down, waiting for some news, all the time fretting over Daniel's condition.

After what seemed like an age to her – it was in fact just over an hour – the surgeon arrives.

"The operation was successful and we were able to remove the bullet intact. There is some tissue and muscle damage but the bullet did not hit anything else. He will be a bit drowsy for a while, but I am sure you would like to sit with him."

"Thank you, Doctor. My dear Daniel, once again you are in the wars saving me from these dreadful people. God, I look forward to when we can go away from all this and live in peace," she says to herself.

"Don't fret, Polly. It will be sooner than you think."

"Daniel, you're awake. How are you feeling?"

"Like I have been run over by a train, Polly. I ache all over."

"I must phone home to let them know you are ok, Daniel, I won't be a moment.

"Daddy, you must contact the police and request a police guard for Daniel, one of the men escaped and I am concerned he might try and get to Daniel in the hospital."

"I am a little ahead of you with that request, my dear, it is arranged. The officer should be with you very shortly. How is Daniel?"

"He is resting, Daddy, but otherwise ok. I will have to come home shortly, to change my clothes and wash, I am still covered with Daniel's blood."

Polly returns to Daniel's bedside just as the officer arrives.

"Good morning Miss, P.C. John Winterton, I am to watch over Mr Bottomley," the P.C. says, surprised by the state of Polly, dishevelled and bloodstained.

"Thank you for being so prompt, officer," she says, looking at her watch. It is 4.00am. She goes off to arrange for some tea for him before going back to Daniel's bedside. He is sleeping soundly, so Polly decides to ask Ben if he will collect her so that she may return home for about an hour to clean herself and change her clothes.

"He is sleeping soundly, Daddy, so I thought I might return home and wash and change and collect what is necessary. I must also call Fitz as soon as possible and tell him what has happened."

The children are all awake when she returns to the house, asking questions about Daniel.

"Daniel is recovering. He has had an operation to remove a bullet from his chest, but he will be ok, so please do not worry."

"What happened, Polly? There is blood everywhere, did the men hurt you?"

"No they didn't hurt me, George, the blood you see is from the one that Daniel shot."

"He will be ok, won't he Polly?" Maisy asks with concern in her voice. She is very fond of Daniel and was horrified to hear that he had been hurt.

"Yes, he should fully recover, Maisy, and I will look after him. Now I must have a wash and change all my clothes. Mummy, will you help me please?"

Margaret follows Polly to the bathroom and is astonished at the amount of dried blood all over Polly's chest and arms. Polly also has scratches on her back and marks on her wrist from being dragged down the stairs and across the hallway, and she has red marks across her chest and legs where she was hit by the men whilst trying to abduct her. Her face is also bruised from being hit.

"Daniel must have lost a lot of blood, Polly, you are absolutely drenched."

Polly finishes washing and has a complete change of clothes. She takes Daniel a change of clothes, his dressing gown, and his shaving requirements.

"I will see you all later. Can you take me back now, Daddy, please?"

Ben drives Polly back to the hospital, and tells him she will call later with any news; Daniel is awake and talking with the police officer when Polly returns to his bedside.

"My dear Polly, I see you have organised everything. I have just been telling John, what happened.

"It must have been very frightening for you, Miss. You are lucky to have such a good friend."

"Yes I am, John, but I have to say he is much more than a friend to me."

The officer leaves the room as Polly pulls up a chair to Daniel's bedside.

"I will call Fitz later, Daniel, he must be told about this and decide what has to be done. These people must be getting desperate, following us to my parents' house."

"It's a concern, Polly. I never considered they would follow us anywhere outside of London. We will have to be aware of this in future. By the way, do you have your pistol in your bag?"

"Yes I do. Why do you ask, Daniel?"

"I just want to be sure that you are prepared at all times, after what has happened." He is shaken by this turn of events and recognises that he must take extra precautions to protect her when they return to London.

"Do you feel well enough to talk to the police later, Daniel? I told D.I. Wishart I would ask."

"I shall be ok to speak with him once the doctor has been round. I suggest that you go and speak with Fitz when he is here, and his officers can talk with you at home."

"Very well Daniel, now shall I get you some breakfast?"

"I think I will have a little nap first, Polly, I'm feeling rather tired."

"Yes of course, I will go and get myself some tea. You rest and I will be back soon," Polly replies kissing him on his forehead before leaving him to sleep while she looks for the doctor.

"Can you give me any more details, Doctor? How long will you have to keep Daniel in hospital?"

"I would suggest that he stay overnight and providing there are no complications you can take him home tomorrow after rounds. You have to be aware that bullet wounds can be unpredictable, and Daniel's body has suffered more than once from such wounds. However, with care and attention he should fully recover from his ordeal."

"Thank you Doctor, I will take good care of him, I promise."

She goes off to collect a cup of tea, before returning to Daniel who is sleeping soundly. She sits down beside him, reflecting on the terrifying events of the early morning, trying to understand what is happening and how they will have to conduct their lives from now on. It is obvious that the communists were behind this latest attempt to kill Daniel and abduct her, and those instructions could only have come direct from Moscow. What is concerning is that they were followed to Polly's parents' and the attempt made in the house, with no regard for any members of the family. It was a well-planned action carried out by professionals. Polly will portray this to Fitz when she calls him. She looks at her watch; it is just eight o'clock, as Ben arrives to ask how Daniel is progressing.

"So far so good, Daddy. There are no complications and provided nothing changes, we can have him home tomorrow. I really thought I had lost him this time, I know I have always regarded him as

Superman, but even he had his weakness," she says, holding on to Ben for reassurance.

"I really believe that he is indestructible with regard to taking care of you, Polly. There is a saying that 'love conquers all', and Daniel's actions over the years to protect you epitomise that saying perfectly," he replies, looking down at Daniel who continues to sleep soundly.

The doctor arrives with Daniel still sleeping, but wakes him so that he may take a look at the wound. All is well and the wound is redressed.

"Hello Ben, thanks for calling in. Sorry about the mess at your place, I seem to have made a bit of a habit of messing up over the years."

"You do indeed, Daniel, and thank God for that."

"We are going back home for an hour, Daniel. I must call Fitz and tell him what has happened, bye for now," says Polly, squeezing his hand and kissing him on the cheek.

"Take good care of him for me, John, please," says Polly to the police officer as she leaves the hospital with Ben to return home.

"You will have to consider your position in the Home Office, after this latest attempt Polly. Would you like me to speak with Beatrice? She may be able to help."

"Let me talk to Fitz about Daniel first, Daddy, he is my priority at the moment."

"Yes of course, my dear."

Polly calls Fitz and recites the details of the previous night to him, expressing her concern for Daniel's life given the lengths the Russians have gone to, in an attempt to kill him.

"My dear Polly, I am so sorry, please convey my thoughts to Daniel. We have to take immediate action on this. I am going to send Conrad to you, do you think your parents could accommodate him until Daniel is well enough to travel?"

"Yes and thank you so much for offering my family protection, Fitz, I do appreciate that."

"It is no more than you deserve. Now Conrad will travel up this morning by car, so that he can drive you both back when Daniel is fit. It will be a safer and more comfortable journey for you both. Meantime, I will talk with Quentin Blake and see about making some arrests. At the very least we must be seen to responding vigorously to this latest attempt on you and Daniel. You are both key to our fight against the communists and must be protected. Is there anything else we can do for you, my dear?"

"Daniel may require some more ammunition, Fitz. He emptied his pistol, and used one of the intruders' weapons as well, so I don't know whether he has any spare with him or not."

"I will get Conrad to bring a box. Do you have your pistol with you, Polly?"

"Yes I do, Daniel has told me that I should carry it with me at all times."

"That is sound advice considering the recent events. Please convey my regards to Daniel, call me at any time if you feel it necessary, both Conrad and Daniel have my home number, and do take special care of yourself, my dear. Bye for now."

Polly goes to tell her parents that Conrad will be arriving later in the day.

"I will go and make up a bed in the spare room for him, Polly, the children will have to share for the moment. And I expect you will want to be in with Daniel when he comes home, so I will see if we cannot make you more comfortable in there."

"Thank you, Mummy. Yes, I will stay with Daniel when he is brought home, now I will call the police and tell them that Daniel will talk to the D.I. at the hospital, while I will talk with them here."

D.I. Wishart arrives at the hospital, while Polly is still at home, accompanied by a PC.

"Good morning Daniel, how are you feeling?"

"Aching like hell, but I'm told I am on the mend, thank you."

"What the hell happened last night, Daniel? The place looked more like a battlefield than a suburban house," the D.I. asks.

"It would seem the Soviets are hell-bent on getting rid of me; they sent five men by the way, were you able to catch the one that escaped?"

"We weren't able to find him yet, but we will keep looking. Two of your visitors were Russian nationals, they are screaming for diplomatic assistance. I have been on to the security services and they have asked that we hold on to them."

"They seem to think the Russians will deny any knowledge of them anyway."

"Yes, I'm sure they will, they never like admitting to anything, especially if they lose."

"How were you able to overpower them, Daniel?"

"Well, they were also after Polly, I know from a previous fight with them that they wanted to take her back to Russia. Apparently, young attractive woman are sought after over there. Anyway, two came for me and two went after Polly. I shot the two in my room, got a bit of a graze on my arm, but nothing serious. When I went after the two with Polly, they were downstairs, and as I reached the stairs, the fifth man shot me in the chest. Fortunately, I was able to get two shots off at him which stopped him. Then, I managed to struggle down the stairs and get a round off to one of the two dragging Polly to the doorway. He let go of Polly, and other one ran off. Don't remember a whole lot after that, I know Polly was screaming when she came to help me. The next clear picture I have is seeing her when I woke up after surgery."

"Your actions certainly saved Polly, now you might like to know that we have determined that the other two men are both from London, we believe them to be communists also, recruited to kill you. We may be able to trace the fifth man from them, I will let you know. We'll let you rest now Daniel, I expect you will be at Ben's place for a while yet, so we know where to find you if we need you," says the D.I. as he leaves Daniel's room.

Daniel lies back and is just about to drop off to sleep, when Polly returns with Conrad.

"My dear chap, you really must stop shooting up the countryside. I thought you were on holiday! Seriously, how are you feeling?"

"Getting better all the time, I shall be going home to Polly's shortly."

"This is a bad business, Fitz is furious, there will be arrests and reprisals I shouldn't wonder."

"Well, if nothing else, Conrad, the Soviets have shown their hand, so we can move forward and make what arrests are necessary and throw them out of our country."

"Daniel, please do not get angry or upset, you have to remain calm. The last thing we want is for you to cause any complications with your injuries."

"You're right, Polly, I will keep quiet for now. Will you ask the doctor when we might leave?"

Polly goes to find the doctor, as Daniel turns to Conrad.

"Have MI5 found out who the men were who came after us, Conrad?"

"We believe they were sent direct from Moscow, Daniel, so much for being specialists, and they were to take Polly back with them."

"For God's sake don't mention that to anyone else, Conrad. Polly knows that they tried to abduct her but I do not want her to dwell on it too much," Daniel replies, as Polly returns with the doctor and a chair to transport Daniel to the ambulance.

"Now Daniel, you must remain in bed at least until the weekend. I will get someone to come and see to you, as you will need to have your wound looked at before then. Polly, please make sure that he does as he is told."

"You can be sure that he will do as you have told him, Doctor, I will see to that."

So after thanking the doctor for his help, Daniel is wheeled to the ambulance by Polly.

"I will see you both back at the house," says Conrad as he drives off.

Polly arrives with Daniel, who is wheeled in by the officers, who then carry him upstairs to his room. Conrad goes to unpack leaving Polly with Daniel, as Margaret enters his room.

"My dear Daniel, how are you?" she asks with concern on her face.

"I am very much on the mend thank you, Margaret, and in good hands."

"You gave us quite a fright, the children will be so pleased to see you back home. Now Polly, is there anything else you need before I make us all tea? I have given you a couple of pillows and some blankets for when you stay in here, is there anything else?"

"Nothing else Mummy, I will be down in a moment for our tea. Mummy tried to get the bloodstains from your pyjamas, Daniel, but it was impossible, so I will get you some new ones as soon as possible. In the meantime, you can use a pair of Daddy's."

"Ok Polly, whatever you say will be fine."

"I expect you and Conrad will want to have a word, but please do not overdo things, Daniel. I will be back with some tea shortly."

Conrad is met by Polly as he approaches Daniel's room.

"Please do not spend too much time with him, Conrad, he needs to rest."

"Just want to say hello and tell him I am here for him, Polly."

Conrad enters Daniel's room to be warmly greeted.

"Thanks for being here, Conrad. Polly and I really appreciate you coming at short notice. It was a bloody close thing the other evening, I don't want to fight against those odds again. While you are here, you can liaise with Fitz for me. The sooner some arrests are made, the sooner the Soviets will know we mean business. And it may put back any plans they had hoped to put in place regarding the unions. My main concern at the moment, Conrad, is Polly and her position at the Home Office.

"I am convinced that Sally Nugent and Jarvis are more than just members of the Red Hand organisation, but cannot prove it at the moment. If they are, they will know what happened here, so we have to consider their next move."

"I think it unlikely that they will attempt anything more here, Daniel. These things take time to plan. You have just put four of their men out of action, which means they will have to find four more."

"The point is, Conrad, we cannot wait for them to attempt another attack on Polly and myself, we must put out of action as many of them as we can, even if only for a short time, while we gather more intelligence."

Polly arrives with some tea for Daniel and insists that Conrad leave him to rest.

"We have a visitor that you may want to speak with downstairs, Conrad, so I suggest you go and say hello," says Polly with a mischievous smile on her face.

"Who has arrived, Polly?" asks Daniel as Conrad leaves the room.

"My Aunty Pauline, you remember that she and Conrad became close friends when you stayed here together? How are you feeling? I'm not sure what is going to happen over the next few days, but I will stay with you and make sure that you get the rest that the doctor ordered. My god, Daniel it is only just beginning to sink in how close we came to losing you. When you are better, and we are back in London, we must talk about us. I know we have always said that we have a job to see through first and I agree with you, but I want us to be together as well, Daniel, before it may be too late," says Polly holding on to his hand firmly.

"Conrad and I touched on changes that may have to be made, Polly, and when we get back, you and I will have a chat, I promise. And if we agree that changes to our life together have to be made also, then so be it, I will be delighted."

"Thank you, Daniel," says Polly, hugging him gently, before she leaves him to rest for a while.

Daniel sleeps soundly for a couple of hours, Polly looking in on him from time to time. Conrad is pleasantly surprised to meet with Pauline again, and they spend some time in the garden together. It was well known that they became close during the difficult times experienced by the Spencer family some five years ago, and they seem to be enjoying each other's company again.

Margaret often wonders just what did happen between them, but did not wish to pry, knowing that her sister would have told her had she wanted to. After lunch, Conrad asks Ben if he might have a word with him in his study.

"Fitz asked me to convey his thanks for allowing me to stay with your family again, Ben, although I never expected the circumstances to be so similar to my last stay with you."

"You are very welcome Conrad, I just wish the circumstances

were different."

"Indeed. Now I have had a word with Daniel, and we both feel that it is most unlikely that anything more will happen here at your home, Ben. Daniel has put four of their best men out of commission, and it will take time for them to be replaced."

"Yes, I agree, and regarding further visits, we are well protected with alarms and security measures, still in place from when you were here last, Conrad."

"Do you still have your weapons, Ben?" asks Conrad.

"Yes I do, and they are in good working order."

"That's good, it's just about being careful."

"What do you think will happen regarding Polly and Daniel, Conrad? It seems that these people are hell-bent on getting rid of both of them one way or the other. Do you think Polly's position has been compromised?"

"What I believe, Ben, is that the communists haven't yet established that Polly is doing anything for the security services, and until they do Polly is in no more danger than she has ever been. Unfortunately that doesn't help her cause, since they are targeting her to get at Daniel. Whilst he is recognised as her guardian, they will try and get to him through her. I don't believe they have any idea of any romantic attachment between them, if they were, I fear they would have attacked Polly more severely.

"What you and your family can be sure of is that Polly will be watched over by the best men for the job. MI5 have recognised her help in bringing down this Soviet organisation within the Home Office, and Fitz is especially fond of her and will make damn sure that no harm will come to her. And then there is Daniel. There isn't a man alive that will take Polly while he is breathing, Ben."

"I thank you for your honesty Conrad, I had no idea my daughter was seen as such an asset. Margaret and I have never doubted Daniel's feelings for Polly and how he has put his life on the line many times for her. But to hear how much she is appreciated by government officials is indeed heartening."

"I know Polly very well, Ben, and I am sure she is destined for high office one day, you mark my words. Now, I wonder if I might use your phone to contact Fitz for an update?"

"Of course, help yourself and thank you once again."

"Good morning Fitz, have arrived safely and Daniel is recovering back in Polly's home."

"That's good news, Conrad, now we are going to make some arrests and rattle a few cages as soon as MI5 can organise their agents. We feel that by making some arrests and generally being a nuisance, they may show their hand. What we need is more information about Sally Nugent and Percival Smith. Daniel was sure they were more than just Red Hand operatives. But until we can get a look at their messages, via Polly, we shall have to wait. I am going to ask Quentin if he can find out about any reactions to the Soviets losing four men in the attacks on Polly and Daniel. Meanwhile, do take care of the family, Conrad, and I will be in touch."

"Bye for now, Fitz," says Conrad, as he replaces the receiver and leaves the study.

When the children come home from school they are delighted to find Conrad has come to stay, George in particular.

"Conrad, are you going to stay with us to look after Daniel?"

"I am going to look after all of you, George."

After dinner, Polly goes up to be with Daniel, who has enjoyed his meal.

"You obviously enjoyed your meal, Daniel. Mummy will be pleased."

"I always enjoy any meal in your home, Polly, there is no substitute for home cooking."

She sits with him for a while before taking his tray downstairs.

"I am going back upstairs to stay with Daniel for a while, Mummy."

"Very well Polly, we will see you later."

Polly sits with Daniel, listening to the radio. He eventually drops off to sleep, so Polly leaves him for a while, going down to say goodnight to everyone, before putting on her pyjamas and settling down beside him in an old easy chair.

She would prefer to be beside him, but circumstances do not permit at present. She soon goes off to sleep herself, but is woken by Daniel twisting and turning. She gets up from her chair to put his covers back on, and realises that he is dripping in sweat. Putting on the bedroom light, she sees that sweat is pouring from him. She gently nudges him to wake him, concerned that he may be having some reaction to his injury.

"Daniel, wake up. Are you ok? You are dripping wet with sweat."

She takes off his pyjama jacket, and is horrified to see that he has bloodstains on his bandages.

"I feel a bit warm Polly, I must admit. Can you get me some water please?"

"Daniel, you are bleeding. God, your wound must have opened, and you have a temperature. I must wake Mummy." Polly dashes from the room to fetch Margaret.

"I will call Doctor Wilson; he has a fever and could have a wound infection."

"Oh my god, he will be alright won't he, Mummy?"

"Let me go and phone the doctor, Polly. You try and make him more comfortable."

Polly gets Daniel some water and bathes his face, before wiping the sweat from his body.

"The doctor will be about ten minutes, I will go and make some tea for when he arrives."

Polly looks at the clock. It is 2.00am. She looks at Daniel, who appears ok apart from the sweat.

The doctor soon arrives and examines Daniel.

"I see you have been in the wars again, Daniel, now let's have a look at your wound. Polly, would you get me some hot water please, and something to bathe the wound?'

Polly goes off and returns as the doctor has removed Daniel's bandages to reveal a very inflamed bullet wound.

"There is some infection in the wound, Polly. I will disinfect it and clean away the small particles at the entrance. I can only think that a tiny speck of the bullet came away during surgery. Fortunately, it has worked its way to the surface, so once we have removed it Daniel should be ok. His fever should begin to subside within a couple of hours or so, and I will prescribe some penicillin. I will call again after lunch today, but if there are any problems call me at once, do you understand?"

"Yes of course Doctor, I believe Mummy has made you some tea." Polly takes the doctor downstairs to the parlour and Margaret hands him his tea.

"See that Daniel takes one of these tablets every four hours Polly, please, and I will see you all later for an update."

Margaret sees the doctor to the door, and Polly returns to Daniel to find Conrad with him.

"He has a fever, Conrad. His wound was infected, but the doctor says he will be ok now. My god, you gave me a fright Daniel, you really did."

"Sorry to be a nuisance, Polly, you go back to bed now. Conrad and I will see you in the morning."

"Please don't give me any more frights Daniel, please," says Polly as she kisses him gently on his forehead.

"Sorry about that, Polly, I just want to recover and get back to normal as soon as possible." There is a degree of frustration in Daniel's reply.

"Get some rest now and please do not worry about getting back to normal until your wound has healed. Your body needs time to recover, Daniel, and you must give it that time."

Daniel soon gets back to sleep, but Polly frets about this latest setback and wonders herself when they will get back to normal as she drops off to sleep. She eventually wakes around 7.00am and goes down to make some tea and toast. Margaret joins her and asks about Daniel.

"Sleeping soundly, Mummy, but he did give me a fright."

"He will recover, I am sure, but you must convince him to rest his body. A bullet wound takes time to heal, and you have to be sure that there are no bits left inside. If there is any residue remaining, his body will reject it, as it appears to have done this time."

"I understand, Mummy, and will watch over him very carefully, believe me."

Doctor Wilson calls around four o'clock and everyone is relieved that the wound infection seems to be clearing up satisfactorily. After redressing the wound, the doctor is satisfied that it should now heal completely, given time.

"Plenty of rest is what is required, Daniel, and you will soon be as good as new, well in your case almost as good as new," the doctor says with a smile.

"I will see that he gets all the rest needed, Doctor, and thank you for taking care of him. I am going to help Mummy with dinner, Daniel, is there anything you need?"

"Ask Conrad to pop in, would you please?"

"How are you, Daniel? Has the wound infection cleared?"

"Yes, thanks. Now I wanted a word about when we return to London. I shall probably be off next week, so will you look after Polly's transport for me please?"

"Won't she want to stay off with you, Daniel? She will not be happy leaving you on your own."

"I am hoping that the doctor will give me the all clear to travel back on Monday. Polly will then only have to lose one day off work. If the doctor gives me the all clear to travel, then I should be ok to look after myself during the day."

Conrad smiles before replying, "You may have a bit of a fight on your hands with Polly over leaving you alone, Daniel, I can't see her leaving you alone while you are recovering."

"I will see what happens over the weekend. I am hoping to get up for an hour or so on Saturday."

Just then, Polly returns to the room accompanied by D.I. Wishart, leaving him to talk with Daniel.

"I hope you don't mind my calling, Daniel. I thought you might like an update on the identities of the intruders. I have made a note of my conversations with MI5 which you may find useful. Two of the men are Russian nationals, sent to kill you and return to Russia with

Polly. The other two are mercenaries for hire, one is German, the other Spanish," says the D.I., handing the file to Daniel.

He continues. "There is every possibility that their trial will take place at the Central Criminal Court because of the seriousness of the assaults on Miss Spencer and yourself. When national security is involved we like to leave it to the experts. Get well soon and give these people what they deserve," says the D.I. as he leaves the room.

Thursday and Friday pass without incident and when Saturday arrives, Daniel speaks with Polly about next week's arrangements. Polly is naturally concerned by his suggestions.

"I am hoping we can return to London Monday afternoon, Polly, once the doctor has given me the ok. I want you to go back to work on Tuesday, suspicions may be aroused if you are away for any longer. And we need some more information on the Red Hand agents."

"Daniel, I really do not want to leave you alone all day, I am worried that something might occur regarding your injuries. I would feel much better if I were with you."

"Let's see what the doctor says first, Polly, he will know if I am well enough to be left alone. I really do want you to get back to normal as soon as possible. Now, I would like to get up for an hour this afternoon."

"I am not sure that would be a good idea, in fact I think you should stay in your bed until the doctor says otherwise. I cannot bear to think of anything else happening to you so for now at least, please stay in your bed and rest."

"Ok Polly, I do not want you to get upset over this, I will stay where I am for now."

"If you feel like it, you can sit in my chair for a while later, and see how you feel."

"I would like a wash, or even a bath. It seems an age since I have had a bath."

"I can help you with a bath, Daniel, but you must be careful not to get your bandaging wet."

Daniel is unsure how to respond to Polly's offer, but as usual, Polly sees no reason why she should not help Daniel with his bath.

"Thank you Polly, if you can help me to and from the bathroom, that will be fine."

So Polly goes off to prepare the bath for Daniel, and returns to help him walk to the bathroom. Then without any hesitation, she pulls off his pyjamas and helps him into the bath.

"I will leave you to soak, Daniel. Call me when you are ready."

Daniel enjoys his soak, feeling a little embarrassed at Polly's actions, but to Polly it seemed the most natural thing to do. Daniel needed help so she gave it without hesitation. After a while Polly appears and leans over the bath to help Daniel get up before wrapping him in the bath towel. She leaves him to dry himself before returning to help in back to his room.

"I have left you clean pyjamas. I will leave you to put them on while I organise some lunch."

"Thank you, Polly. Perhaps I should say hello to Maisy, Daisy, and George while you are gone, I'm sure they would like to see me."

He spends some time with the three children, George asking him about the bullet that he had taken from him, while Maisy is upset at seeing him with his bandages showing. Little Daisy is just overcome by it all.

"You will get better won't you, Daniel? Promise me."

"I promise you Daisy, I will get better. I have Polly to look after me so I will be better in no time." Maisy is sitting beside Daniel, holding on to his hand.

"Thank you for saving Polly, Daniel. I do not know what we would do without her, or without you."

"Thank you Maisy, and thank you for coming in to see me. I am just sorry that we could not have spent more time with you all during the holiday, but there will be other times, I am sure."

"We could spend some time with you in London," says George.

Polly enters the room with some lunch for Daniel as the children leave, Maisy kissing Daniel on the cheek before she moves from his bed.

"Bye Daniel," they say together.

After lunch, Polly sits next to Daniel on his bed, holding on to his hand.

"I have just been speaking with Mummy about your suggestion of me leaving you to go back to work from Tuesday. She is also concerned about you being left alone, but agrees we should let the doctor decide what is best. So that is what we will do."

Daniel gets up for a few hours over the weekend and enjoys a spell in the garden with the children.

George is disappointed that they cannot play a game of cricket, but is promised a game when Daniel next visits. Polly stays close, hovering as if expecting Daniel to collapse in front of her, and Conrad gives Ben a hand cleaning his car. Sunday comes and goes before they know it, and Daniel and Polly begin to prepare for their return to London. On Monday morning, Polly calls Mrs Wright, telling her that she will not be returning to work until Tuesday, because of family business. She does not like deceiving her, but in this case she has no real choice.

"Thank you for letting me know, Polly. I look forward to seeing you tomorrow at 9.00am sharp.

Doctor Wilson arrives around ten o'clock and examines Daniel's wound before giving him the all clear to travel to London the next day.

"Your wound is healing well, Daniel, but you must rest for the remainder of the week. You should be free to go for a walk over the weekend. I will leave you two more dressings which Polly can apply, after that you should be fine."

Daniel and Polly both thank the doctor for all his help, and finalise their packing ready to begin their journey back to London after lunch.

"I cannot thank you both enough for taking care of me and for letting Conrad stay as well. I hope when Polly and I next visit you that there will not be as much trouble following us."

"It's been our pleasure, Daniel. You are always welcome in our house, you know that. You too, Conrad."

After lots of hugs and goodbyes, they finally depart for London, arriving at the apartment around 4.30pm. Polly had brought some items for dinner from home, which Margaret had bought on Saturday. After arranging to collect Polly at 8.30am on Tuesday, Conrad departs, leaving Polly and Daniel to themselves.

"I am still not happy about leaving you tomorrow, Daniel, and will ask Conrad to give you a call around lunchtime anyway."

"And I shall be talking with Fitz, so I won't really be spending too much time alone, Polly."

"I just wish that this business was all over, I worry about how much more punishment your body is taking. Our lives seem to be made up of fighting one battle after another with these people with no end in sight."

"There is an end in sight, Polly, we will get the evidence about the Red Hand operation, I am sure of that. They seem to trust you delivering their messages and sooner or later they will pass clear proof of their complicity with the Soviets. When that day comes, we will arrest those responsible and put them away for a long time. So believe me, Polly, the end is very much in our sights."

So Polly reluctantly agrees to return to her work on Tuesday, leaving Daniel in the apartment. Conrad assures her that he will call him at lunchtime to make sure all is well, as he escorts her to the Home Office. On arrival, she immediately goes into Mrs Wright's office to apologise for returning late.

"Not at all, Polly, an extra day is no matter. You will catch up, I am sure. Now off you go, you have a lot of work to do."

Polly begins her rounds in haste, and when arriving in Sally Nugent's department is stopped and questioned by her.

"Where on earth have you been these last two weeks, Polly?" She almost demands an answer.

"I've been on holiday, Sally, why do you ask?"

"We had work to be done, urgent work. Do you realise how much time we have lost?"

"What are you talking about? I simply had a holiday, that is all."

"And where did you go on this holiday that was so important?"

"I went home to my parents, now I must get on."

"Well please see that Percival gets this file as soon as possible."

"Yes of course, Sally, I will see that he gets it as soon as I have completed my collection."

So Polly has only been back at work for about an hour and she has files that need to be photographed for Daniel's department. In fact she will have more to photograph before the end of the day, as she is handed a file by Percival Smith's secretary.

Conrad escorts her back to the apartment and updates Daniel on the day's events.

"There have been some arrests, Daniel, but we are still waiting for definitive proof of the connection between Moscow and the Red Hand."

"Well I have these pictures for you, Conrad, so there may be something here."

"Thanks Polly, I'll get off now and pick you up in the morning. Bye for now, Daniel."

Polly tells Daniel of her day and Sally Nugent's questions about her holiday.

"I think she was miffed because I didn't tell her I was going on holiday, and she has no one else to deliver her messages. Now I will get us some dinner," says Polly, as she goes off to the kitchen.

After dinner, they both sit listening to music before going off to bed. Polly is tired from her first day back, and Daniel is tired also from his first full day out of bed. The following day, Conrad develops the film and realises they have at last got some real evidence of the Red Hand's connection to Moscow. Percival Smith and Sally Nugent are given instructions from a Valentina Sharopov, that they must carry out specific actions. Smith must secure assurances from the Permanent Secretary to press for strike legislation, and Sally Nugent must urge her union colleagues to mount a campaign of civil disobedience. She is asked to plan a detailed series of events that will coincide with the dockers calling for an all-out strike, giving Smith the ammunition to seek anti strike laws. She calls a union meeting and asks that the members carefully consider their positions with regard to the dockers. They must support their action with a campaign of disruption within government departments. Anything that can be done to cripple the machinery of government must be done.

Polly is apprehensive about her own position, seeing just how forceful Sally Nugent has become. It is obvious that the union members are confused about what should be done. Whilst they understand that the dockers have some reason for their actions, they do not see how any action they may take, given that they are not allowed to strike, can be of any help to them. This confusion will play into Sally Nugent's hands. She will be able to make all the suggestions she wants and lead union members how she pleases. She walks around for most of her day looking to encourage staff to slow down the government machine in any way they can. She urges them to take sick days and more cynically, damage telephones and other machines to interrupt communications between departments. Polly is aware of what is happening but tries not to let it keep her from her duties. However, she is becoming more concerned that Sally will find out about her work for the security services.

She lies beside Daniel on his bed and seeks his reassurance.

"My dear Polly, she knows nothing of your activities, and when and if she does it will be too late, she will be in prison. You must stop fretting over Sally Nugent. There is nothing that she can do to harm you, believe me," he says, putting his arm around her.

"You are right, Daniel. I shall stop thinking about her and get on with my work, nothing else matters now."

And so, apart from the union meeting, Polly's week has been uneventful, and she looks forward to the weekend. They are hoping to go for a walk round the Kensington Gardens on Saturday, after shopping. Daniel really wants some fresh air. Upon returning to the apartment, a worn out Daniel sits down while Polly checks his wound and applies a fresh dressing. Thankfully, it is continuing to heal satisfactorily.

"Do you think there will be arrests next week, Daniel? I am very concerned about Sally Nugent's behaviour. She becomes more agitated every day," Polly asks with some concern in her voice.

"She may be getting pressure from her Soviet masters, they must be desperate to see some sort of action taking place."

"I just want to see her and Smith put away. I will not feel safe while she is free to take whatever actions she sees fit."

They talk for a while about what may happen before Polly, too, goes off for her bath returning in her robe.

"We shall have to take another holiday when all this is done, Daniel, to make up for the one we never had," she says with a smile as she snuggles up to him on the settee.

"Now that sounds like a very good idea, that really is something to look forward to."

After making another cup of tea around ten o'clock, Polly and Daniel go off to bed early. Polly follows Daniel to his room, and climbs into bed beside him. No words are spoken, it just seems the natural thing to do. She turns off the light and turns toward him before going off into a sound sleep. Daniel lies there, pondering her comments whilst being very aware of her closeness.

He, too, hopes that they are able to make arrests very soon, if only to ease Polly's concern regarding Sally Nugent.

Daniel returns to work on Monday morning, anxious to catch up with events and resume the fight against the communist enemy.

"It's good to have you back Daniel, you gave us all a bit of a fright," says Fitz, clasping his hand.

"Good to be back, Fitz, I have some catching up to do. Tell me, what is the news with the dockers and management?"

"They have agreed another meeting. I am wondering whether the events that you were involved in has caused them any problems. There are still sporadic walkouts but that is all."

"Perhaps they are planning something, I need to speak with the dockers as soon as possible."

"Quentin is anxious to act on the information supplied last week from Polly's pictures. I believe he wants to have a public display of the arrests in the Home Office. He wanted you to be available if necessary, so now that you have returned, I expect him to move very quickly," says Fitz.

"Well please let me know when this is to take place, Fitz, so that Polly can be warned to stay out of the way. She is very concerned about the behaviour of Sally Nugent recently and will not want to be anywhere near her when any arrests take place."

"I believe they are to take place tomorrow, but I will ask Quentin to verify. And we need to make sure that Elizabeth Berkley will be released as soon as practical. I believe that you gave her some assurances. Initially, she will be arrested with the others, but I will see that she is released as soon as possible."

On Tuesday morning, police officers and MI5 agents enter the Home Office building at ten o'clock precisely, sealing all exits. They take away Percival Smith, Sally Nugent, Martin Frobisher, David Burroughs, Gordon Hastings, Roberta Phillips, and Elizabeth Berkley. Sally Nugent and Percival Smith protest at the actions of the police, the other members go quietly. There is a large press presence and some television reporters, as Quentin Blake makes a statement.

"After months of investigation and reconnaissance by members of the security forces and Scotland Yard detectives, we have, this morning, arrested several known members of the Communist Party engaged in subversive activities here in the Home Office. They will all be charged with conspiracy and subjected to the full force of the law in due course. That is all I have for you at the moment. There will be further statements when follow-up arrests are made."

And with that, Quentin Blake leaves the Home Office to return to MI5 headquarters at Millbank.

Polly goes into her office, closes the door, and breaks down with tears of relief. She is sitting reflecting when there is a knock on the door. She opens the door to two police officers and a man in plain clothes.

"Miss Polly Spencer, will you come with us please? We need to ask you some questions."

"Am I being arrested?"

"No, you are not being arrested, but you need to come with us please."

Polly goes to collect her bag, and unnoticed by the officers, quickly dials her code into the phone. She puts her undelivered files in the drawer and locks it before locking door to her office.

"I have to hand my key to Mrs Wright, please, so that she has access while I'm away."

Polly is detained with the arrests of members of the Red Hand and is terrified of the implications. Upon being told of Polly's attempt to contact him, Daniel discovers that she has been detained, and immediately contacts Fitz and Quentin Blake to help in getting her released. The police at Bow Street station, however, insist she must be processed and remain at Bow Street until processing is completed, and this is further complicated by the discovery of her pistol.

"Because of the seriousness of the charges against these people, the discovery of a firearm on one of them needs to be addressed," the police officer records.

Blake, Fitz, and Daniel travel to Bow Street to insist on her release, and Fitz calls on Commander Spratt at Scotland Yard to intervene, pointing out that Polly is Ben Spencer's daughter!

"I apologise for contacting you, Commander. My name is Fitzroy Jones of Special Ops, MI5. I was hoping you may be able to help me?"

Fitz then briefly outlines what has happened and how Polly has been detained with the agents of Red Hand.

"I will make some calls. I understand your concerns for Miss Spencer and hope we can resolve the situation speedily," replies the commander.

"Just how much longer do you intend processing Miss Spencer, sir?" asks Daniel, becoming annoyed at the delays.

"Miss Spencer could face serious charges, we are talking about conspiracy here."

"Good god man, are you stupid? It was the actions of Miss Spencer that brought the conspiracy to a head. Without her efforts no conspiracy would have been uncovered," says Daniel, becoming more and more agitated at the attitude of the officer.

"And I am sure her help will be taken into consideration by the courts."

Daniel leaps forward and has to be restrained by Fitz and Blake as he grabs the officer's tunic.

"You bloody fool, she is not responsible for any wrongdoing, quite the opposite. Now go and fetch me your chief inspector or I will get him myself, do you understand?"

By now Daniel is ready to take matters into his own hands. After further debate and argument, during which Fitz has to again restrain Daniel, the police finally release Polly into Daniel's custody. She dashes to his side, sobbing in relief at seeing him.

"It's ok Polly, let's get you home."

"Daniel, I was terrified that the police were going to charge me with the Red Hand agents, thank you for rescuing me. Thank you Fitz and you too, Mr Blake."

The chief inspector responsible for detaining Polly is warned of repercussions for his role in detaining a key member of the Civil Service, who was tasked with assisting the security services fight against communism.

'Believe me, sir, I will see to it you pay for your incompetence in this case," says Daniel as he leads Polly out of the police station.

Meanwhile, the members of the Red Hand organisation are charged and remanded in custody.

Sally Nugent and Smith are charged with conspiracy to bring down the democratically elected government and replace it with a communist-led republic. They are charged as Soviet agents reporting directly to their masters in Moscow, a known Russian agent being specifically named in a memo from Sally Nugent to Percival Smith. Marion Frobisher, David Burroughs, Gordon Hastings, Roberta Phillips, and Elizabeth Berkley are charged as members of the Communist Party, and with membership of an organisation seeking to bring down the government, namely Red Hand. The trial will be held at the Central Criminal Court, and further arrests of those involved in the conspiracy, are expected.

Daniel returns to the apartment with a tearful Polly, still angry at her treatment by the police.

"I will personally see that the officer concerned will be disciplined for his behaviour towards you, Polly."

"I am just so happy to be home, Daniel, so please calm down." Polly goes off to make some tea, and suggests they go out and have some lunch before returning to work.

"Ok Polly, we still have a lot to do, and the sooner we start the better."

Daniel looks at his watch, it is just one o'clock. They both return to their work after their lunch, where Fitz and Quentin are waiting to talk with Daniel.

"Is Polly ok now, Daniel? It must have been rather upsetting for her."

"Yes, she is fine thank you, Fitz, though I want that police officer dealt with; his actions were unprofessional towards her and I want that fact duly noted." Daniel is still angry at what happened, as Fitz notices.

"I will see to that, Daniel. You have my word. Now Quentin is anxious that we push on to see what links the Red Hand may have with the communists causing trouble at the docks. We need some names that we can question as soon as possible. Government is becoming concerned about the possibility of shortages because of shipments held up in the docks. We have the evidence secured by Polly, from Sally Nugent to Smith, advocating that civil war should be an option in order to achieve communist domination in the country and the Empire. What we now need is evidence of the communists' intervention in union actions to close the ports and precipitate strikes and riots of union members."

"What about Conrad and I taking another look inside Communist H.Q.?"

"It's a consideration, Daniel, but this time you must get in and out without their knowledge."

"I suggest that we go in on a Sunday evening. There is a chance that the building may be empty at that time."

"Well speak with Conrad and do as you see fit," Fitz replies.

"We need some definite evidence that the Soviets are driving this unrest and using the docks as their main campaign area. Do what you can, Daniel," Quentin Blake adds.

Daniel meets with Conrad and Paul Horsley to organise a visit to the Communist H.Q. as soon as possible. Paul Horsley, an expert in covert operations, suggests that they look at a map of the layout, and when they enter, first check that the building is empty before they begin looking at any files. They do not want another confrontation, nor do they want the occupants to know of their visit this time.

"I will give you some listening devices which you can place on doorways to detect if anyone is inside, and listen to their conversations if necessary. Also, I have been experimenting with some glasses which will give you excellent vision in almost complete darkness. They should be useful. Finally, these miniature headphones can be used to listen to the tumblers on a safe lock. There must be something useful to look at in their safe. And don't forget your miniature cameras."

"Thanks for the help, Paul, all of these items will be very useful to us. Conrad and I hope to make the visit this Sunday. The sooner the better," says Daniel.

"I will have your equipment ready for you by lunchtime Friday."

Conrad and Daniel sit and discuss what they have to do, realising that they will not have another chance if anything goes wrong.

"If anything goes wrong, we might not be around for another chance!"

"We will plan our operation on Friday afternoon, when we have had chance to check the equipment. Tomorrow, we will see if there is any news from the dockers' dispute. See you in the morning, Conrad."

Polly is a little apprehensive on returning to work and knocks on Mrs Wright's door, unsure of what to expect.

"My dear Polly, please come in and sit down. I was annoyed that the police found it necessary to take you away with Sally Nugent and her colleagues. There was absolutely no need for that. Now that the communists have been removed, I can tell you that Beatrice Carrington had made me aware of your activities on behalf of the security services, and I know she will want me to congratulate you on your work."

Polly sits listening to her, dumbfounded at what she is hearing. Mrs Wright has been aware all along of her activities. She would never have guessed.

"Thank you, Mrs Wright, I had no idea."

"Beatrice was reluctant for you to be put into such a dangerous position without some way out if you were discovered. I would have been your way out. Only Beatrice and I were aware of this arrangement. That way, it was hoped that we could give you the best cover possible. Your work was too important to be put at risk. Fortunately, you managed to overcome any problems as they arose, and your handling of Smith's indiscretion towards you was admirable. Anyway, your job from now onwards should be more routine, Polly, so I will leave you to get on," she says as she hands Polly her office keys.

"Thank you Mrs Wright, and thank you for watching over me."

Polly goes off to her office, thinking over what has just been said. She spends the rest of the day going about her business, and is pleased to note that there is a much better air about the offices. Staff are chatting more openly and there are no longer suspicious eyes following her everywhere. At the end of the day, she goes home with Daniel, telling him of Mrs Wright's comments about her position.

"Beatrice Carrington is indeed very special, Polly. She wanted to be absolutely sure that you were safe. I must thank her when I next speak to her."

They sit down for dinner, and Daniel mentions the visit planned for Sunday evening to the Communist H.Q. Polly is horrified that he should again put himself in danger so soon after what happened at her parents' home.

"Do you really have to do this, Daniel? You were injured the last time, and your latest wound has barely healed."

"We have some special equipment to help us move about easier, and we hope to crack the safe this time. If we can get evidence of the communists receiving instructions direct from Moscow, our work will be done."

"Well I just hope that you will be done with any more dangerous assignments after this one, Daniel. You are too precious to me for anything else to happen to you," Polly replies with concern in her voice.

"Now, can you speak with Penny tomorrow and invite her round to the apartment on Sunday?"

"Yes, ok. It will be good to have a natter, I know she will want to know why I was arrested."

"Yes of course, I had forgotten about that, Polly, we shall have to think of some excuse relating to your position. I suppose that your liaising with members of Red Hand during your work might be seen as suspicious."

"Ok Daniel, I will say that I was questioned because I speak with them most days, but the police were satisfied that making contact with them is part of my job."

The following day Polly asks her friend Penny Carstairs if she would like to visit her on Sunday evening, and Penny is delighted. More than anything, she will ask questions about her and Daniel, which will amuse Polly. Daniel, meanwhile, is informed that there will be no court trial of the men who abducted him and Polly from outside the apartment. The only two men that the police were able to apprehend, were the two shot by Daniel.

They were both Russian nationals, Alexei Malakhov and Boris Lazaroff, and will be expelled back to Russia at the earliest opportunity. Daniel is obviously relieved at not having to put Polly through yet another ordeal in court.

"The security services believe that there would be no benefit in having a trial, and were concerned at putting you and Polly in the public eye with Russians in the dock. They will be punished enough for failing their mission here."

"I am delighted, Fitz, it means that Polly does not have to go through another trial."

When Polly hears the news she is also pleased, while appreciating that there may be others, as well as the conspiracy trial at the Old Bailey.

"Any way that can reduce the number of times we have to go to court will always be welcome by me Daniel, it is always upsetting to see the men responsible for harming you and insulting me. I know that there are two more potential trials, one relating to the men that broke into the apartment, and one regarding the men that attacked us at home."

"I do not look forward to them, but realise that we have to have a trial to put away the men responsible. Anyway, I spoke with Penny and she will be delighted to visit us on Sunday."

"That's good Polly, I expect we shall enter the HQ around eight o'clock so will be back here by ten."

Polly is worried about Daniel's return to the Communist H.Q. and just hopes that he and Conrad come to no harm. What they are doing is extremely dangerous, but Daniel has to find the evidence to stop the Russian connection once and for always, so the risk is worth it in his mind.

He collects the equipment from Phil Horsley on Friday, and asks Conrad to call for him around seven o'clock on Sunday evening. Daniel and Polly enjoy their weekend together, as they always do, but they are both aware of what has to happen on Sunday evening. Daniel does his utmost to make certain that Polly does not dwell too much on what he has to do.

"It will all be over in no time at all, Polly. You will enjoy your evening with Penny, and I will return safe and sound, I promise."

"I am sure you are right, but I can't help but worry," says Polly, curling up beside him after taking her bath. They did not go out on the Saturday as they both wanted to spend the evening together with their thoughts. Daniel contemplating the dangers of going back to the Communist H.Q. and Polly worrying over what happened the last time he went. Polly finally falls asleep, so Daniel carefully lifts her from the settee and carries her to her room. He places her in her bed, and kisses her on her forehead before leaving the room.

They decide to go out for Sunday lunch, and enjoy the rest of the afternoon together. Penny arrives just after six, and Conrad calls for Daniel around 7.30. Daniel is relieved to get away from Penny's questions relating to Polly. He has his difficulties at times with one eighteen-year-old, handling two is beyond his comprehension!

"We'll see you later, Penny," Daniel says, as he and Conrad make for the door, followed by Polly.

"Please be careful and come back safely," Polly whispers to him as she kisses him on his cheek.

Daniel had prepared all his equipment before Penny arrived and had two weapons concealed about his person. He also has the listening devices and the night glasses, and stuffed in his inside pocket is a balaclava.

"Here we go again, Conrad. I suggest we make for the safe as soon as we have checked the upstairs rooms for any occupants. If it has what we need we may not have to look any further."

The taxi drops them off at Covent Garden, and they enter the building exactly as before, by a rear unlocked window. They put on their balaclavas and night vision glasses, which prove to be very effective, allowing them to see reasonably well in the inky black darkness.

They climb the stairs to check on each room for any signs of occupants. No one is in the building, they are completely alone. Daniel leads the way back down the stairs to the front office where they saw the safe on their previous visit. Conrad remains at the door while Daniel attempts to open the safe. After several attempts he still hasn't been able to open it, when he realises that he may have to move the dial right and left to secure the combination to open it. Sure enough, the first time he tries, the tumblers make a different sound, and after about twenty attempts he hears the distinctive sound of the lock opening. He tries the handle, which moves freely and the safe door opens. Daniel removes a bunch of files and looks at the wording on the covers.

"The British Empire, how it can be controlled. Ground strategy to break down law and order. The Trade Union Movement and its weaknesses. Red Hand operation in the Civil Service."

Daniel quickly photographs each page without reading them, although he does notice a number of names. The information is very detailed; it is obvious that there are long-term plans detailed in the files. Daniel decides to glance at the one titled, 'Red Hand operation in the Civil Service', and notices Sally Nugent and Percival Smith mentioned by name and details of their 'handlers'.

This is what he has been looking for, definite proof of Soviet interference in the activities of the Civil Service.

"How's it coming along, Daniel? We should be getting out soon, if not sooner."

Daniel carefully replaces all the contents of the files and places them back in the safe before closing and locking the door.

"Let's get out of here," says Daniel, as they move silently to the back of the building and out via the unlocked window, before carefully replacing it as they found it. Covent Garden is bustling with people so they easily merge in with those around them. They make their way back to King Street and walk towards Duke Street where they hail a cab. Daniel looks at his watch. It is just after 9.15pm.

"I believe that was a job well done, Conrad, even if I do say so myself. We have some damning evidence here, so you may as well take it ready for the morning."

The cab drops Daniel at his apartment and takes Conrad home.

"Daniel, you're back," says Polly, realising that Penny will have noticed her show of affection towards him.

"I hope you two had a good evening, would you like some tea, Penny, before I get you a taxi?"

"Thank you, Daniel."

"We were talking about all the excitement in the week, Daniel. I have never seen so many policeman, and inside the Home Office building, I wonder what will happen to those people they took away."

"If they are found guilty, they will be punished, I imagine that is what will happen."

"Did you and Conrad have a good evening, Daniel?"

"Yes we did, Polly, we had a really good evening," Daniel replies with a smile.

After Penny has left, Daniel outlines their findings from the visit to Communist H.Q.

"That sounds fantastic, Daniel. I am so relieved that it went well and you and Conrad are safe. I will make you a sandwich and then I will go and have a bath."

Daniel sits eating his sandwich, reflecting on a job well done. The coming week will be a flagstone in the investigation against the Soviets. Who knows, once this evidence is presented and the conspiracy trial completed, perhaps the Traffic Light Syndrome will move to amber?

"Daniel, can I be with you for this evening? I am so relieved that all went well, I just want to sleep by your side, do you understand? Sometimes I just have to be near you."

"I understand, Polly, and is there any point in my making a protest at all?"

"No point at all, Daniel," says Polly as she hugs him.

They finally go off to Daniel's bed and Polly goes off to a blissful sleep in his arms. Daniel lies there, adrenalin still pumping from the evening's events at Communist H.Q. When he does finally relax, he decides that he will wait no longer to ask Polly formally to marry him.

Monday morning sees Conrad develop the photographs from the Communist H.Q., and the findings are sensational. There are names and dates relating to the strategies in place to exploit the trade unions and create civil disorder, use of the Civil Service to insert a Red Hand member into government, and to continue to make strides into the colonies with a view to ultimate control.

All the information will eventually be passed on to the security services, MI5, so that it can be used in the conspiracy trial. But before that, Fitz instructs Daniel to utilise the information immediately to stop further escalation of problems in the docks. He will pass on the information he has secured to Hennessey, and arrange a meeting with his colleagues. They must make contact with the union and inform them of communist interference. Meanwhile MI5 will make some arrests. As far as the conspiracy to infiltrate government, Daniel will watch the agents concerned until they can be detained pending the trial. This is key for Daniel, since it is the Red Hand that have sought to involve Polly, and he wants to be sure that they do not implicate her in any way.

"I will speak with the Prosecution Service, Daniel, and ask them when they would prefer those concerned to be detained for questioning. Meantime, if you see any signs that they may be leaving the country, you must stop them," says Fitz.

"There are two names that are mentioned with regard to meetings with Sally Nugent and Percival Smith. They are Sergey Sokolov and Mikhail Litvin. I will put a twenty-four hour watch on them until the security services take over. Can you liaise with Quentin Blake, and ask him to inform you as soon as he is ready to act, please, Fitz?"

"I will talk to him this morning, Daniel. Now how soon can you meet these union men? The government is getting very concerned at what is happening in the docks; there are stoppages every day, and the effects are starting to show with some food shortages already."

"I will call Peter Hennessey this evening to arrange a meet."

Polly's days at work are now becoming more settled and organised. She is no longer bothered by any Red Hand members, and for the moment, the union members are happy to leave things as they are. No one, other than Polly, really knows why the arrests took place and no one seems to be too concerned. She is relieved to see Elizabeth Berkley back at her desk, and suggests they have lunch in the canteen. Elizabeth is one of those people that no one seems to notice, and no one did notice that she was missing for a few days.

"How are you, Elizabeth? I am so glad that you are back with us."

"I am very well, Polly, and relieved that I was released so quickly. Please thank those responsible for me."

"Do you intend to stay in the service, or would you prefer to move on to something else?"

"I have always enjoyed my work, Polly, and I hope I can stay in my job until retirement. Now that Red Hand has been broken up I want to be able to do my job without being afraid any more. You have no idea how that makes me feel."

"Well I am pleased for you, Elizabeth, and I am sure that your help will not go unnoticed. Meantime, you and I will remain good friends."

"Thank you, Polly. I will always remember your kindness towards me and hope we will always be good friends."

Polly enjoys the rest of her working day, unaware that she is soon to receive the most exciting news of her life.

"Did you have a good day, Daniel? What did you discover from your visit last evening?"

"We have all the information we need to prove that Soviet agents have been planning to infiltrate government and create civil unrest in the country to further their aims," Daniel replies as they enter the apartment.

"That's wonderful news, does that mean that we shall be able to live some sort of normal life sooner rather than later?"

"Once the conspiracy trial has been concluded, I hope that the Soviet menace will be at an end at least for the foreseeable future. But before that trial, you and I have two further Crown Court appearances. But things are looking a lot better than they were a week or so ago, Polly. And because our circumstances seem to have improved, there is something I want to ask you."

"You sound very serious, Daniel. I do hope you have not been keeping some bad news until last."

"Not bad news, Polly, but most definitely good news I hope."

CHAPTER 10

"I hope this does not come as too much of a surprise, Polly, but I want us to get married."

Polly stares at Daniel, open-mouthed, speechless, and almost in a state of shock. Daniel's comment has completely surprised her. She has always known that they would get married some day and there is no doubting their love for each other, but she just did not expect Daniel to ask her at this time.

"Yes, yes, yes, Daniel, I want us to get married too. I'm a bit puzzled by your timing though!" she says through her tears.

"I just don't want to wait any longer for you to be my wife, Polly. However, we have to keep our marriage a secret until after the conspiracy trial at least."

"Anything, Daniel, I don't care about anyone else knowing, I will know and that's all that matters," says Polly as she jumps on Daniel's lap and hugs him while planting kisses on his cheeks.

She is ecstatic over what he has said, realising that her dream will soon come true. Polly has loved this man since she was a schoolgirl, and he has cared for her, protected her against all adversities, and has grown to love her in the process.

"When can we marry, Daniel? How soon can we be man and wife?"

"I am hoping Friday, Polly, at Kensington Registry Office. I will ask Conrad to be my best man and witness. No one else will know, not even your parents. Whilst there is still a risk of reprisals towards you and myself, I cannot risk anyone taking advantage of you as my wife. So, for the time being my dear Polly, to everyone you will still be Miss Spencer. But, when we are alone you will be Mrs Bottomley."

"I shall especially enjoy being Mrs Bottomley, Daniel. Can we go somewhere for the weekend? It is a long weekend so we will have an extra day to ourselves."

"I will find us somewhere not too far away, close to town so that you can have a look at your favourite shops."

"I am so happy, Daniel, I could scream," says Polly, as she goes off to have a bath.

The rest of the week will drag for both of them, but with so much to look forward to they put all of their efforts into their work. Daniel contacts Hennessey and asks if can set up a meeting with Liam Cassidy and Jimmy Rush as soon as possible. They meet up on the Wednesday along with Polly, and Daniel tells them that he has definite proof of communist interference in their union activities and that it is being organised from Moscow. This revelation shocks them.

"You saying that commies from Russia are organising the strikes?"

"That's exactly what I am saying, Liam, and it is their intention to infiltrate the TUC and influence policy. Once they have agents on your TUC Council, they will have all the power they need to manipulate policy decisions and organise disruption."

"What do you want from us, Daniel? We want to help."

"Find out whether Michael Doyle is in league with them. Does he know that the actions are being driven by outside agents? If you think that he does not know of the interference from Moscow, then contact me again. Do not tell him about me yet, that may cause me a problem, I have to be sure that he wants to make a difference and rid the union if the Soviet interference."

Daniel and Polly leave the three union men, Daniel hoping that they can arrange a meeting with Doyle, when he can introduce himself officially.

"Do you think they believed you, Daniel?"

"I hope so, I need them to convince Michael Doyle to meet with me, and if they are not convinced they will not be able to convince him."

As soon as an opportunity arises, Daniel tells Conrad that he and Polly are to get married.

"That is the most wonderful news, Daniel. I am so happy for you both, and honoured to be your best man. No two people are better suited to each other, and rest assured your secret will be safe with me."

On Thursday, both Polly and Daniel request Friday as a holiday, which is readily granted. Then on Friday morning, they visit a jeweller in Chelsea to get their rings, before going into town for Polly to buy her wedding suit.

Then, at four o'clock on Friday August 22nd, Daniel and Polly are married at Kensington Registry Office with Conrad as the best man to witness the occasion.

They share a glass of champagne with Conrad before making their way to the hotel in Bayswater that Daniel had managed to arrange at short notice. After registering as Mr and Mrs Bottomley, they go for a walk in Hyde Park before dinner.

"This is the very best day of my life, Daniel. I have dreamed many times of being your wife, and now I am Mrs Bottomley at last."

"I believe that has always been my dream too, Polly, and you and I will continue to be a formidable team as man and wife."

"Do you think anyone might notice a difference in our behaviour, Daniel? I know I shall be glowing from now on, really I will," says Polly, holding his arm tightly.

"It will be difficult, I know, but my concern is for your safety. There are still people who want to destroy our happiness, so let's not give them an incentive by revealing our marriage to anyone."

"There are so many things that I want to do for you, Daniel, now that I am your wife. When everything is settled, I would like us to have a house, somewhere in the country perhaps."

"That will be something to look forward to," Daniel replies with a smile.

They walk for another half hour or so in the sunshine before returning to the hotel for dinner.

They laugh and smile through dinner, oblivious to all around them with eyes only for each other.

Finally, they retire to their room and embrace for a few moments, soaking up their closeness.

"Go and clean your teeth or something Daniel, while I get ready," says Polly, pushing Daniel toward the bathroom. Daniel goes off to the bathroom and returns a few moments later to find Polly in their bed. He quickly undresses and joins her.

"Hold me, Daniel, and make love to me."

She is warm to his touch as Daniel embraces her, kissing her firmly on her lips. He caresses her breasts as his hand wanders down her body before gently pushing his fingers inside her. Polly moans and strokes him gently before guiding him inside to complete their union. They stay coupled for some time, Polly moving her body about beneath him to make the union more pleasurable. Daniel is a big man in every respect and Polly revels in his firmness.

"Stay inside me Daniel, I want to feel you inside me," she says as she clasps her legs around him. Daniel stays inside her for as long as he can before they both climax with each other's pleasure.

As expected, they sleep rather late on Saturday, Daniel waking first, enjoying the touch of Polly's body beside him. She eventually opens her eyes, seeing Daniel beside her.

"Good morning Mrs Bottomley, may I say how beautiful you look this morning."

"Thank you Mr Bottomley," she says, as she wraps herself around him seeking another union, to which he readily obliges. They stay entwined for what seems forever, their lovemaking intense and blissful to both of them.

"I love you Daniel. I love you so much," she says as she thrusts her body upwards. They stay joined with each other, thrusting in unison, their bodies moving as one. Polly has waited so long for these moments and makes sure she gets all the pleasure their lovemaking can give. After one final thrust and gasp from each of them, Daniel moves away from her and lies by her side. And there they both lie, reliving the moments of their first night together.

"Come along Daniel, I want to do some shopping today, but first I will order some breakfast."

Daniel and Polly delight in each other's company for the next three days. Their lovemaking is long and passionate, each exploring how they can pleasure the other.

As they enter the apartment on Monday afternoon around five o'clock, Polly asks the question, "Daniel, do you think we might buy ourselves a new bed? It would be nice to begin our time together in a new bed, don't you think? After all, we will be spending some time in it," she says, smiling mischievously.

"Of course, Polly, but for now I'm sure we shall manage," says Daniel, as he lifts Polly in his arms and carries her to his room, where they swiftly disrobe before enjoying each other again. Their lovemaking is intense and they remain entwined for some time before falling asleep in each other's arms.

Tuesday morning arrives too soon for both Daniel and Polly. They have to adjust to being who they were last Thursday, before they were married. So that they will be constantly reminded, they hang their wedding rings on gold chains around their necks. Polly has a positive skip in her step as she goes about her business, and Daniel finds it difficult to concentrate. However, he is brought down to earth by Fitz asking if he has any information about the unions.

"I am waiting to hear from Hennessey, Fitz. I have asked the two dockers to sound out Michael Doyle regarding direct interference from Moscow. If I can convince Doyle, the dockers will turn against any direct Soviet interference from Moscow."

"Keep at it Daniel, we must put the final pieces in the jigsaw for when we present the conspiracy trial."

Daniel and Polly need time off for the trial of the four intruders to the apartment, which is scheduled to commence Monday next, September 1st. Polly outlines the details to Mrs Wright.

"I don't expect it will last all week, Mrs Wright, but I will keep you informed. I just want to see these men punished for what they did to Daniel and myself. And there will be another trial coming along as well. You may recall, I asked for an extra day off when I had my holiday after the last trial of the men that attacked Daniel and I on the train?"

"Yes, I remember you mentioning something about family business?"

"Yes, well I wasn't telling you the whole story, it wasn't family business as such. My parents' house was broken into by five men who tried to kill Daniel and abduct me!"

"Good god, Polly, I had no idea of the danger you are exposed to with Daniel," says Mrs Wright, clearly surprised at Polly's revelations.

"Daniel was shot and seriously wounded in the attack, and we weren't able to travel back to London until the Monday, hence my extra day, and I do apologise for having to deceive you."

"I fully understand, Polly, and I hope it goes well next week."

Daniel was hoping to have heard from Hennessey before the start of the trial, but that has not happened. He asks Fitz to keep him informed while he is out of the office.

"As soon as Hennessey makes contact, I will contact you."

On Saturday, the new bed arrives, much to the delight of Polly.

"It's beautiful, Daniel, I really can't wait to try it for size!"

"Well I think we should do that as soon as possible, in case there is any flaws in it," he replies as he begins to undress Polly. The bed is thoroughly tested, throughout a wonderful weekend, by the two of them, and they are both more than satisfied with its performance.

The trial of the four men accused of entering Daniel's apartment is not expected to take too long. The evidence is overwhelming and the defence is offering no evidence.

Frederick Marston, Paul Jeffries, Joe Butler, and George Baker are jointly charged with breaking and entering the apartment. They are also accused of grievous bodily harm to both Daniel Bottomley and Miss Polly Spencer. They are further charged with violent indecent assault on Miss Polly Spencer.

"The evidence you will hear relating to the accused is beyond dispute. You will have to decide what level of punishment is appropriate for their actions," the Crown argues in his opening statement.

"What you may also have to consider is who initiated these attacks, since it is patently obvious that they were well planned, and I do not believe those accused capable of planning such attacks. Mr Bottomley's work with the security services may very well have a bearing on what happened, although quite why Miss Spencer was so badly treated may warrant further investigation. I will begin the prosecution by calling on Mr Bottomley."

The Crown begins by asking Daniel to describe the events of the evening in question. Daniel outlines how he and Polly arrived at the apartment to find four men inside pointing guns at them as they entered the lounge area.

"Firstly, in answer to your comment about who may be responsible for this, I believe these men to be Communist Party members, since they implied that I had broken into their H.Q. and stolen information. Only party members would have knowledge of any break-ins at their H.Q."

"Thank you for that, Mr Bottomley. Please continue to tell the court what happened that evening."

"The intruders tied me to a chair and gave me a bit of a beating to try and get information from me. They kept asking what information I had about the Communist Party from my alleged visit to their H.Q. I told them that I had not been to their H.Q. so was unable to give them any information. They did not believe me and continued with their beating. They had taken Polly into her bedroom, threatening to harm her if I did not cooperate. Fortunately, they paused for a moment, and while they were looking away from me I rushed at them, knocking them to the floor against the wall. The noise must have been heard in Polly's room and her two attackers came into the sitting room, obviously wondering what all the noise was about."

"Please go on, Mr Bottomley."

"Miss Spencer, who must have been very distressed from her appearance, bravely came to my rescue. She followed them into the sitting room and shot two of them to save me from any more punishment. Without her intervention they would most certainly given me another beating. She then ordered one of the men to untie me and I secured the two uninjured men. Miss Spencer then called for the police."

"You mentioned the evidence relating to the Communist Party, Mr Bottomley, would you care to elaborate on that comment please?"

"The fact that the men talked about me allegedly entering the Communist Party H.Q. leads me to believe they were sent to punish me for that alleged break-in. There is no evidence to support their accusations that I was responsible, but they were looking for someone to blame."

"It is true, is it not, Mr Bottomley, that your work involves investigating communist activities?"

"It is no secret that the communists pose a very real threat to many western nations, and have done for some time. We have to remain on our guard against this threat, and part of my job is to investigate evidence presented to me by the security services. So yes, it is true."

"Are you saying that you work for MI5, Mr Bottomley?" the judge asks.

"No sir, I do not work for MI5. I am a lowly Civil Servant investigating any leads which are passed to me by the police and the security services, and handing my reports to my boss. That is all."

"Yes, well thank you for your evidence, Mr Bottomley," the Crown concludes, before calling Polly to give evidence.

"You are Miss Polly Spencer and you live with Mr Bottomley. Is that correct?"

"Yes sir, Mr Bottomley, my appointed guardian. My parents decided it would be a good idea for me to have someone to stay with when I secured my position in the Home Office. My family have known Daniel for more than five years and we all trust him completely."

"Yes, thank you for that, Miss Spencer. Now will you tell the court what happened on the night in question please?"

"Daniel and I arrived from work to find four men inside his apartment, pointing guns at us. After some discussion, when they mentioned a break-in at Communist H.Q. and Daniel's discussions with trade unionists, they tied Daniel to a chair and took me into my bedroom. As soon as they had me in my room, they forced me to strip down to my underwear and questioned me about my position at the Home Office. They seem to believe that I had some sort of secretive position, which is nonsense, and were convinced that I was not telling them the truth. They manhandled me before slapping my face. They ripped off most of my blouse, one of them grabbing at my breasts, all the time shouting at me to tell them what my job was. Whilst one held me by my shoulders the other one hit me several times, and then tore off my skirt and grabbed and squeezed me between my legs. They were behaving like beasts…"

Polly cannot stop herself from sobbing uncontrollably, recalling her ordeal in all its detail.

"Miss Spencer, would you like a break?" enquires the judge.

"No thank you, sir, I would prefer to carry on and finish."

"Please continue, Miss Spencer."

"The man touching me pushed me back into the chair and hit me several times in the stomach. It was very painful and I screamed out. They then picked me up and dropped me onto my bed. I was terrified what they were going to do to me as they moved towards me, leering. I closed my eyes, fearful of what might happen next, then there was a loud noise from the sitting room where they were holding Daniel. The two men dashed from my room, giving me the opportunity to grab my pistol from my dresser. I dashed after them and shot the two that were beating on Daniel."

"Miss Spencer, are you saying that you keep a pistol in your bedroom?" the judge asks.

"I carry it with me at all times, Your Honour. Daniel and I have been subjected to a number of attacks over the past few months, and it was decided I needed it for my own protection," Polly replies to the judge, who listens with a surprised look on his face.

"My lord, there have been two trials concerning attacks on Miss Spencer and Mr Bottomley. Would Your Lordship like transcripts?"

"Yes I would. Please continue, Miss Spencer."

"It was as Daniel has testified, after restraining the two uninjured men, I called for the police, who arrived shortly afterwards."

"We have heard of the beating that Mr Bottomley suffered, can you tell the court about your injuries, Miss Spencer, please?"

"I had bruising around my neck and face, and suffered heavy bruising and pinch marks to my stomach and thighs. I had to go back to hospital a second time after becoming unwell and was told that I had a burst blood vessel in my lower abdomen as a result of being punched."

"And have you fully recovered from your injuries?" the Crown asks.

"Yes thank you, sir."

"Very well Miss Spencer, you may step down. We shall adjourn for lunch and I will hear the police and medical evidence after lunch," the judge concludes.

The rest of the day is taken up with the police evidence and with medical details of the injuries inflicted on Polly and Daniel. The following morning the Crown presents his summary to the jury, followed by the judge's summation.

"This trial has been short in delivery, since there is no doubting the guilt of the accused. There is an uncomfortable undertone attached to what has happened, which in time may affect us all, namely communist intrusions into our society. However, we are not here to discuss the Communist Party, rather to discuss the intrusion into Mr Bottomley's apartment, and the brutal assaults on him and Miss Spencer. There was obviously no robbery intended, since you four waited for Mr Bottomley and Miss Spencer to arrive. You intentions were solely to inflict harm on them in pursuit of information. The fact that you mentioned the Communist Party H.Q. is of no matter. We are not here to prove or disprove what might have gone on there, or who may have participated in what might have gone on. What is beyond dispute is that you four men carried out prolonged and brutal assaults. That you chose to be especially callous toward a young woman is contemptible, and could have long-term effects on her. Whilst I would not usually condone the use of firearms, I believe in this case that it was a justifiable response to what was a terrifying attack. In fact, it is not unreasonable to conclude that had Miss Spencer not used her firearm, she would have most certainly been inflicted to a more serious sexual assault and Mr Bottomley to a more severe beating. My recommendation to the jury is that you find all four accused guilty of the charges. Will you please now retire to consider your verdicts?"

The jury members file out of the courtroom as the accused are led away to the cell to await the verdict. Polly and Daniel go off for some lunch, Polly still upset about having to relive the events of that evening as Daniel tries to offer her comfort.

"I don't expect the jury will take too long with this one, Polly. The evidence was pretty conclusive. I was watching their responses when you were giving your evidence. It was obvious that they were disgusted by the behaviour of the accused."

"It was upsetting having to go through what has happened to us, but I know it is the only way to put these people away. I hope they rot away their whole lives in prison."

After about an hour, the Crown barrister tells them that the jury has reached a verdict and as expected, the jury find all four men guilty of all the charges.

"Frederick Marston, Paul Jeffries, Joe Butler, and George Baker you have been found guilty of the charges brought against you by this court," the judge begins.

"On the charge of breaking and entering the apartment of Mr Bottomley, you will each serve three years. On the charge of grievous bodily harm against Mr Bottomley and Miss Spencer, you will each serve seven years in prison, and on the charge of violent indecent assault on Miss Spencer, you will each serve a further seven years in prison. The sentences will run consecutively. Officers, take them away. The court is now adjourned," the judge concludes.

Polly and Daniel return to the apartment and Polly holds onto him, so relieved that the trial is over.

"Hold me Daniel, I just want you to hold me for a moment. I know we have lots to do but I just need a moment."

"We have as long as you like, my dear Polly."

However, after a few short moments they both decide to inform their offices that they will be returning to work tomorrow, Thursday, and Daniel is delighted to hear that Hennessey has left a message.

"Hello Daniel, Doyle has agreed to meet with you, and he and I will see you in the Lamb and Flag Thursday at 7.00pm. Please do not bring along the young woman this time."

"This could be just what we have been waiting for, Fitz. If Doyle is happy to meet it must be a good sign, providing the message that was portrayed to him explained fully the communist plot."

"It might be an idea if Conrad is close by just in case Doyle is followed. He doesn't have to sit in at the meeting."

"Very well, Fitz. Doyle's colleagues will follow him, in which case I may need some help."

Daniel puts down the phone and turns to Polly with a smile on his face.

"Do you think that you will be able to spend some time with Penny tomorrow evening without her guessing that you are now Mrs Bottomley?"

"I will be most discreet, Daniel. I quite like the idea of no one knowing, it means I have you all to myself." She smiles, hugging Daniel and embracing him. She has just bathed and is seated beside him wearing just her robe. Daniel is quickly aroused by her closeness to him and their embrace becomes more passionate. He slowly opens her gown and fondles her breasts before carrying her through to their bedroom. She slips off her robe and Daniel gasps at her beautiful body. As he gets in beside her Polly reaches down between his legs and pleasures him, stroking him gently at first before becoming more forceful. After enjoying exploring each other's bodies for a while, Polly slips beneath him, giving a sigh of relief as she feels his firmness inside her.

"I love you so much, Daniel," she says, as she clasps her legs around him.

"I love you too, my dear Polly," he replies, as they both enjoy each other before lying side by side holding hands.

The following morning Polly invites her friend round for the evening, and Penny is delighted. They have become close friends working together and share common interests. And of course, it will give Penny the chance to ask Polly all sorts of questions about Daniel, again!

Daniel arranges with Conrad to go to Covent Garden that evening.

"I will call around 6.30pm, Daniel, and will stay outside of the pub to keep an eye on things."

"I'm not really sure how this evening will pan out so it will be good to have backup, Conrad. If Doyle is genuine in wanting to rid the union of Soviet interference, there could be members that do not trust him and may follow him to our meeting."

Daniel is unsure of how Doyle will react when he meets him in this new role and not as a journalist. He will be annoyed at being deceived, that is certain, but hopefully will understand the reasons behind the deception.

Conrad duly arrives at Daniel's apartment just before 6.30pm, and becomes the focus of Penny's attention. He has always been a bit of a ladies' man, enjoying the company of many over the years that Daniel has known him.

"Hello Polly, and you are Penny I presume. I'm delighted to meet you. Perhaps we can get together some time when you are not busy?"

"Thank you Conrad, I would like that very much," replies Penny, blushing at Conrad's directness.

"Come along Daniel, let's not keep your colleagues waiting. Bye ladies."

They make their way to Covent Garden by taxi, stopping about 100 yards from the Lamb and Flag. Daniel walks ahead as Conrad hangs back, looking for any suspicious characters outside the pub. It appears all clear as he watches Daniel enter. Daniel spots Doyle and Hennessey at the end of the bar and walks towards them.

"Mr Bottomley, why are you here? Nothing was said about any press."

"I am not press, Michael, I am the person who asked Peter to bring you to this meeting."

"What do you mean you're not press? You told me you were a reporter, what the hell is going on?" says Doyle, looking round anxiously.

"Michael, I had to find out what your feelings were towards what is happening before I could give you proof of the Soviets' interference in your union affairs."

"I am well aware of the communist position within my union, Mr Bottomley. We want a fair share for our members in return for our services, nothing else. We are not interested in what the Soviets want, we are in control," Doyle says indignantly.

'Are you sure about that, Michael? I can give you clear evidence that the Soviets intend to infiltrate the union at the highest level, the TUC and seek to put forward their own agenda. They have no interest in workers' rights, they seek only to enforce their ideals. They want to precipitate unrest through all out strikes, and take advantage of the chaos that follows. Once they succeed in breaking down law and order they want to propose a totalitarian state run by Moscow, where the state recognises no limits to its authority and seeks to control every aspect of public and private life. Confrontation not negotiation is what the Soviets practise, Michael."

Doyle looks stunned at Daniel, who orders some beers and ushers him and Peter Hennessey to a side table. He brings over the drinks and sits down.

"How do you know all this, Mr Bottomley? Who are you exactly, are you working for MI5?"

"No I do not work for MI5, Michael. I have a specific job trying to stop the Soviets from achieving their aims, by any means. I do not work in any particular department, I have a free hand to go about my task as I see fit. And I need your help in this."

"How can I possibly help? I am just an ordinary bloke who acts as a union official."

"You have told me that you are an active member of the Communist Party, Michael, and that you agree with some of their ideas. I want to know if your colleagues think the same way, or are there sinister moves being planned that confirm what I have just told you?"

"You want me to spy on my comrades for you? Because I will not do that."

"No I do not want you to do that, I want you to find out if any of them are talking to Soviet agents, and also if the group known as the Red Hand are known to any of them."

"The Red Hand, I have heard of them. They want to take over the Civil Service Union and make it more democratic. "

"Did you know that you cannot be a member of the Communist Party and be a Civil Servant?" says Doyle, confident that his comments will make Daniel see that he knows what is going on.

"The Red Hand was a group of agents working in the Civil Service with the sole aim of getting one of their members into a senior position whereby he or she could influence government policy. Their intention, before they were arrested, was to influence the government into introducing anti strike laws to cause unrest within the union movement. Civil unrest causes anarchy, which in turn will feed the Soviet idealists."

"You say they have all been arrested?"

"And charged with conspiracy against our democratically elected government."

"What you have told me clears up some incidents that have occurred recently; new faces are showing up at meetings to discuss the management offers. They do not speak but take notes on what is being said. I never paid them too much attention, but am now beginning to wonder if they were sent by the Soviets to stir up trouble amongst the members."

"Would you be able to find out who they are, Michael? It could be a great help, Michael."

"I will do what I can, Mr Bottomley. You have given me a lot to think about, but I will not give you information that is union business, I believe in the trade union movement and will not be a part of any attempt to destroy it. However, if what you say is true, then these people will do just that and I will not be a part of any scheme to undermine what the movement stands for. As soon as I have anything, I will let Peter know and we can meet again. Next time can we meet on a Saturday lunchtime?"

"Wherever you wish, Michael, and please call me Daniel, and again I apologise for deceiving you."

"Ok Daniel, we'll be in touch," says Doyle as he and Hennessey depart.

Daniel goes outside to find Conrad, who has been wandering around Covent Garden.

"How was your meeting, Daniel, good news?"

"Yes it was, Conrad, and when we meet next time, I believe he will deliver the last pieces of the jigsaw to conclude the conspiracy trial. He was genuinely stunned by the information that I gave him about the Soviets and Red Hand. Once we have the additional evidence to link the Soviets with Red Hand and the unions, the Crown will have all the information it seeks for a public showpiece to embarrass the Soviets and bring the perpetrators to justice."

The taxi pulls up outside the apartment block in Thurloe Street, and Daniel goes up to his apartment after thanking Conrad and saying he will see him in the morning.

"Daniel, you're back. We were wondering where you were," says Polly, as she struggles not to run into his arms in front of her friend.

"Yes, our meeting went on for longer than expected, I hope it won't make you too late home, Penny?"

"Not at all, Daniel. I was hoping your friend Conrad might join us."

"There will be another time, Penny, and I wouldn't be at all surprised if he does not make contact with you anyway. He spoke of you while we were out earlier."

"Did he? I will really look forward to hearing from him, he seems a very nice man."

Daniel smiles as he returns to the apartment where Polly has made some tea. He briefly outlines what went on and how the light at the end of the tunnel is getting brighter.

"I really hope so, my dearest Daniel. Now that we are married, I do so want to be with you all the time and lead a normal life," she says, holding on to him before kissing him on the lips. They sit in each other's arms, quietly enjoying being together, each with their own thoughts for the other. It would be ideal to have a normal life sometime, thinks Daniel, and his meeting with Michael Doyle may have brought that time closer.

Polly, too, dwells on being able to be a housewife and welcome Daniel home each evening. With these thoughts she drifts into a deep sleep. Daniel carefully carries her to the bedroom and removes her top clothing before putting her in bed. He returns to the lounge to finish his tea and sits with his thoughts for a while before he too goes off to bed. Polly is still sound asleep as he slips in beside her. He looks at her, sleeping soundly, appreciating just what she means to him and the sheer joy at their now being married, before he too goes off to sleep.

When Daniel meets up with Fitz the next morning, he is delighted that Daniel has been able to convince Doyle to look closely at union activities.

"His input could be very useful, Daniel, and you have obviously convinced him of the Soviet menace. I appreciate that he seems a dedicated union man with only the interests of his members at heart. It must have come as something of a disappointment to him that his union was being infiltrated by people with no interest in the needs of the membership. I have also spoke with Quentin and he is anxious that we can secure enough evidence against the Soviets to close down their operation in this country. He is under no illusions about their intentions and he knows that they will not stop their activities, but at least we have slowed them down for a while. We have to keep at them, Daniel, and make their operation as difficult as possible for them."

When Polly and Daniel arrive from work for the weekend, they have notification of the trial of the men who entered Ben Spencer's home. The trial date is set for Monday 15th September at Leicester Crown Court, one week from Monday next, a lot sooner than Daniel thought.

"God, Daniel, it seems we move from one case to the next."

"I know it seems that way, Polly, and this one has come round quicker than I thought it would. This is probably because the caseload in Leicester is not so great as London. Anyway, the sooner it comes round, the sooner it will be over, and we get to see your family again, meantime."

"Yes, that is true, I must call Mummy and arrange to stay over. I would have liked us to stay in a hotel so that we could be together, but I don't want Mummy and Daddy to wonder why we are not staying with them."

"I am sure we will find a way. I don't like having to deceive your family, Polly, but for now we must leave things as they are. I'm sure they would understand. Anyway, there is plenty of time to fill between now and then and I'm sure you will find us something to do together!"

"What do you mean, Daniel?" Polly replies, laughing as she drags him toward their bedroom. Their lovemaking is always intense and Polly continually seeks new ways to give Daniel pleasure. He just loves her for what she is, his wife and companion whom he loves dearly, and who will spend the rest of her life by his side.

They finally sit down to dinner, before relaxing together listening to music. Polly calls her parents over the weekend to arrange their visit for the trial at Leicester.

"It will be nice to see you both again, my dear Polly. How long will you expect to stay?"

"I expect we will be with you for most of the week, Mummy. It's difficult to say, really."

"Well, you are both always welcome, Polly. I shall arrange a late Sunday lunch, and we will see you then. I know the children will be delighted to see you both, especially as your last visit was so terrible. It will give them a chance to catch up and George especially will be pleased to see Daniel again."

The weekend passes all too quickly, and on returning to work on Monday, Daniel is pleasantly surprised to have a message from Hennessey waiting for him in his office. Doyle believes that he can help Daniel and will spend the week looking for evidence of Soviet interference within the union. He will make contact with him later in the week to tell him where they might meet on Saturday lunchtime. He tells Fitz of the message from Doyle and of the trial due to start next week in Leicester.

"That is good news, Daniel. It would seem that Doyle is anxious to help. Hopefully, he will have some real evidence. We must arrange to have you call me over the weekend to give me a report on your Saturday meeting, but we can talk more about that on Friday before the weekend."

"I did not expect him to get back to me so soon. He must be anxious to move on this, Fitz. It's just a pity that I cannot meet with him sooner. I believe he is concerned for his safety on this, hence wanting to meet at the weekend."

"I understand his caution, Daniel. There is a lot at stake. We must accept the fact that he may be compromised through talking to us, so we have to go along with whatever he decides. Anyway, it's only a few days to wait."

On the Thursday morning, a concerned Polly is summoned into Mrs Wright's office.

"Please come in, Polly, and sit down. Your work since you joined us has been first rate, and I would like to thank you for all your efforts as my Corporate Liaison Officer. You have handled your responsibilities very professionally through a very difficult period within the Office."

Polly is shocked by Mrs Wright's comments, it would seem that she is being dismissed.

"Thank you Mrs Wright, but I don't understand. Am I being dismissed?"

"Good lord no, you are going to be offered a more senior position, this time in the Foreign Office. You will clear today's work by lunchtime and be at the Foreign Office building by two o'clock. You will report to Mrs Marjorie Warner, Director of Strategic Planning. She will brief you on your new post and give you all relevant details of what your new position will involve. I am not sure when they want you to start. Obviously it will not be this week or next because of the trial. I would think they will want you soon after that. Anyway, come back and let me know after your interview this afternoon. Good luck and very best wishes, my dear."

"Thank you Mrs Wright, I have enjoyed my work here and I hope we can keep in touch," says Polly, who is absolutely delighted with the news and can't wait to send a message to Daniel.

And so after lunch, Polly locks her office and makes her way across Whitehall to the Foreign Office, and is directed to Mrs Warner's office on the first floor. She knocks on the door before entering.

"Hello Polly, I'm Marjorie Warner. Please come inside." Marjorie Warner is a strikingly attractive woman, in her early forties, immaculately dressed in a blue suit and white blouse. She is indeed an imposing figure, every inch the professional Civil Servant.

"I expect this has all come as a surprise to you. Well, we have been watching your progress for a while and Mrs Wright has spoken very highly of you. Despite how young you are you have shown a high degree of maturity in going about your business. I refer to your handling of the Red Hand organisation approaching you to act on their behalf, and your no small contribution to their downfall. Your close ties with Daniel Bottomley has meant you have become a formidable team, as the security services have found out."

"Thank you for your comments, Mrs Warner, Daniel and I do work well together, we have known each other for a long time."

"Yes, we are familiar with Daniel's role when you were still at school and the dreadful incidents that you and your parents endured at that time. And it has not escaped notice just how close you and Daniel have become. He is your guardian, I believe?"

"Yes he is. I moved in with him, in January when I secured my position at the Home Office. My parents saw him as the obvious choice since they knew him very well."

"Yes, quite so, Polly. Well we are now more concerned with what you can do for us here at the Foreign Office. We have recently set up a new department to deal specifically with the Soviet menace in our colonies. You have been involved with their activities in Britain, and will continue to do so, but we are becoming increasingly concerned of their efforts to destabilise our Commonwealth interests. This new department will be handling sensitive information from our Commonwealth friends, giving details of Soviet activities in those countries. We need someone with knowledge of the Soviets, and with a high security rating. They will be responsible for sifting through the details and handing them on to an appropriate member of staff to deal with. You will be our Soviet Strategies Analyst, but before we go any further, let me introduce you to your departmental head," says Mrs Warner, pressing a button on her phone.

"David, I have Polly Spencer with me. Would you join us please? David, this is Polly Spencer."

"Miss Spencer, I am delighted to meet you. I have heard a lot about your activities against the Soviets, from your position in the Home Office. I am sure we shall all benefit from your expert knowledge of the Soviets. I know you will prove an admirable addition to the team."

"Thank you Mr Fellows, I hope I can be of use to you," Polly replies, somewhat overwhelmed by the cheery manner and compliments from David Fellows. He is a large man in his fifties, formerly with MI6 and specially selected for this new department to combat the Soviet threats in the colonies. His pleasing jovial manner hides a ruthless former agent with the British Security Service, who has been involved in activities in Eastern Europe and in Germany.

"I had no idea you were so young, Miss Spencer, but I know we will work well together. I believe you are an acquaintance of Daniel Bottomley. I know of Daniel's activities with the security services, he is a bit of a legend. I understand that you and he have been the target of some especially nasty attacks recently?"

"Yes sir, there have been a number over the past few months, in fact there is a trial beginning next week relating to an incident at my parents' home."

"Really? I had no idea. What happened?" asks David Fellows.

"Daniel and I went to stay with my parents for a few days in July. We had just been through a previous trial, and wanted a few days' holiday before returning to work. Both of us always enjoy going to my parents' home and were both looking forward to it very much. Five men broke into my parents' home and tried to abduct me and kill Daniel. It was a terrifying experience, but fortunately for me, Daniel stopped them, shooting four of them. He was, however, badly hurt in the fight whilst I just had a few bruises."

"Good lord, so Daniel saved the day. He always was the man to have on your side, even when I knew him. So, I understand from your file that you have known him since you were at school, and he is now your selected guardian while you are in London, is that correct?"

"Yes sir, I have known Daniel for more than five years, during which time he has saved my life on more than one occasion. My family will always be grateful to him and so will I."

"Yes, I'm sure you will, Miss Spencer. Now let me tell you a little bit about your new role in our department. My title is Director of Strategic Planning and my job will to coordinate the data from the colonies and decide what actions to take. Your job will be to analyse that data as it is received and assess the significance before passing it on to the relevant personnel. I will brief you more fully regarding the personnel when you are settled in your new position. Suffice for me to say, Miss Spencer, that the position carries a good deal of responsibility since you will be handling very sensitive information. However, we feel you are uniquely suited to this position, despite your age, because of your involvement in Soviet activities in Britain, and because of your high security clearance we believe there is no one better suited."

"Now Polly, when would be the earliest that you would be able to take up this position?" asks Marjorie Warner.

"As soon as the trial in Leicester is over, I would think week beginning 22nd September."

"Very well, I shall set out your terms of contract from that date, and ask that you report to me at 9.00am on the day. Meantime, I would ask that you only tell those that need to be told of your new position. Mrs Wright will be aware, of course, and I am sure you will want to discuss it with Daniel."

"Welcome aboard, Miss Spencer, I am sure you will prove to be a worthy addition to our team," David Fellows adds as he shakes Polly's hand.

"Thank you, sir. Thank you very much. I will do my very best not to let you down," says Polly, as she leaves and makes her way back to the Home Office. She sits in her office thinking over what has been said, and realising that her career is about to become more important and more dangerous, dealing direct with the Soviet menace.

This does not in any way detract from her success in being handed such an important role in the Foreign Office, and she cannot wait to tell Daniel about her new job. She talks excitedly about it on their way home and inside, she smothers him in kisses, telling him how happy she is.

"You have done well, Polly, and it is no more than you deserve. I am pleased for you."

"Thank you, Daniel. I really don't know what will be expected of me, but I will do my best," she says, hugging him as they sit on the settee.

"I have to telephone Hennessey to find out where we are to meet him on Saturday," says Daniel.

"Ok, I will have a bath while you are talking with him." Polly goes off to the bathroom as Daniel dials Hennessey's number.

"Hello Daniel, I was expecting your call. Michael has been in contact and asks to meet you in Whitechapel. There is a pub called the Black Bull not far from the tube station. He will be waiting for you at noon. I believe he does have some information about our friends and is anxious to pass it on to you."

"That sounds very encouraging, Peter, Black Bull in Whitechapel it is. I will see you then. By the way, I shall have my colleague Polly with me."

"That's ok, it might be an idea for a woman to be with us, it stops people from being curious about strange men in the pub. See you Saturday."

"Is the meeting arranged, Daniel?" asks Polly, joining him in her robe.

"Yes, we will meet him in Whitechapel. I believe it has a large Jewish community there. Anyway, noon on Saturday," he replies as Polly snuggles up beside him.

He is conscious of Polly wearing nothing beneath her robe, since she has not tied the drawstring. He decides to go and make them some tea before he becomes too aroused, so goes off to the kitchen. And while he is there, he makes some cheese on toast for supper. Friday is spent clearing any outstanding business before they both go off for the trial in Leicester beginning on Monday.

"You will let me know what happens tomorrow, Daniel, when you meet up with Doyle? We are almost ready to present all our evidence to the Crown."

"Can I call you Sunday evening, Fitz, when we are at Polly's home?"

"That will be fine by me, we never do anything special on Sunday evenings."

Polly, meanwhile, discusses her move with Mrs Wright, telling her that she won't be able to tell anyone of her move under instruction from Marjorie Warner.

"I wonder if you might have a word with Elizabeth Berkley and Penny Carstairs for me please. I would have liked to have said something, but will catch up with them both when I have settled in my new post."

"Yes of course, Polly, leave that with me. Now off you go for your last round of collections."

The rest of Friday passes quickly for both of them, and they arrive back at the apartment just after five o'clock. After a quiet evening together they enjoy an early night.

"Do you think I will get an increase in my salary, Daniel, with this new job, and more responsibility?" Polly asks as they lie together on Saturday morning.

"I am sure you will, Polly, and it is no more than you deserve. You are very highly thought of in both the Home Office and the Foreign Office."

"And when the trials are all finished and we can get on with our lives, can we look for our own house? I do so much want us to have a house together."

"I look forward to looking for a house for us Polly, I have lived in this apartment for too long."

"And we will need somewhere bigger for our family, won't we?" says Polly, laughing as she climbs on top of Daniel and kisses him passionately. They lie together for a while before Polly falls asleep, still on top of Daniel. He gently moves her and gets up from the bed.

They spend some time shopping on Saturday morning before setting off on the short journey to Whitechapel by tube. They leave in plenty of time, Daniel wanting to show Polly what life is like in the East End of London.

Whitechapel Road is busy on Saturday morning, and they spend some time looking at the array of shops and market stalls. There is a thriving Jewish community in the area and this is evident everywhere, with many men sporting the long beards and kipas on their heads. All this is new to Polly, who is fascinated by what she sees. However, just after midday, they enter the Black Bull and notice Doyle and Hennessey sitting in the corner of a busy bar.

"Michael, I don't believe you have met Polly. She is a work colleague of mine."

"Hello, Miss, pleased to meet you."

"I'm pleased to meet you, Michael," says Polly, extending her hand.

"I have made some enquiries since we met, Daniel, and what you said appears to be true. There is definitely some sort of plot by outsiders to influence union decisions. I was really disappointed to find that two of my members have conspired with these 'commie' agents. The sooner you put them away the better, I say," says Doyle, obviously shocked at what he has discovered.

"How did you find out about your colleagues' involvement with Russian agents?"

"Two members, Bill Hornsby and Jack Makepeace, mentioned to me that they had been talking with the men we had seen at meetings. The men had approached them and urged them to push the membership harder for an all-out strike. They were told that they would achieve nothing without a violent struggle against the bosses, and were offered money to secure a vote for the strike. They spoke with me and were pretty scared of what these men were suggesting. I think they suddenly realised what is happening, but it's now too late to change their minds. Now they want me to join with them and get the members out. They are really scared of these men, Daniel, and have turned to me for advice. They have met with two of them, a Leonid Rafikov and Boris Ruchkin, but they are convinced they are being watched by others," Doyle replies, obviously apprehensive at what he has discovered.

"They are probably being watched by other agents who are reporting their progress. Your colleagues are in great danger, Michael. You must urge them to do as they have been asked. If the Russians suspect anything they will be dealt with most severely. And you, Michael, must encourage them without getting involved. Don't really know how to advise you there. But you must not meet with any of the Soviets, because they will be taking pictures so that they can blackmail members who try to change their minds later on. Also, you must only meet with Hornsby and Makepeace at your union offices on official union business. It is vital that your evidence cannot be tainted by the Soviet agents."

Daniel's comments have shocked both Doyle and Hennessey, and they are both looking very apprehensive. Daniel realises that he has to somehow reassure them of how he can help.

"Peter, I suggest that you do not meet or make contact with Michael again, at least until this is all over. In fact, can I suggest that you leave now? If you have any further information that you feel may help, I suggest you use a telephone box only." Hennessey nods, gets up, and leaves.

"I will give you a number, Michael, which you have to memorise, that you can use to contact me. Now, it is important that you appear to be helping your colleagues, but only through your union channels. You must be very careful what you say to them in case there are any recording devices in your union office. I will get someone to keep an eye on you to see if you are being watched. And you must not mention any of this to your family members; the less they know the better for everyone.

"If you believe that you or your family are being threatened in any way, you must contact me immediately. Do you understand what I have been saying, Michael? It is absolutely vital that you do as I have asked," says Daniel firmly.

"My god, Daniel. What have I let myself into? I just want what is best for my members, and thought the Communist Party would give me that. I had no idea what their intentions were," Doyle replies with fear in his voice.

"And one more thing, Michael, you may be asked to testify and tell the court what you have just said to me."

"How can I testify, Daniel? If what you say is true they will harm my family. I can't put them in danger, not for any reason at all. I'm sorry, I can't help you there."

"You don't understand, Michael. These people do not need an excuse to harm you. They may do it to make an example of what they do to anyone who interferes with their plans. So long as you are prepared, and you are now prepared, you will be ok. And once we have put these people either behind bars or expelled them from our country, you will be safe. If you still have to be protected, then that will be arranged, I promise you. Your meeting with me and telling me about the communist interference shows that you want to be rid of them, so let's do it. You just have to be watchful, they don't know that you know, and that gives you an advantage. Let's use that advantage to see that they are stopped from destroying your union and our country."

Doyle sits, drawing sharply on his cigarette, aware that his life is about to change. He cannot tell his family to be careful, they will want to know why. And if he tells them, he will be putting them in danger. He has two boys and two girls and he has to protect them. He knows that what Daniel has said is the only way he can protect his union, but at what cost?

"How do I know they are not already watching me and my family?" asks Doyle, looking round the pub and becoming edgy.

"There is no reason why they should be watching you, Michael. They have your two colleagues working for them. If they had wanted you they would have approached you already. Of course, that is not to say that they won't approach you sometime. Let's cross that bridge when we get to it. For now, go home and enjoy your weekend with your family. This is the number where I can be contacted. Leave your message and I will get to you as soon as possible, anytime, anywhere.

"What you have done, Michael, does you credit and I admire your convictions. Let's see them through to the end."

"Very well, Daniel. Thank you for being honest with me, I appreciate that. I will contact you shortly with an update on this. Bye, Miss, nice to have met you," says Doyle as he gets up and leaves, anxiously looking around a he does so.

Polly and Daniel leave the Black Bull after a few moments and catch the tube back to Kensington. Polly wanted to look round Whitechapel, but Daniel thought it best that they return to their own surroundings, since Jewish communities can be very suspicious of strangers. On returning, they sit down to lunch in a restaurant in the High Street that they have used many times.

"Daniel, Polly, nice to see you both again," the waiter says.

"So what do you think Doyle will do, Daniel? The poor man looked really scared after you had spoken with him."

"I am confident that he will see it through; he does not have any real choice now that he has made the move to uncover the activities of the Soviet agents. He is a man of strong convictions, Polly, I really believe he wants to help, but is fearful for his family and that is understandable."

After a good lunch, they go off and do some shopping locally, but since they will be away for most of next week, there is not much they need to get. They have the rest of the afternoon and the whole of the evening to themselves, and Polly is determined that they should enjoy it with each other. They sit with each other on the settee and she turns to him, saying: "Do you realise, this will be our last time together as man and wife for a week, Daniel? What should we do with ourselves, do you think?" says Polly with a mischievous smile.

"What do you mean, Polly?" he replies with an equally mischievous grin.

Polly takes his hand and leads him toward their bedroom, helping him remove his clothing. They embrace passionately as they climb into bed. Polly gently strokes Daniel as he kisses her breasts before they couple and make love. Afterwards they sleep in each other's arms before Daniel gets up to make some tea.

"I'm going for a long soak, Daniel. Can I have my tea in the bath please?"

He takes her tea into the bathroom, before sitting down and reflecting on his conversation with Michael Doyle. He believes they have everything necessary for the Crown to present their case.

There is now a wealth of evidence to charge four Russians with espionage and conspiracy and four British nationals with conspiracy, and it is possible that the security services may have more suspects under investigation. For Daniel, the conspiracy trial and conclusions will mean the end of a long fight to rid the country of the Soviet attempts to impose a communist state on Britain. It has been a difficult fight with both himself and Polly subjected to serious assaults and even assassination. None of this has stopped him from going on to complete his work, nor will any further attempts by the communists. When he reflects on the vicious attempts to harm and abduct Polly and the beatings he has endured to stop such attempts, he becomes even more aware of just what the country is up against. The Soviets will not stop in their efforts to enforce their ideals on the British people and know they have an ideal opportunity in a country still suffering from the ravages of war. There is still genuine poverty in Britain. There are many buildings still showing the aftermath of bombing. The country is taking too long to really recover, and the Soviets are exploiting the misfortune of it all. However, Daniel is optimistic that the British people will show their strengths and rise to the challenges that they face, not least the communist menace that threatens. And he is only too aware that neither he nor Polly can ever be safe until his work is completed and those accused are put away or deported. He is still deep in thought when Polly bounds into the lounge and sits down on his lap.

"You were deep in thought there, Daniel," she says, as she hugs him and plants a kiss on his lips.

"Just going over what has happened over the past weeks, and looking forward to seeing an end to it all. I know we have next week's trial to get through, but I am hoping that the conspiracy trial should see the end of it all and then you and I can announce our marriage to everyone."

"Why Daniel, you really are a sentimental romantic at heart, and I love you even more for that."

CHAPTER 11

Daniel and Polly arrive at Polly's home on Sunday afternoon, around 2.30, looking forward to their visit on the one hand, but wishing the circumstances were better on the other.

As usual, they are warmly greeted by the children especially, with lots of hugs and kisses.

"Polly, Daniel, it's been such a long time since we saw you."

"Well here we are, George," says Polly, hugging him and her sisters before going through to the parlour.

"My dear Polly and Daniel, it's so good to see you again."

"Thank you Mummy, it's always good to come home."

The family sit in the parlour chatting before Daniel is approached by Maisy. Polly has gone into the kitchen with Margaret and the others have gone into the garden.

"You look different, Daniel. Is everything alright?"

"Yes thank you, Maisy, are you on another one of your fishing trips?"

"No, I just wondered if you and Polly had decided when you were going to get married, that's all," says Maisy, hoping for a response.

"You will know soon enough, Maisy."

The family enjoy a pleasant meal, and sit round afterwards discussing the trial.

"I believe we now have enough evidence to go ahead with a major conspiracy trial. The results should be able to shut down the Soviet operation in Britain for some time. We know the threat will never go away completely, but the trial will send a message to the Soviets that we will fight them with everything we have in order to maintain our democracy. I expect that some of the accused will be expelled, so they will not be looking forward to the verdicts. The Soviets do not like failures and the government is keen to give the trial maximum publicity so as to cause maximum embarrassment. Now, I have to contact Fitz to tell him what happened at the meeting yesterday. Can I use the study, Ben?"

Ben nods, so Daniel goes off to make his call to Fitz and relates to him what happened at his meeting with Doyle in Whitechapel.

"It seems that Doyle is going to help us after all, Daniel. His information is sound enough already for us to mount surveillance on the four men he mentions. They will no doubt lead us to any other conspirators, and it might be an idea to ask Quentin if he can keep an eye on Doyle. Whilst we need to be absolutely sure of his intentions, we also need to protect him. It will be difficult for him to act as if nothing has changed when he is with his colleagues, and when he is with his family. So we must watch for any signs of changes to his routines. He is going to be under a lot of pressure trying to act normal with so much going on around him, so should he make contact while you are away, we might have to consider Conrad meeting him. I will discuss that with you of course, before making any decision. Anyway, good luck with next week, Daniel."

Daniel puts down the phone before joining Polly as they finally go up to their rooms, deciding on an early night ready for the trial tomorrow. Daniel lays there, thinking how strange it is not to have Polly beside him, but respecting the need to keep their marriage secret.

For Polly, the events surrounding the invasion of Ben's home were particularly unpleasant, but she has the strength that her marriage to Daniel has given her, to help her through the ordeal.

After an early breakfast, Ben runs them to the station to catch the train to Leicester. The Crown Court is only a short journey from the station, and they both arrive in good time.

"Good morning to you both, I am Jonathan Barwick, Q.C. for the

Crown. Most of this morning will be taken up with procedures and my presentations. I'm sure Justice Blythe will have something to say also. Since two of the accused are Russian nationals, they will have representation supplied for them since they do not recognise the court's jurisdiction. The other two men have their own counsel. Ok, so unless you have any questions, I think we should go in now."

Daniel and Polly follow the Crown barrister into court and a few moments later the judge, Justice Peregrine Blythe, enters.

The four accused are brought into the court and the charges read. One of the men walks with the aid of a stick whilst another has severe lacerations and scarring on his face, both men suffering their injuries as a result of the firefight with Daniel.

"Demetrius Bukovsky, Vladimir Comaniche, Karl Obermann, and Pedro Fuentes, you are jointly charged with breaking and entering the home of Mr Ben Spencer at Crabtree Lane, Milton Parva.

"You are also charged with grievous bodily harm and the attempted abduction of Miss Polly Spencer, the attempted murder of Daniel Bottomley, and the discharging of firearms with intent to endanger life."

The two Russians refuse to enter a plea, the other two accused plead not guilty; one of them has to write down his answers since his voice box has been damaged.

The Crown barrister then stands to deliver his opening introduction to the court.

"This really is a very unpleasant case, as you will determine from the evidence. When someone breaks into your home, in itself that is a violation. To break into a home and attempt to kill one occupant and kidnap another is despicable and must have been very frightening to the occupants, not least Miss Spencer's parents and siblings who were also present in the house at the time.

"These four men entered the house with the intention of killing Mr Bottomley and abducting Miss Spencer. The evidence will prove that conclusively. Their actions prompted a fierce fight with firearms used extensively, as is evident from the wounds of the men in the dock. Their condition is evident of the desperate efforts made by Mr Bottomley to stop them from killing him and abducting his ward, Miss Spencer. In fact he, too, was seriously injured from gunshot wounds.

You will hear police evidence of just how ferocious the fire fight must have been, and how terrifying the aftermath was for the family, and medical reports on the injuries to Mr Bottomley and Miss Spencer.

"It is not beyond the realms of possibility that the accused were acting on specific instructions. Whether those instructions were delivered by a foreign power is open to debate, and that debate will be for another court to decide. What is reasonable to assume, given Mr Bottomley's work, is that all four men had instructions to kill him because of previous incidents, which are duly recorded, that have occurred to both him and Miss Spencer. You will hear that two of these men are in fact guns for hire. Who hired them and why? Again, that may be a question to be answered at another time. However, it cannot be ignored, especially as the other two accused are Russians, and I have no doubt that there may be foreign interest in the trial outcome. What you have to decide, after you have heard all the evidence, is the significance of any foreign power influence in all this, and whether it should be highlighted and reflected in any decisions you may make.

"The idea that a foreign power send men to our country to kill and abduct our citizens from inside their homes cannot be tolerated under any circumstances, and I hope that our government will make the strongest possible protests to those concerned. We are living in dangerous times, it would seem. It is not exactly a secret that communist agitators are at work in our country. These people would seek to destroy the very fabric of our society. Men such as Mr Bottomley are to be applauded for doing their best to protect us," the Crown concludes his opening argument.

A member of the defence team stands to make his opening argument.

"My lord, I just want to make the jury aware of why they are here. The prosecution have tried to imply that the accused may be part of a giant conspiracy by a foreign power, in order to influence the verdicts and so secure harsher sentences. There is no direct evidence to support that theory and I hope they will see that as the trial progresses."

"Thank you gentlemen, we will now adjourn for lunch and begin hearing evidence this afternoon," The judge says as he adjourns proceedings for the lunch break.

Immediately after the lunch break, the Crown calls Daniel to the stand.

"Can you tell the court your name and your occupation please?"

My name is Daniel Bottomley and I am a Civil Servant."

"If you could be a little more specific, Mr Bottomley," the judge requests.

"I work in a department that investigates any information relevant to the government's stand against communists and communists' attempts to influence our society, sir."

"Thank you. Please continue, Mr Barwick."

"My lord, with reference to the defence barrister's comments, I would like to ask Mr Bottomley a pertinent question, if I may? Mr Bottomley, I believe that you and Miss Spencer have recently concluded another trial relating to a break-in at your apartment when you were severely beaten, is that correct?"

"Yes sir, that is correct. The four accused were found guilty. May I add that Miss Spencer also suffered severe injuries in this attack while also being seriously indecently assaulted by her attackers?"

"Yes, thank you Mr Bottomley. Now tell me was their not also an attack in July, previous to the one in your apartment, when you and Miss Spencer were both abducted?"

"Mr Barwick, can I ask where all this is going?" the judge asks impatiently.

"I am almost there, Your Honour. Can you answer the question, Mr Bottomley, please?"

"Yes there was, Miss Spencer and I were abducted at gunpoint from outside my apartment block and taken to an old warehouse in Soho."

"And may I ask what happened at the subsequent trial of your abductors?"

"There was no trial. The only two that were caught by the police were Russian nationals and they were expelled by the government. The security services realised that it was not to anyone's advantage to have a trial at this time. They had very specific reasons for their actions, you can be sure of that," says Daniel.

"Russian nationals, you say, and quite a coincidence that two of the accused here today are also Russian nationals. I hope the jury members take note of that fact when they consider the evidence, before considering their verdicts. Thank you for that, Mr Bottomley, now if I may continue," the Crown barrister goes on.

"Can you tell us what happened on the night in question at Mr Spencer's home, please?"

"I was woken by a noise at about 2.00am. I am a very light sleeper so any sound will wake me. As soon as I heard the noise, I got out from my bed and reached for my pistol."

"Were you expecting trouble, Mr Bottomley, reaching for your pistol?"

"Not expecting it especially, sir, but surprised that Miss Spencer and I were once again targeted in her family's home."

"Yes, please carry on."

"I had just got up and moved to my bedside when two men entered my room, firing their weapons a number of times towards my bed. I caught a ricochet bullet which grazed my arm and responded by shooting back, hitting one man in the chest and the other in his face. Since both men were badly injured, I felt it was safe enough to leave them and go after Polly's – Miss Spencer's – attackers.

"You were aware of Miss Spencer being attacked?"

"Yes I was, she was calling for me hysterically and I saw the men turn to go down the stairs just as I reached the door of my bedroom. They were part carrying, part dragging Polly between them. I dashed down the landing and knocked on Mr Spencer's bedroom door before turning to go down the stairs."

"Yes, Mr Spencer's bedroom is to the left of the staircase as you look up the stairs, is that correct?"

"Yes sir. I called to Mr Spencer to watch over the injured men in my room. However, I must have been off my guard, because as I turned to go down the stairs another man shot at me, hitting me in the chest. I did not realise there was a fifth man in the house and was caught completely by surprise. I staggered momentarily, then returned fire, hitting him in the stomach and in the neck. He fell unconscious to the floor at the base of the stairs. However, by this time, I was bleeding pretty badly from my own injury, but managed to get down the stairs."

"And what was happening to Miss Spencer in the meantime?"

"Polly was being dragged across the hallway towards the front door. She was desperately trying to break free of these men, screaming and kicking, and I was fearful that they would make off with her, but was struggling to stay conscious from my injury," recounts Daniel, visibly upset at having to recall the events of that evening.

"I know this must be distressing for you but please go on, Mr Bottomley."

"I managed to reach the bottom of the stairs, but realised that my pistol was empty, so I picked up the pistol belonging to the man lying unconscious at the bottom of the stairs. Polly was putting up a hell of a fight as the two men pulled and grabbed her round her waist, trying to get her out of the house. One of the men now had his back to me as they wrestled with her trying to get her out of the door. I fired twice and hit him somewhere at the top of his thigh, causing him to release his hold on Polly. Unfortunately, the other man ran off before I had a chance to fire."

"You must have been in a pretty bad way by now, Mr Bottomley?" the Crown asks.

"I managed to stagger part way down the hall before collapsing. I could hear Polly screaming at Mr Spencer to call an ambulance, after that it gets a bit hazy until I woke up in the hospital with Polly beside me."

"Mr Bottomley, let me just clarify this. You shot and incapacitated four of the five men that were in the house, is that correct?" the judge asks.

"Yes sir, as I mentioned, I was unable to stop the fifth man from escaping."

"And you did this whilst you were seriously injured yourself. I am astonished at your actions, Mr Bottomley, both in stopping these men from shooting you and in your efforts to save Miss Spencer from being abducted despite what was to prove to be a serious wound to your chest. There can be no doubt that but for your actions, Miss Spencer would have been abducted that night," the judge concludes.

"I have no more questions for Mr Bottomley, my lord."

The defence had no questions to ask Daniel so he is asked to leave the witness box.

"Ladies and gentlemen of the jury, the evidence you have just heard has been both harrowing and graphic. Because of this and the time, I believe now would be appropriate for an adjournment for today. I will see you all again tomorrow."

And with that, the judge adjourns proceedings for the day. Daniel and Polly meet up with the barrister, who thanks Daniel for his evidence.

"It seems you impressed His Lordship, Daniel. Always a good sign. Now enjoy the rest of today and I will see you again tomorrow," the Crown barrister says as he sees them to the door.

Polly and Daniel hail a taxi to Leicester Station and return to Carswell, eventually arriving back at Polly's home around five o'clock. Polly decides to go and have a bath, the day's proceedings being rather upsetting. Daniel, meanwhile, follows Ben into his study.

"A difficult day, Daniel, but I expect tomorrow will be more so with Polly in the witness box."

"I will be there for her, Ben, but yes, reliving that night will not be a pleasant experience for her. She is very strong willed and will cope, of that I am sure. And by the way, Ben, we haven't told you about her new position, have we? She has been offered a job in the Foreign Office."

"That is wonderful news, how did this come about?" says Ben, bursting with pride at his daughter's achievements.

"There is a new department established to combat the communist menace in the colonies. It is headed by a chap called David Fellows, formerly of MI6. He had been made aware of Polly's achievements by Fitz, and asked that she be offered the position. I expect she will take up the new post once the conspiracy trial is out of the way. This is a very big promotion for her, Ben. She is most definitely destined for high office.

"As well as Fitz, MI5 have been very impressed with her work in the Home Office. I must confess she surprises me sometimes with her enthusiasm for the cause."

The two men leave the study for the parlour where Polly has just arrived after her bath.

"My dear Polly, Daniel has just been telling me the news about your new job. Our daughter has been offered a position in the Foreign Office no less," says Ben, hugging Polly.

All of the family rush to congratulate Polly, who is rather overwhelmed by their reactions, but no less delighted.

"We are all so proud of you, Polly," says Margaret.

"Thank you, Mummy. I am not sure why they selected me, but I will do my best, and I have Daniel to help me," Polly replies, holding on to him and smiling. Polly never misses an opportunity to show her feelings for him, and they do not go unnoticed.

"I may even get a salary increase, which will be very useful. David Fellows has only briefly outlined the position to me, but it sounds really exciting, Daddy," she says as she sits next to Daniel, holding on to his arm.

"Will you have to travel all over the world, Poll, because will you bring me back some stamps if you do?" asks George.

"My new position means I have to be available in the Foreign Office, George, so no visits to foreign countries, I'm afraid. But if I know of someone who is travelling abroad, I will ask them to bring you some stamps back with them."

"Wow, thanks Poll."

"It would be nice if your new position kept you away from danger, Polly, I really wouldn't want you and Daniel to be exposed to even more dangers with your new position. The last few months have been hell for all of us," says Margaret tearfully.

"Daniel and I will overcome whatever difficulties our positions put us in, Mummy. We have survived so far, and together, we will survive anything, won't we Daniel?"

"What we will always endeavour to do is stay away from any trouble, Polly. I do appreciate your concerns, Margaret, but I will always have

Polly's interests at heart and watch over her wherever she may be," he replies, holding Polly close to him as if to reassure Margaret.

"I know you will, Daniel, I just worry for you both sometimes. A mother's privilege, you know."

"Come along now Mummy, let's go and organise some dinner," says Polly, jumping up from the settee and taking Margaret's hand.

"Margaret is right, of course. You and Polly have been subjected to terrible ordeals these last few months, Daniel. Most people would have not been able to survive what you have had to endure. Polly still believes you are invincible, you know."

"I would never intentionally put her at risk, Ben. I care for her too much to do that. Unfortunately, circumstances have dictated that we have been put into some difficult situations recently. And, these people know no boundaries, as the attacks here have shown. Polly and I both long for the time when our work becomes more routine, with the only danger being boredom."

"Somehow, I do not believe that either of you really want routine to be what your work involves. Perhaps a little routine would help though," says Ben with a smile.

"Well, perhaps you're right, I would certainly not want to dent Polly's enthusiasm, and she really is an inspiration to me."

"Your relationship is truly very special, Daniel, we all see that, and I know that you will protect her with your life, as you have done many times."

Polly, meanwhile, is in the kitchen with Margaret and seeks to reassure her.

"Daniel will always be there to protect me, Mummy, so please do not worry. And my new job will not put me into any direct contact with anyone from the colonies. All of my contacts will be by correspondence and telephone."

"But what about Daniel's work, Polly? That will still expose you to some danger, won't it? He will still be in direct conflict with the communist menace."

"Once the conspiracy trial is over, Mummy, the threat will have all but disappeared, and so will the danger."

"Very well my dear, but I cannot help but worry for you both."

Polly had dropped her peeling knife while they were talking, and as she stood up Margaret could not help but notice the ring on the end of the chain. Polly quickly tucks the chain inside her shirt, hoping Margaret did not notice. But Margaret has noticed, and smiles to herself.

On Tuesday morning Polly and Daniel arrive back at court, knowing that Polly will almost certainly be called first to give her evidence of the night she was attacked.

"Will Miss Polly Spencer please take the stand?" the court usher instructs.

"Will you confirm your name and occupation for the court, please?"

"My name is Polly Spencer and I am a Civil Servant at the Home Office."

"And will you tell the court, in your own words, what happened to you, at your family home on the night in question, Miss Spencer?"

"I was woken suddenly by two men grabbing me and forcing me out of my bed. I struggled as they grabbed at my pyjama jacket, which they almost ripped off in the struggle. They were very rough with me, not saying anything, just dragging and pulling me. No matter how hard I tried, I couldn't stop them from taking me from my room. I screamed for Daniel, as they carried me along the landing, still trying to break free from them."

"And where would Daniel Bottomley's room be in relation to yours?"

"Daniel's room was next to mine, closer to the staircase, so they would have to pass it to get to the stairs."

"Thank you. Please go on, Miss Spencer."

"As I was being dragged past his room, I heard the gunshots. The two men carrying me continued to the staircase and began carrying me down the stairs. No matter how hard I tried, I just could not free myself. My pyjama jacket was hanging off and I tried desperately to cover myself, but one of the men was dragging me by my arms. I noticed the other man at the bottom of the stairs, and he fired just as we got to the bottom of the staircase. One of the men dropped me as there was more gunfire, which must have been Daniel from the top of the stairs."

"And what happened next?"

"The men grabbed my hair and began dragging me across the hall to the doorway. I was trying to stop them and grabbed at the doorway of the study and they hit me across my bare chest to make me release my hold. I was screaming for Daniel as they got as far as the door. Despite my kicking and screaming, I was sure they would get away with me. No matter how hard I tried, I could not stop them from dragging me closer to the front door," Polly says, holding back her tears and gripping the front of the witness box.

'Would you like a break, Miss Spencer?" the Crown asks.

Polly declines and after a few moments, continues.

"Then suddenly one of the men dropped me. He had been shot by Daniel and couldn't hold on to me. I grabbed at the other, trying to release myself from him, but he let go of me anyway and ran off. I got up from the floor, having fallen on the man who was wounded, to rush to Daniel who was staggering across the hallway now bleeding heavily from his chest wound. Mummy and Daddy came down the stairs and I remember shouting to call an ambulance. There was blood everywhere, most of it Daniel's. I was hysterical thinking he was going to die. I'm sorry, can we stop?" Polly asks, sobbing uncontrollably.

"Mr Barwick, a short recess, I think," says Judge Blythe as Polly rushes over to Daniel.

They sit in the court entrance for a moment as Polly rests in Daniel's arms.

"That must have been very difficult for you, Polly."

"I'm ok now thank you, Mr Barwick," Polly replies as she gets up and returns to the courtroom.

"Are you ok to continue, Miss Spencer?"

Polly nods and the Crown barrister asks her to continue.

"As I said, Daniel was bleeding badly. I held him in my arms, talking to him, terrified that he might die there and then. I was also covered in his blood since my pyjama jacket had been ripped off in the struggles. I have never been so scared as I was at that time, I could not believe what was happening to me in my parents' home. I kept talking to Daniel and I remember Mummy covering me with something, then the doorbell rang and the ambulance arrived. The ambulance officers treated Daniel before they could move him, giving me time to go and put on some clothes so that I could go with him to the hospital."

"And do you have any idea why these men should have carried out these attacks on you and Mr Bottomley, Miss Spencer?"

"There have been a number of attacks on Daniel and myself over the last few months."

"Yes, we are aware of that, and His Lordship does have details, but can you say why?"

"I have no idea. My work as a Civil Servant is mainly administration, delivering mail to various offices, hardly something that would cause offence. In previous attacks, reference has been made about Daniel's work and even threats that I would be taken to Russia."

"You have previously been threatened with abduction to Russia, Miss Spencer?" the judge asks, visibly shocked by this latest revelation.

"Yes sir."

"And why do you suppose the Russians would want to abduct you and take you to Russia, Miss Spencer?" the Crown continues.

"I can only think that they want to punish Daniel in some perverted way. I try not to think too much about their threats of abduction, it's too terrifying to understand."

"Yes, quite, Miss Spencer. The Soviets are not known for their hospitality. Now what happened once the officers had treated Daniel in the hallway?"

"When we arrived at hospital, he was given emergency surgery to remove the bullet from his chest. Thankfully, there was minimal damage internally, so he was allowed home to my parents' house after a couple of days. Unfortunately, there was a complication – a tiny fragment of bullet must have been left inside him, causing a fever. The doctor was able to remove this as it had worked its way to the surface of his skin. Once this was removed, we cared for Daniel at my parents' home and were finally able to return to London the following week."

The Crown barrister sits down, and a defence barrister stands.

"Why would the Russians want to punish Mr Bottomley, Miss Spencer?"

"I have no idea, sir."

"Perhaps something to do with his work, He works for the security services, does he not?"

"I believe he answered that question yesterday," Polly replies angrily.

"I believe that you also work for the security services, Miss Spencer, and may have brought some of these events on yourself."

"My lord is this really necessary, and is there a question here?" the Crown barrister asks.

"Yes, is there a question here?" asks the judge.

"No sir, I have nothing further to ask this witness," the defence barrister concludes.

"May I question the witness further, Your Honour?" the Crown asks. "Miss Spencer, do you have any definitive knowledge linking Mr Bottomley with the security services?"

"No sir, I do not."

"And do you, Miss Spencer, work for the government security services?"

"No sir, I do not."

"Thank you, Miss Spencer. My lord, we shall be hearing from a member of the security services later in this trial, and I trust he will enlighten the court."

"Thank you Mr Barwick, perhaps we should now adjourn and continue after lunch."

After lunch, D.I. Wishart is called to the stand.

"You are Detective Inspector Wishart of Carswell police, is that correct?"

"Yes sir, that's correct."

"And will you tell the court the circumstances surrounding your call to the Spencer residence on the night in question?"

"I received the call, from Mr Spencer, around 2.30am. He said there had been an intrusion at his home and shots fired. I dashed round, accompanied by my sergeant and a W.P.C., to be greeted by a scene of total carnage. There was a man in the porch with a gunshot wound in his leg, and just inside the hallway, Mr Bottomley was propped up against the wall, bleeding heavily and being comforted by Miss Polly Spencer. She was very dishevelled and covered in blood herself. There was another man at the bottom of the staircase with wounds to his stomach and neck. Mr Spencer told me that there were two more men injured upstairs, and I instructed my officers to bring them down. They were both injured – one had a chest wound the other had a serious injury to his face," the D.I. replies.

"So, there were five men in total suffering gunshot wounds and four of those five were intruders. Is that correct, Detective Inspector?"

"Yes sir."

"And do you see the alleged intruders in court today?"

"Yes sir, they are the four men in the dock."

"And what happened when you were eventually able to question these men?"

"I was able to positively identify two of them as Russian nationals."

"And how were you able to do that, sir?"

"With the assistance of the security services," the D.I. replies.

"Thank you, Detective Inspector."

"Detective Inspector, you say the security services positively identified these men?" a defence barrister asks.

"Yes sir, that is correct."

"And what made you contact the security services?"

"Because I believed they would want to be made aware of Russian nationals attacking British citizens in their own homes," the D.I. replies.

"Don't you think it reasonable that these men took their actions because Mr Bottomley is a member of the security services?"

"I have no idea why they took their illegal actions, sir. I only deal in facts, and the facts were very clear to me."

"Detective Inspector, did you not find it unusual that Mr Bottomley was carrying a firearm?"

"Providing the carrier has the required licence, anyone can carry a firearm."

"Is the defence going somewhere with this line of questioning?" the judge asks.

"No further questions, my lord."

The rest of the afternoon is taken up with details from the doctors of the wounds sustained by the accused and by Daniel, as well as details of Polly's injuries. The court is then adjourned for the day.

"I understand that Mr Fitzroy Jones will be called tomorrow, Daniel, to outline the security services' findings. You know him very well, I believe?" the Crown barrister asks as they leave the courtroom.

"He is my Operations Commander, Jonathan. Yes, I know him very well."

"As well as asking him for the security services interest in this case, I will be asking him about you, Daniel. There has been some underhand methods adopted by the defence to cast doubt on your integrity. I want that to be dispelled by Fitzroy Jones tomorrow."

Polly and Daniel return home, relieved that their contributions have now been completed. Daniel decides he must call Fitz for an update, but is a bit taken aback by Polly's comments about Margaret noticing her ring.

"Are you sure Margaret saw it, Polly?"

"I know she saw it, Daniel, and she also noticed how quickly I tried to hide it. I hate deceiving my parents about this, Daniel, especially over something so wonderful and precious to me."

"We shall not deliberately deceive them any more than necessary, Polly. If your parents comment on the ring around your neck then we will tell them, of course. Now I must call Fitz."

They had been sitting in Polly's room drinking tea, and both go downstairs, Polly to the parlour and Daniel to the study.

"Daniel, dear chap, how goes it? I am just about to leave for leafy Leicester," says Fitz cheerfully.

"Both Polly and I have given our evidence, Fitz, so the trial is coming to an end."

"Good. You will be pleased to know that your Mr Doyle has been in contact. He is anxious to see you again sometime next week. He would not say what is was about, but did sound edgy."

"He is scared, Fitz, and looking for reassurance. We are keeping an eye on him so he should be safe enough, but if the communists find out he has been speaking to us, he will be in trouble."

"Anyway, he will be in touch with you again next week, I got the impression he is waiting on something. Now I must dash, I will see you in the morning, Daniel. My regards to Polly."

Daniel returns to the parlour, to find Polly, Margaret, and Ben looking rather sombre. Polly moves towards Daniel as he enters, her eyes brimming with tears, as she reaches out for his hand.

"Daniel, Ben and I wondered if there was something you and Polly might want to share with us?" Margaret asks awkwardly.

Daniel holds Polly close to him and looks at her before answering Margaret.

"Polly did mention your observation yesterday, Margaret. With our apologies for the delay, Polly and I are delighted to tell you that we were married on the 22nd of August at two o'clock."

Margaret bursts into tears, Polly bursts into tears, Daniel and Ben shake each other's hands enthusiastically, and the children arrive to see what all the noise is about. They too burst into shrieks of delight for Polly and Daniel.

"My dearest Polly and Daniel, we are so happy for you, truly we are. There is no couple anywhere more suited to each other," says Ben.

"And I am so happy I could burst, I now have a big brother at last," says Maisy.

"We would so much have liked you to all be there, Daddy, but it had to be kept secret after all that had happened to us. We wanted to wait until after the trial, but Daniel said why wait for each other? We love each other so much, and felt that we were sacrificing our happiness because of circumstances beyond our control. It was never our intention to keep such wonderful news from you, but there really was no other way. Only Conrad knows, because I needed a best man and witness. Other than that we are still Mr Bottomley and Miss Spencer, and will remain so until after the conspiracy trial. We only had the weekend away, before returning to work as normal on the Tuesday," says Daniel.

"I wanted to tell the world, Mummy, I really did. I have loved Daniel for so long, and if I had waited much longer to be his wife I would have screamed!"

"Can you put on your wedding rings, just for this evening please?" asks Margaret.

Daniel and Polly take their rings from round their necks and place them on each other's fingers

"We thought it would be nice if I wore Daniel's round my neck, and he wore mine around his."

"Thank you, Mr and Mrs Bottomley," smiles Margaret.

"I always knew you would marry Polly, Daniel. I told you, didn't I?" says Maisy.

"Yes you did, Maisy and you asked me about it many times, didn't you?"

"It's so wonderful to be able to tell you all. Keeping it a secret has been so very stressful, hasn't it Daniel?"

"I can honestly say that it has proved to be a very difficult venture, we have had to tread so very carefully and avoid all the difficult questions. Now at least we can relax in your home, if not anywhere else for a while."

"And when the trial at the Old Bailey is over we shall have a huge party as our wedding reception for all of our friends, isn't that right Daniel?"

"We most definitely will, Polly. Most definitely."

"I can only repeat how happy we all are for you both. You have been a member of our family for some time now, Daniel. Through the difficult times of five years ago, you put your life on the line for all of us, not least Polly. At first, Margaret and I thought that Polly's feelings for you were from gratitude, as you were her saviour so many times. But it soon became obvious that you were both beginning to have feelings for each other. And we are most grateful that you treated our daughter with so much respect when she was younger. As for Polly, she had made up her mind about Daniel very early in all this."

"The way that you talked of him, Polly, convinced Margaret and I that you were always going to be together. And here you are as man and wife."

"Thank you Ben and Margaret for those kind words. Our relationship came about through adversity in the dark times of '47. That was the time I met a very beautiful young girl who had been subjected to terrible ordeals, and would suffer even more as time went by. I went from being her protector to being her friend and companion. The time we spent together will always be precious to me and to Polly, I am sure. Eventually, our very special friendship grew into our love for each other."

"I always knew that we would marry someday. Yes, Daniel saved me many times, but I always felt comfortable with him as well as being safe in the difficult times. I have spoken to you many times about my feelings, Mummy, and I know that you were waiting in anticipation for Daniel and me to make the announcement. I remember when I moved in with Daniel, wondering how long it would be before we became husband and wife. Our relationship was very special from early on. As I have said to you many times, I cannot imagine my life without him by my side," Polly replies, hugging Daniel and kissing him on his cheek.

And so after all of the congratulations, the hugs and kisses and the speeches, the family settle down to dinner with a glass of wine for celebration. Daniel and Polly eventually retire, into the same room, as Mr and Mrs Bottomley, and enjoy the night together.

The following day, Daniel and Polly arrive early at the court in time to speak with Fitz, who is in conversation with the Crown barrister.

"Polly, Daniel, good morning to you both."

"Good morning, Fitz. Did you have a good journey?"

"I did, yes. This is my first visit to the Midlands and to Leicester."

"Fitz will be called first today, he will be asked to give evidence on behalf of the security services and specific reference to Daniel's work. I would think that today should see the conclusion of evidence, unless the defence wishes to call any of the accused, which is unlikely. Ok, shall we go in?" says the Crown barrister.

Proceedings duly commence with Fitz being called to the witness box.

"Will you confirm your name and occupation please?"

"My name is William Fitzroy Jones and I am Special Operations Commander with the security services."

"And what exactly does that entail, Mr Fitzroy Jones?"

"I head a task force specifically to fight the growing menace to our society of communism."

"Do you work for MI5?'

"No I do not, my position is completely independent of MI5. It was decided by the government, to carefully monitor the Soviets not long after the end of World War Two. My department monitors any communists that we suspect may be trying to create problems for our democratically elected government."

"And can you tell the court where Mr Bottomley fits into all this?"

"Let me tell you a little about this man. Daniel Bottomley received a number of commendations for his services in World War Two in Europe and in Africa. When war ended, he worked with the security services after resigning his commission, feeling sure he could contribute more without the constraints of the military. He is my most senior operative in the fight against communist infiltration within the Civil Service and the trade union movement.

"It is as a direct result of his actions and that of his team, that the Crown are preparing a conspiracy trial. The trial will show just how far this conspiracy has progressed within our country."

"Mr Fitzroy Jones, the Crown called you to give evidence because they want to show to the jury the possible link between the attacks that took place at the Spencer home and the Soviets. Can you enlighten us at all? Is there perhaps a link or are we being overzealous in our attitude towards the communists?" the judge asks.

"During his work for the department, Daniel has discovered specific evidence of Soviet plotting against the state. This evidence will be detailed in the conspiracy trial to take place at the Old Bailey later in the year. In discovering these links he has been engaged in direct physical contact with Soviet agents, who attempted to kill him and abduct his ward Miss Polly Spencer. During these skirmishes, he has been successful in incapacitating a number of them, not without some injury to himself and Miss Spencer. I believe that the attempt by the men in the dock to kill him and abduct Miss Spencer, at the Spencer family home, was in revenge for his actions against the Soviets."

"So, it is your opinion, that the accused were hired by the Soviets to kill one British citizen and abduct another from within a family home?" the Crown ask.

"That is correct. Daniel and his team have successfully broken down Soviet attempts to initiate their members into government office and influence trade union members, on a number of occasions. He has suffered a number of injuries, one very serious, for his actions. Also his ward, Miss Spencer, has been the subject of some nasty attacks on her personally. You might say he has become a thorn in their side. You need to appreciate the sort of people we are dealing with. They have sought to harm a young woman, Miss Spencer, on a number of occasions, a young woman who has no political aspirations – she works at the Home Office. Their actions toward her can only be described as spite for their own failings. Without men like Daniel Bottomley, our country would be a lot less safe. He is to be commended for his work within the security services along with so many more unsung heroes."

"Thank you, Mr Fitzroy Jones. I'm sure the defence council will want a word."

"Mr Fitzroy Jones, I represent Mr Obermann and Mr Fuentes. Can you tell me why we should believe a word of your fairy tale about a communist conspiracy in Britain? Is it not just the imagination of the security services working overtime?" the defence asks with disdain.

"The threat to our security is very real, sir, as will be most definitively proved at the Old Bailey. The evidence is conclusive, no one is imagining anything. I wish I could say we were."

"I would like to ask Mr Fitzroy Jones another question if I may, Your Honour."

"After lunch, Mr Barwick. We shall adjourn for lunch," says the judge.

Polly and Daniel find a restaurant close by the court and asked Fitz to join them. Polly goes off to call home before ordering, leaving Daniel and Fitz.

"This was a bad business, Daniel, attacking you and Polly in Mr Spencer's home."

"I am sure the judge will take that into consideration, he has been very inquisitive about what is going on."

"I have just spoken with Mummy, Fitz, and she asks that you have dinner with us this evening."

"It will be my pleasure, Polly, and thank you for the invitation," Fitz replies with a smile.

After lunch, Fitz is recalled to the witness box by the Crown.

"Mr Fitzroy Jones, how long have you worked for the security services?"

"Since the end of the war in one capacity or the other."

"And is it true that, apart from being a decorated soldier you have received numerous commendations for your work with the security services?"

"Well, er, one does one's best, you know," Fitz replies rather awkwardly.

"What is you point, Mr Barwick?"

"I am merely showing the integrity of this witness, my lord. Not the sort to make up fairy stories."

"Very well. Please continue, Mr Barwick."

"Whilst the Crown will be able to establish the guilt of the accused beyond all reasonable doubt, it is important for the jury to be aware of just what is at stake here. Mr Fitzroy Jones, you mentioned earlier specific attacks on Mr Bottomley and his ward Miss Spencer?"

"Yes, there have been several attacks, in one case the perpetrators, Russian nationals, were expelled by Her Majesty's government. In the other incidences, Miss Spencer has been brutally assaulted and badly beaten, simply because she was in the company of Mr Bottomley. They were attacked on a train, in the apartment of Mr Bottomley, and they were abducted in the street. These attacks were not the work of opportunists, they were obviously well organised. And in the case before this court, but for the astonishing heroism of Mr Bottomley, we would have been dealing with an abduction of one British citizen and the murder of another."

"Mr Fitzroy Jones, your evidence has indeed been enlightening. Just what bearing it may have on the outcome of this trial, is for the jury to decide. And I am sure that they will seriously consider what you have said when they retire. What is clear to me, is the lengths one individual will go to in order to inflict his will on another. We have previously heard Miss Spencer's evidence relating to her attempted abduction. This young woman has been the subject of several abduction attempts. I am concerned why these attempts were made, and who instigated them. If, as the Crown suggests, this attack on Mr Bottomley and Miss Spencer was instigated by Soviet agents, then this is very serious indeed and will need to be addressed at the highest authority. We live in a democratic society and have no place for thuggery by foreign instigators.

"I now propose that we now adjourn for the day and I will present my summation to you in the morning."

Polly and Daniel meet with Fitz in the court reception area to arrange for him to have dinner with Polly's family in the evening.

"Dinner will be at seven o'clock Fitz, if you catch the train to Carswell and ask for the Spencer's house, Green Gables, the taxi will know where to take you," says Polly.

"I will see you both later then, bye for now," says Fitz, as he walks out of the courthouse.

Daniel and Polly arrive home to discuss the arrival of Fitz for dinner.

"You are full of surprises, Polly. Yesterday your marriage, today we are to meet Mr Fitzroy Jones."

"I know, Mummy, but I just felt we could not let him come to Leicester without inviting him to dinner. And Daniel and I have decided that we will tell him of our marriage. If he cannot keep a secret then no one can! We both know him very well, and I really do want you to meet with him."

"Well I think that it's a wonderful idea. Now Polly, come along and see what I have sorted for our dinner this evening," says Margaret, as she moves off to the kitchen followed by her daughter.

Fitz arrives around 7.15pm and is introduced to the family by Polly.

"Fitz, this is Mummy and Daddy and this is Maisy, Daisy, and George."

"I am so very pleased to meet you all. You have a wonderful family, Polly, and may I say to Mr and Mrs Spencer, you have a truly remarkable daughter."

"Well thank you Fitz, and please, Margaret and Ben, and yes we are rather proud of her ourselves," replies Ben.

"Fitz, before we go any further, Polly and I need a word with you in the study if you don't mind."

"Well of course, dear boy, please excuse me everyone," says Fitz, as he follows Polly and Daniel into the study with a puzzled look on his face.

"What on earth is the matter, Daniel!"

"Absolutely nothing, Fitz, we just wanted to give you the news that Polly and I were married on August 22nd."

"That is absolutely wonderful news, Daniel. Many congratulations to you both," he says, as he kisses Polly on the cheek and gives Daniel a firm handshake.

"We only told Mummy and Daddy yesterday, we both wanted to wait until after the conspiracy trial, but decided we could wait no longer. Conrad was our best man, but apart from Conrad no one else knew."

"I can understand that you want it to remain secret for the moment, and I will not mention it to anyone until you say otherwise. Had I known sooner, I would have brought champagne instead of wine, but no matter. Now come along, let's go and join your family, Polly."

"It's a real pleasure to make your acquaintance at last, Ben. I feel as if I have known you and your family for quite some time. Daniel wasn't with my department when he spent his time with you some five years ago, but I am familiar with all the circumstances."

"They were dark days, Fitz. Daniel and Conrad, were all that stood between us and disaster on more than one occasion. We have a lot to thank both of them for, both the family and for their assistance in helping me close down the black market operation. Now I am honoured to have Daniel as a member of my family."

"He is a very special person, Ben, your daughter has chosen well. Although I have to admit I did have some idea of their feelings for each other. And they make a formidable team. Polly has been an asset in our fight against the communist menace."

"So I suppose we could say we are both fortunate to know them. Now, Ben, let me have a look at your beautiful garden if I may."

"Certainly Fitz, follow me."

Daniel was already in the garden entertaining Maisy, Daisy, and George.

'You will still come and see us now that you and Polly are married, won't you Daniel?"

"Of course we will, Maisy, and you can come along and see us during school holidays."

"Really, Daniel? And perhaps we can go and see some cricket?"

"Certainly, George. The ladies could go shopping, and you and I could go to the Test Match."

"I think my sister is the luckiest person in the world marrying you, Daniel."

"Well thank you very much for that, Daisy," he replies, smiling.

Fitz proves to be an excellent guest, with lots of stories to tell about himself and life in general. He never misses an opportunity to compliment Ben and Margaret about their beautiful daughter, and her contribution to the security services' efforts to rid the nation of the communist menace threatening our society. And he gives a special mention to Daniel's contribution, and the sacrifice he has made for his country.

"While we have men like Daniel working with women like Polly, we have nothing to fear, Ben. They are a formidable team in more ways than one. I therefore offer a toast to Daniel and Polly, may your happiness together last forever," says Fitz, raising his glass.

"Thank you for that, Fitz. Polly and I do appreciate your comments. We are both looking forward to the conclusion of this trial and the big one at the Old Bailey. We can then officially become Mr and Mrs Spencer and get on with our lives. Meantime, we know what needs to be done."

"Tell me Ben, do you still have problems with black market business locally?"

"There will always be spivs at work, Fitz. The best way to put them out of business, is to end rationing altogether. Only then, will they have nothing to offer."

"And that is one of the reasons why we have to stop theses damn communist agitators. They are causing problems at the docks every day. We have tons of perishables rotting on the boats and on the quayside waiting to be moved," says Fitz.

"I am hoping to meet with them next week and see where we are with the dock strikes, Fitz, it is becoming serious. The longer it takes to settle, the more the communists will gain momentum."

"Well Mr Doyle seemed anxious to make a contribution, Daniel, although he was very frightened of being discovered."

"Did you meet with the dockers Polly?"

"Yes Daddy, I go with Daniel whenever I cannot arrange for a friend to stay with me, and I can make a difference. Sometimes the men will feel more relaxed if a woman is there."

"At first, Ben, I just didn't want to leave Polly alone, but she has proved useful. The men definitely seem more relaxed when she is there."

"Your daughter has a calming influence on everyone she meets, Ben," Fitz comments with a smile.

"Any idea how long it will be before the conspiracy trial begins,

Fitz? Daniel and Polly have spent so much time in court recently, it will be a relief when it is finally all over."

"Yes it will, Margaret. We are not far away from a date now. The bulk of the evidence is already with the Crown. Any additional evidence that we secure in the meantime can only strengthen the case. But I understand how you feel, and will be glad when it is all over myself."

"We shall be relieved as much as you, Mummy. Daniel and I want to look for a house as soon as we have some spare time."

"Another celebration for us all to look forward to, visiting your new home," says Margaret.

"Meantime, Daniel, let's get those traffic lights off red once and for all," says Fitz, and proceeds to tell Ben and Margaret the significance of his comment.

The rest of the evening goes by quickly, and Ben calls for a taxi for Fitz around 10.30pm.

"It's been a wonderful evening, Ben and Margaret, I trust we shall meet again at Polly and Daniel's party, thank you so much for inviting me," says Fitz as he leaves for Carswell Station.

"What a charming man. I am so glad that you suggested he come for dinner, Polly," says Margaret, as they sit having tea before going up to bed. Daniel and Polly sit for a while talking about the evening and the trial, before going up to bed.

"I am so glad that we have been able to tell the family, and Fitz, about our marriage, Daniel. I want to tell the world about us, but am happy to wait so long as we are together," says Polly, as she snuggles up to Daniel and embraces him.

Daniel removes her nightdress, then gently feels between her legs as he kisses her breasts. Polly gasps with pleasure at his attentions and moves her hand down his body to pleasure him. His firmness excites her as she strokes and rubs him before guiding him inside, thrusting her body upwards to secure maximum penetration. Their lovemaking is always passionate and they have learned to control their pleasures to lengthen their period of coupling. Finally they subside and lay side by side, breathless and bathed in sweat, before falling asleep in other's arms.

The following morning Polly and Daniel set off for the courts to listen to the closing arguments. The Crown has a very strong case which is documented by the Crown barrister Jonathan Barwick Q.C. There are no excuses that can be offered for the appalling attacks on Polly and Daniel in the Spencer home. The fact that Russian nationals were involved, is cause for concern, which the judge is expected to comment on. In conclusion, the Crown asks the jury to find the four men guilty of all the charges.

There is very little that the defence barristers can offer in defence of their clients. They ask the jury to consider the facts and not be influenced by the questions of national security. The barrister representing the Russian nationals recognises that his clients will most probably be deported anyway.

After about an hour of deliberations by the relative councils, the judge begins his summary.

"This has been a decidedly unpleasant case for a number of reasons, not least the terrible assaults on Mr Bottomley and Miss Spencer. That Mr Bottomley is alive to tell his story is in itself remarkable. And without his heroism, Miss Spencer would surely have been abducted to a foreign power. The further use of foreign nationals in carrying out this crime is also disturbing, illustrating the lengths that they were prepared to go to achieve their aims. And it is the international scope of the men who carried out the assaults that should cause everyone to be concerned about what the events of that night were all about. These men should be made to pay heavily for their crimes, which were inexcusable. That a foreign power should seek the assistance of hired guns to carry out these assaults on British citizens will need to be addressed by a higher authority. However, that it happened at all is why we are here. You four men in the dock brutally assaulted a young woman, Miss Spencer, in a determined effort to abduct her to a foreign power. There is no doubt in my mind that was your intention, and we can only guess at what might have happened to her if your efforts had been successful."

Polly and Daniel listen intently to his comments and she squeezes his hand tightly on hearing his remarks.

"We cannot allow foreign nationals to ride roughshod over our laws, if they do they will be punished severely, as would British nationals who behaved in this way. The attack was obviously well planned; five men do not enter a property without a preconceived idea of who will be doing what. Their indiscriminate use of firearms, with no regard for the Spencer family, including three young children, was despicable. You should consider the fact that this was a family home that was attacked, with no regard for the occupants. When you consider your verdicts, consider all of the facts. Asks yourself, do you want to live in a country where a foreign power seeks to force its ideals on us no matter what it takes? Will you send a message from the British people to those concerned that this behaviour will not be tolerated, and reflect that in your final verdicts? My recommendations to you is that you respond in the strongest possible way in giving your verdicts. I urge you to find all four of the accused guilty of all the charges against them. Upon receiving your verdicts, I will add what I consider to be appropriate with regard to the use of foreign nationals being used to commit brutal assaults on British citizens. Now please go and consider you verdicts. For now, this court is adjourned."

The jury return after just one hour of deliberation and they record verdicts of guilty on all charges for all four men.

"Demetrius Bukovsky, Vladimir, Karl Obermann, and Pedro Fuentes, you have been found guilty of all the charges against you. All that remains is for me to pass sentence. This I will do after considering my options. The court will reconvene in the morning."

Daniel and Polly enjoy the rest of the day together, before returning on Friday morning to hear the judge's ruling.

"The four men in the dock have been found guilty of serious charges of assault, attempted murder, attempted abduction, and breaking and entering. You will be charged collectively of all of the charges listed.

"On the charge of attempted murder, you will each serve seven years. On the charge of attempted kidnapping, you will each serve seven years. On the charge of grievous bodily harm, you will each serve seven years. And on the charge of breaking and entering illegally, you will serve three years. All sentences to be served consecutively. I also recommend that upon the termination of your sentences that you be deported to your country of origin, although in the case of the Russian nationals, it may well be that the security services have other ideas. I thank the jury for their diligence in this difficult case. That concludes my deliberations, this court is adjourned."

"Well they certainly got what they deserved, Daniel, I'm sure you and Polly agree on that. It was apparent from the start that the judge was deeply disturbed by the use of foreign nationals and wanted to send a message. Well goodbye to you both, it was nice to have met you."

Jonathan Barwick Q.C. shakes their hands before going back into the court buildings, whilst Daniel flags down a taxi for the station.

"Do you think Mummy and Daddy would mind if we returned to London today, Daniel? I know it sounds mean, I just want to get away and be with you," says Polly, as the taxi pulls up outside Leicester Station.

"I'm sure they will understand, Polly, and we have had a whole week with them so it is time to get back home." Daniel hopes his comment will reassure Polly. When they arrive at Carswell Station they inquire about train times to London to find there is one at 4.30pm.

"Of course we understand, dear. You are married now and have things to do before returning to work. We have all enjoyed your being with us and hope that it will not be too long before we see you again."

"Thank you Mummy, I knew you would understand."

They arrive in good time to catch the 4.30pm train, and arrive at Euston around seven o'clock.

By the time they get back to the apartment, it is nearly eight o'clock, and they are both very tired from the day. Polly runs her bath, while Daniel looks for something to eat.

"I will call home over the weekend to say hello to Maisy, Daisy, and George. I felt a bit mean leaving without saying goodbye," says Polly, sitting next to Daniel on the settee.

"Can we show off our rings while we are out shopping tomorrow, Daniel? I do so want to wear my ring in public."

"Yes of course, Polly."

Polly hugs Daniel and kisses him on the lips. He allows his hand to wander inside her gown and he gently fondles her, before picking her up and carrying her to their bedroom.

Afterwards Polly lies in Daniel's arms and says: "We should get something to eat, Daniel. I am hungry, are you?"

Daniel goes off to make something to eat and Polly puts on her nightdress and gown.

She spends Sunday looking forward to starting in her new position at the Foreign Office.

"I had almost forgotten about the new job, being away all week, Daniel. Now I really am looking forward to making a new start. I just hope that I can live up to everyone's expectations of me."

"I'm sure you will be just as successful in your new position as you were at the Home Office, Polly. You have become an asset to the Civil Service."

"Thank you for that, Daniel."

Monday passes quickly for Daniel, and in the evening he makes contact with Hennessey.

"Daniel, Michael is keen for another meeting, and has suggested that he meets up with you again in Whitechapel at the Black Bull at noon. He is very nervous of being found out, so does not want to meet anywhere he will be known," says Hennessey.

"Tell him Polly and I will be there, Peter, and thank you."

This is good news for Daniel, who is hoping for some clear evidence of Soviet interference in the unions.

Monday is very special day for Polly, since she is to start her new job as Soviet Strategies Analyst at the Foreign Office. She is both apprehensive and excited as she enters the reception area where she is asked to go up to Mrs Warner's office. She has bought a new outfit for her new job, comprising a two-piece suit and a white blouse. She enters Mrs Warner's office and is warmly greeted by her.

"Polly, do come in and sit down. Now, I understand that a trial date has not yet been finalised, but I would like to make your appointment official. Whilst I appreciate that there will be some disruption while you are giving evidence and so on, that does not prevent us from installing you in your new role, it is really important that we make a start. Now you will have two assistants to help you with the vast amount of data that arrives each day from the colonies. You alone could not possibly be expected to sieve and coordinate what is received on a daily basis and also be effective in analysing its importance. David Fellows thought it might be an idea to let you have your own office, so that you can be easily identified by staff. Your two associates will still be situated in the main office. Now let me introduce you to them before you go to your station to meet with David."

Just then, two members of staff enter Mrs Warner's office.

"Polly, this is Rachel Nichols; Rachel has been working in our data processing for a while now, she will be able to help you identify processes that we operate as required. And this is Peter Bartholomew; Peter is a communications expert, who has been working with communications, helping to listen in and identify suspect conversations. Peter has spent some time in South Africa, and has first-hand knowledge of Soviet interference in that region. Peter, Rachel, this is Polly Spencer, Polly has joined us from the Home Office, where she has played no small part in bringing down a communist-inspired organisation that were trying to infiltrate government. She is also a close associate of Daniel Bottomley, who is heading up the task force that has been responsible for bringing a number of Russian citizens and Soviet agents to trial."

"I have heard about Daniel from my colleagues at MI5. He has a fearsome reputation throughout the service, Polly. I am very pleased to meet you and will enjoy working with you, I am sure," says Peter, shaking Polly's hand.

"And I have heard of you, Polly, from my friend in the Home Office, Penny Carstairs," says Rachel.

"You are a friend of Penny's? Then I am sure we will get along fine, Rachel," says Polly, shaking her by the hand.

"Ok, now that we all know each other, Peter, Rachel, back to your office and tell David that Polly will be along shortly. Now Polly, what we haven't yet discussed is your pay grade. You will be pleased to know that you will be put on HEO grade, that of Higher Executive Officer, which will mean a significant increase in your salary. The details are in your package here," says Mrs Warner, handing Polly a large envelope.

"It also gives you a number of additional benefits that you can use. Now before you go to your department, can I just give you a few words of advice? Your position will no doubt be questioned by some because you are so young. Office gossip will soon be aware of who you are and questions will be asked. Believe me when I say, no one is better suited to the job than you, and no one is more experienced! You have proved yourself to be a credit to the Service and displayed abilities far beyond your years; your activities have preceded you, Polly. I am sure you will show the same enthusiasm, fortitude, and diligence in your new position, as well as giving instruction to your two associates. May I wish you all the very best in your new post, and remember, I am always here if I can help."

"Thank you very much, Mrs Warner, I will do my very best for you," says Polly, as she leaves the office and heads for her new department. The Soviet Studies offices occupy two floors. Polly is situated on the first one of the two and she has to walk the full length of the office to reach David Fellows. As she walks into the office she senses all eyes are upon her, the male occupants being especially interested in what they see. Polly is a very attractive young woman, slim build with long dark hair, dressed in a blue suit and white blouse. She feels many pairs of eyes following her as she walks through, and is almost relieved when she reaches David Fellow's office, where Rachel and Peter are waiting for her along with Fellows.

"My dear Polly, how nice to see you again. You have met with Rachel and Peter, I believe?"

"Yes I have, Mr Fellows, and I am very pleased to be here."

"Now your office is adjacent to mine, and Rachel and Peter will be within your line of sight in the main office. How you organise the allocation of the data is entirely up to you. At the moment, it is a bit hit and miss.

"Staff take the details as they come through irrespective of where they are coming from or the degree of importance. From tomorrow that will all change, all data will come through to you Polly and you will decide how Rachel and Peter can be most effective in helping you clear it. There will be a lot of planning for you to arrange and we do have a lot of work to do in this department. We are at the forefront of the battle against the Soviet menace in our colonies. We need to be able to quickly assess any dangers to key personnel and to colonial government operations. We also need to be aware of any threats relating to colonial assets, mineral wealth, water supplies, forestry, and wildlife. Polly, this will be very much your responsibility. You will have to decide how to separate the data for Peter and Rachel to assess and then it will need to be handed over to the relevant person in the office for action. This is a huge task, but I will always be here for help and guidance should you need it. Rachel and Peter, I have already mentioned to you Polly's record against the Soviets. Use her experience whenever you think it may be useful. Believe me, she has a wealth of knowledge so don't be put off by the fact that she is young. She has more knowledge and experience than anyone in this office, and close-hand unpleasant experiences of Soviet methods of intimidation. Ok, now off you go, I will leave you to get acquainted and make ready for a start tomorrow."

Polly leads Rachel out of the office and into her own, which is spacious with a round table in one corner and her desk in the other. Now she must speak with her two colleagues as their superior, which will be a new experience for her.

"Rachel, Peter, I would like to make a start after lunch today in preparation for tomorrow. I would like you both to go down to stationery and collect some filing trays, about a dozen in all, and some tags that can be used to identify what they are holding. Also see if you can find a wall map, highlighting the Commonwealth countries, and some coloured pegs to insert onto the map. And a board and easel would be useful," Polly begins, hoping she doesn't sound too officious.

"Now, I think that we should split the Commonwealth down the middle for reference purposes."

"After lunch we will list the main countries on the blackboard ready to itemise their deliveries into the relevant filing trays. We also need to devise some way of highlighting the most urgent from the others."

"Perhaps we could use different coloured folders to put them in?"

"Yes, that's a good idea, Rachel. I suggest we add red folders to our stationery list. Ok, now you two go off for lunch, I will get a sandwich and a soft drink and stay in my office to make a few notes. I will see you in about an hour," says Polly, as Rachel and Peter go off to lunch.

Polly sits down at her desk and reflects on the huge task she has been given. She will have direct responsibility for overseeing the fight against Soviet threat in the Commonwealth, which is an enormous area of the world. The effectiveness of that fight will depend on the efficiency of her team, and how the threats are assessed and speedily passed to the relevant member of staff for action. She begins to make a list of the main countries in the Commonwealth when there is a knock on her door. Polly looks up to see Daniel standing in the doorway.

"Daniel, what a lovely surprise, what are you doing here?" she says, as she gives him a hug.

"I thought I would take a look at your new Empire. Actually, I spoke with David Fellows this morning and asked him if I might drop by."

"It is a nice surprise to see you. Look, I have my own office and my own staff now, Daniel, and I also have been given a pay rise," she adds with a big smile.

"It is no more than you deserve, Polly, you have worked very hard and earned this position and do not let anyone tell you otherwise. It's just as I told your parents, my dear. You are destined for high office, Mrs Bottomley," he says, also with a smile.

They continue chatting, about Polly's new job and what it will all mean to her. As usual Polly's enthusiasm knows no bounds as she outlines to Daniel what she is proposing to ensure the office runs smoothly. Daniel is sitting on her desk and Polly is holding his hand when Peter and Rachel return from lunch.

"Rachel, Peter, let me introduce you to Daniel. He has called in to keep an eye on me."

"I have heard a lot about you, Daniel, I'm Peter Bartholomew."

"And I'm Rachel Nichols, Daniel. Polly's friend Penny has also told me about you."

"Well, you know more about me than I know about you, but I am very pleased to meet you both. Now I must let you get on, bye for now, Polly. See you later."

"Bye Daniel, see you at five o'clock," she says as she plants a kiss on his cheek.

Peter and Rachel look at each other, somewhat surprised at Polly's show of affection.

"Now can you two go along and get the stationery items? You might just have a word with David, in case he has to sign anything."

After about half an hour or so, Rachel and Peter return with all the stationery items that Polly has requested.

"We have all the items you requested, Polly, except the easel, which is being brought to you separately," says Rachel.

"Ok, now Peter can you fix the wall map? I suggest this wall so that it faces my desk, and Rachel, you and I can place the trays on the table together with the folders."

The board and easel, together with chalks, duly arrives as requested and once it has been erected, Polly lists the main Commonwealth countries for them to consider.

"Now, I would suggest that the main areas that will be under threats from Soviet interference are predominantly in Africa, namely Rhodesia, Nigeria, Kenya, and of course South Africa. You will be able to help me with Africa, Peter, especially South Africa."

"Yes Polly, the threat in South Africa is very real. The Apartheid regime creates all sorts of problems with its programme of segregation. The government continues to introduce more repressive laws against black South Africans, which will only create more resistance. The ANC will continue to grow stronger and the communists will seek to take advantage. There are dangerous times ahead, I'm afraid," Peter replies.

"So, you will need to keep a special watch on any information from the townships, Peter. If what you have told me is happening, then we must stay on top of any information we receive from there. That will be an absolute priority for you. Now do you have any contacts in any other parts of Africa?"

"Just South Africa, Polly."

"No matter, it makes sense that you look after the other information from the rest of the African continent, it may be connected. The other area of concern must be Asia, so Rachel, you look after anything from India and Pakistan. I don't know much about Asia myself, but the Soviets must be seeking expansion and influence over such a vast continent. And you should look after Singapore also, Rachel, one of Britain's most successful colonies that needs to be protected. Find out what you can about what is happening there since the end of World War Two.

"This leaves us with our dominions of Canada, Australia, and New Zealand. We shall have to see just what is arriving over our desk and move accordingly. What we do know is that Australia is very active against the communists. So, if you could mark up some name tags to reflect the list on the board, and we should be about ready," says Polly. She is anxious to put in place a structure for dealing with the intelligence as it arrives, so that it can be distributed to the appropriate officer as soon as possible. She explains this to Rachel and Peter as soon as they have finished sorting the name tags.

"What we have to now decide is how best to sort out information in order of urgency and precedence, I am going to call it 'The Traffic Light System'. So red items most urgent to be acted upon as soon as possible, amber for consideration and should be looked at within a reasonable timeframe, and green for filing under consideration. We can then transfer this data, using the coloured pins, onto our map for easy reference."

"That way we can see at a glance if a pattern may be emerging, and it is always there for reference. That's brilliant, Polly," Peter replies, obviously impressed with Polly's tactics.

"Thank you, Peter. The more effective we can make our efforts, the easier it will be for us and for those officers following up the leads. Please remember that we are dealing with a soulless, ruthless regime, intent on destroying our democratic process both here in our own country and in our Commonwealth. We must do whatever it takes to stop them. Anyway, enough of my 'soap box' talk, I do tend to go on a bit once I start. Now, do you have any other suggestions?"

"What about some tea, Polly? It's just about time for the tea trolley."

"Now that is a very good suggestion, Rachel."

They sit around the table to have their tea, and Peter comments on Daniel and his exploits within the service.

"It was indeed a privilege to meet him after hearing so many stories about his exploits, especially against the Soviets."

"I had no idea he was so famous, he will be very pleased to hear what has been said. He is my guardian and I have lived with him since I took up my post in the Home Office in January."

"Have you known him very long, Polly? If you don't mind my asking."

"Not at all Rachel, it's no secret. Daniel and I have known each other for over five years, since I was thirteen. He and his colleague lived with us for a while to protect my family from attacks by black market criminals that my father was seeking to bring to justice. It is no secret that he saved my life and my family on more than one occasion. And, it is no secret that he and I have been involved in a number of skirmishes with criminals and Soviet agents, over the last few months. You may have heard about the upcoming conspiracy trial, well that is all about what has been happening for some time now. In fact we were at a trial in Leicester only last week, where four men were given heavy sentences, two of them Russians."

"Gosh, Polly, I had no idea you had been so involved," says Rachel, rather overwhelmed by what she has just heard.

"My involvement has been as a direct result of my living with Daniel. The Soviets have made several attempts to get at Daniel by using me. He has suffered a number of severe injuries over the time we have known each other, many of them protecting me. I hope I did not embarrass you when he was here earlier, but I am very fond of him and often show my affections, forgetting where I am," Polly comments with a smile, feeling for Daniel's ring around her neck.

"So you know all about me. Now then, Peter, tell me about South Africa."

"I was there for about two years. It really is a beautiful country, but it will tear itself apart with its laws of separation. I enjoyed my time there with the diplomatic corps and was able to get around and see the sights and of course the weather was wonderful. I was sorry in some ways to return, but as I mentioned earlier, I fear for the country, I really do."

"And what about you, Rachel, what have you been doing?"

"Pretty boring I'm afraid, I have been with the Service since I left school. My father is with MI6, and he helped me secure my position in the Foreign Office. He will be very pleased that I have secured this special position and will be delighted to know I am working for you, Polly."

"Ok, now I have a list of the various officers here with their responsibilities. Rachel, can you type me some copies so that they are to hand for reference? Perhaps you and Peter could have a look at them while I go and have a word with David about what we have been doing."

Polly goes off to David Fellow's office and outlines her proposals to him. He is very impressed with the fact that Polly has made the preparations so soon after arriving at her new post.

"Thank you for your diligence, Polly. Your enthusiasm is duly noted. There is a lot of work to be done by your section, and an early start can only be to your advantage."

"Thank you for that, David. I would hope that by the end of the day tomorrow we should be well established.

"So how do you think this first day has gone, you two? Better than you thought or not?" Polly asks them.

"I believe we are all set to begin sorting files in order of prominence before their distribution to the relevant workstation. We are ready to begin this operation, Polly," Peter replies.

"Good, now there is just one more point I would make. If you have any suggestions or ideas that you believe will help our operation, please write them down on the board, and we will discuss them at the earliest opportunity. Will you do that for me please?"

"Absolutely, Polly," they both reply. And with that, they go off for the end of the day. Polly has made the arrangement for Daniel to begin collecting her from directly outside of the Foreign Office; there is no need for any personnel not to know who he is.

"So, how did you enjoy your first day as the boss, then?"

"I'm not really a boss, Daniel, I am just overseeing what needs to be done, that's all."

"You have been given a good deal of responsibility, Polly, and they must think very highly of you to put you in charge of such a key part of the Foreign Office operations."

The rest of Monday evening passes by quickly before they go off to bed for the night.

On Tuesday, Daniel and Polly receive notification of the conspiracy trial. The date is set for Monday 13th October and they talk over what will happen and the significance of it all over their evening meal. Polly is somewhat edgy and expresses her feelings to Daniel.

"We have just finished one trial and we are about to be involved again, Daniel. And goodness knows what sort of questions we will be asked, it just seems never ending."

"Now Polly, just focus on a week or so beyond the trial, what we can be doing once it is all over. Don't worry about what is going to happen on the 13th. Think beyond the trial dates, Polly, we will have so much to do," says Daniel, trying hard to reassure her, but appreciating just how she must be feeling having to go over so much again.

They eat the rest of their meal in silence, and Polly goes off to have her bath. After a brief moment, Daniel follows her into their bedroom where she is undressing. He enters the room to find her standing in her underwear.

"My dear Polly, please do not be concerned about what will be happening at the trial," he says, as he embraces her and kisses her on her cheek.

"I'm sorry, Daniel. Sometimes it all seems too much, I just want to be with you always."

Daniel removes her top as Polly steps out of her pants and lies down on the bed. He lies beside her before embracing her as she begins removing his clothing. Soon they are lying naked together in a firm embrace.

"Please do not worry, Polly, there is so much to look forward to once the trial has ended," he says as he fondles her breasts, then moves his hand down her body, feeling between her legs. They kiss passionately and Daniel soon becomes aroused as Polly strokes him, holding him firmly before she guides him inside. There lovemaking is, as usual, intense and Polly screams with pleasure when she comes to fulfilment, before they both lie back in each other's arms and enjoy the moment.

On Wednesday morning, Daniel meets with Fitz and Winterton from the Ministry to discuss the continuing action in the docks.

"Is there any news on this, Daniel? I was hoping that we had solved the problem once the arrests were made of those standing trial," Winterton comments.

"I have a meeting this weekend with my contact. I am hoping that he has asked to see me with some definite news. There are communist agitators in the docks that are manipulating these strikes, Jeremiah, and I am hoping that my source will be able to give me some names. With the trial date now scheduled, I really do want to bring our work to a conclusion."

"Is your contact in a position to give you names, Daniel?" Winterton asks.

"Yes, I believe he is. He is himself very much inclined to communism and has been asked to make a bigger contribution to the strike actions. Providing he doesn't lose his nerve, he will be an asset to our investigation. We are watching him to make sure he does not come to any harm, so all we can do for the moment is hang on until Saturday."

"We need his help, Daniel, so be sure to keep him on our side. His being on the inside will be invaluable in this fight. We want to be able to have the docks operating smoothly for the start of the trial which is less than two weeks away now. It will not look good if the press focus on what is happening in the docks rather than giving the conspiracy trial the headlines which we are hoping it will generate."

"He is on our side, sir, I can assure you of that. The fact that he has asked to meet again has to be good news. He must have something to tell me, so let us hope that it is what we are waiting for, that is, definitive proof of conspiracy in the docks," Daniel replies, hoping that his comments will reassure the man from the Ministry.

Polly, meanwhile, settles into her new job with enthusiasm, and soon has the operation running very efficiently. The data is processed as soon as it is received by Rachel and Peter. With Polly's guidance they decide on the level of importance of each piece of information. Sometimes, it is difficult to decide if the information is relevant at all, or whether some overenthusiastic aide in the High Commissioner's Office has decided to act on his own. Polly has a filing tray for such information marked 'Pending further investigation.'

The Foreign Office is the coordinating centre of information from the colonies, usually through the High Commissioner's Office. This is backed up by local security agencies liaising with British intelligence, and monitoring the movements of suspected communists within the trade union movement and the Civil Service, and including the introduction of proposed legislation to ban the Communist Party in some of the colonies. Australia has been at the forefront of the fight against communism in the colonies, anxious to maintain the Empire. And it is from Australia that intelligence is passed to Polly, which causes her serious concerns. The High Commission hands information giving some details of an assassination attempt on a government agent in Britain. Whist they cannot name him, it is obvious from their description of his activities that they are referring to Daniel. Polly immediately speaks with David Fellows, who contacts Fitz.

"Fitz, it's David Fellows at the Foreign Office. Polly Spencer's section has just received some rather disturbing news from our Australian Office, concerning Daniel. I wonder if the two of you might come over as soon as possible. We need to look at this threat right away."

Fitz and Daniel duly arrive at Polly's office, where David Fellows, Rachel, Peter, and Polly are waiting. Polly especially is very apprehensive about the information received.

"Daniel, Fitz, take a seat. You can sit next to me, Daniel, please," Polly insists, before she proceeds to give details of the information received from Australia.

"This information came from our Australian office. During their routine monitoring of conversations by the communists, they came across a passage that referred to a British agent that had caused them a lot of problems. They then go on to mention that he has a young ward that they have attempted to abduct so as to curb his activities. They continue by deciding to ask Moscow to put together a team to kill the agent and deal with his ward as they see fit," says Polly, as she hands her copy to Daniel and Fitz.

"They are determined to try and kill Daniel, so you must take action to protect him, Fitz."

"We must take action to protect both of you, Polly. You were also referred to in the conversations, please don't forget that."

"Well yes, but the threat to Daniel's life frightens me more than the threat to me. They cannot get to me while he is alive, as they have found out when they have tried previously. We have to protect you, Daniel, we have to do whatever is necessary to stop these people," Polly replies, holding on to his arm, and looking at him with affection mixed with fear. Her display of feelings toward Daniel do not go by unnoticed, as Fitz replies.

"We will do everything that can be done to protect you both, Polly, believe me. Now let's begin by covering your journey to and from the workplace. I will have a car put at your disposal, and Conrad and one other agent will be with you for the journey. Daniel, Conrad will be with you at all times that you are outside of either our office or your apartment. And you and Polly will continue to carry your firearms at all times, of course.

"Now, we shall have to make some arrangements for when the trial begins the week after next. You, Polly, have no need to leave this building other than to leave for home. So when you leave at the end of the day, might I suggest that Peter goes with you to the waiting car? Will you do that, Peter?" asks Fitz.

"It will be my pleasure, sir, anything I can do to help."

"Thank you Peter, I appreciate that."

"I shall get on to the High Commission in Australia and ask them to let us know immediately they have any more news on this Fitz, and I will send out a message to all the relevant offices to ask them to be especially diligent over this. Should I hear anything, I will contact you immediately," David replies to Fitz.

As the meeting breaks up, Polly asks Daniel if he will stay a moment. She closes the door when everyone has left and turns to him.

"You will promise me that you'll take every precaution until we can catch these people, Daniel. I love you so much and do not want to become a widow so soon after becoming a bride," she says rather tearfully as she holds on to him.

"We have been through so much together, Polly, and we have

survived. No one is going to get the chance to kill me, I promise. Now I must go, we will pick you up at five o'clock. I love you," he says, kissing her on the cheek before he leaves her office. Rachel and Peter return to the office, rather overawed by what they have heard.

"Gosh, Polly, has there really been several attempts to abduct you, and do you carry a firearm all the time?"

"Yes I do carry a firearm with me, Rachel, and yes there have been a number of attempts to abduct me. But for Daniel, they would have taken me long ago.

"You have to appreciate just how ruthless the people we are dealing with are and to what lengths they will go to in their war against democracy. Now, we must not let this latest information divert us from our work with the rest of the colonies. It may be that the communists may reach out to another country to look for someone to carry out the attempt on Daniel, so please carefully check everything that comes into the office. Please let me know immediately if you receive any information you believe may be relevant."

"We will be on the lookout for any suspicious conversations from now onwards, Polly, and protect you and Daniel in any way we can."

"Thank you for that, Peter."

"I think I can speak for both myself and Rachel, when I say that we both admire the work that you and Daniel have carried out for our country. We will do whatever it takes to keep you both safe by being extra diligent in our activities. That the Russians would go to such lengths in order to eliminate one person indicates just what your Daniel, must have done to so upset them," Peter replies, then smiles when he realises how he has described Daniel to Polly!

"Yes, he is very much my Daniel, Peter, you have no idea," says Polly with a beaming smile.

So for the remainder of the week, Polly and Daniel settle into being escorted to and from their work accompanied by Conrad and one other member of the team. And Polly is always escorted to the pickup car by Peter as an extra precaution. No further information arrives from any of the colonies about the proposed attempt on a 'British agent'.

For their trip to meet with Michael Doyle on Saturday, it is agreed that Conrad will travel with them but will wait outside the Black Bull pub. They do not want to put off Doyle by introducing a new contact. As usual, Whitechapel road is bustling with people selling their wares. This street scene fascinates Polly, who looks forward to being able to spend time there in the future.

"When we have some time, Daniel, I would love to explore an old fashioned street market," she says as they approach the doorway into the Black Bull pub.

Doyle is already inside, waiting anxiously for their arrival, and greets both of them with a handshake. They sit down and Doyle begins telling them what has been happening in the docks.

"A lot has happened since we last met, Daniel. I have been to some meetings with guest speakers, but I can't find out who they are because no one is willing to say who they are or where they are from. One of them did have a strong Irish accent, however. They are demanding that we do not sit down with the bosses. They say it's a trick to prevent us from calling out the members, but they continually refuse to have a mass meeting and vote for or against an all-out strike. My guess is they don't believe they will get a mandate from the members for an all-out stoppage, and are trying to get the management to offer some sort of unacceptable terms to the workers. At the moment, these outsiders have no real reasons that will encourage the men to withdraw their labour. They are continuing to stir up trouble and call out the men in small groups. And I have heard that there are outsiders being paid to bully workers into strike action. Perhaps you could sort that out. If you could find some sort of proof, and get the papers to mention it, then we could get back to the negotiating table."

"I will see what can be done to confirm that, Michael. Now, it seems to me that the agitators are becoming desperate, wouldn't you say?"

"They seem to be trying more and more bullying tactics to get their way. There have been a lot of incidents where men have been beaten up by gangs of thugs, and I know some have had threats made to their families," Doyle replies. Polly is making some notes as Doyle speaks, and asks him if he can give any names.

"Their names would be useful, Michael, and whether they attended hospital. We could then check their details."

"I will get the names of any that went to hospital, but I dare not give you any other names. You will have to rely on the press finding them out for you."

"Ok, Michael, you have given us plenty to discuss. Now if you could get those names to us as soon as possible, we can talk with the press and hope they will discredit the troublemakers. Send the information to me in the usual way using the number I gave you. Only contact me again if you have any new information, I do not want you putting yourself at risk at all."

"Thank you Daniel, I will be careful. Goodbye Polly, I will call when I have anything else for you," he says as he moves away and into Whitechapel Road. Conrad enters the pub and walks over to where Daniel and Polly are seated. Daniel gives him the main details from their conversation.

"It's encouraging to hear that the troublemakers are losing the fight, Daniel. We need to make this public as soon as possible. Do we know a journalist that will best portray what is happening?"

"Fitz will know a man who does, no doubt; as soon as we get the names of the dockers that have been attacked by these thugs, we will be able to get something into print."

The three of them eventually leave the Black Bull to return to Kensington where they have some lunch together. Conrad then walks with them back to their apartment.

"See you both Monday," he says, as he hails a taxi.

"Well Daniel, I think it may be best if we do not leave the apartment this weekend. We have to keep safe, I do not want anything to happen to you. Problem is, I really cannot think what we are going to do with ourselves!" says Polly with her mischievous smile as she hugs Daniel.

"Oh, I'm sure you will think of something, in fact I'm sure you will, Polly. You always do!"

After a wonderful weekend together, marooned in their apartment, Daniel and Polly set off to work on Monday, accompanied by their escorts. Daniel and Conrad meet with Fitz and outline the conversation with Doyle from Saturday.

"This is encouraging, Daniel. As soon as we have those names, we can get a journalist to follow up on our behalf. I have a colleague in Fleet Street who will handle this for us. Once we expose the troublemakers, the dockers' management should be able to reach agreement with the men. And it would be a bonus if all this could be wrapped up before the trial. We really do need to be able to show everyone that we are winning before the trial starts."

"If that happens, and the trial conclusions are as we expect, Fitz, then we can move the Traffic Lights to amber, and who knows what will happen after that day?"

The remainder of Monday and Tuesday are uneventful, then on Wednesday, Daniel receives names, from Michael Doyle, of the dockers that were treated at hospital after being attacked.

Fitz calls his colleague in Fleet Street for a meeting, to discuss how the information can be put into a feature article in the press as soon as possible.

Polly, meanwhile, receives further news about the plot to kill Daniel. On Wednesday morning Peter passes her a memo from Australia, with some devastating information. They believe a team has been assembled and has left for Britain. Polly sits down with Rachel and Peter to discuss the implications of this message.

"Peter, will you contact Australia and ask them for more detail on this? We must know who these men are and when they are arriving in Britain. Rachel, can you check carefully if there is any information that may be relevant to this coming from elsewhere? I want to be able to track these men, so they can be detained as soon as they set foot in Britain. Nothing must happen to Daniel, he must be protected whatever it takes. Do you both understand?"

"As we said before, Polly, we will do everything we can to protect you and Daniel. It is obvious that you care for him," Rachel comments.

"Close the door, Peter. What I am now going to tell you does not go outside of my office, do you understand? Because of the exceptional circumstances I feel I must let you into a secret."

Peter and Rachel look at each other, curious at what Polly is about to say.

"I am sure that you have both become aware of the closeness of Daniel and I. We make no secret of our feelings for each other. Officially, Daniel is still my guardian, but in fact we are married. We became Mr and Mrs Bottomley on the 22nd August."

"We are very happy for you both, Polly."

"Thank you Rachel, now please do not tell anyone about this. We do not want to give the Russians any more reasons for attacking Daniel or me. If they knew of our marriage, I am sure they would find some way of using the information.

"Daniel and I will announce our marriage officially after the conspiracy trial. For now, I have Daniel's ring around my neck and he has mine around his," says Polly, showing them the ring. "So now you are aware of just how much Daniel means to me and I rely on you both to help me protect him against this threat on his life. I cannot and will not allow anyone to take him away from me, so let's look at what we know, and see if we can determine who these people are," Polly concludes. She has revealed her secret reluctantly but felt that it was necessary given the exceptional circumstances.

"The Australian agents must be our best bet for further information, I will get onto them straightaway."

"And I will get onto the Australian airports and see if they can give us any information about who has left for Britain recently. There won't be too many at this time of year," says Rachel.

"Ok, I will go and speak with David and update him on what we are doing to find these people," Polly replies as she leaves her office. She updates David Fellows on what they are doing to try and locate these men and asks him if he thinks there is anything else that can be done.

"You have covered everything, Polly, and I'm sure they will surface soon. We have to keep on with the investigation. Do let me know if there is anything you need."

She decides that she will make a call to the High Commissioner's office to see what further information they may have uncovered. It is late evening in Canberra when Polly makes contact, but the office is most helpful.

"Polly, my name is Bruce Harvey. We may just have a lead for you. Four men left Sydney bound for London yesterday. All four are known to have communist sympathies. We would have told you sooner, but the booking clerk that recorded their details went off sick. I really am sorry, I hope that you catch them."

"Thank you Bruce, you will let me know if you hear anything else, won't you?"

"Absolutely."

"Well, it appears that the men sent to kill Daniel are already here in London," Polly tells Peter and Rachel. Then she contacts Fitz and briefs him on the information she has just received from Sydney.

"I will talk with MI5 on this, Polly. They will be able to help with watching movements of communist personnel. They can also watch the Communist Party headquarters, these men may be staying there. Rest assured, Polly, everything will be done to protect you and Daniel."

"Thank you Fitz, I appreciate that. Bye for now."

On Thursday morning Daniel meets with Fitz and a reporter to discuss how he might portray the activities in the docks and discredit the communists at the same time. He can follow up on the names of the men who were attacked. He has a friend who is a nurse who may be able to help with details. He is anxious to make a good story from what he has heard and wants to follow it with an inside look at the conspiracy trial.

"I have a certain amount of licence here. Whilst I do not have to actually prove what I am saying, I can make assumptions and leave the reader to draw his own conclusions. These communists need to be stopped and the power of the press is one weapon that can bring them down. Believe me, Fitz, I will do everything I can to show these people for what they are, cowards and bullies," the reporter concludes.

On Thursday, and Friday, the wires to the Foreign Office are hot with additional information relating to the efforts to kill Daniel and abduct Polly. Most worrying is unconfirmed reports that separate ransoms are being offered for Polly's abduction and Daniel's assassination. This could lead to rogue operators making attempts. Because of this additional danger, extra security is placed at the Foreign Office. Daniel's place of work is confidential, only the members of the team know the way into the 'tombs' as they are known, so there is no reason to post any security in the immediate area, it would only serve to reveal Daniel's whereabouts. Despite all this extra security about them, they are both relieved when they are dropped off safely at the apartment on Friday, and look forward to the weekend. No additional security is provided over the weekend, but they both carry their weapons with them at all times. In any case, they only go out for a short time on Saturday, for the remainder of the weekend they stay in the apartment.

Spending time alone together does not present any problems for them, in fact quite the opposite. Their love for each other means that they welcome every opportunity to be together to express their feelings for each other in their lovemaking. However, all good things must come to an end at some time, and on Monday morning they are collected for another working day. When Polly arrives at her office, there is further news from Australian, confirming that four men have arrived in Britain with instructions to kill Daniel and abduct Polly. On hearing this, Fitz decides that he should ask MI5 to detain the men as soon as possible. The suspects have been watched since they landed, but have not left the offices of the Communist Party headquarters. It is decided that they will wait until darkness, on Monday, to raid the offices. Although Daniel wanted to be in on the raid, Fitz decides that he should stay away until the men are detained.

The raid is carried out in the early hours of Tuesday morning, but despite a thorough search of the building, there is no sign of the four men. They have somehow managed to give the security services the slip. On Tuesday morning there is a debrief to discuss how they could have lost the four men. Fitz is furious that the security watch allowed the men to get away, and they now have no idea of where they may be. The Australian office is unable to give them any more details of the men or any of their contacts in Britain. However, events take over much quicker than anyone had anticipated.

On Tuesday afternoon, Polly receives a call from Home Office reception, asking her to report to Mrs Wright. She has some outstanding papers that require her attention. Rachel and Peter are out of the office, so she leaves a brief message, slips on her jacket and goes off to see Mrs Wright. She walks across the road from the Foreign Office, not noticing the car that has stopped just ahead of her. A man gets from the car and approaches her.

"Excuse me, Miss, I am trying to find my way to Whitehall," he says as he draws level with her. Polly turns to give him directions, not noticing the second man, as the car moves up beside her. She is suddenly grabbed by both men and pushed into the back seat, as the car speeds of eastwards. She struggles desperately as the two men shove her down to the floor. Her skirt is ripped as she twists in the confined space, desperately trying to fight off the men holding her. "Keep still, you bitch, you cannot escape. We will soon be at our destination, then we'll deal with you," the older man tells her.

"Where are you taking me? What do you want?"

"Well, we are all going on a little trip in a day or so, but first we have to put you somewhere safe. Now shut up and keep quiet, no one can hear you or help you.

"We are going to teach you a lesson and your Mr Bottomley will not be able to do anything about it. He has caused my colleagues a lot of trouble and now he will pay for that by losing you, my dear, forever," he replies, as he hits Polly hard across her face and neck.

"Yes, that's what you get for struggling, now let's have a look at you."

The man rips off her blouse, grabbing at her breasts and legs. Eventually, after about twenty minutes or so, the car pulls up alongside the gangplank of an old freighter. Polly is manhandled up the gangplank by the men who enjoy themselves, groping her as they walk to the back of the ship and down into the ship's hold. The hold is almost pitch black, very damp, very dirty, and the floor is covered in water.

The men rip off what's left of her top clothing, continuing to paw at her whilst making lewd comments. They sit her down on an old wooden bench in just her underwear, securing her hands and feet to the ends of the bench, which leaves her feeling very vulnerable. They jeer and laugh as they continue to molest her, speaking in Russian but leaving her in no doubt of what they have in store for her. Then, another man enters the hold and speaks directly to Polly.

"Hello Miss Spencer, my name is Vladimir Barinov, I am very pleased to meet you. I had no idea you were so young. I am here to tell you that your interference in our affairs will cost you your life, you and Mr Bottomley. Eventually, you will be disposed of at sea. However, before that, I am going to let my crew have you. Some of the men have had no leave for a while and will be very glad of some female company. Then, when they have finished you will be thrown overboard."

"You're evil and despicable people. My colleagues will continue to look for you and kick you out of our country. And when Daniel will finds you he will shoot you dead, Mr Barinov."

"Well you won't be any use to him any more when I have done with you. As I have told you, Polly, you will be kept here until we sail in a couple of days' time, before we dump you overboard with the rubbish. Oh, and I forgot to mention, the rats come out in the evening and should enjoy feasting on you. Scream all you like, my dear, no one will hear you. I'll come and see how you are getting on in the morning," he says as they close the hold door shut, leaving Polly in a large, damp, and dark hold.

She sits whimpering, looking round the room and listening for any noises, but all she hears is steam hissing and clunking sounds from the ship's boiler. She is also shivering both from the cold and from fear as to what might happen to her. Although she is cold, she manages to drop off to sleep to be woken by something running over her feet, then up her legs. She screams as she realises that a rat is sitting on the bench between her legs, then moving on to her pants before resting on her lap. She screams as she tries desperately to free herself. She can now hear more than one rat squealing and shuts her eyes as she continues to try and free herself from the ropes that bind her. The rats are biting at her legs and feet, running over her at will. Polly is becoming more and more hysterical as the rats squeal, biting her at every turn. Eventually, they disappear as one or two chinks of light appear in the hold. Polly is almost delirious with fear, and screams and screams until she is hoarse. Eventually, Barinov returns to find Polly exhausted from her exertions and dirty and dishevelled from trying to free herself. Her legs and feet are covered in rat bites and her bounds have cut into her skin as she has struggled to escape.

"Oh dear, you seem to have been visited by our little friends during the night, Polly. Not to worry, the crew will bathe you and treat your wounds before you entertain them. "

"I have a crew of eight and some of them are very mean, so I expect they will enjoy giving you a beating as well as having their way with you. Stepan especially will want to give you a thrashing. He is an expert with the whip, as some of the crew will tell you. Then there is Oleg and Yakov, both sadists who enjoy hurting women, believing they should know their place. They will enjoy giving you a beating and will shave you as well. And then last but not least, there is Nikolay, who enjoys using a knife. Nikolay knows how to slice skin like peeling an orange. And the fact that you are so young will be a bonus, since most of the men are in their fifties and will especially enjoy such a young body. You will want to die by the time they have done with you, Polly, believe me. They all know that we shall be disposing of you when we are out to sea, so will no doubt be especially keen to carry out their own fantasies. Anyway, you will discover soon enough and wish that you had not meddled in business that did not concern you. We shall be casting off around lunchtime, and the men will collect you shortly after they have completed their tasks. I will see you again, because I want to watch the men enjoy you."

"You are a beast and an animal, and I hope you and your crew rot in hell!" screams Polly.

Barinov returns to the room, hits Polly hard across her face, before ripping off her top and grabbing at her breasts.

"That is just a taste of what my men will do to you. That and so much worse, believe me, you little bitch!"

After about an hour, Barinov returns with a member of his crew to take Polly up to the mess. The man is huge with a bushy beard and his appearance scares Polly, fearful of what he might do with her. However, he picks her up gently and smiles as he carries her up the stairs, caressing and stroking her. The crew are waiting and cheer and clap as she is carried into the mess. Some of them attempt to touch her, but the big man holding her resists them, pushing them away angrily.

"She needs some attention to her wounds and rat bites. We will have her soon enough, I want to clean her first."

The men do not protest but leave him with Polly. He sits her down at the table, and attends to the cuts on her wrists and ankles, enjoying being able to touch her. She is terrified, sitting there trying to cover herself as she only has on a pair of torn and dirty pants. The men are shuffling closer, unable to take their eyes off her, muttering to each other and laughing and jeering while all the time becoming more excited at the sight of Polly, who is virtually naked.

"Never mind cleaning her, Boris, the men have waited long enough to have her, haven't you boys? Isn't she just what we have been waiting for? Didn't I tell you I would find you a treat?" says Barinov, smiling. The men cheer and move towards Polly, making obscene gestures. She clings to the bearded, man hoping he will save her. But he is a willing participant into what they are expecting from her.

"Ok, get her pants off, spread her out on the table and hold her down. Now, who's gonna do the bitch first?" Barinov shouts enthusiastically.

*

Conrad and Daniel realise that something is wrong when Polly does not arrive to be driven home. It is 5.20pm, so Daniel goes inside the Foreign Office to speak with David Fellows.

"I have not seen her since lunch, Daniel. Let me check in her office."

"She was going over to see Mrs Wright about some paperwork still outstanding. Let me call Mrs Wright for you to see when she arrived."

David Fellows calls Mrs Wright to be told that she has not seen Polly at all today. Daniel realises that something is now seriously wrong and fears that his wife has been abducted.

"I'm so sorry, Daniel, is there anything I can do at all?" asks Fellows.

"If you could try and find out when she was last seen and call me on this number please," Daniel replies, giving his number. He heads back to the office and tells Fitz and Conrad of his fears.

"Good god, Daniel, not again. Do we have any leads at all?"

"Nothing yet, Fitz, I have asked David Fellows to try and find out when she was last seen, so we have somewhere to start. I am going to contact Hennessey and ask him to set up a meeting tomorrow morning as early as possible. If Polly has been abducted by the Russians, it makes sense that they would hide her on one of their own ships."

"There are a lot of ships to choose from, Daniel, and we have no idea where they are docked."

"That's why I need to speak with the dock workers, Conrad. If anyone knows, they will. Fitz, can you have a word with Blake and see if he has heard anything at all? I cannot believe that an abduction can be carried out without detailed instructions from high up."

"I will speak with Blake immediately."

"Conrad, can you come with me back into the Home Office? I want to ask Mrs Wright if we can talk with any of the Red Hand members who were not arrested. We need their addresses."

Daniel and Conrad return to the Home Office and secure the addresses of the five Red Hand members. They are Marlon Frobisher, David Burroughs, Robert Denham, Gordon Hastings, and Roberta Phillips.

"Thank you Mrs Wright, I will let you know when we have anything," says Daniel, as he and Conrad go off to question the five members of Red Hand. Daniel pulls no punches when he and Conrad make their calls to the Red Hand members.

"You need to tell us anything that you know which will help us find where Polly Spencer is being held. Any bits of conversation you may have heard from Sally Nugent, Percival Smith, or any other member of your organisation, that may give us an indication of where she may have been taken. You need to think very carefully. If you are able to help us it could make a difference to how you are viewed by the authorities. We know you are members of Red Hand. No decisions have yet been made as to whether you may be charged. Your help in finding Polly will influence the authorities in how you are finally dealt with," says Daniel, first to Marlon Frobisher and then to all five members in turn. It is generally agreed that she could have been taken to the docks, since the Soviets have threatened, on more than one occasion, to take Polly to Russia. And they all agree that the only person who would know any more details would be Sally Nugent.

By the time all five members have been interviewed it is almost midnight. Daniel talks with Fitz and arranges to secure access to Sally Nugent, who is being held in Holloway. They arrive at Holloway around 1.00am. The governor has been told of their visit and has

Sally Nugent in an interview room upon their arrival.

"Mr Bottomley, Polly Spencer's guardian as I recall. What on earth are you doing here?"

"Miss Nugent, I am here because Polly has been abducted, we think by the Russians."

"We think. Who is we, Mr Bottomley? Not the BBC as you said when we were first introduced?"

"My colleague and I are very anxious about what might happen to Polly, Miss Nugent. I believe that you were quite fond of her when she was working at the Home Office?"

"Yes, I liked Polly, but I had no idea she was betraying our cause with her innocent smiles. How do you think I can help you, even if I wanted to?"

"Miss Nugent, you had a high position in Red Hand and I am sure that you would have met with Russian agents at some time. At this moment, I have no interest in what you did, I just want to know if you have any idea who may know what has happened to her, or where she may have been taken."

"I don't really care what has happened to her, Mr Bottomley, you and your colleagues will never find her if the Soviets have taken her, you can be sure of that."

"Now listen to me very carefully, I can make your life very miserable in prison. I can arrange for you to be mistreated by prisoners and guards alike, in fact it can be arranged that you simply disappear, do you understand?" Daniel replies, raising his voice and standing over Sally Nugent.

"Now Miss Nugent, shall we start again? Can you help us locate where Polly may be?"

"Alright, she is most probably being held in a ship ready to take her to Russia or God knows where, I don't know. They have arrangements with some of the ships' captains to take people back without asking questions."

"Any names that you heard in your conversations?"

"No, my conversations did not involve me talking with ships' captains. I only know this happens because one of the agents has a colleague who works on such a ship. He didn't tell me the man's name or the name of the ship. If they have taken her, you will not be able to save her, believe me. The agents I have been in contact with are ruthless men who will kill you for the hell of it."

"What about your colleague, Smith, would he be able to help us?"

"Smith was just an incompetent yes-man, he was never in contact with anyone of any note. I did all the planning, I was the person that made any decisions. All I will say to you, Mr Bottomley, is find her quickly, because if they have not already sailed she may be dead anyway. Now I have nothing more to say to you," she replies, as she summons the guard to take her back to her cell.

Daniel speaks with MI5 regarding possible Russians that may be involved, but they can offer no real assistance, since their activities rarely involve Russian sailors. So Daniel seeks help from the dockers themselves. They offer a number of alternatives, and one ship sticks out as a possible choice. An old Russian freighter, the *Katrina*, is moored in the East India Dock. It has been there for about three days, but has not unloaded or loaded any cargo during that time, so it may well be where they are holding Polly. Daniel and Conrad and two colleagues from their department of special operations, decide they have to chance their arm and board the *Katrina* to look for Polly.

It is mid-morning when they finally climb the gangplank onto the deck, before making their way towards the crew's quarters and the mess hall. As they enter the corridor, screams can be heard coming from inside the mess hall. Daniel and Conrad burst in to find Polly stretched out naked on the mess table, held down by two of the men. They catch the men unawares, and Daniel shoots both of them holding her and a third who tries to use her as a shield. Conrad meanwhile, has shot Barinov in the arm as he stood by the door.

"Daniel, please Daniel, help me!" Polly is screaming and shouting hysterically. She is covered in the blood of the men he has shot. He grabs a blanket to cover her as she dashes toward him, before backing out of the room, with Conrad acting as his cover, the other sailors waiting their chance to attack them. Daniel lifts Polly into his arms as they dash down the corridor, then down the steps towards the main deck, hotly pursued by the remaining crew members who are being urged on by Barinov.

"Stop them, don't let them escape. Kill all of them except the girl."

Although he has cover from Conrad and his men, Daniel still manages to sustain a gunshot wound to his shoulder and another to his lower arm. Operating solely on adrenalin, he manages to carry Polly to the safety of the quayside and the waiting vehicles.

"Daniel, you have been shot. My god, you're bleeding all over the place," Polly screams hysterically.

"You're safe now, Polly," Daniel replies, as he hands Polly over to the police, who by now have arrived in force, before he collapses on the quayside. Both Daniel and Polly are rushed to hospital, accompanied by Conrad.

Although severely traumatised, Polly refuses to leave Daniel's side until he has been looked at by the doctor. One of the nurses has found her a gown to put on, as she waits anxiously by Daniel's side. The bullet that hit him in the shoulder is still inside him, so that will have to be removed. The other one went straight through his outer arm.

"We have to get him into surgery, Miss, and he has lost a lot of blood but he should be ok."

"Thank you Doctor, and it's Mrs by the way. I am Daniel's wife."

"My apologies, now let me take a look at you."

Conrad, meanwhile, has made a call to Fitz with the good news, and he and a colleague will stay at the hospital with Polly and Daniel to watch over them.

The doctor examines Polly and is concerned about how deep the wounds to her wrists and ankles are. Also he suggests a course of antibiotics to combat any infections from the rat bites.

"Your wrists and ankles will take a while to heal, Mrs Bottomley, and I see you have some bruising to your breasts also. Is there anywhere else I need to look at? Did any of your captors sexually assault you?" the doctor asks.

"Thankfully no, Doctor."

"Good, well before I apply any bandages, I am going to ask the nurse to give you a wash. You are in a bit of a mess with all this dried blood on you."

After she has been washed and her wounds treated, the nurse finds Polly some underwear, and a robe to put on over her hospital gown. She asks the nurse if she would ask Conrad to come in.

"My dear Polly, how are you? That was a close call back there."

"I am much better thank you, Conrad, but I need a phone, and can you find out what has happened with Daniel for me please?"

"I will get a chair, and we will go and look for him together, the phone can wait for now. I have contacted Fitz, so he will pass on the good news."

Daniel has had his surgery and is in a recovery room, conscious but very groggy from the anaesthetic, as Polly goes to his side.

"Daniel, my dear Daniel, how are you feeling? I thought they had killed you, there was so much blood," she says, leaning over and kissing him.

"Feeling a bit frail, Polly, but what about you? Did they…?"

"I'm ok, Daniel, nothing happened apart from being groped by some of them, but nothing else, I promise. You were just in time, you saved me again my dear Daniel," she replies tearfully.

Conrad returns with some tea and a phone trolley for Polly.

She phones the Foreign Office and speaks with David Fellows, who expresses relief that she is safe. She then speaks with Rachel and asks her to come along to the Royal London Hospital as soon as she can and bring Polly's bag with her.

"Of course, Polly, we are all so pleased to hear that you are safe."

Polly enjoys her tea as Daniel slowly regains consciousness, and after a short while Rachel arrives with her bag.

"Thank you, Rachel. Now I wonder if you would mind running an errand for me. I need some clothes, underwear, shirt, and trousers please, and would you find a shirt for Daniel? His is soaked in blood and will have to be thrown away. Conrad, can your colleague go with her please?"

"Certainly Polly, is there anything else we can do for you?" Rachel asks.

"No, that will be all, Rachel, and thank you," Polly replies, giving her the keys, and noting the apartment address and alarm code. Polly sits for a while with Daniel, and slowly begins to realise what has happened. She was abducted by Russians, subjected to a terrifying experience in the ship's hold with rats, held prisoner by Russian sailors who threatened her with unspeakable atrocities, which they would surely have carried out, then when they had finished with her they were to throw her overboard when the ship was at sea. She suddenly bursts into tears, and clings on to Daniel.

"Daniel, I am so relieved that it is over, I am not sure whether these are tears of joy or what they are. I am just pleased to be with you and that you are ok. I understand from the doctor, that your wounds should heal satisfactorily, just more scars for your display," says Polly, wiping her face and trying to compose herself as Conrad comes into the room with Fitz.

'My dear Polly, and you too, Daniel. How are you both? This is a bad business, I have spoken to Quentin and I want some action against the Soviets over their behaviour towards Polly especially," says Fitz, visibly angry over the recent events. Over the months that he has come to know Polly, he has become very fond of her and finds the behaviour of the Soviets despicable.

"We are both recovering, thank you, Fitz. Daniel has had the bullet removed, we are just waiting for the doctor to come and have another look at him. They were going to kill me, Fitz. After they had finished with me, they were going to throw me overboard at sea," Polly replies, fighting hard to hold back her tears, really struggling to compose herself.

"Now then, Polly, please don't upset yourself. You and Daniel are safe here and Conrad will stay with you. We shall be making a formal protest to the Russian Embassy over this dreadful business. They need to be told of the government's concerns and give assurances that the men concerned will be punished severely. Now is there anything at all that you and Daniel need before I leave?" asks Fitz firmly.

"We are ok now, thank you Fitz, and thank you for calling on Daniel."

Meanwhile, Rachel returns with the clothes that Polly asked for and hands back her keys. She is genuinely upset about what has happened, and asks Polly if she can help any further.

"Anything we can do for you at the office, Polly, please say so. Everyone is so disgusted at what has happened, and send their regards to you and Daniel."

"Thank you Rachel, and thank everyone for their concern, we do appreciate it. Daniel and I will be away next week when the trial begins, so I will be relying on you and Peter to keep things running smoothly. I am not sure how long Daniel will be kept in hospital, I will let you know about that as soon as I know. Meantime, thank you for fetching my clothes, I must go and change now."

Polly goes off to change into the clothes Rachel has collected for her and returns as the doctor arrives. He spends some time looking at Daniel's injuries before speaking with Polly.

"The bullet in his shoulder did not cause any internal damage, thankfully. It was quite high up in the shoulder region, so it missed the bone and main tissue. The wound to his arm, whilst going straight through, will need to be dressed regularly until it closes. The bullet ripped through the muscle, so the stitching will remain in place for a while. We'll keep him in overnight, but you can take him home tomorrow after I have had another look at him."

"Thank you very much, Doctor. I will stay with him tonight if you don't mind, and Conrad will remain also."

Polly has very little sleep during the night, fretful herself as she relives her ordeal, and also concerned over Daniel's latest injuries. She has some flashbacks of what happened to her and also what could have happened to her. She keeps hearing Barinov's voice telling her what his men will do with her. She sees one man approaching her with a razor ready to shave her while two men stand ready with a whip. Meantime, they are all gathered round her, feeling and squeezing her naked body. She wakes suddenly, bathed in sweat, as Conrad taps her shoulder.

"Polly, are you ok? I have bought you some tea, were you having a bad dream?"

"Yes I was, Conrad, a really bad dream. What time is it?"

"It's six o'clock. So how are you coping? You have suffered a terrible ordeal and will need time to recover."

"I am coping, Conrad, but I fear for Daniel sometimes. His body racked by more wounds, I wonder how much more it can take. Two more bullet wounds to add to all the others he has taken while saving me."

"He will be fine, Polly, and remember he has the greatest healing medicine of all, your love and care. But you need to take care of yourself too, you have had another terrible experience, and should draw on Daniel's strength to help you through all this."

"Thanks Conrad, I do appreciate your concern, and for all the efforts you have put in with Daniel. Now will you stay a moment while I go to the bathroom? I need a wash."

Daniel wakes around seven o'clock, and seems to have had a restful night.

"Good morning Daniel, how are you feeling this morning?"

"Much better thank you, and how are you my dear Polly? Did you manage to get any rest?"

"I had some rest, but my main concern is you. I hope the doctor will allow me to take you home later this morning. Now let me go and organise you some breakfast," says Polly, as she heads off towards the cafeteria, leaving Conrad with Daniel.

"How are you, my friend? Better for a good rest I hope?"

"I think I am being well taken care of, Conrad, and not just by the hospital staff!"

"Very true, Daniel, Polly worships you as well you know, and is constantly organising things for your benefit. But you will have to be careful with her, when she eventually sits down and goes over what has happened. It is obvious to see that she is very frail at the moment. When I woke her earlier she was obviously having a bad dream and was bathed in sweat. She is going to need all of your love and attention."

Polly returns with some toast, a pot of tea, and three cups. They sit together enjoying their tea and toast and trying to put yesterday's events to one side for the moment.

"I hope the doctor will let me take you home today, Daniel. I can best take care of you in the apartment."

"Well I feel well enough to leave, so hopefully, he will give me the all clear."

"We will take the car when we do leave, Daniel, and drop you off as before. I am not convinced that the communists have given up just yet, so we must remain on our guard at all times."

"Well, if they are planning anything else, Conrad, they had better hurry themselves. It's now Thursday and the trial is due to start on Monday."

The doctor calls on Daniel at nine o'clock and gives him the all clear to go home, but he must rest and give his wounds time to heal.

"And you must take care of yourself too, Mrs Bottomley, you have obviously been through a traumatic experience which will be with you for some time. However, you taking care of Daniel may be just what you need to occupy your mind right now."

He gives Polly additional dressings for Daniel's wounds and cream for the rat bites she has on her legs and feet. The bites are still sore and she has had to cover some of them because they are quite deep.

"Thank you, Doctor. I will see he gets all the rest he needs and I will take care of myself too," says Polly with determination in her voice. Conrad helps Daniel to the bathroom where he washes and dresses for the journey home.

One of the colleagues assigned to watch over Daniel and Polly arrives with the car and they are driven back to their apartment in Kensington, arriving around 10.30am. After thanking Conrad for all of his help, they go up to their apartment, relieved to be back home safe and together.

"I am so glad to be back home with you, Daniel. Now I want you to settle on the settee because I really do need a bath."

"Ok Polly, you enjoy your soak. I will make a couple of calls in the meantime."

His first call is to the Spencer's home to tell them what has happened. Margaret answers the phone and is clearly distressed when Daniel tells her what has happened.

"Oh my god, Daniel. You have been shot again rescuing our daughter, how are you both? Did they hurt Polly at all?"

"I'm afraid they were rather rough with her, Margaret, and she has a few bruises, but it was the threats of what they were going to do to her that has so frightened her, and the rats didn't help. I am going to take her away until Sunday to try and get her to relax and forget what has happened. I thought we would go to Stratford on Avon again. We both have fond memories of Stratford and I hope to be able to give her a quiet time where she can enjoy the fresh air and pleasant surroundings."

"Well that sounds a wonderful idea, Daniel. I know I don't need to say this but thank you again for saving our daughter. We will speak to you soon I hope, enjoy your short break."

Daniel then makes contact with Fitz for an update on the police activity regarding the freighter where Polly was held captive.

"No news on that, Daniel, but I have asked the Minister to speak with the Russian ambassador and express our anger and disgust at the behaviour of the Russians. He was appalled when I told him what had happened. The Russians will be embarrassed by it all, I am sure, although they will probably deny all knowledge. Whatever happens, you can be sure it will be mentioned at some time during the trial."

Daniel tells Fitz of his plan to take Polly away for a short break before the trial, to which he agrees it will be a very good idea.

"I just hope that she will be strong for next week. The trial will be very wearing and will be a long haul. Anyway, I will call you Sunday evening for an update, Fitz, bye for now."

Daniel has just put down the phone when Polly arrives, having had her bath and changed into fresh clothes. She looks better for having her bath, although Daniel does notice how pale she is and she is showing signs of strain on her face. For now he decides not to make any mention of how she may feel, hoping that a weekend away will help.

"I'll make some tea and see what we have for lunch. Who were you talking to, by the way, Daniel?"

Daniel tells Polly about his phone calls and tells her that he wants to take her away for a short break before the trial begins.

"Daniel, that will be marvellous. Where shall we go, do you have somewhere in mind?" says Polly, smiling with excitement, her face lighting up with expectation.

"How about Stratford on Avon again and stay in the same hotel as we did five years ago?"

"What a wonderful idea, Daniel, but you will let me share your bed with you this time, won't you?" she says, laughing out loud.

"This time, you may share my bed. It will be my pleasure, Mrs Bottomley!"

And so for the next hour or so, Daniel and Polly sit together reminiscing over the trip they made to Stratford on Avon five years ago, when Polly was still at school.

"I can still remember how embarrassed you were to find me in your bed that morning. Thinking about it now, Daniel, you must have been terrified and horrified, a thirteen-year-old sharing your bed! I remember wondering what all the fuss was about, but you, my dearest Daniel, explained everything to me beautifully. I loved you then in my own way, you know, and I love you more than ever now. Unfortunately, all I can offer you for now is a kiss, my dear, because you are in no fit state to put up with the rigours of lovemaking!" says Polly, laughing and giggling.

It does Daniel good to see her enjoying herself so much after her ordeal. After a few days away, she should be feeling so much better, he hopes. However, that evening and night prove to be especially difficult for them. They had decided that they would travel to Stratford on Avon on the Friday morning after a night's rest. Daniel has contacted Conrad and asked if he might drive them to the station in the morning. They spend the rest of the evening talking about what they might do over the next three days before finally going off to bed for the night. Much as they would have enjoyed making love, they decide that physically, it might not be a good idea for Daniel. However, they do find pleasure in other ways before finally drifting off to sleep.

After what seems to be a short time, Daniel is woken by Polly screaming and thrashing about, obviously reliving her ordeal at the hands of the Russian sailors. Daniel tries desperately to console her, and she finally collapses into his arms, sobbing uncontrollably.

"God, Daniel, have you any idea what those men would have done to me if you had not arrived when you did? They acted like animals, and I will never forget what that man Barinov said. I want you to kill him if you ever get the chance. The man is evil."

Polly is shaking with a mixture of rage and fear, as Daniel seeks to console her.

"What happened to you was terrible, but we must try and move on, my dearest Polly. You are safe with me now, we have some good times to look forward to so please try and get some sleep," he says, as he kisses her tenderly.

They both drift off into sleep again, but Polly again wakes Daniel. This time she has dashed from their bed and crashed into the bedroom door, frantically trying to open it.

"Daniel, Daniel for God's sake help me, we must get away!!" she is screaming and shouting.

He holds Polly tightly talking to her, trying hard to console her, but not sure whether she is awake or in the middle of a nightmare. Eventually, she calms down, and Daniel wraps her in her robe. She is bathed in sweat so he fetches her a towel and gently wipes her face.

"You must try and calm down, Polly. You will make yourself ill with screaming so much," he says as he sits beside her stroking her face.

"My god, Daniel. What have I done? Your pyjamas are covered in blood; let me see," she says as she helps him remove his top. His exertions have opened up both his shoulder wound and the one on his arm.

"I will have to dress both these wounds for you, I am so sorry Daniel."

"Don't worry, Polly. We can soon clean up the wounds."

Polly carefully bathes Daniel's wounds and puts on fresh dressings, before finding him another pair of pyjamas. Thankfully, attending to Daniel has completely taken her mind off her nightmares, and within half an hour or so appears calm and composed. Polly removes her nightdress and gets back into bed wearing just her robe. They lie together, not saying much, and finally drift off back to sleep in each other's arms.

Conrad arrives around ten o'clock and drives them to Euston to begin their journey to Stratford on Avon. On arrival they are shown up to their suite, and Polly is at last showing signs of feeling better.

"How are you feeling, Polly? Better for our being here with such fond memories?"

"Yes, Daniel. This was where I first climbed into your bed. I so wanted to be with you but was too young to realise what I was doing. Not so now, though, please take me to bed, Daniel."

The time spent in Stratford on Avon definitely helps Polly since she sleeps soundly on Friday and Saturday, although their lovemaking probably helped! On Saturday, they spend time walking by the river and wandering around the many gift shops. In the evening, they manage to get two tickets for the theatre. Whist Daniel is not a big fan of Shakespeare, Polly is an absolute fanatic and has read many of his plays, so visiting the Royal Shakespeare Theatre is a special treat for her. They have another night of joy and passion together and on Sunday take a trip to Blenheim Palace. It had been opened to the public only this year and was already proving a great success. However, they do have to get back to London and arrive back at the apartment about seven o'clock. They both agree what a wonderful break it has been and both feel refreshed for the trial ahead.

"It was a marvellous weekend, Daniel, and thank you for such a wonderful time."

"We still have some time left, Polly, and I am getting fitter all the time," he says as he guides Polly through to the bedroom, where they hastily undress. They lie together, as Polly pleasures him orally before stroking him. Daniel, meanwhile, fondles her before he moves his hand slowly down, resting between her legs, stroking her gently. She moans with pleasure as his stroking becomes more intense. Then he too becomes excited as she continues to stroke him more intensely before guiding him inside. Polly's intensity during their lovemaking becomes almost frantic. It's as if she is afraid that each time may be the last time.

"I love you so much Daniel, promise me that we will always be together," she says, looking into his eyes from beneath him.

"Always and forever, Polly," he replies, still struggling a little with his injuries. Realising that Daniel's movements may be restricted, Polly manoeuvres herself until she is on top of him, then raises herself up to make their coupling even more pleasurable. She screams with delight as Daniel continues to give her maximum pleasure.

"Shall we get some dinner, Mr Bottomley?" asks Polly, turning towards him after a while.

"Yes, I think that would be good, Mrs Bottomley. Some nourishment before we continue, I think."

"And then, what do you suggest, Mr Bottomley?"

"Oh, I am sure we shall think of something, Mrs Bottomley," smiles Daniel, as he holds Polly in a firm embrace and kisses her passionately.

CHAPTER 12

The conspiracy trial begins at the Old Bailey on Monday 13th October. Despite Polly's ordeal the previous week, she and Daniel want the trial to go ahead as scheduled. She looks pale and frail, but is encouraged by Daniel promising that they will go away again as soon as circumstances permit. With two Crown barristers and three defence barristers, there is some time lapse before the accused are brought into the dock. In total, there are seven men and one woman, and they are all being charged with similar crimes.

The accused are Sally Nugent, Percival Smith, Bill Hornsby, Jack Makepeace, Leonard Rafikov, Boris Ruchkin, Sergey Sokolov, and Mikhail Litvin.

The four British nationals are accused of conspiring, through the Civil Service, to influence government by installing a communist agent into a ministerial position. They are further charged with treason against Her Majesty's government with intent to secure a foreign power in place of a democratically elected government, conspiracy to overthrow the sovereign government, and conspiring to enforce the will of a foreign power on British citizens.

The four Russian nationals are accused of espionage against the sovereign state of Her Majesty's government.

All eight of the accused are also charged with conspiracy to commit murder on British citizens to further their attempts of overthrowing Her Majesty's democratically elected government.

All the accused plead not guilty, and there are protests from the dock questioning the legality of the trial. The Russian nationals accuse the court of illegally holding them against their will. They demand that they be released and all charges dropped and claim that they are entitled to diplomatic immunity for all charges. The judge dismisses the protests, pointing out diplomatic immunity does not apply in cases of espionage and goes on to warn the accused that they will be removed to the cells if they do not behave.

Some time is taken up with the selection of the jury, but eventually, the leading prosecutor, Philip Walters Q.C., begins his presentation.

"The case before you is both frightening and sinister in its content. You will be transported into a dark, silent world, where all manner of activities are practised to further an ideal foreign to our country. Some of the evidence you will hear will sound far-fetched and unbelievable. Murder, kidnapping, extortion, are all part of the everyday workings of these people who would seek to impose the will of their masters on us all. They have no time for the legal rights of the individual to make his or her own choices. They would force their will on you no matter what. They would destroy the very fabric of our society, and that of our Empire. You will hear of the heroic work of our security services in bringing the accused to trial. You will especially be witness to the incredible heroism of two of our citizens in all this, namely Daniel Bottomley, who is in fact attached to the security services, and Miss Polly Spencer, a Civil Servant in the Foreign Office. The individual sacrifice of these two people in securing the evidence before you today, cannot be measured. You will hear of several attempts to stop Mr Bottomley from securing the evidence placed before you, by abducting his ward, Miss Polly Spencer. Mr Bottomley has been shot on several occasions, and is in fact recovering from two bullet wounds at present.

"These two people have risked their lives to secure the evidence that will be presented to you and prove the accused guilty, and for that we owe them our gratitude. Traitors do not abide by rules, they believe they can impose the will of others on their fellow citizens and secure favour for their actions. They are not interested in democracy, even though it is that democratic way that has permitted them to speak freely and seek change by force. What the accused in the dock do not appreciate is that they would not be permitted to behave in such a manner in a Soviet state. Dissidents are despatched, never to be seen or heard of again. That is what they would impose on the British people. The evidence to be presented by the witnesses is overwhelming both from the point of proving beyond doubt, and by its sheer weight. I propose to open for the Crown by calling Miss Polly Spencer to the stand."

Polly goes into the box and is sworn in by the court usher. The gallery is full and all eyes are on this attractive young woman, with long dark hair, held in a ponytail. She is wearing a two-piece suit and a white shirt, buttoned down at the wrist to hide her injuries. She also wears black stockings to hide the rat bites and injuries to her ankles. Although still pale from her recent ordeal, Polly is still a striking picture for all to see.

"Will you tell the court your name and occupation please?"

"My name is Polly Spencer, and I am a Civil Servant in the Foreign Office."

"Now I believe you have only recently moved to the Foreign Office from the Home Office. Is that correct, Miss Spencer?"

"Yes, I was offered a position beginning 22nd of September."

"And can you tell the court what your previous position at the Home Office entailed?"

"I was the Corporate Liaison Officer. When I first took up my post in the Home Office in January, my movements were limited to certain departments, and I was situated in an office. However, I was asked to keep my eyes and ears open by Daniel, since the security services knew there was a secret organisation within the Civil Service, but had been unable to get any proof of its existence. So I was given a more expansive role, that of Corporate Liaison Officer, so that I had more freedom of movement. There are a lot of messages passed between staff relative to their own particular position, and too much time was being used to get information from A to B, meaning staff were away from their workstations more often than was ideal. I was responsible for all collection and distribution of messages sent between members of staff, giving everyone more time to attend to their duties."

"And when did the circumstances surrounding your position change, Miss Spencer?"

"I believe it was sometime in July, when I was approached by a member of staff, Mrs Elizabeth Berkley. Elizabeth was a member of a secret communist organisation within the Civil Service. Its main aim was to try and secure one of its members into a senior position so that they might eventually influence government policy. Their aim was to place someone in the Permanent Secretary's office."

"Miss Spencer, are you saying there was an organisation, within our Civil Service, scheming to overthrow Her Majesty's government?" Judge Thornton asks.

"Yes sir."

"Thank you. Please go on, Miss Spencer."

"And why did Mrs Berkley contact you, Miss Spencer, rather than anyone else?"

"Because my position allowed me to move freely into all departments, she presumed that the security services would be interested in what I might uncover. Daniel – Mr Bottomley – and I met with her to see what she had to say and it was decided to take her at face value and see what information she may have. Unfortunately, the Red Hand, the name of the secret communist organisation, were very careful. As a member your only contact was with whoever passed information to you and whoever you had to pass it onto depending on its significance. No one knew who all the members really were, only the one that handed the file to you and the person you handed it on to."

"So what happened next, Miss Spencer?"

"I was approached by Sally Nugent to deliver messages for the Red Hand membership."

"So you were asked to be their messenger. Have you any idea why they would place so much trust in you?" the prosecution ask with surprise.

"No not really, I suppose they considered me safe because of my age and because I had only been in the Service for a short while."

"And how old are you, Miss Spencer?"

"I am eighteen, sir."

"So by delivering messages directly to Red Hand members, you were able to discover their identities, but not what the messages were about, surely?"

"Not at first, I used to have a look at them and try to remember important bits and pass them on to Daniel's department using a closed telephone line. Ideally, the security services wanted to actually take a look at the messages to be able to find out just what they were about. So it was decided that I would photograph any Red Hand documents handed to me before passing them on to the recipients. That was decided the best way to secure the information."

"You took pictures of the documents before handing them on to the members of this illegal organisation, Miss Spencer?" the judge asks, fascinated by what he is hearing.

"Yes sir."

"And how were you able to photograph and pass on the pictures, Miss Spencer?"

"I used a miniature camera to take the pictures in my office before passing on the files in the normal way. Then, at the end of the day, I would take the camera home and hand the film to Daniel for processing."

"And this was done during the normal course of your day, and no one had any idea of what you were doing?"

"I was very careful, sir, but no one had any reason to think I was doing anything other than my job, and Red Hand had their business running smoothly through me. At least that is what we hoped they would think."

"And what about the threat of installing a member in high office, close enough to have a role in decision making?"

"Yes, well, I think we will leave Miss Spencer's reply until after lunch, Mr Walters," says the judge.

Polly steps down from the box and hurries over to Daniel. There is a buzz around the court, and when they move out into the hall, Polly is besieged by reporters. Daniel and Conrad manage to get her outside and drive off in a taxi to find somewhere for lunch.

"It's a good thing we suggested you stay close, Conrad, it looks like the press are going to be buzzing around while the trial continues."

"This is hard work, Daniel. I had no idea they wanted to know so many details. I feel as though I am telling the court my life story in the Civil Service."

After lunch, and fighting her way through the reporters again, Polly returns to the witness box.

"Now Miss Spencer, you were talking about the attempt of Red Hand to secure one of their members into a senior post within government?"

"Yes, Mr Percival Smith was the person selected, and he achieved the position of Undersecretary at the Home Office."

"And what did you find out about his activities in his new position?"

"Nothing really, because he was dismissed from his post after a short time."

"Oh, and why was that, Miss Spencer?"

Polly hesitated before replying with some embarrassment.

"He was reprimanded for an indiscretion with a member of staff."

"Can you be more specific, Miss Spencer?"

"Yes sir. He made lewd remarks towards me and touched me inappropriately when I was in his office delivering a file," Polly replies, blushing on hearing the murmur from the gallery.

"So this indiscretion must have been a setback for the organisation?"

"Yes it was, and it was entirely of Smith's own making. Sally Nugent was particularly angry about what happened, both towards me and to Mr Smith. She had been openly discussing civil disobedience and strike action within the Service to destabilise the government. She was very determined that the communists should secure a strangle hold within the Service. Mr Smith's indiscretion was a setback to their activities and she blamed me for that. However, the security services were relieved to find an excuse to get Smith moved from his position. And there was no reason for them to be suspicious over his dismissal."

"And during this time and afterwards, Miss Spencer, I understand there were a number of occasions when your life was threatened, and these threats were directly connected to what you and Mr Bottomley were involved in?"

"Yes sir, there have been a number of occasions, during which I have been abducted twice and physically attacked, while Daniel has sustained gunshot wounds protecting me."

"Miss Spencer, are you telling the court that we will hear evidence that links the Soviet threats to our government, with these abductions and physical attacks on you, and to Mr Bottomley's injuries in protecting you?"

"Yes, my lord. In fact two of the men responsible were deported soon after one of the abductions and some of the other men involved are in the dock today."

"Yes, I see from my bundle of evidence that you and Mr Bottomley have been witnesses in a number of trials recently, all involving shootings and attempts to abduct you."

"Yes sir, that is correct."

"I find this persistent targeting of a young woman in order to get to a member of the security services astonishing and very worrying."

"Thank you, Your Honour. I should like to elaborate, if I may, on these attacks and the link between them and this trial. The prosecution will show that the attacks on Miss Spencer and Mr Bottomley were in retaliation to his activities for the security services. We shall hear more about his activities when he gives his evidence."

"Very good, Mr Walters. Please carry on."

"Now Miss Spencer, perhaps you could tell the court a little more about the attacks on you and Mr Bottomley during the period that you have been in the Home Office?"

"The first attack took place when three men broke into Daniel's apartment. It was never proved that this was anything to do with the Soviets, although I had been stopped in the street and warned about asking questions in the Home Office."

"Really? What happened then, Miss Spencer?"

"Sally Nugent and a man stopped me and warned me to stop asking questions or face the consequences. The man was quite forceful, grabbing me and pushing me against the wall."

"Please continue with details of the first attack, Miss Spencer."

"The attack was obviously directed at me personally, since they passed Daniel's room to get to me. The two men hit me hard and tried to indecently assault me, ripping off my pyjamas and threatening me with a knife. Fortunately Daniel was able to stop them, although one of the men stabbed him before they escaped."

"It must have been very frightening for you?"

"It was, and but for Daniel it could have been much worse," Polly replies, looking across to where Daniel is seated.

"Thank you Miss Spencer, I am sure you would like a break from all this, so we will adjourn until the morning, gentlemen."

Polly rushes to Daniel, anxious to be near him as they leave the court to face the press. Polly is besieged by dozens of cameras and reporters, all wanting to ask questions about how she tricked Soviet agents into giving her information.

"Miss Spencer, weren't you scared of what would happen to you if the Soviets found out that you were passing information from the Red Hand communist organisation?"

"We were always very careful, weren't we Daniel?" she replies, turning to Daniel for support, and holding on to him tightly.

"Polly was watched over very closely to make sure that she would not be detected. Her safety was always a priority."

"You are Miss Spencer's guardian, Mr Bottomley. What does that mean exactly?"

"Please, no more questions, thank you," says Daniel, as he and Conrad force their way through the crowd together with Polly and drive away.

"I had no idea this was going to happen, Daniel. I hope they have not found out where we live," says Polly anxiously. Unfortunately, despite Conrad driving round for some time, there are more press outside their apartment block in Kensington. Fortunately, they manage to slip in unnoticed, using the side entrance.

"I need a soak, Daniel, before I do anything at all," says Polly, going into the bedroom while Daniel makes some tea, and looks out of the window to see a number of press outside the apartment entrance. He was considering going out for a meal, but they will have to make do with what they have. After her bath, Polly has a look at Daniel's injuries.

"Your shoulder is getting better, but the bullet holes in your arm do not appear to be closing, Daniel," she says, concerned that the entrance and exit of the bullet are still open.

"We shall have to watch the wound in your arm closely. If it does not show signs of improving, we will go back to the hospital."

They spend the rest of the evening going over what has happened during the day and Daniel expresses his concern at how the press are attracted to Polly.

"I had no idea the press would react this way towards you, Polly, I am so sorry."

"It's ok Daniel, so long as the communists are punished and we stop the Soviets, it will be worth it. I find it amusing that they want to talk to me about what has happened."

"Well as long as it does not upset you. Now I will call Conrad and ask him to collect us from the side entrance in the morning, we do not want to be besieged again."

Polly and Daniel settle down for the evening and enjoy a quiet night together. They are both rather tired from the day's events and fall asleep in each other's arms. On Tuesday morning, Conrad manages to collect them from the side entrance, unseen by the press, and drives back to the Old Bailey.

"Have you seen the paper, Daniel?"

Polly and Daniel are pictured beneath the headline: "Young heroine foils Soviet plot."

"Good god, what on earth are they doing? I did not realise that Polly would become such a target for the press," says Daniel, as he and Polly read through the article covering the trial.

They arrive at the Old Bailey and again struggle to get through the reporters and photographers.

"Now Miss Spencer, you were telling the court about the attacks on yourself and Mr Bottomley. Please continue."

"The second attack occurred during Easter weekend when Daniel and I were travelling to the Midlands to spend the holiday with my family. Four men attacked us in our railway compartment. They gave Daniel a terrible beating and indecently assaulted me. However, he managed to stop them from hurting me too badly. I had a lot of scratches and they ripped off most of my clothes, but Daniel suffered terrible injuries from the attack and was unable to resume his work for almost two weeks," replies Polly, distressed at being reminded of what happened and struggling to remain composed.

"Are you ok to continue, Miss Spencer?"

"Yes, thank you my lord, I will be fine.'

"So, what happened next, Miss Spencer?"

"Two attacks directed at me were considered too much of a coincidence, and the security services wanted to be able to get proof as soon as possible that the Soviets were involved.

"That is when I began a more active role in looking at the documents that came to me. Daniel had other business to attend to so I concentrated on communists within the Civil Service."

"And then there was another attack on you both, is that correct?"

"Yes. Daniel and I were abducted at gunpoint from outside our apartment. We were driven to an old warehouse in Soho, and questioned about an alleged break-in at Communist Party Headquarters. One of the abductors was called Alexei Malakhov, so the Soviets must have decided to become involved directly. Again Daniel was given a beating and I was bruised, but threatened more than physically hurt.

"The abductors told Daniel that if he did not tell them what information he had from the alleged break-in at the Communist Party H.Q. then I would be transported to Russia."

"Your abductors actually said that, Miss Spencer? They would take you to Russia?"

"Thank you, my lord. So what happened next, Miss Spencer?"

"They left us for a while, and we managed to free ourselves. We ran out from the warehouse as they were returning and Daniel shot two of them, the others escaped."

"Miss Spencer, you say Mr Bottomley shot two of them?"

"Yes sir."

"Where on earth did he get his weapon from?"

"The men had left our clothes and my bag in the room where we were being held, so Daniel was able to use my pistol which was still in my bag."

"Good lord. You carry a weapon with you, Miss Spencer?"

"Yes sir, I do. Daniel decided I had to be prepared should I be attacked."

"Miss Spencer, you continue to surprise me."

"Thank you, my lord. Now tell us about the next attack, Miss Spencer. This took place again in Mr Bottomley's apartment, is that correct?"

"Yes, the intruders tricked the concierge into letting a man in posing as a gas engineer, and he left the door unlocked. When we arrived home in the evening, four men were waiting in the apartment. After binding him to a chair at gunpoint, they again questioned Daniel about the break-in and also referred to the Red Hand organisation at the Home Office. They took me into my bedroom and made threats against me also."

"Can you be more specific regarding these threats?"

"One of them held me while the other ripped off my blouse and skirt, before indecently assaulting me. I was slapped across my face, then punched hard a number of times in my stomach. The men then removed the remainder of my clothes and threw me on the bed."

"Please go on, Miss Spencer."

"Well, although Daniel was tied to a chair he managed to rush at the two men and bring them to the ground. The two men with me heard the noise and went to see what was happening. As soon as they left my room, I put on my robe, grabbed my pistol from the drawer, and followed the men into the lounge. I then shot two of the men who were all attacking Daniel."

The gallery gasped and then cheered at Polly's actions, absorbed in what she has said. The judge orders quiet and addresses Polly.

"You shot two of the men who were attacking Mr Bottomley?"

"Yes sir, if I had not, they could have killed him."

"Miss Spencer, you show maturity far beyond your years. I think now would be a good time to take lunch."

Once again, Polly rushes over to Daniel and, together with Conrad, they manage to get out of the courts and go off for lunch.

After lunch, the Crown barrister asks Polly to continue.

"Miss Spencer, continuing on from before lunch, I understand that you suffered a serious injury from this last attack?"

"I'm afraid so. The bruising to my lower abdomen from the punches I received, caused me to be violently sick a couple of days later. Daniel took me to hospital to be examined and the doctor was concerned that the attack may have cause me permanent damage, since it was close to my womb. Thankfully it was just bruising and eventually the bruising subsided."

"And are you are fully recovered from the attack, Miss Spencer?"

"Yes. Thank you, my lord."

"Thank you, my lord. As I have mentioned, details of these attacks and sentencing involved is with your bundle. Now Miss Spencer, tell me about the next attack on you and Mr Bottomley."

"After the trial in July, we decided to spend a week with my parents to get over what had happened and enjoy some time with my family. I don't get to see them as often as I would like so this holiday at home was eagerly awaited. However, after an enjoyable weekend, five men broke into my parents' house, and tried to kill Daniel and abduct me."

"Miss Spencer, are you telling the court that this was the intention of the intruders to your family's home, to kill Mr Bottomley and abduct you?" the Crown asks Polly.

"Yes sir, that was established at their trial."

"Please go on, Miss Spencer."

"Two of the men went into Daniel's room, but he must have heard the noise coming from my room next door and was ready for them. He shot both men as they entered. The other two men dragged me out of bed and along the landing towards the stairs. I struggled desperately to get away from them, and they ripped my pyjama jacket in the struggle. They were carrying me down the stairs as Daniel reached the top, but was surprised by a fifth man at the bottom of the stairs, who shot him in the chest, seriously injuring him. In spite of his serious injury, he shot back, injuring the man and he also managed to shoot one of the men trying to get me out to their car. The other man let go of me and ran off. Once again, Daniel had saved my life and prevented me from being abducted. However, he had a serious gunshot wound to his chest, and was covered in blood from his chest wound and barely conscious. Mummy and Daddy then came downstairs and telephoned for an ambulance and the police. It was terrible, I thought he would die..."

Polly becomes rather upset by this time, having to relate such distressing details of that night.

"Are you ok, Miss Spencer? Would you like to stop for a moment?"

"I am fine, thank you sir.'

"So, Mr Bottomley shot four men attempting to abduct you and kill him, and he did this on his own?" the judge asks, continuing to be shocked by Polly's evidence.

"Yes sir, Daniel had saved me once more and this time there was no doubt that the Russians were behind this since two of the men were Russian nationals, and are now in prison with the other two."

"And I believe there was a further attempt to abduct you very recently, Miss Spencer. Is that correct?"

"Yes sir, this occurred only last week. From my new position at the Foreign Office I was handed information from Australia, that four men had left for Britain with the intention of killing a British agent and abducting his young ward to Russia. There were also ransoms offered."

"Can you tell us what happened to you regarding this latest attempt to abduct you to Russia?"

"On Tuesday last, I received a message that I was required at the Home Office. Without thinking, I set off, leaving a note on my desk for my colleagues. As I crossed the road to go to the Home Office I was stopped by a man and asked for directions. As soon as I was engaged in conversation, a car drew up and I was pushed into the back seat, then driven to the docks. I was taken to an old boat and carried up the gangplank and into the ship's hold where I was stripped to my underwear and tied to an old chair."

"That must have been very frightening, Miss Spencer. Can you tell the court what happened next, please?"

"A man calling himself Barinov, came and told me they were going to throw me overboard when the boat was at sea. But first..." Polly struggles to compose herself, remembering vividly the events of only last week.

"Please sir, may I stop for a moment?"

"Of course. Fifteen minutes' recess, usher."

Polly rushes from the witness box to Daniel and holds him tightly, sobbing uncontrollably.

"Daniel this is hard for me, I really am struggling."

"I know it is, Polly, but it will soon be over. This is the last piece of unpleasant information that you have to recall. There isn't long left today, so the sooner you finish, the sooner we can go home," he says, holding her to him to give her comfort and reassurance.

Polly continues to hold onto Daniel before finally recovering. She knows that she must finish giving her evidence, and returns to the witness box after the recess.

"Are you feeling better, Miss Spencer? Are you happy to continue?"

"Yes. Thank you, my lord."

"Please continue, Miss Spencer. You mentioned that you were going to be disposed of at sea, is that correct?"

"Yes, but before that was to happen, I had to spend the night in the hold, and then I would be given to his crew."

"What did he mean by given to his crew?"

"He told me that I would be given to his men to do with as they wanted knowing that I was to be disposed of when they had finished with me. He went into details of what they might do with me and seemed to enjoy telling me. Please don't ask me to repeat what he said."

Polly's remarks drew gasps from the gallery, and the words 'shame on them' could be heard.

"And I understand that you were bitten several times during the night by rats, Miss Spencer?"

"Yes, the hold was filthy, dirty and pitch black. The rats came out soon after I was left alone. I was bitten on my feet, legs, and stomach, one of them actually sat on my lap as he nibbled at my stomach. It was horrible," Polly replies again, struggling to compose herself.

"Yes indeed. Please go on, Miss Spencer, if you would."

"Barinov came the next morning and indecently assaulted me whilst I was tied to the chair. Then I was carried up to the mess hall where the crew were waiting. One of them attended to my bites and took off what was left of my underwear. Barinov then began urging the men on, telling them what to do with me. His comments were despicable and disgusting. Then the man who had been cleaning my wounds lifted me onto the mess table and two men held me down.

Barinov was goading them to begin, shouting and laughing. They… I was…" Polly again finds herself unable to carry on, tears running down her cheeks.

"Take your time, Miss Spencer, the court appreciates how difficult this must be for you."

Polly takes a deep breath, determined to finish her evidence as soon as possible.

"Then, just at that moment, thank God, Daniel arrived with his colleagues. He shot the two men holding me, I think Conrad also shot Barinov, and we managed to escape down to the quayside, but not before poor Daniel was shot twice."

"Mr Bottomley sustained yet more gunshot wounds?"

"Yes sir, he is currently recovering from a wound to his shoulder and one to his arm."

"So Miss Spencer, you and Mr Bottomley have been repeatedly targeted by the Soviets, it would seem, in the fight against Soviet domination of our country. Before I hand over to the defence, my lord, I would like to ask Miss Spencer about her relationship with Mr Bottomley. I believe it is relevant, and I want to avoid the possibility of her integrity being brought into question."

"Very well, Mr Walters, but do get on."

"Thank you, my lord. Now Miss Spencer, can you tell the court what is your relationship to Mr Bottomley?"

"Daniel was asked to be my guardian, by my parents, when I was given a position in the Civil Service. I have lived in his apartment since January."

"And how did your parents come to choose Mr Bottomley to be responsible for you while you are in London?"

"My parents and all of my family have known Daniel for over five years. He lived with us, along with his colleague, when my family were threatened by criminal gangs during Daddy's fight to break up the black market racketeers in 1947."

"Could you elaborate for us, Miss Spencer?

"During the war years and after, Daddy fought an endless battle with black market gangs. He was with the Central Office for Information, and used his position to track down racketeers to the highest levels of government."

"Was his work dangerous?"

"Only because the men responsible for the racketeering were making huge profits and saw Daddy's operation as a threat to their business."

"And tell us where Mr Bottomley fit into all this?"

"The racketeers threatened Daddy by abducting me on more than one occasion."

"More than one occasion, you say, Miss Spencer?"

"Yes, they abducted me two or three times. They also took Mummy, and on one occasion took Daddy and me. Daniel was placed in our house to protect me initially, then when the attacks became more serious, his colleague stayed with us also. Each time they took me or attempted to take me, Daniel rescued me. Because of what happened, Daniel and I became very close, as I am sure you will understand. I was only thirteen years old and the subject of kidnappings and beatings." Polly struggles again as she recalls the events of five years ago.

"Miss Spencer, would you like to stop for a break?" the judge asks, as the gallery becomes noisy, listening to Polly with interest.

"No thank you sir, I am ok."

"So Mr Bottomley and his colleague lived with you for several months?"

"Yes. Daniel took me to school each day and collected me at the end of the day, and he slept in my room each night."

"He slept in your room?"

"Yes sir, in a chair. The men actually took me from my room on one occasion when they broke into our house. I became so frightened that I asked Daddy if Daniel could stay in my room to keep me safe."

"Yes, it must have been very frightening for you and your family?"

"Our house was set on fire and an explosive device sent by mail, and they poisoned our dog!"

"There were a number of trials relating to this, my lord. The details are available if required."

"You say that an explosive device was delivered?"

"Yes sir, fortunately the only person in the house at the time was Daniel. He was suspicious of the noise coming from the parcel and placed it at the bottom of our garden. When it did go off, it wrecked most of the back of the house and garden."

"It appears that you are no stranger to adversity, Miss Spencer."

"Thank you, my lord. And tell me, Miss Spencer, when did Mr Bottomley eventually move back to London?"

"As soon as the conspiracy trial was concluded and all of the accused sent to prison."

"And you kept in touch?"

"I did. I spent some of my holidays with him and he stayed with us sometimes."

"And because of what you had endured and because Daniel had been able to save you from these terrible events, you became very close to him?"

"Yes sir, he is very special to me."

"Thank you, Miss Spencer. Please remain in the witness box." The Crown barrister concludes his examinations.

"Thank you Mr Walters, the defence will begin its cross tomorrow. For now we are adjourned."

Once again Polly, Daniel, and Conrad have to endure a frenzy of reporters and photographers. Polly has become the press heroine and they cannot get enough of her.

"Miss Spencer, tell us how you feel about those men who abducted you."

"How close are you with Daniel?"

"Do you really carry a firearm with you all the time?"

The questions are endless, but finally, they make it to the car and Conrad speeds away to take them home. Polly is hiding her face in Daniel's chest, completely exhausted and overwhelmed by what is happening. No one had any idea that Polly would become such a celebrity, but in such austere times, the public were looking for someone to lift their spirits, and Polly seems to have done that. A beautiful young woman who has fought off every attempt to silence her, and her man, from uncovering the Russians' attempts to overthrow the government. That Polly is so young means that she is become the pin-up of young and old alike. Schoolgirls want to emulate her and mothers want to cherish her.

"What are we to do, Daniel? We are being pursued wherever we go now, the press have become almost a menace to us."

"We must try and get used to it for a little while, Polly. At least until the trial is over. When that happens, we will give a press interview and try to answer all their questions at the same time.

"I am however, going to make a statement when I begin my evidence and tell the court that you and I are married. I do not want to hear any more comments and innuendo relating to you and me. I love you too much for anyone to tarnish that love."

"Does that mean we can wear our wedding rings at last, Daniel? That's wonderful," he says, hugging him.

"Ow! Mind the wounds, Polly. I am still very frail you know!" he replies, laughing.

"Sorry Daniel, let me go and make some tea and organise dinner."

The two of them enjoy their evening, and Polly is delighted to receive a call from home commenting on the coverage of the trial.

"Everyone is asking about you, Polly. You have become quite a celebrity. How are you and Daniel coping?"

"We are ok thank you, Mummy, and tomorrow Daniel is going to tell everyone that we are married to stop the comments about us once and for all."

"That's wonderful news. How is Daniel by the way, are his latest wounds healing?"

"Yes they are, but you know Daniel, he's indestructible!"

"You be sure to take care of him and I hope it all goes well for you both for the remainder of the trial."

After dinner, Polly has her bath, then she and Daniel enjoy each other for the rest of the evening and through the night, their lovemaking as intense as always. They are collected by Conrad on Wednesday who shows them the latest news headlines.

"Russian bear foiled by young heroine and her guardian."

"Stuff of dreams for the press, Daniel."

"I suppose it was to be expected when we went to trial. As long as they are all put away for a long time it will be worth the publicity."

They fight their way into the court and Daniel has a discreet word with the Crown barrister Philip Walters before they enter the courtroom, informing him of his intention to make a statement regarding his relationship with Polly.

"I understand fully, Daniel, and I believe you are making the right decision. You can bet the defence counsel will make an issue of it this morning."

Polly enters the witness box for the third day ready to face questions from the defence team.

"Miss Spencer, my name is Donald Capel and I represent Sally Nugent and Percival Smith. Now the court has heard how you collected evidence about this alleged secret organisation and passed it on to the security services, is that correct?"

"Yes sir, that is correct."

"Do you really expect the court to believe that the members of this so-called Red Hand willingly gave their secret messages over to you to do with as you wished?"

"No sir, they were handed to me to be delivered to their members indicated."

"And how did you know that the document was being delivered to a member of the alleged Red Hand and not just a member of staff, Miss Spencer?"

"Their files were marked with a red fist holding a red sickle. That is how they were identified," Polly replies, as members of the gallery mutter approvingly.

"When were you recruited to this so-called organisation, Miss Spencer? You were a member, were you not?"

"No sir, I was not a member."

"But were you not arrested and detained by the police, when the Home Office was raided?"

"Yes, but I was released shortly afterwards. Because it was known that I handled Red Hand files, they assumed I was involved. The only reason I was kept overnight was because I was carrying a weapon."

"Yes, so to recap, you were in regular contact with all members of the organisation, you were trusted to deliver confidential messages for them, and you were arrested at the same time as all the other members. And yet you say you were not involved in their activities, is that correct?"

"Yes, that is correct."

"Now can I ask you about your so-called guardian? What exactly is your relationship to this man that you live with all alone?"

There is a buzz around the gallery in anticipation of Polly's response.

"Daniel was appointed as my guardian by my parents, when I secured my position in the Home Office, but I have already mentioned this to Mr Walters."

"Yes, do move on, Mr Capel!" the judge remarks.

'Miss Spencer, you are actually asking the court to believe that this man is your guardian and nothing else. You are a beautiful young woman and he is a good-looking man after all." The defence presses Polly. Thankfully, the judge intervenes to save her any embarrassment.

"Mr Capel, I asked you to move on. Do you have any further questions for this witness?"

"No, my lord. Thank you, Miss Spencer, I have no more questions. Remain in the box please."

Polly breathes a sigh of relief as the second defence barrister stands.

"Miss Spencer, my name is Bernard Johnson and I speak on behalf of the four Russians in the dock. Now these abductions and assaults that you have vividly detailed for the court, did they really happen like you said?"

"I'm not sure what you mean. I gave my evidence, explaining what has happened. Apart from the last attack, everything else has been dealt with by the courts."

"Yes, yes, Miss Spencer, but are you absolutely sure that you have been the victim of a Soviet plot? Could this not have been some thugs looking to hold you for ransom, and nothing to do with Russia or communists?"

"I can assure you, sir, the evidence tells the true story.'

"Yes, but Miss Spencer, is it not true that it was the idea of the security services to use these attacks to smear the Russian people and the British Communist Party?"

"If you believe that you are very much mistaken," Polly replies angrily.

"We shall see, Miss Spencer. Now I should like to ask you a question about Mr Bottomley. Was it not convenient for him and the security services to be nominated as your guardian?"

"Daniel was nominated as my guardian because my parents trusted him to take care of me whilst working in London. My family knew him well and he was the obvious choice. Really, Mr Johnson, some of your questions are nonsense."

"It is my contention that you conspired with Mr Bottomley to attack the Soviets and so further the aims of the security services to destroy the Communist Party in this country."

"As I said earlier, if that is your opinion Mr Capel, you are very much mistaken."

"I have no further questions, my lord."

"Very well, Mr Capel, then now would be a good time to stop for lunch. Miss Spencer you may step down."

Polly and Daniel go off to lunch with Conrad, again besieged by the press. The reporters seem particularly delighted at the way Polly handled the cross examination. After lunch Daniel is called into the witness box. He is tall and well-built with dark hair, and is wearing a grey suit and has an upright bearing left over from his career in the Army.

"Will you confirm your name for the court please?"

"Daniel Bottomley."

"And what is your occupation?"

"I work in special operations for the security services."

"Could you be more specific please?"

"My department works independently of MI5 with special reference to identifying the threat of communism and the Soviets in our country."

"Now Mr Bottomley, we have heard a lot about you and Miss Spencer and your relationship to her. Because of this speculation, I understand you would like to make a statement before we proceed, is that correct?"

"Yes. As you say there has been much speculation about the two of us what we do and the fact that I was appointed her guardian. There have been comments of how close we may or may not be to each other and the fact that we live together in my apartment. I can state here and now that Polly and I love each other very much and we were married on the 22nd of August."

There are cheers and applause from the gallery, which overwhelms Polly, who sobs with delight.

When the noise dies down, the judge orders a fifteen-minute

recess so that the court may get back to normal. Polly rushes over to Daniel and they leave the courtroom together.

"The whole world knows now, Daniel. I am delighted. We need to celebrate as soon as possible," says Polly, beaming with delight.

The press are clamouring to get into the area immediately outside the courtroom but are prevented. They call out to both of them but Polly and Daniel ignore their requests for picture. After the short recess, Daniel returns to the witness box and apologises to the judge for the disruption.

"Now Mr Bottomley, we have heard about Mrs Bottomley's activities on your behalf. Can you tell the court what other areas you explored in pursuing the communists?"

"There has been a great deal of trouble in the docks over the past few months, and we have been compiling evidence of communist activity there."

"Yes, and I understand that this all came about from a message you received some time ago?"

"Yes. I received a message when the print unions were on strike from a union member who asked to speak with me."

"And how did he know how to make contact with you, and how did he feel you could help him?"

"Some five years ago, when Polly's father was engaged in the fight against black market racketeers, I was part of a task force that closed down the operation at Milford haven. The man who contacted me was in the attachment of army personnel who assisted in the operation, and he remembered me from that time. He must have talked to his commanding officer who directed him to me."

"Yes of course, and what did your contact have to say?"

"He expressed concern at the communist interference in the running of his union and believed that they had a hidden agenda. This man was a dedicated trade unionist, who believed that the working man should have a say in his destiny, not be dictated to by anyone, including union agitators."

"And what conclusions did you draw from his conversation?"

"That we had to find out what was happening in the docks and what the communists were planning. The unofficial strikes were causing severe problems with tons of food being destroyed, and raw materials held up, causing problems for the manufacturing industries. I was instructed to get information on the activities of the Communist Party and how the Soviets may be involved."

"So how did you go about getting your information?"

"We paid a visit to the Communist Party Headquarters and had a look around."

"What do you mean by paid a visit, Mr Bottomley?'

"We broke in and looked at the files that were not locked away, sir."

"I see. Please go on, Mr Walters."

"We found enough evidence to convince us that the communists were being given instructions from Moscow. Then we had a lucky break when Elizabeth Berkley approached Polly. We then set up an operation so that Polly could get close to the Red Hand and give us information. You have heard just how successful she was."

"Indeed, Mr Bottomley. Now what about your activities against the agitators in the trade union movement, how did you get on there?"

"My contact persuaded some of his colleagues in the docks to talk to me. To begin with I posed as a reporter trying to get an inside story. It was obvious from what I was told that the genuine grievances of the men were being sacrificed for the political ends of the communists. The men I met were aware of this and asked if they could help to change it. They were good trade unionists who only wanted what was best for their members. You will have an opportunity to speak with one of them later."

"Do go on, Mr Bottomley."

"As you will know from her testimony, while we were pursuing the communists, Polly and I were having to put up with numerous attempts to abduct her, in the hope it would stop me from bringing them to justice."

"And it was during your efforts to prevent Miss Spencer – I beg your pardon – Mrs Bottomley, from being abducted that you were injured several times, I understand. How are your latest injuries, by the way?"

"Yes, I did sustain one or two wounds, and I am healing well, thank you sir."

"Thank you, my lord. Now I'm sure the court would like to know what the circumstances were that led you to ask someone so young and inexperienced to carry out the dangerous task of securing information from a communist-inspired organisation?"

"Quite simply we were at a loss how to move forward. We couldn't infiltrate the organisation, we didn't even know who the members were. We thought Polly may be able to listen and learn and she jumped at the chance to help. So it was decided to give her a more responsible position, allowing her to move freely through both the Home Office and the Foreign Office. Being so young and having no political agenda, she was ideally suited to be put into a position of trust. Polly is very determined to be successful in her job and she proved to be invaluable, especially as the Red Hand agents trusted her completely. The information she passed on showed a link between the organisation and Russian agents in Britain. MI5 were able to photograph Smith with known Russian agents, which confirmed the details that we were receiving from Polly's efforts."

"Thank you, Mr Bottomley. Now I wonder if we might refer back to your findings relating to trade union interference by the Soviets."

"Mr Walters, I think now might be a good time to adjourn for today," says the judge.

As Daniel leaves the witness box there are screams of abuse from the dock.

"We will kill you eventually, Mr Bottomley, and your pretty young wife, be warned!" one of the Russians shouts.

"Get those men down to the cells at once," orders the judge.

Daniel seems completely unmoved by the threats as he and Polly move towards the court entrance. Once again they are besieged by the press wanting details of their marriage. "When did you first realise that Daniel was the man for you?" Polly is asked by the reporters.

"I suppose I must have loved him right from the first time I knew him, when I was still at school."

And when did Daniel first realise he loved Polly? He refers to their unusual relationship caused by his being her protector. They were constantly together, apart from when she was actually inside school. Polly never left his side and he was completely devoted to his task of protecting both her and the Spencer family.

"You have to have lived through our experiences to understand how close we became. Then when Polly came to live with me, she brought something special to my bachelor life, and then I found myself being her protector yet again before I fell in love with her. We kept our marriage secret only because we feared the Soviets might try to exploit our love for each other. Now gentlemen, please, that's enough for now. We have a long way to go yet before the trial ends. We will talk to you again then, thank you," says Daniel, as they move toward the waiting car.

"Well Daniel, apart from everything that is going on, how do you see the trial progressing?"

"It's going well, Conrad. If you were a betting man you would bet on a clear victory for us and we have not finished yet."

"It's so satisfying to be officially Mrs Bottomley, Daniel. I can't wait to start telling the shopkeepers, the postman, the milkman and…"

"Yes, ok Polly. I think you should put your ad in the Times. What do you think, Conrad?"

"Absolutely Daniel, that sounds a marvellous idea."

Once again they use the side entrance to the apartments to avoid more press and the photographers.

They are getting used to the routine for the moment, but Daniel is uncomfortable with the publicity and hopes that, when the trial is done, they might be able to lead a rather more normal life. Polly, it would seem, is quite relaxed by it all. That the whole world knows she loves Daniel is just what she needed, and she is thrilled by what has happened. However, on Thursday morning there is a sinister occurrence which puts the whole trial into perspective. Daniel had just started to give his evidence when there is an explosion somewhere within the building. The courtroom shakes and dust is everywhere, but there is no damage within the courtroom itself.

"Get the prisoners back into their cells please, and clear the courtroom," the judge calls.

Daniel grabs hold of Polly and rushes to find Conrad, who is just outside the entrance. Staff and barristers file out in an orderly fashion. Daniel can see dust and debris at the back of the court entrance, but the walls and ceiling are intact.

"What has happened, Daniel? Do you think it was a bomb?"

"I'm pretty sure it was a bomb, Polly, probably planted underneath the courtroom, but not powerful enough to create any damage to the courtroom or the surrounding area. Conrad, go and identify yourself to the senior police officer and see what you can find out. I will stay with Polly in case anything else is planned."

Conrad returns after a short while, telling Daniel what he has found out.

"The device was planted in the boiler room, not very big, but it has done a lot of damage in the boiler room itself. As far as I can determine, no one was inside the room at the time."

"I will talk to the barrister and then we will get away from here. I am not convinced that they will not try something else now that they have a diversion," says Daniel, as he goes off with Polly to find their barrister. He suggests that proceedings will be postponed for the day and they report back on Friday morning, so they quickly move away from the Old Bailey and decide to go into work for the day. Conrad drops Polly outside the Foreign Office, where she receives warm applause from everyone as she enters her office.

"Many congratulations, my dear. You and Daniel have become quite famous, but what are you doing here, should you not be at court?" asks David Fellows.

Polly tells him about the explosion at the Old Bailey, and her decision to come into work and make herself useful. Daniel had decided it would be the safest place for both of them.

"A wise decision, I would think, Polly, and there is much to do."

Polly goes into her office and views the mountain of outstanding files to be looked at. Peter and Rachel look rather harassed, so Polly calls them into her office. They both congratulate Polly again on her marriage and on her newfound fame from the press.

"Thank you both, now let's see what we have here. I have the rest of the day to help with all this so I need you both to try and arrange the files in some sort of order and I will see what can be done."

"There has been a lot more information from Australia, Polly. They seem to be having some sort of purge against all communists there."

"They are trying to ban them, Rachel. I do not believe that is the right way because all that happens when you ban an organisation is that they go into hiding. They do not go away, they just become more difficult to keep an eye on, and so give you more work. So let's see what has been happening in Australia."

Fitz is delighted to see Daniel and Conrad, but concerned at what has happened.

"I was shocked when I heard, Daniel, they are obviously trying to stop proceedings. Do you know when the trial will be able to carry on?"

"The Crown barrister told us to report back tomorrow morning."

"Anyway, things have settled in the docks, and the management have taken the initiative and called all the representatives to a meeting. I think we may have a breakthrough."

"That's good news, Fitz. It will go quiet at least for a while because many of the troublemakers have been removed or gone to ground. The management should take this opportunity and press home what is needed to settle the dispute."

"Yes indeed, and how is Polly recovering from her ordeal? I had completely overlooked that."

"I think she has too, so much has happened since last week, and I have let her enjoy what has been going on around her."

"Good idea Daniel, I think now that she is officially Mrs Bottomley, nothing else seems to matter."

Daniel asks Fitz if he can use a pool car for the weekend, to which Fitz readily agrees.

"I am going to take her home for the weekend to get away from all the publicity, Fitz. It will do us both good."

At the end of the day they are collected by Conrad and return to their apartment. Polly calls her parents to tell them that they would like to come home for the weekend, and Margaret is obviously delighted.

"It will be an honour to have such celebrities in our home!"

"Thank you Mummy, it will be a relief to get away from all the press following us everywhere. I do so want to be able to sit down with everyone and just enjoy being with you. Then going for a walk with Daniel afterwards."

Daniel and Polly spend their evening together before returning to court the next day. The proceedings are to go ahead after the judge has made a statement.

"Yesterday's events were shameful and will not be tolerated, and those responsible hunted down and brought to justice. This is a court of law and the law will be administered and will not be put off by such actions. Furthermore, I would add that any further outbursts from the dock will be held in contempt. Thank you. Mr Walters, please continue."

"Thank you, my lord. Now Mr Bottomley, we were talking about Soviet interference in the trade unions. What did you determine from your investigations?"

"Both within the Civil Service and the trade unions in the docks, the communists were seeking to cause maximum disruption that would eventually lead to civil unrest. The court has already heard about their intentions within the Civil Service and they saw the trade union movement as an ideal place to create upset and disruption. They have members who are powerful speakers who can sway an audience with their ideals and promises. However, their intentions did not sway everyone and genuine members of the trade union have become worried about what is happening. That is why I was contacted. I have spoken with some of the members, even communist members. They, too, are concerned about Moscow's agenda. They only want what is best for their members, not what Moscow would force on them."

"Are you telling the court that some members of the Communist Party resent what is happening?"

"Yes I am, and you will be told more about this later on in this trial."

"Please go on, Mr Bottomley."

"I have spoken at length with members who have told me of intimidation and threats to anyone who questions their intentions. Despite several overtures by the dock managers, the dockers have been told that only an all-out strike will achieve their aims. Of course an all-out strike will cause more hardships for the public. We still have rationing in our country, and the Soviets are seeking to exploit our hardship, and they have been planning their operations for some time.

"They are very good at playing the waiting game. They had to wait some time to get their man in an influential position in the Home Office and when it happened, it was to have triggered a predetermined series of events."

"Can you be specific, Mr Bottomley?"

"With a man in a high position in the Home Office, his job would have been to encourage the Secretary to put forward the idea of industrial legislation to ban strikes in key industries.

"It would only need this information to be leaked for the communists to call the men out on strike. Once they had achieved their aim, the government would have no alternative but to use the military to get essential supplies moving from the docks. This move would put the British public against the British public, and civil unrest would naturally follow. Once the flames had been fanned by the agitators, Soviet representatives would step in and call for a people's revolution. From here it is not difficult to determine how it could unfold."

"And that is what was being planned by the communists, Mr Bottomley?"

"That is what the Soviets were planning, my lord, and using the members in Britain to put their plans into practise. Make no mistake, we are dealing with an evil ideology that would throttle all free speech and replace it with a kind of political slavery," says Daniel, speaking directly to the judge.

"So how did you succeed in finding the final pieces of the jigsaw so that this conspiracy trial could take place?"

"By paying a second visit to the Communist H.Q. and getting into their safe. There were details of times and dates relating to the placement of a member into a position of influence in government. Also a plan to escalate the strike action to the industrial heartlands of the Midlands, as soon as the dockers were effectively locked out, was outlined. There was even mention of paying members to visit the Midlands and start unrest among union members by visiting branch meetings. It is well known that the Electrical Trades Union has communist members, so that is where they were to start. They also intended to strangle the transport system by calling out the railway unions. It was all detailed and planned."

"A disturbing thought, Mr Bottomley. Thank you. Please remain in the box, I'm sure the defence barristers would like a word."

"Mr Bottomley, my name is Bernard Johnson, I speak for our Soviet friends. Now sir, you have painted a pretty grim picture here today, I am almost scared to travel home this evening, with such threats hanging over us."

"You may well be scared, sir, for what happened to my wife, I would not wish on anyone. Not even you," replies Daniel sharply, drawing laughter from the gallery.

"Yes, now let me ask you about your so-called visits to Communist Party Headquarters. You broke into the premises, didn't you, and then their safe, isn't that what you did, Mr Bottomley?"

"There are no rules in the war against foreign government agents, Mr Johnson. No right and wrong, no one you can turn to for advice. You get caught and you are either shot or disowned by your government, so please don't ask me to justify or condone what I do. If it wasn't me doing it, someone else would take my place."

"You say we will hear more about the trade union interference, is that correct? And if so, what exactly do you mean?"

"British citizens, genuine trade union members, will be giving evidence against your clients."

"There is no evidence, this trial is a sham!" shouts one of the Russian accused.

"Please sit down, sir. The next time, you will be removed to the cells," the judge remarks.

"You will see just what this trial is when you get sent away for the rest of your life, sir, or even worse for you, sent back to Russia,"

Daniel responds, and is warned by the judge.

"My apologies to the court, my lord."

"Very well Mr Bottomley, perhaps we should all have some lunch and calm down. We are adjourned until this afternoon."

Daniel looks up at the dock as he leaves the witness box and stares hard at the Russian who was hassling him. He leaves the courtroom and goes off for lunch with Polly and Conrad.

"Bravo, Daniel. You were brilliant in there, wasn't he, Conrad?"

"Good show, Daniel. It was good to see the barrister stuttering, and I enjoyed your comment to the Russian, I think everyone did."

After lunch, Daniel returns to the witness box ready for more questions.

"You say that you found this evidence of a conspiracy to remove our government at the Communist Party H.Q. Is that correct?" the defence barrister continues.

"Some of the evidence, yes, I'm sure you will have seen it also."

"And how do we know that it is genuine, Mr Bottomley? How do we know that you haven't made it up?"

"You don't."

"What, you mean that it could well have been made up, sir?"

"If you really believe that, Mr Johnson, you are in the wrong job," replies Daniel, drawing laughter from the gallery again.

"Mr Bottomley, please confine yourself to matters at hand. I will not have my courtroom used for flippant chatter."

"My apologies, my lord."

"Now can we refer to Mrs Bottomley's efforts in all this? Do you really expect the court to believe that she was able to collect sensitive details from the members of an alleged secret organisation, take them back to an office, photograph them, return them into their files and deliver them on to one of the alleged agents? Is that what really happened, or did you make it all up, Mr Bottomley?"

"Well sir, the lady in the dock would be able to substantiate part of what you are asking, and your bundle of evidence should substantiate the rest for you."

"My lord, will you instruct the witness to answer the question?"

"Mr Bottomley, please answer the question."

"My apologies, my lord. Do I expect the court to believe that Polly collected sensitive details from Red Hand members? Yes I do. Do I expect the court to believe that she took the files back to her office and photographed the contents? Yes I do. Do I expect the court to believe that she then delivered them to members of the Red Hand organisation? Yes I do. Because that is precisely what she did."

"Mr Bottomley, can I ask you, what did you do in the war years? Were you a serving member of Her Majesty's forces?"

"Yes I was."

"And so these men, these Russians, would have been your allies – our friends. You are now asking the court to believe that the Russians are our enemy. Are you not mistaken in all this?"

Daniel thinks carefully before he replies.

"Sir, any man who belongs to the country that has attempted to kill me on more than one occasion, has abducted my wife, thrown her into a filthy ship's hold where she was bitten by rats, then abused her in the most unspeakable manner, are no friends of mine or my country. And I will tell you now, that should I ever meet Mr Baranov, I will kill him myself for his actions towards Polly."

"Isn't that what this is all about, Mr Bottomley? A vendetta by you against my clients?"

"Your clients will have the opportunity to defend themselves if they wish, although I doubt whether you will want the Crown to question them. Don't you understand, sir? In a communist courtroom there is no presumption of innocence until proven guilty, no jury, no trial defence. Just prosecutors shouting and a crowd, yelling support for the verdict and sentence. This is the difference between our country and Russia, not economics or democracy, but rule of law. There is no rule of law in Russia."

"Your Honour, will you direct Mr Bottomley to answer the questions put to him?"

"I think Mr Bottomley has a point to make, but yes, please answer the questions as they are put to you."

"May I ask the barrister to repeat the question he wishes me to answer, my lord?"

"I asked whether you had a vendetta against my clients, Mr Bottomley?"

"Why would I have a vendetta against your clients? That suggests a feud or a fight of some sort. My fight is against the communist ideal, but I will admit that I have become angry with their cowardly methods. They have tried on many occasions to harm my wife, even attack us in her family's home. They have become frustrated that their ambitions to turn our country into a communist state have not succeeded. So you could say they have a vendetta against Polly and me for what we have done to stop them from achieving their aims."

"I have no further questions, my lord. Thank you." The defence barrister sits down, rather frustrated with his efforts.

"Mr Bottomley, my name is John Griffiths, I represent the trade union members. You have said that we will hear more about the communist involvement with the union in this trial. Can you tell me what you mean by that?"

"You will hear evidence of communist interference in the running of the trade unions. That this interference will include intimidation, threats, and violence against anyone who speaks against them, and evidence of a conspiracy reaching into government by using a communist to attempt to influence government policies."

"Yes, yes, but what about actual witnesses, Mr Bottomley?"

"Well you will have to ask the Crown about witnesses, Mr Griffiths. I do not have a list as you well know."

"So you are suggesting that my clients were party to this conspiracy by acts of violence and intimidation against union members, and you know of this because of what, you were told?"

"Yes, I was told, and anyone working the docks will tell you of beatings and threats. I have the evidence for anyone to see. Your clients were misguided, believing that the communist agents were working for the benefit of the membership."

"Perhaps the intimidation came from you, Mr Bottomley. Perhaps you issued threats against my clients and their colleagues if they didn't tell stories about the communists."

"That, sir, is rubbish and is not worthy of a response."

"Really! You won't say whether anyone will confirm your claims, you use illegal entry to gain access to legitimate business premises, and you urge management to bully the union members back to work. Is that correct, Mr Bottomley?"

"You are talking rubbish, sir. I have already answered the first part of that question, the second part has already been dealt with by one of your colleagues, and as for the third part, I can only say I have no idea what you are talking about. You flatter me if you think I have such influence on management."

"Don't try and be flippant, Mr Bottomley. You know what I am saying. You have been using your office's influence to force management of the dockers to bully the men into submission. Profits before people. The government is fearful of union labour and relies on men like you to do the dirty work of smearing union leaders, hoping to reduce what powers they have. You are both a trouble shooter and a trouble maker. Isn't that true, Mr Bottomley?"

"What is true, sir, is that you have a vivid imagination. I would like to be able to say yes to your question. To have so much power could be the answer to many problems. With so much power you could run a country single-handed. You wouldn't need a government, would you? But no, I'm afraid it just isn't true."

Once again, murmurs and some laughter can be heard in the courtroom.

"Mr Bottomley, do you deny that you have deliberately fabricated your evidence and evidence apparently yet to be heard? Evidence that maliciously accuses the communist of conspiring against our government?"

"I do deny your accusation, sir, and would suggest that you look at the information you have been given relating to your question. Is it not customary to prepare your case before you blindly go forth in the courtroom?"

"I suggest you watch your tone, Mr Bottomley, you may be held in contempt."

"What for, sir? Telling you to be prepared before making ludicrous accusations that you cannot substantiate?"

"Your manner and attitude, Mr Bottomley, suggests to me that you are a man who likes his own way no matter what the consequences."

Daniel stares at the defence barrister without commentating. There is a strange hush in the courtroom.

"Is that correct, Mr Bottomley?"

"My apologies, I did not realise there was a question in there. I thought you were thinking aloud. Do I like my own way? I think we all like to have our own way, don't we? No matter what the consequences? Well that would depend on what those consequences were."

"Would you care to elaborate?"

"Elaborate on what?"

"Elaborate on consequences, Mr Bottomley."

"If the consequences meant the difference between the life or death of my wife or family, then yes, no matter what the consequences. If the consequences meant the difference between saving someone's life who was in imminent danger, then yes, no matter what the consequences.

"But for your benefit, Mr Griffiths, if the consequences meant that someone be treated unfairly or illegally, then no consequences could excuse such behaviour."

"We have heard testimony relating to you using a weapon on several occasions to get your way, Mr Bottomley, is that correct?"

"No sir, it is not correct."

"But Mr Bottomley, your wife has testified to you having shot several people, are you saying that did not happen?"

"Yes sir, that is correct."

"But you just said that was not correct. Which is it to be, Mr Bottomley? The court is confused."

"It is you who are confused, sir. The men that I shot was to save either my wife from being abducted or to save myself from being killed; it was not to get my way. It was a consequence of life or death. Do you understand that or would you like me to repeat it?" replies

Daniel, becoming angry at the barrister's tone of questions. Again the courtroom and the gallery mutter and laugh.

"You, Mr Bottomley, are trying to confuse the issue here. You don't have the evidence to prove your theory, you have shot and sometimes killed those who got in your way, and have used your position to satisfy your obsession with a legal organisation, the British Communist Party."

"And you, sir, are an idiot and a buffoon if that is what you truly believe!"

"Your Honour I must protest!"

"Mr Bottomley, please refrain from insulting the defence barristers.'

"Your Honour, I thought my comments were appropriate after what he had said."

"I demand you hold this man in contempt, Your Honour."

"Gentlemen, I think now might be a good time to adjourn for the weekend and give those concerned time to calm down," the judge replies.

The courtroom is in uproar, and people in the gallery are standing and applauding loudly. Daniel steps down from the witness box, walks past the defence barrister, smiling.

"You have not heard the last of this."

"Whatever you say, sir, whatever you say, Mr Griffiths," Daniel replies as he moves off to Polly and they leave the courtroom together. Conrad helps them push their way through the press and the crowd that has gathered, many people cheering Daniel and saying, "Well done," to him.

They had packed their weekend suitcases and were driven to collect their car before setting off for Carswell.

"Good show, Daniel. That barrister was out of his depth and you showed up his inadequacies perfectly," says Conrad.

"Well I thought you were brilliant, Daniel, and so did everyone in that courtroom, apart from Mr Griffiths, that is," comments Polly.

Conrad takes them back to the car pool area where Daniel collects a car for their trip.

"Enjoy your weekend, both of you. If you get the car back here for eight o'clock Monday Daniel, and I will drive you both to the courts.

"Thanks Conrad, see you Monday," he replies, as he and Polly get into the car and begin their drive north across London. The traffic is rather heavy but they eventually reach the A41 then onto the A5 Watling Street, which will take them almost the whole distance to Carswell. They arrive at Polly's home around 7.30pm to be overwhelmed by the family greeting.

"Polly, Daniel, wonderful to see you both," Margaret says.

"Daniel, we have missed you, but we have read about you and Polly in the papers," says George.

"Daniel it's so good to see you, how is the trial progressing?"

"Daniel has been brilliant, Daddy. You should have seen the way he handled the defence barristers."

The family go through to the parlour where Margaret has prepared some dinner. Polly and Daniel are hungry from a long day and enjoy their meal. Afterwards, Polly goes to have a bath, and Margaret takes the opportunity to ask Daniel more about her abduction.

"Polly was subjected to a particularly nasty assault, Margaret. Quite apart from being bitten several times by rats. The trial has been a real help to her; she has had something else to focus on which has meant she hasn't had too much time to think about what happened previously. When the trial is over and we get back to normal, she may have some sort of reaction, I honestly don't know."

"And what about you? You were injured yet again?"

"Yes, but I am healing, Margaret, and will soon be fit again."

"Have you been shooting villains again, Daniel?"

"Evil men who wanted to harm Polly, George."

Polly returns having had her bath, dressed in her night clothes. She has put on pyjamas to hide her rat bites, but the marks to her ankles and wrists can still be seen. Margaret notices them, but says nothing for the moment.

"Daniel was wonderful in court today, Daddy. He really showed up the defence barrister."

"It's not always a good idea to antagonise barristers, Polly, he may react unfavourably.

"Well Daniel will handle him, he saved me again you know, Mummy. The men who abducted me were going to kill me. Had Daniel not arrived when he did I would be dead by now."

"He is indeed a remarkable person, Polly, and I want him to know that."

"Thank you, Daddy. I sometimes think I am the luckiest person in the world to have him as my husband, and I have you and Mummy to thank for that for it was you who invited him into our house such a long time ago. Do you remember?"

"We do remember, Polly, and thank God that we chose him," Ben replies as Daniel enters the parlour, refreshed after his wash. The family discuss the trial in some detail and are shocked to hear about the explosion yesterday.

"They never stop, Daniel. Thankfully no one was injured," says Ben.

"These people do not care who they hurt, the end justifies the means to them, it seems."

After more discussions on the trial, Daniel and Polly decide to go up to bed. For them, it has been a long day.

"Goodnight both, we will see you in the morning," says Margaret.

Polly goes with Daniel to the bathroom to examine his wounds. The hole in his arm is at last closing, and his shoulder is healing as Polly applies a clean dressing to both injuries.

They get into bed and reflect on a heck of a day.

"It's been a difficult day, Mr Bottomley," says Polly as she strokes him gently.

"I think we coped rather well, Mrs Bottomley," he says, as he helps her out of her pyjamas.

They lie there, exploring each other and enjoying each other's touches. Polly's stroking of Daniel becomes more and more intense before she slips beneath him and guides him inside. Daniel strokes and caresses Polly as their union finally reaches its conclusion. They lie side by side then, in each other's arms, before drifting off into a deep sleep.

Saturday morning sees Polly go off to Carswell with Margaret, while Daniel stays to entertain Maisy, Daisy, and George and talks with Ben.

"Thank you for saving Polly again, Daniel. It sounded as if she was very badly treated by the Russian seamen. The paper said something about her being bitten by rats while she was tied, it must have been horrible for her."

"Yes Maisy, but I am hoping that being here with you and everyone will help her. Your sister is very stubborn and determined in everything she does, but she has been through a lot over the past few months, and is rather frail at the moment. We all love her, Maisy, and that will help, I'm sure."

"Well, if it wasn't for you we wouldn't have her, so thank you for taking care of her so well," Maisy replies, hugging Daniel, who smiles and thanks Maisy, before going into the study.

"Daniel, my dear friend, how are you? More wounds to heal from your heroics in saving Polly."

"The wounds are healing fine, but like you I wonder what the Russians may do next. I am puzzled by their unprofessional manner in targeting Polly and myself. Can they really be so small-minded as to seek revenge at the expense of what they were hoping to achieve? It doesn't make sense to me, Ben."

"It is rather odd, perhaps it is that you have taken out their experienced operators and they are finding it difficult to replace them. I would think they may pause to regroup after this trial. It is attracting publicity throughout the world. I have no doubt and they will want to wait for circumstances to improve for them. But that does not mean you should let your guard down, Daniel. You will be in their sights for some time, I am sure."

"We have Conrad permanently at our disposal now, driving us to and from our work. And of course, Polly never goes out alone. I have additional security on the apartment, that is really all that we can do, Ben. We hope to move out of London soon and buy a house. Polly has always said that we need a house so that we can start a family. Now that information is between you and I, Ben, for now."

"Of course, Daniel. She does seem to have everything planned, doesn't she? And this new position too is quite a step up for her?"

"You have no idea how much she is valued, Ben. Her boss, David Fellows, thinks very highly of her, and the two colleagues under her appreciate her expertise. I believe she will go a long way in the Service and I will not let anything happen to her if only to see her achieve the success she deserves."

Polly and her mother return from shopping with new clothes and a plentiful supply of groceries. Despite continuing rationing of some items, there is no real shortage in the countryside.

"Sorry we have been such a while, Daddy, but everyone wanted to congratulate me on being married to Daniel, and of course they asked about the trial. I even met some of my school friends who wanted to ask about my new husband."

"Well you and Daniel have become celebrities, Polly, so it is natural that everyone wants to talk to you. And now that you and Daniel are married, means more questions, I suppose."

Daniel decides that they should have a meal locally in the evening to give Margaret a break, and since it has been a while since they all went out together. The meal and occasion is enjoyed by everyone, even though they are interrupted several times by well-wishers. Polly takes it all in her stride and Daniel is relieved to see her so happy after her ordeal. On Sunday morning, Polly asks that they all go to church.

"It has been a while, Mummy, and I just feel that it will be good for Daniel and me. I have asked the vicar if he would bless our marriage and he has agreed. It will make the marriage complete for both of us and I am sure that some of our friends will appreciate seeing us together."

"It will be a wonderful service, Polly, and I am so pleased that the vicar agreed."

The Sunday service is enjoyed by everyone, many people bringing flowers for Polly. She is radiant, smiling as she shows off Daniel to everyone. After the service the vicar addresses the congregation directly.

"I am sure we are all delighted to be able to witness the blessing of Polly and Daniel's wedding here today. Of course we have known Polly for many years and Daniel has been with us for some time. They are a wonderful couple who are striving to make our world a better place and for that we thank them. However, for today let us wish them well as they dedicate their marriage to God in our service of prayer and dedication."

After the service, Daniel, Polly, and the family join with some friends for a celebration drink in the Carswell Hotel before returning home for lunch. Polly has invited the vicar to join them and thanks him for blessing their marriage.

"It was my pleasure, Polly, and may I say I have not seen such a radiant bride for some time. You are a very lucky man, Daniel."

"Thank you sir, and thank you for a wonderful service."

The family return home to enjoy lunch together before Polly and Daniel prepare to set off back to London.

"Thank you for a wonderful weekend, Mummy. It was so relaxing to get away from everything that has happened. And we have our reception to look forward to very soon. We will let you know the details as soon as we have them."

After lots of hugging and kissing, they set off around four o'clock. They are both better for the weekend away, and Polly is delighted to have been able to have their marriage blessed.

"It makes up for not having the traditional church wedding, Daniel, don't you think?"

"It was a really good idea, Polly. I had no idea that you had planned it."

"It was only when Mummy and I were in town Saturday that it was decided, and we managed to find the vicar in."

When they arrive back in Kensington, they are relieved to see that there are no press about. Polly decides on a bath as soon as they are inside, and afterwards they settle down to a quiet evening together. Since they are both tired from the journey they decide on an early night, but not before they enjoy each other with their lovemaking.

They take the car back on Monday morning and Conrad is waiting to drive them to the Old Bailey. Polly has chosen to wear a black skirt and matching jacket with a silk blouse. They force their way through the press yet again before entering the courtroom to shouts of, "Good luck!" from the gallery. Daniel enters the witness box to again confront the defence barrister John Griffiths.

"Mr Bottomley, you will recall your rather insulting remarks before the weekend adjournment?"

"I thought they were entirely appropriate to your questioning."

"Your Honour, I again ask you to find this man in contempt."

"Mr Griffiths, please do get on and stop whining."

"To recap, Mr Bottomley, you fabricated evidence against my clients to smear the Communist Party. Isn't that correct?"

"No sir, it is not correct."

"You burgled the headquarters of the Communist Party hoping to pass on information to the management of the docks to be used against trade union members, isn't that correct?"

"No sir, that is not correct."

"Mr Bottomley, your actions for the most part were illegal. Can I ask, were you carrying a weapon when you entered the Communist Party Headquarters?"

"I carry a weapon at all times."

"Are you saying you are carrying a weapon at this moment?"

"As I have already said, I carry a weapon at all times."

"I ask the court to consider whether we want members of the public roaming our streets and shooting anyone who gets in their way."

There is a silence as the defence barrister seeks to press home his statement.

"Mr Bottomley, how do you respond to my comments?"

"Sir, I am not here to respond to comments, only to questions."

There is laughter and jeering from the gallery in response to Daniel's reply.

"I challenge you to substantiate the outrageous claims you have made against my clients, genuine trade unionists who serve their members to the best of their ability. You would deprive their members of representation to serve your own ends."

Again, there is a silence in the courtroom, as the barrister waits on Daniel to respond.

"Mr Bottomley?"

"I am waiting for a question, Mr Griffiths. As I have already said, I am not here to respond to comment."

"You have nothing on us, Bottomley, and you know it!" shouts Jack Makepeace.

"Mr Griffiths, please tell your client to be quiet. They will get an opportunity to have their say if and when you put them in the witness box," the judge responds angrily.

"I apologise, my lord, but it is frustrating to be treated with such arrogance by the witness, and I ask you again to consider my contempt request."

"You cannot hold a witness in contempt for responding to your comments, Mr Griffiths. Do you have any more questions?"

"Yes my lord, thank you. Mr Bottomley, you say you met with trade unionists who expressed concerns. Would you elaborate please?"

"The concerns were about the influence that communists were able to exert over the rank and file membership. The men who I spoke to were genuine trade unionists who…"

"Yes, we have heard all that already. Your genuine trade unionists seem to be conspicuous by their absence, do they not?"

"The Crown will decide whether to interview more members, I am sure."

"Oh, so you decide who is to be interviewed do you, Mr Bottomley?"

"I don't believe I said that. Did I say that, my lord?"

"Mr Griffiths, please!" the judge says, becoming agitated, as an usher approaches him and whispers in his ear.

"I have just been informed that smoke has been detected coming from beneath the building. Please leave the court in an orderly fashion. The court is adjourned but those concerned please make yourselves available."

Daniel leaves the box and moves towards Polly before guiding her out into the grand hall where Conrad is waiting. The smoke is more noticeable here as Daniel asks Conrad to see what he can find out. The press are eagerly waiting on Polly and Daniel outside of the building.

"Mr Bottomley, who do you think is responsible for this latest interruption?"

"The same people who were responsible for the explosive device, I would say."

"Do you think the judge will abandon the trial after this latest attempt to stop the proceedings?"

"No, I am sure the judge will not be intimidated by this. He will insist on justice being done."

"Mr Bottomley, you seem to be having a bit of a fight with the defence team."

"They are only doing their job, but I have to admit some of their questions are a bit unprofessional."

"And what about you, Mrs Bottomley, Polly? Are you feeling better now after your ordeal of two weeks ago?"

"Yes, I am feeling much better, thank you. Daniel and I look forward to the end of the trial so that we can get back to work."

"What would you say to those men who took you if you had the opportunity to face them?"

"If the occasion were to occur, it would be a case of who killed them first, Daniel or me. The civilised world has no place for them," Polly replies with a tear in her eye.

"Can we have some pictures of you together please, before you go? Thank you."

The photographers gather to take pictures, when Daniel notices that Conrad has returned.

"Thank you, gentlemen," says Daniel, as he steers Polly through the crowd.

"The fire seems to have started in the labyrinth of tunnels beneath the courts. In the old days, they were used to take prisoners to the gallows. There is a disused yard at the end where some waste bins were kept. Someone had set the contents alight and pushed them into the tunnels. The court clerk has suspended proceedings for the day and suggested you report back normally tomorrow."

"Someone is trying very hard to stop the trial, Conrad. When it is all over we must investigate. Meantime, let us hope we have no more disruption," Daniel replies as they arrive back in Kensington.

Daniel contacts Fitz to update him and suggests they begin investigating the fire as soon as possible. Polly also phones her office and asks how they are coping. She tells David Fellows about the fire and asks if there has been any chatter about plans to disrupt the trial.

"Nothing that we know of, Polly, but I will ask Peter and Rachel to check for you."

"Thank you, David. Can you transfer this call to my office? I would like a word."

"Hello Rachel, I have just been speaking with David." She relays her comments about any messages that may have been intercepted that could indicate who is causing the disruption, mentioning the fire.

"Gosh, Polly, was anyone hurt? It seems that someone is determined to stop the trial."

"Thankfully, no one was hurt and the trial will continue no matter what." Polly puts down the phone, and really does wonder how many more interruptions there may be before the trial is over. She sits with Daniel, reflecting on what has happened.

"Do you think the Soviets will keep trying, Daniel?"

"I wouldn't be at all surprised. They know they are losing and the publicity must be hurting."

They have some lunch before settling down again, enjoying the peace and quiet of the afternoon. Polly snuggles up to Daniel and kisses him passionately. Daniel responds and goes to pick her up to carry her to their bed.

"No, Daniel, let's stay here, just make love to me please."

And afterwards they lie together before falling asleep in each other's arms.

"Come along Daniel, we need to make some dinner, and it will soon be time for bed," she says, laughing out loud.

Daniel is delighted that she really seems none the worse now for her terrible ordeal of two weeks ago. Conrad collects them on Tuesday and, after the usual struggle past the press, Daniel again enters the box to hear the judge make a statement to the court.

"As you know, yesterday's proceedings were interrupted by a fire in the tunnels below the courtrooms. This is the second attempt to stop this trial and I would say this to those concerned. If we have to finish the trial in the street outside, we will do so. I will not allow anyone to interfere with the court's work. Justice will be served no matter what it takes. Mr Griffiths, you may proceed."

"I have no more questions for this person, my lord."

"My lord, may I ask Mr Bottomley some additional questions?" the Crown barrister enquires, to which the judge nods.

"Mr Bottomley, during the course of events that have been discussed at this trial, have you ever deliberately killed anyone to further your aims and ambitions?"

"No sir, I have not."

"And have you fabricated any evidence that you have given at this trial?"

"No sir, I have not."

"And have you attempted to bribe any witnesses to lie or give false evidence?"

"No sir, I have not."

"And have you tried to influence any decisions that the management of the docks may have made or will be making regarding the dockers?"

"No sir, I have not."

"And will you tell the court why you carry a firearm at all times?"

"To protect myself and my wife from further attacks on us by the Russians. They have made no secret of their intentions toward both of us."

"Thank you, Mr Bottomley."

The judge instructs Daniel to leave the witness box.

Again there are shouts of abuse from the dock towards Daniel as he leaves the witness box.

"You have nothing on us and you will pay for your interference, Mr Bottomley!" the Russian nationals shout.

"Please talk to your clients, Mr Johnson. I will not tell you again."

The Crown barrister now calls Mrs Elizabeth Berkley. A slight woman in her fifties, Mrs Berkley looks very nervous. The Crown barrister asks her for her name and occupation.

"My name is Elizabeth Berkley and I am a Civil Servant at the Home Office."

"Mrs Berkley, I will get straight to the point. Are you a member of the Red Hand organisation?"

"Yes I am."

"And as a member of that organisation you are a communist sympathiser, is that correct?"

"Yes it is. My husband was a member of the party when he was an academic, and I went along with him. I was not an active supporter of the party, I simply followed my husband."

"Did you husband ever talk about the communists seeking to overthrow our government?"

"Good lord, no. My husband was a believer in the communist ideal, but he was also loyal to the King. He simply believed that the working class should have a say in how they were governed other than a cross on a ballot paper."

"Now let me ask you about Red Hand, Mrs Berkley. What made you become a member?"

"I was approached, by Sally Nugent. They knew of my husband and encouraged me to become a member. I think they saw me as some sort of figurehead. I went along with their request because I thought it was what my husband would want."

"What did you think about the radical thoughts of overthrowing our elected government and forcing the communist ideal on the electorate?"

"I never really thought about what might happen at first, it was only when Sally Nugent became more and more vocal in her demands for disobedience and disruption in the workplace that I realised what she was trying to achieve."

"So what did you decide to do?"

"I made an approach to Polly Spencer as she was then, now Mrs Bottomley."

"What made you approach an eighteen-year-old office girl who had only been in the service a few months?"

"I just felt that there may have been a specific reason for Polly being given a position where she could roam freely throughout the building. And she was ideal, being a newcomer. I asked to meet with her to see what she might be about and when she arrived with Mr Bottomley, I was sure that she was in fact helping the security services."

"And what did you do then, Mrs Berkley?"

"I offered to give her any information I could about Red Hand members. I was not very helpful, however, since Polly was given all the relevant details about them by Sally Nugent herself."

"So Sally Nugent told Mrs Bottomley, Polly, all the relevant details about a secret organisation that was operating within the Civil Service?"

"Yes, that is correct, so there was no need for me to make any further contact with Polly that might jeopardise her position. I still regard her as a friend, though, in spite of what has happened."

"Thank you Mrs Berkley, please remain in the box."

"Mrs Berkley, my name is Donald Capel for the Red Hand members. Why aren't you in the dock with them?"

"I suppose I am not considered to be a threat, just a participant in the organisation. I don't know other than that."

"Were you not present at the meetings when Sally Nugent allegedly advocated civil disobedience within the service and the intention to place a member into an influential position?"

"Yes I was, together with the other members of Red Hand."

"And why did you not express you views if you were concerned?"

"Sally was a very forceful person, not the sort you would argue with. That is why I contacted Polly, Mrs Bottomley."

"Is it not true, Mrs Berkley, that you are giving your evidence for the Crown in exchange for your freedom from prosecution?"

"No sir, the Crown have not made me any promises, I do not know what will happen to me, only that I have been dismissed by the Service."

"I have no further questions, my lord."

Mrs Berkley is excused by the judge and the Crown call on Michael Doyle, who is asked to confirm his name and occupation.

"My name is Michael Doyle and I work in the docks as a stevedore."

"Mr Doyle, are you a member of the Communist Party?"

"Yes, I am an active member of the party."

"And can you tell us why you decided to contact a member of the security services?"

'I have been a committed member of the Communist Party and an active trade union member a long time. I believe the workers should have a say in the running of the businesses they work for, an equal share, and I believe in a government working for the people. But I do not believe that our aims should be achieved by any means, even revolution. It was becoming obvious to me that there were strangers joining the trade union with their own agenda. They were not interested in what we wanted, their only interest was in creating strikes, causing civil unrest, and capitalising on the chaos that would surely follow."

"So what did you decide, Mr Doyle?"

"I had talked with a colleague of mine in the E.T.U."

"Excuse me, Mr Doyle. The E.T.U?"

"The Electrical Trades Union. I had spoken with him about this and he said he would make some enquiries and get back to me. I now know he contacted Mr Bottomley."

"How did he know, Mr Bottomley?"

"From his army days just after World War Two. He was on some sort of mission that Mr Bottomley fronted with his colleagues to break up black marketeering rackets based on the coast."

"Ah yes, I believe they have been mentioned. Please continue."

"When I first met with Mr Bottomley, I thought he was a journalist. At least that was what he told me. I gave him an interview outlining what the unions in the docks were after, putting our case so that the public could get a perspective on what was happening. I was and still am committed to getting the best deals for the workers. Mr Bottomley listened and said he would pass our message on. What he was really doing, of course, was finding out what was happening in the docks, what influence outside agitators were making and the mood of the men."

"So to begin with you were deceived by Mr Bottomley?"

"I suppose so, but I was suspicious of him anyway, as I am of all journalists."

"And what happened to make you change your mind towards him?"

"The mood of the agitators was becoming more aggressive towards my members, men were being attacked and beaten if they spoke against anything that was being proposed. It was becoming obvious that there was a group acting within the framework of the committee representing the members, that had an agenda completely different from the one that had been originally suggested by the union membership. Any attempt at discussion or debate was not permitted. The talk was of all-out strike action to teach the management a lesson. We should encourage members to talk to their colleagues in other unions and tell them to strike against this government, especially those in the transport unions. Their sole concern was to bring down the government. What they had planned after that, I don't know and I don't think they did either. There was talk about moving men into the Midlands manufacturing areas, but I wasn't really involved so I am not sure how far they were with this. The next time I spoke with Mr Bottomley, he had Mrs Bottomley with him. We met in a pub in Whitechapel, and I told him of my concerns. He wanted me to tell him everything I knew about the so-called conspiracy. From the start, I made it clear that I would not divulge any genuine union matters to him, nor those of the Communist Party itself. I spoke only about the events that were happening in the docks, the events that were scaring me and my fellow trade unionists."

"You say you would not divulge any genuine union business or party business to him. Did he ask you?"

"No, he wasn't interested in any union business or Communist Party information. He wanted to know why I was so sure that what was happening was not in the best interests of the trade unions and their members. I told him what I have outlined here today, and it seemed he did have some ideas of what was being planned. I was confirming what he already knew."

"And did he offer you any money or ask you to do anything specific?"

"He certainly did not offer me money, and I would not have accepted it anyway. I did not meet with him for money, I wanted to know if he could help my members. And as for asking me to do anything specific, no, he didn't. All he asked was that I listened to what was happening and if he believed that he should tell me, then make contact again."

"And did you contact him again?"

"Yes I did. When we first met and he told me who he was I was sceptical and suspicious. But he had also talked to some of my colleagues, unknown to me, and told them what the communist agitators were doing. They did not involve me because they were unsure of where my loyalties were. Then when I realised that those two, Makepeace and Hornsby, had met with Rafikov and Ruchkin, I knew I had to make a decision. I was approached to take part in the initiative to call an all-out strike. When I met with Mr Bottomley a second time and told him what had happened, he urged me not to meet with the Soviets. If I did my evidence would be worthless, if I testified."

"Did Mr Bottomley ask you to give evidence of this union conspiracy by the Soviets?"

"He told me I may be asked to testify, yes. He also told me that we should not meet again and gave me a number if I needed to contact him urgently. I told him I was scared for my family and he said he would arrange for them to be protected along with me. Nothing official, just that his colleagues would watch over us."

"And did you ever know that you and your family were being watched over?"

"No, I just hoped we were. Nothing happened anyway, so it must have worked whatever it was that they did."

"Do you feel threatened at all now, Mr Doyle?"

"I am not scared, just for my family. But I want this intimidation to stop and go back to representing my members as I have done before. I want to see them get a fair deal and I will fight hard to get that."

"Thank you, Mr Doyle. Please wait there for the defence barrister."

"Mr Doyle, I represent your colleagues, Mr Hornsby and Mr Makepeace. They are your colleagues, are they not?"

"I'm not sure anymore, they seem to have switched their loyalty to the Russians, and they definitely are not on our side."

"How much did you say you were paid by Mr Bottomley to make up your story?"

"I wasn't paid anything, and if you say that outside the court you will regret it."

"Are you threatening me, sir?"

"Yes, if you make that comment outside of this courtroom."

"Mr Doyle, you must not make threats to the court officials."

"I am sorry, sir, but that man is slandering me in court and I will not put up with that."

'Yes, very well Mr Doyle, now can we get on please?"

"Mr Doyle, you are a communist?"

"Yes sir, I am a member of the Communist Party."

"And yet you ask us to believe that you are not part of this so-called conspiracy by the communists."

"What has been happening over the last few months in the docks has nothing to do with the British Communist Party. We do not seek to impose our beliefs on the union members, or intimidate them, and we have no interest in seeking to overthrow the government. We believe there is an alternative way that the workers can be given a bigger say in their destiny. We want to use our strength to negotiate better deals for the membership and eventually to run businesses with cooperatives. That is what we want, sir."

"And what did the Russian colleagues offer you when you met with them?"

"I never spoke with nor met any Russians, or anyone other than the members I knew and had represented for some time."

"These men are attending your meetings and talking with members, and you, a representative of those members, never sought a conversation with them?"

"Firstly, they did not openly attend any official branch meetings. Our meetings were usually small in number and I would have recognised any strangers. Our minutes will confirm who attended the meetings and they are available for inspection by anyone. Who they may have approached in the docks, I have no idea. Docklands is a vast area so they could have wandered about anywhere."

"So this so-called conspiracy was taking place underneath your nose, Mr Doyle, and you expect the court to believe you knew nothing about it?"

"At the beginning of the dispute, I knew nothing because there was nothing to know. When it became obvious to me that outsiders were attempting to influence decisions, I talked about this with some of my colleagues and one of them, who also was concerned, introduced me to Mr Bottomley."

"Ah, the infamous Mr Bottomley, the man who solves his problems by shooting people."

The court erupts into uproar and Daniel stands up, demanding an apology.

"Mr Griffiths, you will apologise to the court for your comments."

"Just making a point, my lord. I apologise for my comments, although the court has a right to judge the testimony of a man who goes round shooting people on our streets, don't you think?"

"My lord, will you hold this man in contempt before I do

something I might regret?"

The courtroom is in turmoil and Daniel remains standing, threatening to move toward the barrister.

"Mr Bottomley, please sit down. Mr Griffiths, I will speak with you in my rooms now. The court is adjourned for lunch."

After lunch, the judge returns and makes a statement to the court.

"I have asked Mr Griffiths to confine any further questions he may have to Mr Doyle and not make any comments relating to previous witnesses. And I repeat to you, Mr Bottomley, please refrain from making statements from the floor of the court. Mr Griffiths, please continue."

"Thank you, my lord. Now Mr Doyle, these colleagues that you mentioned, will they be giving evidence today?"

"I do not know, sir."

Doyle looks across at the Crown prosecutor who informs the judge that additional union members will not be giving evidence for the Crown.

"So, Mr Doyle, we have just your word for these so-called conspiracy plots?"

"I believe Mr and Mrs Bottomley would have mentioned the information I passed to them."

"Yes, Mr and Mrs Bottomley. What do you really know about these two people, Mr Doyle? Have you any idea who they really are?"

"I don't quite understand what you mean. Isn't who they are known to the court?"

"Well, Mr Bottomley says he works for the security services, and Mrs Bottomley says she works for the Foreign Office. I just wonder who they really work for, who gives them licence to hunt down and kill Russian nationals. Does anyone know?'

Daniel is halfway down the aisle towards John Griffiths before he is restrained by the court security guards.

"You will recant Griffiths, or suffer the consequences of your nonsensical rambling" shouts Daniel, as he wrestles with the two security guards.

"Mr Griffiths, I am holding you in contempt for this latest outburst, and adjourning proceedings for the rest of the day. Mr and Mrs Bottomley, please refrain from making any derogatory comments about these proceedings to the press."

The judge leaves the courtroom, concerned that the trial is becoming disrupted by outside influences. John Griffiths is taken away by the court officials, and Daniel and Polly leave to face the press once more.

"Mr Bottomley, do you think these interruptions are being deliberately orchestrated?"

"All I would say to you about this, is if John Griffiths is the best that the defence have to offer, then I am relieved that I am not one of the accused. The man is incompetent."

"And Polly, will you go back to work in the Foreign Office when all this is over?"

"Yes I will. I have only just taken up my position and there is a lot of work to be done."

"You seem very relaxed. Are you feeling better after your ordeal?"

"Yes I am. So long as I have Daniel I will be fine."

Daniel ushers Polly through the crowd accompanied by Conrad.

"What do you think Griffiths is up to, Daniel? Is he being used to try and get the trial stopped?"

"That could be one explanation for his erratic line of questioning. He cannot disprove anything that has been said against his clients or the other accused, so stopping the trial would be ideal for them, especially the Russians."

They soon arrive back at their apartment and Daniel thanks Conrad, adding that he will see him in the morning.

"Do you really think the trial could be stopped, Daniel? I should hate to have to go over my testimony again, it was painful to have to recall those events that happened to us."

"The judge will not allow the defence tactics to stop the trial, Polly. I am absolutely sure he will see it through."

"I hope so, Daniel," says Polly, curling up beside him on the settee. After a restless night when Polly seemed to wake Daniel a dozen times, asking questions about what might happen if the trial were stopped, he gets up around six o'clock, leaving Polly to sleep. He is obviously concerned by her worrying about the trial, and hopes that it will be completed and the accused punished.

They arrive back in the courtroom to hear the judge introduce the proceedings once more.

"Firstly, I have withdrawn my application for contempt of court action against Mr Griffiths after he gave me his assurances. I will not tolerate any more outbursts in this courtroom. To those concerned, I would repeat what I said previously; this trial will be concluded if we have to move it to the street outside. Mr Griffiths, please proceed."

"Mr Doyle, what were you told to say to the court when you met with Mr Bottomley?"

"I wasn't told to say anything. I told him what I had found out and he told me that I may be asked to give evidence."

"And what about protecting your family? Didn't he promise to move them into a hotel miles away in return for your testimony here today? Didn't he say you would be handsomely rewarded for your testimony, and be given the opportunity to move with your family and live elsewhere? Didn't he make those promises to you if you said what he told you to say?"

The courtroom is again in uproar, as is the gallery. Mr Doyle remains calm, but Daniel is finding it difficult to hold himself in check.

"Mr Griffiths, do you have any questions for this witness that do not relate specifically to Mr Bottomley?"

"I believe Mr and Mrs Bottomley manipulated this witness into saying what they wanted him to say. I am deeply suspicious of Mr Bottomley taking Mrs Bottomley to these meetings. Was she for show or did he hope that Mr Doyle would be flattered by a pretty young woman sitting beside him?"

"Your Honour, is he allowed to say such rubbish without any proof?"

"It would appear that he can say what he likes, Mr Doyle, hiding behind courtroom privilege," says Daniel, standing up in the court.

"Mr Bottomley, please, you must not interrupt proceedings from the floor of the court. Mr Griffiths, continue but be careful."

"Thank you, my lord. Well, Mr Doyle, were you influenced in any way by Mrs Bottomley's presence, did it perhaps persuade you to do as Mr Bottomley asked of you?"

"I agree with your comment about Mrs Bottomley, she is a very attractive lady, but her presence at my meetings with Mr Bottomley did not influence what I had to say. And he did not ask me to say anything. There was no reason to, since he did not know whether the Crown would ask me to give evidence. I am my own man, Mr Griffiths, I would not have been influenced by any offers made by anyone. In fact if Mr Bottomley had made such offers, I would have been very suspicious of his motives."

"Didn't Mr Bottomley in fact threaten to have you arrested with my clients unless you gave specific evidence that he issued you with, isn't that what happened?"

"Mr Bottomley neither threatened me nor gave me any instructions."

"Did you know that both he and Mrs Bottomley were probably carrying guns when they met with you in Whitechapel? Wouldn't that have been reason enough for you to agree to anything he said, Mr Doyle? The man is a trained assassin for God's sake, not the sort of person to argue with."

Amid even more uproar in the court, the Crown barrister stands.

"My lord, how much longer do we have to put up with this character assassination of Mr and Mrs Bottomley?"

"Yes, Mr Griffiths, where are you going with this?"

"I believe Mr and Mrs Bottomley manipulated this witness with promises and threats in exchange for his evidence. Mrs Bottomley could only have been there to flatter him and the fact that Mr Bottomley was carrying a weapon must have been intimidating."

"Once again, Your Honour, Mr Griffiths is talking absolute nonsense."

"Am I really, Mr Doyle? You were not flattered at all by a beautiful young woman paying you attention. What possible reason could she have for being there if not to help Mr Bottomley persuade you to say what he instructed you to say? Did she not sit very close to you all the time you and Mr Bottomley were talking? Were you not aware that she was sitting close to you at all?"

"Of course I knew she was there."

"And what was she wearing, Mr Doyle."

"I didn't notice what she was wearing."

"You didn't notice what an attractive young woman sitting close to you was wearing, are you sure?"

"Well I think she wore a white shirt and slacks when I first met her."

"And the second time you met what was she wearing then?"

"I think she wore a black skirt and sweater.'

"Well for someone who said you didn't notice what the young woman was wearing you appear to have noticed rather well. And were you not attracted to this beautiful young woman sitting beside you in a black skirt and sweater, Mr Doyle? This young woman sitting close to you?"

"I was there to talk with Mr Bottomley, nothing else," replies Doyle, appearing somewhat embarrassed by the barrister's line of questioning.

"You say you were not offered any money or the opportunity to move your family in return for giving evidence, by Mr Bottomley. Were you offered anything else at all?"

"What do you mean?"

"Were you offered anything else? You were obviously attracted to Mrs Bottomley, did Mr Bottomley offer you anything else, perhaps some time with alone Mrs Bottomley?"

This time the court ushers are not quick enough and Daniel rushes at Griffiths, grabbing him by the throat and punching him before they are able to pull him away.

"You are a cretin, sir, and I resent your disgusting innuendo towards my wife."

Polly stands up and shouts at the defence barrister.

"Why are you doing this to us? You are a hateful and spiteful man!" she screams. The courtroom once again is in uproar, as the officials struggle with Daniel who has the barrister on the floor.

"Please remove Mr and Mrs Bottomley from the courtroom. We will adjourn for fifteen minutes."

Daniel and Polly are escorted from the courtroom as the uproar and cheering continues.

"Mr Walters, you really must tell this barrister to cease this line of questioning. It serves no purpose other than tarnish Polly's reputation. I don't care what he says about me, but I will not allow such disgusting comments to be made about my wife."

"I will do what I can, Daniel, but you must not attack barristers in the courtroom. The judge will no doubt hold you in contempt for this."

The court resumes after fifteen minutes and the judge makes yet another statement.

"I am at a loss as to how I should react to the recent outburst in the courtroom. Nothing like that has ever happened before, but I have decided to make certain reservations. Firstly, despite Mr Griffith's protestations, I will not hold Mr Bottomley in contempt, but will tell you this, sir. If you ever do anything like that again in my court I will hold you in contempt, do you understand?"

"Yes sir, I understand."

"Now regarding your line of questioning, Mr Griffiths, I would ask you this. Do you have any questions for this witness that do not directly relate to his meetings with Mr Bottomley?"

"No sir, I do not."

"In that case, Mr Doyle, you may leave the witness box. Your next witness please, Mr Walters."

"I would like to recall Mr Bottomley if I may, Your Honour."

"Mr Bottomley, there has been much made of the fact that your wife was with you on the two occasions that you met with Mr Doyle. Whilst not in any way condoning the line of questioning by the defence, some people might be curious and would ask, why did your wife accompany you to these meetings? Would you indulge the court, please?"

"Yes, certainly. You will recall, from evidence given by myself and Polly, there have been a number of occasions when she was attacked and abducted. The attacks were severe and her last abduction was very brutal and distressing. Before we were married, I had an obligation to Polly's parents as her guardian to protect her. So after the first attack on her, we decided that she would never be left on her own and we would always go everywhere together. That was the only way I could give her my full protection. So when I met with Mr Doyle, and with the dock workers previously, Polly came along. I introduced her as a fellow worker who would take notes, which she did. The court has heard what has happened to her even with my trying to keep her safe. I always felt that the best way I could protect her was to always be with her. And you will also be aware that we are escorted to and from our places of work each day by one of my colleagues."

"Thank you, Mr Bottomley. My lord I have no more witnesses for the open court, but the security services will give their evidence in camera."

"Very well Mr Walters, we will adjourn for lunch. After lunch I will listen to the evidence in closed court. I suggest you all leave for the day and report back tomorrow as usual."

Polly and Daniel leave the courtroom together and are besieged once more by the press.

"Polly, what did you think about Daniel hitting the barrister?"

"He is a spiteful man and he got what he deserved," replies Polly, holding on to his arm and looking up at him.

"And Daniel, did you think the judge might hold you in contempt?"

"No more than I deserve, really. It was a stupid action on my part, but I just could not allow that man to continue with his vile insults. I am, however, deeply ashamed of my actions."

"What can you tell us about the evidence that will be given in secret?"

"As you say, it will be secret. All I will say is that some of the witnesses do not wish to be identified and some of their evidence will be highly sensitive, and to hear it in open court might threaten our nation's security."

"Polly, John Brown from the Carswell Times. Do you have any message for the people of Carswell?"

"Hello John, just say hello from Daniel and me and thank them all for their support."

"Daniel, do you think the trial will put an end to this Soviet menace?"

"I hope the trial will show the Soviets that we will not be pushed around. We will fight for a freedom no matter what it takes, but the threat will remain for some time I am sure."

"I understand your new job puts you on the front line of the fight against the Soviets in the colonies, Polly?"

"Yes, and when all this is over, I want to get back to it. The threat to our colonies is as great as it is here at home. I have a small team that helps me assess those threats and take actions accordingly."

"You and Polly look as though you are going to be busy with the Soviet threat, Daniel?"

"Yes we are, but Polly is very good at what she does and her team is very dedicated. Here at home, we must all be aware of the threat. Now I think we have answered enough questions, gentlemen, thank you," says Daniel, moving through the crowd with Conrad to the waiting car.

"We must do some shopping on the way home, Daniel. We have absolutely nothing to eat!"

Kensington High Street is a thriving shopping area and they spend about an hour stocking up on foodstuffs, Daniel and Conrad doing the carrying while Polly makes her selections.

"I will get some lunch arranged, Daniel. Can you put the groceries away please?"

Daniel then moves off to the sitting room and reflects on what happened at court today. He was indeed fortunate not to have been cited for his behaviour, and he decides he will apologise privately to the judge as soon as he has an opportunity. He is growing rather tired of the press attention, but realises that it is unavoidable. Fortunately, Polly doesn't seem to mind, in fact she seems happy to answer any questions put to her. For his part, Daniel will be glad when it is all over and he can return to work.

"Is Fitz going to give evidence, do you know, Daniel?" asks Polly as they sit down to lunch.

"I believe so, and also Quentin Blake has said he will put the case for MI5. He feels that the court should be aware of just how dangerous the Soviet threat is to the country."

"So it should not be too long now, Daniel, then we can arrange our reception for everyone."

After lunch Daniel calls Conrad, who is now back in the office.

"Glad you called, Daniel. We have just been informed that the Russians have made a formal complaint about the trial. That means that they are obviously feeling embarrassed by it all."

"Hopefully, our diplomats will wring a few concessions from them. And for the moment, you and Polly should be able to relax. I don't believe they would try anything after making a move diplomatically."

"Well that is good news, Conrad. Now I want to be sure that Michael Doyle is looked after, so can you take care of him? I don't want any dockers to seek revenge."

"We will continue to keep an eye on him. I will see you tomorrow."

Because the dockers are still in discussions with the dock managers, no official decisions have yet been made. Hopefully removing some of the troublemakers will help and Daniel is determined to see that there is a satisfactory conclusion to the dispute. Polly and Daniel spend the rest of the day together, and Polly calls home to tell her parents what happened in the courtroom. Ben is obviously concerned that Daniel may still be punished for his behaviour.

"Daniel was only protecting me, Daddy, and the press all agreed with him. There was a reporter from the Times there so you may get a visit, I'm afraid."

"We shall have to cross that bridge when we get there, Polly. Now Mummy wants a word."

Margaret is delighted to hear her daughter's voice and on being told of Daniel's actions, cannot hide her admiration for him.

"Your Daniel will never allow anyone to make personal remarks about you, Polly. Anyone who dares will be dealt with in quick time, I'm sure. Give him my regards, won't you?"

After talking with Margaret, Polly is rather quiet, so Daniel leaves her to her thoughts. They listen to the wireless for a while, then have some supper around nine o'clock.

"Can we go to bed, Daniel? I suddenly feel very tired, it must be some reaction from the day."

"Come along then Polly, I could use an early night too."

However, it will be a night that they will both remember for different reasons. It was about one o'clock when Polly becomes restless and disturbs Daniel from a deep sleep.

"No, no, please Mr Barinov, you are hurting me." Polly squirms in the bed, curling herself into a ball almost.

"No, please, your crew, now you... I can't do it anymore. No, no." Polly sits up in bed and starts hitting Daniel hard in his chest. She is screaming and pounding his chest over and over. He feels a sharp pain as he fights to calm her down before she hurts herself. Slowly Polly calms down and responds to Daniel's voice before bursting into sobs.

"Polly, my dear Polly you were having a bad dream. Everything is fine now, you are safe." She is covered in sweat as she finally stops sobbing.

"God, Daniel, I thought the men on the Russian ship had me and you didn't come and they were hurting me, then Barinov was..."

"It's ok Polly, it was all a bad dream, let me get you some water." Daniel gets up from the bed and switches on the light.

"Oh my god, Daniel you're bleeding. Look at your pyjamas, covered in blood.'

Polly leaps out of bed and gently removes Daniel's jacket. His wound has opened, and blood is flowing freely. Polly leads Daniel into the bathroom and is shocked, realising what she has done.

"What have I done, Daniel? I am so sorry," she says as she cleans away the blood to reveal that the wound is teared. Polly dries it as best she can, then pulls the tear together and puts a plaster over it.

"We have to go to hospital now, Daniel, in case there is any internal damage."

Polly goes back into the bedroom and removes her blood-soaked nightgown before getting dressed. She then phones for a taxi. Daniel gets dressed, helped by Polly, and they go off to St Mary's Hospital. They are rather embarrassed, having to explain what has happened.

"It was my fault, Doctor, I had a bad dream and punched Daniel in the chest. I am so sorry to cause so much trouble. Will he be ok?" she says, concerned.

The wound has been torn so will need stitching. Daniel has some internal bruising. You must have hit him hard, Mrs Bottomley."

Polly is very embarrassed by what has happened as the doctor continues.

"Nothing to worry about, I will get him stitched and you can take him back home," he continues, as he goes to find a nurse to apply the stitches and dress the wound.

"Please return early next week to have the stitching removed, and I will give you a couple of spare pads to dress the wound. Looking at you, Mr Bottomley, you are obviously used to wounds, but do be careful both of you."

"Thank you so much, Nurse," Polly replies, as she helps Daniel with his shirt and jacket before going off and getting a taxi back home. It is 2.30am when they arrive back at the apartment and return to bed.

"I am so sorry, Daniel. I promise to behave and will not hit you anymore," says Polly, nestling beside him and kissing him on the cheek. "I would love to be able to apologise properly, but you must not have any exertion in case your stitches break!" she says, smiling.

They manage to get some sleep before Polly gets up around 6.30am leaving Daniel asleep. She makes some tea and toast and takes it back into the bedroom just as Daniel stirs.

"Good morning Daniel, how are you feeling?"

"I'm ok Polly, a bit sore but fine otherwise. Now let's have some breakfast."

Conrad collects them around 8.30am and they go off to the Old Bailey, unsure what today's proceedings will be. They meet with the

Crown barrister in the Grand Hallway of the courts.

"I do not expect the court will be opened at all today, Mr Bottomley. There is a good deal of evidence that the security service wish to put forward. I am sure you will know of some if not all of it. Indeed, you probably supplied a proportion of it yourself. How are you by the way? You look rather pale."

"My wound opened last night and I have had to have it stitched, so we have not had much sleep."

"I hope everything is ok, I imagine bullet wounds can be complicated."

"Daniel is rather well acquainted with bullet wounds, Mr Walters, but I will take care of him."

"Yes, I'm sure. Anyway, as I was saying, I suggest that you go off back home, it will give you time to rest Mr Bottomley, and return tomorrow Friday. I am hoping to begin my summary tomorrow, depending on what the security services have to say."

"Thank you Mr Walters, I will take Daniel home as you suggest."

Conrad drives them back to the apartment and leaves them to return to his office. Since Fitz will be giving evidence today, it makes sense for him to be available if needed. Daniel and Polly decide to catch up on some sleep, and go back to their bed. Daniel goes off very quickly and is very restless. Polly holds him as best she can, making sure she does not disturb the dressing to his shoulder. She is so annoyed with herself for what has happened and hopes that he will soon recover. And she desperately misses being loved by him. His touch gives her so much confidence and she yearns for him to recover so that they might resume their lovemaking. Polly cannot rest so she leaves Daniel sleeping and tidies up in the apartment. She then calls her office for an update, but is told not to worry.

"We are coping, Polly, and will look forward to giving you a full update when you return," says Rachel.

She looks in on Daniel and is surprised to find him still sleeping some two hours since he went back to bed. He must need the rest, thinks Polly, so leaves him and returns to the sitting room. Reflecting on what has happened over the last few weeks Polly knows how fortunate she is to have Daniel. He has saved her life so many times and his body has suffered greatly. But he always recovers and is there for Polly whenever she needs him.

She sits with her thoughts and the wireless and falls asleep herself eventually. She is woken suddenly by the telephone and Conrad asking for Daniel. She looks at her watch. It is four o'clock and Daniel is still sleeping! She asks Conrad to hold and goes to fetch Daniel. When she enters the bedroom she is shocked to find him breathing heavily and with a very high temperature. Polly takes a look at his wound to find there a swelling and redness around it and he appears to be unconscious.

"Conrad I have to get Daniel to hospital, he is unconscious and has a fever."

Polly calls for an ambulance and goes back to Daniel, but despite her efforts she cannot wake him, so she has to wait for the ambulance which arrives in a matter of minutes. She grabs a few items to take with her, Daniel's toilet bits and some clothes, as the ambulance arrives.

The officers make a quick check before placing Daniel on a stretcher.

"He has a fever, Mrs Bottomley. I would guess that his wound has become infected, we must get him to hospital straightaway."

Polly goes with Daniel back to St Mary's, concerned at his worsening condition. He is put on a drip because of his dehydration and the doctor carefully examines the wound area.

"He has an infection of some sort, Mrs Bottomley. The surgeon will have to take a look at him, I'm afraid. I don't suppose you know what sort of weapon was used?"

"I'm afraid not, they were Russians so it was almost certainly a Russian pistol."

"You say they were Russians, so it may well have been an old weapon. In which case the bullet has most certainly infected your husband."

"He will be ok, Doctor, won't he?" asks Polly, becoming more and more concerned.

"We will know more after the surgeon has had a look at him, but please try not to worry too much, he is in good hands."

Conrad arrives as they are moving Daniel to the operating theatre.

"My god, Polly, what has happened?"

"The doctors think it's some sort of infection. He went to sleep after we returned from the hospital earlier and hasn't woke since," says Polly, tearfully holding on to Conrad.

"Now please don't get too upset, Polly, he is a tough character as you well know. He will be fine after a rest, you'll see," he replies, hoping to reassure her.

He goes off to get her some tea as Polly sits forlornly waiting for news of the man that she loves so much and who is her whole life. Conrad returns and wakes her from her thoughts.

"The doctor asked me if I knew what sort of weapon was used. Conrad, have you any idea?"

"My guess is that it is a leftover from the war. The bullets would be old and could well be contaminated with age."

They sit waiting for news, Polly becoming increasingly concerned as the time passes. Conrad does his best to console her, but Daniel is her whole world and she is becoming increasingly fearful for him. After almost an hour, the doctor appears, accompanied by the surgeon.

"Is he ok, Doctor? Please tell me he is ok," Polly asks, her face etched with concern.

"This is Mr Wilson, the surgeon who operated on your husband, Mrs Bottomley."

"Your husband is a hell of a fighter, Mrs Bottomley, and he has had a close shave."

"But he will be ok won't he, Mr Wilson?"

"We have removed the problem. There was bacteria surrounding the area behind where the bullet was originally lodged. It was missed because the muscle absorbed it during the operation. Your husband was hit by an old bullet, probably from the war or even older. Goodness knows what it was made of, and the bacteria had multiplied inside the muscle. The opening of the wound recently dislodged some of the bacteria, causing the infection. That reopening of the wound was fortunate; if that hadn't happened, the infection may have spread and caused more problems. How did the wound happen to reopen, by the way?"

"That was my fault, I had a bad dream and hit Daniel in the chest while we were both asleep," says Polly, somewhat embarrassed.

"Well Mrs Bottomley, your actions may well have saved your husband from something far worse. Now, he will be conscious in about ten minutes or so. We have put him in a side ward and the doctor will monitor his progress for the next few hours."

"Thank you so much, Mr Wilson. I am most grateful to you."

"My pleasure, Mrs Bottomley. Take care of him won't you?"

Polly turns to Conrad and grasps his hand reassuringly."

"He is going to be ok, Conrad."

"I told you so, Polly. Now come along, I will take you to him," says Conrad, leading Polly to the room where Daniel is. He is rather drowsy, but instantly reacts when he sees Polly.

"My dear Daniel, you gave us a fright," she says, gently kissing him on the cheek. She notices that he looks much improved from when he was brought to hospital, and she is visibly relieved.

"How are you feeling, my friend?"

"I ache all over, Conrad. I am thirsty and hungry, but otherwise I am feeling much better thanks."

"I will ask the doctor about what you can have when he comes to look at you, Daniel. As soon as he has had a look at you I will call Mummy."

Polly looks at her watch; it is almost six o'clock and she too is feeling hungry, not having eaten since lunch. She asks Conrad if he can get her a sandwich and some more tea while they wait for the doctor. The doctor arrives as Polly is finishing her sandwich and takes a look at Daniel's wound. She is shocked by the long insertion across Daniel's chest but there is no longer any swelling or redness.

"We shall keep you in for twenty-four hours, Mr Bottomley, before deciding what to do next. You have had a bad infection and we must be absolutely sure there is no bacteria left behind. I expect you will be staying overnight, Mrs Bottomley, so I will get the nurse to find you a blanket."

"Thank you, Doctor. Can Daniel have something to eat now?"

"I will get the nurse to get him some soup. Now I will see you again in the morning, Mr Bottomley."

"Thank you, Doctor."

"Yes, thank you so much, Doctor. I will watch over him until morning. Conrad, will you tell Fitz what has happened for me please? But before you go I must call Mummy."

Polly goes off to call her parents and Conrad sits down beside his friend.

"Those damn Russians, even their bullets are contaminated. You were lucky it seems, Daniel. The surgeon commented that Polly's hitting you in her sleep and reopening the wound set off the movement of bacteria. Had that not happened it could have been much worse."

"So I have to thank Polly for giving me a beating then?" he says, smiling.

"It seems that way, now is there anything I can do for you at all?"

"Perhaps you would call at the apartment and get me some clothes, and I would appreciate an update if you can."

"Polly has asked me to contact Fitz, so I will get an update from him. Now you must rest my friend, bye for now."

Polly returns and asks Daniel if he needs anything before settling down for the evening.

"Having you beside me would be nice, Polly. Apart from that, I think I will take a nap."

Polly settles down beside him and goes over in her mind the events of the last few hours. She really believed she was going to lose the man she loves so desperately. The family have always joked that he is invincible, but the recent events have proved he is only human. The next few days are critical to his recovery and Polly knows that she has an important role in taking care of him. With these thoughts in mind she drifts off to sleep in the chair. Daniel has a restful night. Polly, however, is rather fretful, sleeping only in small parts, listening for any noises from Daniel. She finally goes off and sleeps until six o'clock. Daniel is still sleeping when she wakes, so she goes off to the bathroom to wash. She returns to find Daniel is stirring from his sleep.

"Good morning my love, how do you feel this morning?"

"Hungry and thirsty, Polly, and much better thank you. But I do need the bathroom."

Polly goes off to find a nurse to see if she can arrange for some tea and breakfast and a chair for Daniel. When the doctor arrives around nine o'clock he is very satisfied with Daniel's progress.

"You have made excellent progress, Mr Bottomley. You can take him home this afternoon, Mrs Bottomley, when I have had one more look at him and dressed the wound. Just make sure he gets plenty of rest to give his wound time to heal properly."

"Thank you Doctor, thank you so much. I will take good care of him, I promise," Polly replies, smiling with a sense of relief. The last twenty-four hours or so have been very traumatic for her and she is close to tears knowing Daniel will now recover fully from his set back.

Meanwhile, the security services begin their testimony on Thursday morning, William Fitzroy Jones taking the witness box. His evidence is detailed, outlining the time spent watching the suspects' activities and securing documents from the Communist Party headquarters. These documents proved conclusively that there was a conspiracy in place to overthrow the British Government. There were precise details of times and dates that key personnel would be replaced by Soviets, especially at the Home Office, the Foreign Office and the Ministry of Defence. The Royal Family was to be exiled and Buckingham Palace used as the new seat of government. The Houses of Parliament would be used as the headquarters of the Communist Party in Britain and the colonies. Eventually, Britain would be divided into regions, South, Midlands, North, Wales, and Scotland. There was no mention of Northern Ireland. Each region would be overseen by a committee to be responsible for its running and day-to-day operations, security, transport, power distribution, wealth distribution, supplies distribution, etc. These were just some of the frightening details that were uncovered from the documents secured by Fitz and his team. And it was here that he paid special tribute to Polly and Daniel.

"The efforts of Mr and Mrs Bottomley in preventing the Soviets from their aims, cannot be emphasised too highly. They risked their lives to secure vital information that we were able to act upon. Daniel has been shot and wounded on more than one occasion and Mrs Bottomley subjected to appalling abuse when she was abducted by the Russians. They are both to be applauded for their actions."

Fitzroy Jones went on to detail the activities of the Red Hand organisation. Although they had known of its existence for some time, the security services had not been able to get any real evidence of what it was doing, and what it hoped to achieve. Until, that is, Mrs Bottomley was approached by Elizabeth Berkley, then Sally Nugent. It was Polly's actions, securing vital evidence from their documents, which helped the security services to finally arrest all the members and close down the Red Hand operation. The dual approach by the Soviets, of securing key positions in the Civil Service and taking control of the trade unions, would have had a devastating effect on the democracy of the country. Overnight 1,000 years of freedom would have been eradicated.

"In the security services we use an expression 'The Traffic Light Syndrome' to highlight the dangers the Soviets have posed since the end of World War Two. When the war ended the lights were definitely on green for go. The Soviets were our allies and it was hoped that a new era of peace and conciliation was beginning. Unfortunately, the opposite has happened. The Soviets have continued their policy of expansion and have mobilised a huge army to help them achieve this. The traffic lights moved to amber some time ago, and one wonders when they will move to red," Fitz continues solemnly.

His testimony is challenged by the defence council for the Russians and for the Red Hand members, who endeavour to ridicule his comments, inferring that they are nothing more than scaremongering.

"The evidence is available for all to see, gentlemen, and it is my belief that you will not be putting your clients in the witness box for fear of them incriminating themselves. The Soviet threat is very real and the West needs to fight back with every means at its disposal. Occupation by stealth is very difficult to measure and combat, but we must not let our guard down for one moment if we wish to maintain the traditions we all cherish."

Fitz goes on to explain what safeguards the government will have to employ to stop the Soviet intrusion. Some of them will not be popular as they may restrict free movement, and there has been some discussion of introducing identity cards. What is important is for the public to be made aware of this menace, and hopefully, this trial with all its publicity will do that.

On Friday morning, Fitz concludes his evidence and Quentin Blake speaks for MI5. His evidence speaks of agents uncovering a Soviet plot to infiltrate colonial governments. With the colonies fragmented, British influences overseas would be threatened.

"Our friends in Australia have been very helpful here and I applaud their stance against the communists. It was their office that warned us of the threat against Mr and Mrs Bottomley."

Blake goes on to detail how the Colonial Office is collating all the evidence of Soviet activities and doing what has to be done to counteract any plans they may have.

"This is very much a war we are fighting with a silent menace. They are no armies that we are fighting, the menace is invisible to the man in the street, but I assure the court it is very real. We must employ any means at our disposal to stop the aims of the communists," says Quentin Blake.

As with Fitzroy Jones, the defence attacks his comments and questions what means they are using and would be prepared to use. They accuse the security services of swapping diplomacy for a Wild West attitude, shooting first asking questions later. Democracy is not threatened by the Communist Party but by a government imposing its will on the people and using force to put down anyone who gets in the way. Mr Blake points out the antics of the Soviets on just two British citizens, Mr and Mrs Bottomley, and the ruthless attempts to stop their uncovering the Soviet aims.

"No diplomacy was used to shoot and almost kill Mr Bottomley and brutally assault Mrs Bottomley. The Soviets made their aims perfectly clear the way they behaved towards them. Kill anyone who dares to stand in our way and destroy their loved ones for good measure. That's the Soviet way, sir, as you well know from the evidence presented in this trial. If the Soviets were to be satisfied with what they have and not persist with their desire for global domination, then the world would be a safer place. Unfortunately, they follow in the footsteps of their notorious predecessors, the Nazis, and seek to rule the world through their ideology. Thank God for people like Mr Bottomley who refuse to be bullied by such bigots," continues Quentin Blake.

He goes on to outline just how much effort goes into keeping the country safe. There are some aspects of the work of the MI5 which have to remain secret, of course, but they will continue to do whatever is necessary to keep our country free. The Russians in the dock scream abuse at the MI5 boss who remains indifferent to their protests and responds:

"Sticks and stones, gentlemen, stick and stones."

Donald Capel for Sally Nugent and Percival Smith denies his clients had any knowledge of the Soviets' ambitions. They were only seeking to introduce a communist ideology within the Civil Service trade union.

"But don't you understand, sir. Their very desire to put an agent within the seat of government was to be able to influence decision making. Nugent's comments on more than one occasion about civil disobedience and using any means necessary to achieve their aims, points to revolution not negotiation. The Red Hand was started by revolutionary academics. Whilst we have no proof, I am sure they talked with the Soviets about what was to be done. Had they succeeded, I have no doubt that Sally Nugent would have played a major role in the new order," Quentin Blake concludes.

The Crown begins summing up the case for the prosecution late on Friday.

"Conspiracy trials are difficult to assess because the laymen might not consider a crime has been committed. No one has been murdered or had their house burgled, and because the victim is the government of Her Majesty, it is even more difficult to comprehend. But the most serious of crimes has been committed by the accused in the dock. They have sought to take away from the British people that which is most sacred, their freedom and their democratic right to decide their destiny. All eight of the accused made contributions towards the destruction of our democratic way of life. The Red Hand agents and the trade unionists were the tools used by the Soviets to further their aims and ambitions for our country and for our colonies."

The judge interrupts the Crown barrister here to adjourn the court until Monday.

*

On Monday morning, the Crown continues with its summary, impressing on the jury that the very future of our way of life could rest on their verdict.

"This trial has not been about putting someone away so they cannot do any more harm in society. It's about sending a distinct message to those who would look to destroy our way of life. They have committed offences against all of us with their false dreams. They have attempted to destroy our trade union movement. This is part of the fabric of our society, the right of our working people to decide for themselves and negotiate a fair price for their labours. What they were endeavouring to replace the union movement with was an axis of evil intent. No more one man, one vote, but a State dictating what you can do and how it must be done. Your every move decided for you with no debate. That is what the accused were party to, a conspiracy against our people at home and abroad.

"It's not about the verdict, we all know they are guilty of conspiracy. What you have to decide is to what level each one of the accused is guilty. Now I'm sure you appreciate that they are not the only ones responsible. They are only a small number of the people plotting to destroy us. What we have to do here is send a message so severe in its response that it will deter any future conspirators. There is no maximum sentence for this crime, the judge can impose whatever tariff is appropriate to the findings of this trial. In times gone by they would most certainly have hanged for such a conspiracy. Today, there are choices to consider. They can be subjected to multiple tariffs if found guilty of all the charges. You also have to consider what connections they may have had with the appalling attacks on Mr and Mrs Bottomley. For those attacks alone they should be punished most severely. The abduction charges also carry a stiff sentence and you need to consider which of the accused were complicit. So you have heard the compounding evidence as to the conspiracy charges and I ask you to recommend maximum sentencing for all charges recorded against all of the accused."

The rest of Monday and Tuesday morning is taken up with arguments by the defence barristers.

They offer a range of mitigating circumstances as to why their clients should be found not guilty. Donald Capel, for Sally Nugent and Percival Smith, implies his clients knew nothing of a Soviet conspiracy. They were only trying to improve the conditions of their union members. John Griffiths, for Bill Hornsby and Jack Makepeace, claimed most of the evidence against his clients was fabricated by bribing the Crown witness with favours, and Bernard Johnson's clients refused to accept any of the evidence against them. It was all a conspiracy by the British government to undermine the legitimate operations of the British Communist Party.

"This government will resort to any dirty tricks at their disposal to alienate the working man from the communist ideal. They do not want the British people to know the truth of just what an alternative form of government has to offer. My clients were offering the unions a means of creating a workers utopia, their chance to be their own bosses and forge their own destiny," says Bernard Johnson with an air of conviction in his voice. He continues with his broadcast on behalf of the Communist Party with no real evidence of his client's innocence of the charges, just political rhetoric and communist dogma.

Donal Capel talks of his clients, Sally Nugent and Percival Smith, as though they were the victims of a communist plot and the vindictive actions of Mr and Mrs Bottomley. They had tried to further Polly's career in the Service by giving her responsibility within the Home Office.

She had spurned their offer and made up allegations of intimidation and assault and had tried to imply that they were implicit in the actions to overthrow the British government. This had not been proved by the Crown, says Donald Capel.

"My client's, hardworking Civil Servants, are the victims of a vicious smear campaign by the Crown using the evidence of Mrs Bottomley. Sally Nugent befriended this woman and wanted to promote her within the Home Office. She was rewarded for her efforts by Mrs Bottomley reporting her actions to the security services and implying that there was a conspiracy orchestrated by the so-called Red Hand organisation. Percival Smith, too, saw potential in Mrs Bottomley and offered to promote her within his office. She repaid him with accusations of impropriety, because he responded to her crude offers of favours to him in return for his help. She is a young and attractive woman who used her charms to snare a senior member of staff and destroy his career," Don Capel continues.

Indeed most of his defence summary is aimed at Mrs Bottomley. He implies gross abuse of trust by her and downright lies and deceit in her testimony. Realistically, he does not have any real proof of any of the claims he makes against Polly. Indeed, he has no evidence at all to substantiate his claims. His sole intention is to endeavour to put doubts in the jury's minds as to Polly's integrity, especially as her husband works with the security services. Eventually, the judge asks him to either qualify his accusations or sit down.

John Griffiths adopts a similar defence for his clients, Bill Hornsby and Jack Makepeace.

"I really do fear for democracy in our country when two union members, going about their legitimate business, are accused of conspiracy! My clients are dedicated members of the trade union movement and have been for many years. The evidence against them has been fabricated by the security services on the one hand, and by offering favours to Michael Doyle for testimony on the other. Just what those favours were, we can only guess, especially as Mrs Bottomley would seem to be involved with those favours," says John Griffiths. The rest of his summary, too, is littered with suggestions and innuendo against Mrs Bottomley and the security services.

Again, the judge becomes increasingly angered by his comments towards Polly and asks him to be more specific with his accusations or move on. It is a matter of fact that Griffiths has very little evidence in defence of his clients and concludes his defence. Justice Peter Thornton begins his summation on Tuesday after lunch.

"Conspiracy trials don't occur very often and when they do the evidence is usually very conclusive. This trial has been no exception. I do not propose to dwell on the politics of the evidence. I want to walk you through the facts against the defendants, beginning with Sally Nugent and Percival Smith. They were undoubtedly members of an illegal organisation, Red Hand, who sought to impose their membership on high office. Why did they want to do that? Well you will of course draw your own conclusions, but I would say that it is obvious. Their beliefs were in complete contrast to those of the democratically elected government, so it is not unreasonable to assume that their intentions were to change the beliefs of government with the insertion of their own members. Whatever your political persuasion is, whether you are sympathetic to their cause or not, you are here to decide on what their intentions were and to what lengths they conspired to achieve those intentions. You have heard testimony of meetings between them and Soviet representatives. "

"What was the purpose of those meetings? Was it to further the Soviet ambitions in our country? Were they just trying to improve their working conditions or was there a more sinister reasoning behind their activities? You may feel it was extremely naive of Sally Nugent to divulge the Red Hand operation to Mrs Bottomley. It was to lead to her downfall, Mrs Bottomley being involved with the security services. And Percival Smith proved himself to be completely out of his depth when given the responsibility of high office, seeing it as an opportunity to further his lust for a young woman. The actions of both of these defendants was very unprofessional to say the least, for very different reasons. So are they guilty of all the charges set against the defendants, namely conspiracy to commit espionage, conspiracy to overthrow the sovereign state and replace with a Soviet-controlled regime, and conspiracy to commit murder against British citizens to further their aims? I will continue with my summation in the morning, for now we are adjourned."

The judge resumes his summations on Wednesday, continuing to discuss the role played by Sally Nugent and Percival Smith.

"That these two defendants were the leading members of the Red Hand organisation is beyond doubt, and there will be a further trial of the other lesser members within the Home Office, at a later date. My recommendation to you is that they are complicit in the conspiracy here. Whether they were aware of the murderous intent towards Mr and Mrs Bottomley is for you to consider.

"My thoughts towards the guilt or not of Bill Hornsby and Jack Makepeace are somewhat muddled, I have to say. There is documented evidence that they conspired with Soviets, but did they really know what their intentions were or did they believe that they were only looking after the best interests of the trade unionists? I believe that both of them are intelligent men, who were well able to make up their own minds about whatever the Soviets had planned. They may have been offered inducements, they may have been promised high office in the trade union movement. But what is definitely a matter of fact is their absolute commitment to their cause, namely the Communist Party beliefs. That, they have made plain during union meetings. They wanted to further their cause through the trade union movement. You have to decide if their cause involved conspiracy to overthrow the government and replace it with a Soviet-controlled regime, and whether they would endorse the murderous intentions shown toward Mr and Mrs Bottomley. And finally, we come to the four Russian nationals in the dock. They live in a world where if you are caught, you are guilty. If you are not, then you are presumed innocent. These four men have been caught by the security services holding meetings with the other accused. They were not discussing the weather, of that we can be sure. So what could they possibly have been discussing? Were they conspiring with the other accused to overthrow our government? Were they conspiring to replace our government with a Soviet-style regime? And would they go to any lengths, including attempting to murder British citizens, in order to achieve their aims? You have to consider those facts in the face of overwhelming evidence of their guilt. Please go and consider those facts and record your verdicts." The judge concludes his summary.

The jury is in discussion for all of Thursday. They ask the judge for advice on two occasions, mainly on sentencing tariffs and how they will be met. At ten o'clock on Friday morning they are ready to announce their verdicts.

Polly and Daniel arrived at the court at nine o'clock. Daniel is well on the way to recovery from his latest operation and has been well cared for by Polly. They would not answer any questions from the press, saying only that they would comment when the judge had passed sentence on the accused. In the courtroom, they sit side by side while the judge introduces proceedings. The jury confirm that they have reached verdicts on which they all agree, on all eight of the accused.

"On the charge of conspiracy to commit treason, how do you find Sally Nugent and Percival Smith?"

"Guilty, my lord."

"On the charge of conspiracy to overthrow the sovereign state and replace it with a Soviet-controlled regime, how do you find Sally Nugent and Percival Smith?"

"Guilty, my lord."

"And on the charge of conspiracy to commit murder against British citizens, how do you find Sally Nugent and Percival Smith?"

"Not guilty, my lord."

"On the charge of conspiracy to commit treason, how do you find Bill Hornsby and Jack Makepeace?"

"Guilty, my lord."

"On the charge of conspiracy to overthrow the sovereign state and replace it with a Soviet-controlled regime, how do you find Bill Hornsby and Jack Makepeace?"

"Guilty, my lord."

"And on the charge of conspiracy to commit murder against British citizens, how do you find Bill Hornsby and Jack Makepeace?"

"Not guilty, my lord."

"On the charge of espionage against the British people, how do you find Sergey Sokolov, Mikhail Litvin, Leonid Rafikov, and Boris Ruchkin?"

"Guilty, my lord."

"On the charge of conspiracy to overthrow the sovereign state and replace it with a Soviet-controlled regime, how do you find Sergey Sokolov, Mikhail Litvin, Leonid Rafikov, and Boris Ruchkin?"

"Guilty, my lord."

"And on the charge of conspiracy to commit murder against British citizens, how do you find Sergey Sokolov, Mikhail Litvin, Leonid Rafikov, and Boris Ruchkin?"

"Guilty, my lord."

On hearing this last result there are cheers around the court and protests from the Russians in the dock. The judge adjourns the court for lunch, saying he will pass sentences at two o'clock, and at two o'clock precisely, the judge returns.

"Before passing sentence, may I thank the jury for their deliverance of their verdicts. The trial has heightened emotions for many people. Espionage and treason trials will always be emotional and controversial and this one was no exception. Sally Nugent and

Percival Smith, please stand. You have been found guilty of treason against your fellow citizens, and conspiracy to overthrow the sovereign state and replace it with a Soviet-controlled regime.

"You will go to prison for fourteen years on both counts and your sentences will run consecutively.

"Bill Hornsby and Jack Makepeace, please stand. You have been found guilty of treason against your fellow citizens, and conspiracy to overthrow the sovereign state and replace it with a Soviet-controlled regime. You will go to prison for fourteen years on both counts and your sentences will run consecutively.

"Sergey Sokolov, Mikhail Litvin, Leonid Rafikov, and Boris Ruchkin, please stand. You have been found guilty of espionage against the British people, guilty of conspiracy to overthrow the sovereign state and replace it with a Soviet-controlled regime, and guilty of conspiracy to commit murder against British citizens. You will go to prison for fourteen years on each of the three counts and your sentences are to run consecutively. Furthermore, on completion of your sentences you will be sent back to your country. Bailiffs, take them all to the cells."

The judge pauses for a moment before continuing.

"Before we adjourn, I would like to pay special tribute to Mr and Mrs Bottomley for their services in bringing the accused to trial. Their personal sacrifices in securing the evidence deserve special mention, and I am sure the nation will see that they are duly rewarded. You are indeed a remarkable couple and this country owes you a debt of gratitude," the judge says, looking directly at Polly and Daniel. "This court is now adjourned."

Polly and Daniel leave the courtroom to the applause of everyone present, and including those in the gallery. The trial has been a long one and they have become household names as a result of their activities. They are both somewhat embarrassed by all the attention the press and the BBC television cameras give them and find all of the publicity somewhat overwhelming. Polly is especially sought after. Being so young and strikingly attractive, with her long dark hair and slim figure, the press and public love her, wanting to know more about this young heroine. Polly, for her part, never strays far from Daniel's side, a point which does not go unnoticed. Daniel himself is also asked for interviews, and the public is fascinated about his contribution in bringing so many communists to justice, and they just love the idea of him rescuing Polly from the Russian bear! They both thank the press for all their kind comments as they are driven away from the Old Bailey.

CHAPTER 13

So Friday brings the end of the week and Polly and Daniel believe they can begin to get back to some normality in their lives. Daniel's wound infection has healed and Polly is looking forward to planning their reception.

"I have pencilled in 22nd or 29th November for our party, Daniel. It's only three or four weeks away, and the Savoy will be having Christmas booking shortly, I am sure. I will make a list over this weekend and you must add whoever you wish," says Polly, as she prepares them an evening meal. Although the trial is now over, Polly and Daniel are still very much in the press headlines, but hope that they will not be news for much longer.

"I long for it to be just you and me again," she says, as she curls up beside him after their meal.

"It will be soon, but I have been very proud of how you have handled the press. They all love you, Polly," he says, turning toward her and kissing her on her lips. Polly responds passionately, climbing on top of Daniel. Because of Daniel's injury, it has been a while since they made love, and Polly seizes the moment.

"Take me to bed, Daniel. I want us to make love."

Daniel carries her through to the bedroom and they quickly undress and climb into bed.

"I enjoyed that very much, Mr Bottomley, and thank you."

"And thank you, Mrs Bottomley, it was my pleasure."

"I think I will have a bath before bedtime, I want to be clean and fresh for whatever may happen later," she says, as she leaps out of bed laughing.

They enjoy their Saturday, not doing anything special, just being together. In the evening, they go out for a meal, and they enjoy being able to just be themselves. The main topic of conversation is the reception to be organised at the Savoy.

"I have made a list of some of the guests, Daniel, but it seems to go on forever, it will cost an absolute fortune you know."

"No matter, Polly, it is a once-in-a-lifetime occasion and I want you to have everything that you deserve. And it will give us the opportunity to meet with all of our friends again."

"Thank you Daniel, now let's go home, I am feeling rather tired!" she says with a big smile on her face. They leave the restaurant and call a taxi. They stop outside the apartment block and Daniel notices a van parked a few yards down from the apartment entrance. Then, as the taxi drives off, the van accelerates across the road, driving towards them. The passenger fires several rounds at Daniel, who responds shooting several times at the windscreen, pushing Polly out of the way of the speeding vehicle. The van crashes into the front of the adjoining block, both the occupants dead from gunshot wounds to the head. However, Polly has been hit by a stray bullet and lies bleeding on the pavement.

"Daniel, please, I think I have been shot!" she shouts, holding her chest.

"Good god, Polly. What have they done to you?" he screams as he dashes to her side, carefully pulling her jacket to one side to reveal that Polly has been shot in the upper part of her chest and is bleeding heavily.

"Stay still, Polly, the ambulance is on its way. You will be fine, I promise you."

"Are you ok Daniel, are you hurt?" she asks. So typical of Polly, looking out for him as always.

"I am fine, Polly, please keep still, you are bleeding quite heavily," he replies with some concern.

The ambulance arrives and Polly is given emergency treatment before being driven to hospital. St Mary's is just over a mile away and when they arrive, she is rushed straight into emergency to be assessed.

"How bad is it, Doctor, will she be ok?" asks Daniel, panicking over Polly's injuries.

"We have to remove the bullet as soon as possible, Mr Bottomley, but first we have to establish just where it is so we will take an x-ray of her upper chest area."

"May I see her please?"

"Well just for a moment, then we must get on."

Daniel goes into the room where Polly is and is shocked by what he sees. She is covered in blood around her left breast and is deathly pale, but her eyes light up when she sees him.

"Daniel, I knew you'd come, I feel so tired. You will stay, won't you?"

"I will be here by your side, Polly."

She is taken from the side ward and Daniel stays with her, holding on to her hand.

"The doctors will take care of you, Polly, I will be here when you return," he says with tears in his eyes as his beloved Polly is taken into the operating room.

"Don't worry, Mr Bottomley, we will take good care of her," the doctor reassures him.

He calls Conrad who says he will be along as soon as possible, then sits down with his head in his hands. Polly has been shot and her life is in the balance. He has never felt so helpless, but all he can do is wait. He doesn't want to call home until he has some definite news, so he just sits and waits, then stands and walks up and down, until after what seems an age the doctor appears.

"Your wife will be fine Mr Bottomley, we have removed the bullet and she will be out shortly. She has some damage to the pectoral muscle in her upper chest area. There is a tear, but there is no reason why it should not fully heal, and she is young so she will soon be back on her feet. Any scarring will be minimal, although it may be visible when she wears some items of clothing."

"Thank you so much, Doctor. May I see her now please?"

"Of course, this way."

The doctor shows Daniel to a side room where Polly is resting, still drowsy from the anaesthetic. He goes to her and clasps her hand. She opens her eyes and instantly recognises him.

"Daniel, I feel like I have been run over by a bus."

"You will be ok, Polly, but having had a bullet removed you are bound to feel a bit sore."

"Did you get the men who tried to run us over?"

"I did and they will not be harming anyone again. Now I need to phone home and let your family know what has happened," Daniel replies, just as the doctor arrives. He opens Polly's gown to reveal bruising developing on her chest around the wound.

"The bruising is from the muscle reacting to the damage. It's a good sign, indicating that does not appear to be any complications, Mrs Bottomley."

"Thank you, Doctor. Will I be able to go home tomorrow?"

"As long as your body continues to heal, you should be able to leave around lunchtime. For now though, you need to rest."

"Thank you, Doctor. Now Polly, you rest while I phone home, I will be back in a while."

"You need a change of clothes, Daniel, you are covered in blood."

Daniel looks down at his jacket and his shirt, both soaked with Polly's blood, and goes to wash his hands which also have blood on them. He is just about to make his call when Conrad arrives.

"My god, Daniel. Don't these people ever give up? How is Polly?"

"She's recovering well, no complications so I hope to take her home tomorrow. Could you fetch me some clean clothes? I am going to stay here."

"Of course, I'll get onto that straightaway."

The call to Polly's parents is very distressing, Margaret is obviously in tears and Ben is also struggling. That something like this should happen to their daughter is beyond belief.

"My god, Daniel. These people they should be dealt with severely."

"Those concerned have been dealt with, Ben, they are both dead."

"And no more than they deserve. We will come to London tomorrow, we must see Polly."

"Of course, Ben. I hope to take her home in the morning, but will confirm it with you as soon as I know."

"Thank you. Please give her all our love, bye for now."

Daniel looks at his watch, it is almost midnight. Conrad returns to find Daniel sitting beside Polly, who is sleeping.

"She was lucky in a way, Conrad. That bullet could have killed her."

"Well she will be fine, I'm sure, and she will be in good hands. I will give you a call on Sunday, anything you need, let me know. Bye for now."

"Bye Conrad, and thanks."

Daniel goes back to Polly's beside and a nurse asks him if he would like some tea, which he welcomes. He looks down at her, realising just how much she means to him. She is his whole life, nothing else matters, he lives only for her. To lose her would have been the end of his world. Polly, meanwhile, sleeps soundly all night with Daniel sleeping beside her in a chair. He is woken by Polly around six o'clock.

"Daniel, wake up, I need the bathroom!"

He calls the nurse, who fetches a bedpan.

"I would prefer to walk to a toilet if I may, please, Nurse."

"Very well. I will fetch a chair for you, Mrs Bottomley."

Daniel wheels her to the toilet and she washes while she is there, dampening her hair before asking the nurse if she might have a comb. Daniel tells Polly that he has spoken with her parents and will call them again as soon as the doctor confirms that she can go home.

"They should be along later today."

"Really, Daniel? It will be so nice to have them close by. I just hope Doctor allows me home."

The doctor finally makes his call just after eight o'clock to look at Polly's wound, and is pleased to announce that it is healing well.

"Does that mean I can go home, Doctor?"

"Absolutely, Mrs Bottomley. I will arrange for an ambulance, but take it easy, we do not want the internal stitching to break loose. I suggest you call back on Monday afternoon, when I will have another look and change the dressing."

"Thank you very much, Doctor," Daniel replies as he helps Polly to dress, which is rather awkward since her arm is in a sling to stop any excess movement. She only has a sweater to wear, supplied by one of the nurses, since her shirt and jacket are covered in bloodstains. Then, after the short journey by ambulance, Daniel helps her into their apartment.

"I will call your home before I do anything, and you can have a word."

"Polly, my dear Polly, are you ok?"

"I am ok, Daddy. Really I am, and Daniel is looking after me now we are back home."

"We shall be along as soon as we can catch a train, probably later this afternoon.'

Polly also speaks with Margaret who becomes very tearful, as do the children.

"I am ok now, Mummy. Really I am. Give my love to Maisy, Daisy, and George, and we will see you shortly," she says, hoping to reassure her parents.

"Daniel, I would really love a bath to get rid of the hospital smell. Can you help me please?"

He runs Polly's bath and helps her undress, then supports her as she slowly sits down. He leaves her to soak for a while before returning to help her wash. It's at times like this that he realises just how beautiful his wife is, even with her shoulder strapped and still showing signs of the rope marks on her ankles and wrists from her abduction. When he has finished washing her he gently dries her all over before handing her the towel, then between them they manage to wash her hair and dress her. When they have finished, they sit down together, Daniel holding her hand and Polly resting her head on his shoulder, both very relaxed in each other's company. Then the doorbell rings, and Daniel opens the door to D.I. Manners and W.P.C. Becky Peters.

"Please come in, Detective Inspector, we have not long got back from St Mary's."

"I hope we have not called at a bad time, Daniel, only I was hoping to get your statements while the incident is still fresh in your minds."

"That's fine, Detective Inspector," he replies, as he and Polly relate the events of Saturday.

Polly's parents arrive around one o'clock and are relieved to see their daughter looking so well.

"We didn't know what to expect. We remembered when you were shot, Daniel, and you looked terrible," comments Margaret.

"I am feeling fine, Mummy. A bit sore, but the doctor was pleased how well I had healed in such a short time."

"I assume the damage outside is from the van that tried to run you down?"

"Yes Ben, it was fortunate that I noticed them as we left the taxi."

"Now Polly, let me get some lunch. What do you have in the kitchen?"

Polly's parents spend the weekend with them before returning home on Sunday afternoon. They were both so relieved to see their daughter recovering from yet another ordeal.

"Let us know what the doctor says, Polly, and take care of yourself, my dear."

"I will be fine, Daddy, really."

Daniel decides that he will take the next week off to look after Polly, a point that Fitz readily agrees to when Daniel speaks with him on Monday morning, before he takes Polly for her hospital check.

"Take as much time as you wish, Daniel. Polly is precious to all of us, so look after her."

"Thank you Fitz, I appreciate that."

At the hospital, the doctor carefully examines Polly's wound.

"You seem to be healing well, Mrs Bottomley," he says, as he carefully examines the affected area for any signs of swelling or tenderness.

"How do you feel yourself?"

"I feel fine, Doctor. Thank you."

"Good. Well I will get the nurse to dress the wound for you and suggest you call back on Friday to have the stitches removed. If there are any signs of swelling or tenderness, please come back immediately."

"Ok. Thank you, Doctor."

After having the wound dressed they return to their apartment where Polly busies herself with arrangements for the reception after securing the date of Saturday 22nd November with the Savoy Hotel.

"The Savoy have asked for an approximate number of guests so we need to make a list as soon as possible. We will have at least fifty guests as a guide for the hotel to work with. I would prefer a buffet to a formal seats round a table reception. That way we can mingle with our guests, and it is always difficult to know who to sit next to who anyway when everyone is seated. I think a buffet will be best, I am not keen on the formal sit-down myself, and it will be good to mingle and chat with colleagues who we may not have seen for a while," says Polly.

So over the next few of days, they confirm the invitation list and send out the cards with the RSVPs attached. Polly will get a new gown as soon as they can get into town. On Friday they return to the hospital for Polly to have her stitches removed. Her wound has closed and the doctor covers it with a plaster to prevent any garment rubbing.

"I should remove the plaster after a couple of days and leave the wound to air. And I think that is all for now, Mrs Bottomley."

"Thank you, Doctor. Thank you very much."

Polly calls home after lunch, and asks her parents if they might go home for the weekend. It is Daniel's birthday and it would be nice to celebrate with the family.

"Polly, what a wonderful idea. I mentioned to Daddy that we would like to see you again as soon as you were recovered, and have a celebration for Daniel. Will you be here for dinner?"

Polly asks Daniel if they can be there for dinner and he readily agrees, so they pack a bag, call a taxi, and arrive at Euston Station in time for the three o'clock train. They have an uneventful journey, and eventually arrive at Polly's home around six o'clock. As usual, they are mobbed by the children, who are always so delighted to see their sister and Daniel.

"Polly, what happened? How are you? Mummy said you'd been shot," they chorus.

"Did you get the men that hurt Polly, Daniel?"

"I did, George, and they won't be hurting anyone else."

"Come along children, let Polly and Daniel get inside the house please."

"Sorry, Mummy, we just miss them so much, don't we Maisy?" says Daisy.

They settle down in the parlour and George insists that Polly show him her scar.

"Yes, ok George, and then perhaps Daniel and I can go and unpack?" she says as she exposes her wound for the benefit of George and everyone.

"It could have been so much worse, my dear Polly," says Ben, relieved to see how well the wound has healed.

After dinner, Polly discusses the reception arrangements with Margaret while Daniel goes with Ben into the study.

"How do you read this last attempt, Daniel? Are the Russians still determined to get rid of you one way or the other?"

"I believe the threat will be with us for some time, Ben. I will continue to give Polly all the protection I can, and we will carry our weapons at all times. But we will not allow the threat to affect our lives together. At the moment Polly is busy organising our reception."

"Thank you for that, Daniel. As usual you have a way of reassuring me."

"I think we all have to accept that she is destined for high office in the Service, Ben, with all the responsibility that high office will carry. She is very ambitious and her strength of character far exceeds her age. You must be very proud of her, she really is rather special."

Polly, meanwhile, is going over the guest list with Margaret.

"I thought I might invite Valerie Oakes from school. And Peter and Maureen of course, as well as Beatrice Carrington. Then there is Aunty Pauline and Uncle John."

"You could make contact with most of them while you are here this weekend."

"That's a good idea, Mummy, I will do just that and save some time. I do so much want the reception to be special."

Polly is awake early on the Saturday morning to wish Daniel a very happy birthday.

"Good morning Daniel and a very happy birthday. I will be collecting your present later but would like to give you a little something in the meantime," she says, smiling as she pleasures him before they enjoy some early morning love making.

Later in the morning, Polly goes shopping with Margaret and collects Daniel's present. She has arranged to have some gold cufflinks engraved with his initials at the jeweller's in Cresswell.

When they return, she makes contact with the guests she mentioned and they are all delighted to have been invited. Peter and Maureen Forsyth mention how much they look forward meeting up with so many friends again. Valerie Oakes is also very pleased to be invited and Polly suggests she joins the family for lunch today.

"It's so nice to see you again, and many congratulations to you and Daniel. I think we all knew that you would get married someday," she says, as she hugs Polly.

"I think I have always loved him, Val, and I know I always will," Polly replies, smiling. The two of them chat over lunch, catching up mostly on local news, Polly not wishing to go over the unpleasant ordeals that she and Daniel have been through.

"We have read some of the details about you both, Polly. Are you fully recovered now? What has happened must have been very frightening."

"Yes, it was terrifying and once again my Daniel saved me. I can't tell you how much I love him but I'm sure it is obvious for all to see."

So Val and Polly say their goodbyes, Val saying how much she is looking forward to the reception. The rest of the weekend passes all too quickly for everyone, Polly finalising reception details with Margaret, before she and Daniel set off back to London on Sunday afternoon.

"I am looking forward to returning to work tomorrow, Daniel. It seems ages since I was there."

"Just takes things easy on your first day, Polly, please."

They both return to their offices on Monday, and Polly is given a warm reception by all of her office colleagues. They have followed the events of the trial closely and appreciate the effort that she has put into the convictions of the accused.

"We are all very proud of you, Polly, and hope you are fully recovered from your most recent setback?"

"Yes I am, thank you, David. I want to get back to normal as quickly as possible, I am sure there is a lot to do."

"Peter and I have kept things running smoothly, Polly, but there are a number of documents for your attention," Rachel says.

Daniel, too, has some catching up to do and sits down to meet with Fitz and Conrad. With the Red Hand organisation closed down, all efforts have been directed towards securing agreement within the union movement and the management. Michael Doyle has been leading the dockers in their meetings with management and has proved a tough negotiator. However, the meetings have been constructive and both sides are working to secure a long-lasting agreement. What is noticeable is Doyle has chosen a team for the talks with communist backgrounds, but no allegiances to Moscow.

"After what happened with your Polly, Daniel, we have to remain vigilant as to the threat towards both of you still being very real. In fact the threat in general still remains, as I am sure they will not take defeat graciously. I suggest you keep in contact with both Peter Hennessey and Michael Doyle as they could prove worthy allies in this fight against the Soviets," Fitz concludes.

For the remainder of the week both Daniel and Polly work hard to get their prospective workloads back on track and welcome the arrival of the weekend before their reception. They have arranged a trip into town to buy their clothes for their special occasion. Daniel has no difficulty arranging his wardrobe through Moss Bros, in Covent Garden. Polly however, takes a little more time before deciding on her dress of black lace. When they have completed their shopping, they call on the Savoy to finalise next Saturday's reception. The events manager Roland Palmerston is very accommodating, realising the significance of his two guests.

"The Savoy is delighted to have you as their guests, Mr and Mrs Bottomley, and would like to offer you one of our Riverview suites for your overnight stay with our compliments. I'm sure you will find it suitable."

"Thank you very much, Mr Palmerston. Daniel and I are delighted to accept your hospitality. Now perhaps you can go over the buffet menu for us. As Daniel will have mentioned, we are expecting to have around fifty guests and are looking to have a start at about four o'clock."

Polly and Daniel follow Roland Palmerston into his office and spend some time going over the details of the reception. Once all the arrangements have been finalised Daniel speaks with the manager.

"As you know if you have been following the trial, both Polly and I have been involved in a number of attacks and abductions prior to securing the convictions of most of those responsible."

"Yes indeed, Mr Bottomley, and I understand that you have recently suffered an attack which resulted in a gunshot wound, Mrs Bottomley. I trust you are fully recovered?"

"Yes, thank you Mr Palmerston."

"To continue, Mr Palmerston, I have arranged that four of my colleagues be ushers at the reception, I will see that you get their details. They will in fact take care of our security measures. Polly and I are under no illusions about possible further attacks on ourselves or our colleagues so do not wish to leave anything to chance."

"Good heavens, Mr Bottomley, you do not think the Russians will attempt to disrupt your reception do you?"

"I certainly hope not."

"Well, I thank you for your honesty, I will inform our security officer of your comments." And with a final word from Polly that they will contact him on Friday afternoon with any last minute adjustments, they leave the Savoy and head back to Kensington.

"I had no idea we would be staying overnight at the Savoy, Daniel. That was a complete surprise."

"Well I am sure we shall make the very best of the surprise, Polly!"

The weekend and the following week fly by, with Polly combining her work with final reception arrangements. All her guests have responded to their invitations and Polly and Daniel decide they will make it a long weekend, returning to Kingston-on-Thames on the Sunday for a few days.

They sit together at the end of the week, checking everything is in place for tomorrow's reception. "I think we have everything organised now, Daniel. Mummy and Daddy and the children will arrive here around noon, then they can all change ready to go to the Savoy. You and I will be there no later than 3.30pm to check on any last-minute details with Mr Palmerston."

"Don't forget to pack whatever you need for our stay in Kingston."

"Gosh, I almost forgot, Daniel, thank you for a wonderful idea. You are the most wonderful husband in the world and I love you so much," she says, kissing him passionately. Daniel responds as they embrace before looking at each other, then slowly rising from the settee and moving off towards their bedroom.

"Daniel, Daniel, my wonderful Daniel," says Polly as she embraces him again, feeling his firmness as they begin to undress. They continue with their naked embrace as they both explore each other, becoming more and more excited. Polly feels Daniel, stroking and rubbing him, then continues to excite him orally, Daniel moaning with pleasure at her touch. They explore each other as they have never done, before Daniel slowly glides inside Polly to her gasps of pleasure. Their lovemaking seems to go on forever, before finally, they lie in each other's arms, bathed in sweat after their exertions.

"I love you Mr Bottomley, I love you so very much."

"And I love you too, Mrs Bottomley."

They continue to lie in each other's arms, savouring the moment before going off to sleep. They awake after about an hour and Polly goes off to have a bath while Daniel lies contented, looking forward to their special day tomorrow. He finally gets up and goes to the kitchen to make some tea and look for something for dinner. After dinner, they sit together before going off to bed, chatting about the very special day to come. They have been through some terrible ordeals during the year and their love and devotion for each other has helped them to endure. Many people would not have survived, but Daniel's determination and resolve coupled with Polly's courage has seen them through every adversity. No two people could be better suited to each other, as events over the coming years will prove. Fate brought them together five years ago, when Polly, still a schoolgirl, was subjected to the most horrifying experiences imaginable, to be rescued time and again by Daniel, who became her hero, her saviour, her benefactor, then finally her husband.

"Goodnight Polly," says Daniel, kissing her gently.

"Goodnight Daniel," Polly replies, as they lie down together and fall into a deep and contented sleep.

The following morning, Daniel and Polly go into town to collect their clothes for the reception. Polly's dress is black lace with short sleeves, the shape and style showing off Polly's slim figure perfectly.

"My dear Polly, you look absolutely stunning, doesn't she Ben?"

"Thank you Mummy, I am waiting on two of my friends to help me with my hair, then I will be ready to go."

The children are getting very excited as the time passes and have new outfits to wear for the occasion and Ben and Margaret too are looking forward to the special day.

Finally, after having a sandwich and tea for lunch, Polly and Daniel leave to be at the Savoy by three o'clock. Daniel's four colleagues are already in place, waiting on his arrival.

"Polly, let me introduce you to Ricky Walton, Jeremy Blythe, Paul

Jefferson, and Mickie Palmer. I have asked them to act officially as ushers and watch over proceedings for us."

"I'm very pleased to meet all of you, and thank you for helping us on this special day."

"It will be our pleasure, Polly, anything to help you and Daniel," Ricky Walton replies.

"I have arranged with the manager that he will introduce the guests from their invitations, Ricky and Jeremy will tick them off the list and usher them into the function room, where Polly and I will be waiting to greet them. That way we will not have any unwelcome visitors and we will be able to determine whether any of the guests have failed to arrive. Paul and Mickie will be inside the function room. It is a beautiful setting, but it does overlook the Thames so they will keep an eye on things for us."

"You seem to have thought of everything, Daniel, thank you."

"Only being careful, Polly. I will not let anything or anyone spoil our special day."

After finalising with his colleagues, Polly and Daniel admire the beautiful function room, with its views of the Thames, while they wait to greet their guests. Mr Palmerston has agreed with them that the buffet will be available from five o'clock, with drinks available for the guests as they arrive.

"This is going to be the most wonderful day for us, Daniel. All our friends and family celebrating with us our marriage. I love you so much."

"Thank you, Polly," says Daniel, holding her close before kissing her on her cheek.

The first to arrive are Polly's family, followed by Conrad who has managed to find out that Margaret's sister Pauline is not with her husband. It has been some while since he has seen her and they are both obviously delighted to see each other again. As the guests continue to arrive Polly glows with contentment, soaking up the occasion. Once all the guests have been accounted for, the doors of the function room are closed with Ricky and Jeremy remaining outside. Inside, Polly and Daniel are mingling with their guests, some of them they have not seen for some time.

"Beatrice, how nice to see you again, and thank you for coming."

"My pleasure, Daniel. Hello again, Polly. You look delightful my dear."

"Thank you, Beatrice."

Polly then notices Peter Forsyth with Maureen and goes over to say hello. She has never forgotten Peter and how he was there to take care of her before Daniel arrived.

"Polly my dear, do come along and meet the wife."

"Hello Fitz. I'm delighted to meet you, Mrs Fitzroy Jones."

"Didn't I tell you what a beautiful young woman she was, Ruth?"

"Hello Polly, yes, Fitz has told me all about you, and hello Daniel. What a marvellous occasion for both of you after all that has happened."

Daniel notices Peter Hennessey and Michael Doyle and they both go and say hello to them. They appear to be overawed by the occasion, so Polly does her best to make them feel at ease.

"Michael, Peter, a bit more upmarket than the Lamb and Flag, but I do hope you will enjoy it with us today."

"Thank you Polly, it is not quite what I expected but it's good to be able to share your special day and meet with some of your friends," replies Michael Doyle.

"Polly, you look absolutely stunning," says Rachel Nichols, who has just spotted Polly. They are standing with David Fellows and Marjorie Warner and Polly greets them all again.

"Thanks for the compliment, Rachel. Daniel and I are so pleased that you were all able to come."

"And thank you for inviting us, this is quite an occasion for you both," David Fellows replies.

Polly looks out for her school friends so that she may be able to introduce them to Penny Carstairs. She notices them and walks across with Daniel.

"Penny, let me introduce you to two of my school friends Val and Veronica."

"Polly, you look wonderful," says Val after the introductions.

And so they continue to say hello to each and every one of their guests before the announcement of the arrival of the buffet. The tables are arranged informally, so there is no seating plan. Polly and Daniel sit with her parents and the children, who chatter, excited by the occasion.

"Will we be able to dance after eating, Poll?"

"Yes of course, Maisy."

"Good. So will you dance with me, Daniel, please?"

"Absolutely, Maisy."

After about half an hour of guests sampling the buffet, Ben goes up to the small platform and asks if everyone will pause for a moment.

"I hope you all will indulge me for a moment to say a few words on this very special occasion. We are here to celebrate the marriage of two very special people, my darling daughter Polly and Daniel, truly a remarkable young man. During the five years or so that they have known each other, Polly and Daniel have been the subject of vicious and concerted attempts to harm them. But they have endured, and in adversity have grown to love each other. Circumstances brought them together, and those circumstances would eventually form the basis of their love for each other.

"Some of you know Polly from those early years, others from her employ in the Civil Service. She has matured from a schoolgirl into a young woman over these years, helped by her relationship with Daniel. And Daniel, my dear friend, has proved so many times to be the man to save her from adversity. These two people deserve to be with each other and I ask you to drink to their health and their life together. To Polly and Daniel."

Ben ends his speech to be greeted by applause and cheers as Fitz walks to the small stage.

"Hello everyone, my name is Fitz and I am acquainted with both Polly and Daniel from their workplace.

"Now I am not the sort to heap praise lightly, but I have to say that these two people are quite the most remarkable I have ever known. I am sure Polly won't mind when I say that she is only eighteen years old and yet she has shown a level of maturity far beyond her years in how she has worked to bring down subversives in the Service, while being subjected to some terrible ordeals. She has endured through her partnership and love for Daniel, one of the most remarkable young men it has ever been my pleasure to meet. Polly and Daniel were made for each other and I ask you to join me in wishing them long life and happiness."

Again there is a long round of applause. After it has subsided, Polly and Daniel move forward, and Daniel hands Polly the microphone.

"Thank you Daddy and thank you Fitz for your wonderful compliments. Daniel and I are delighted to see you all here today and thank you very much for coming. We apologise for the initial secrecy about our marriage, but at the time it was decided that it was best kept from common knowledge. In fact we did not intend marrying until after the trial, but decided we couldn't wait any longer! It is true, Daniel is very special to me and to my family and I love him very much. He would never admit to this but many of you are aware of how he has always been there for me. What you may not be so aware of is the cost he has paid for saving me so many times.

"He is my saviour as well as my husband and I know I speak for my family when I thank him for being there for all of us. So before we continue, I ask you to drink to Daniel, my very special husband," says Polly, leaning toward Daniel and kissing him.

The cheers die down and everyone surges forward to engulf Polly and Daniel as the music begins. For the rest of the evening, entertainment is the order of the day as the guests enjoy the fine music of the band. Polly dances with many of her guests, and especially enjoys dancing with her Daddy. Daniel entertains both Maisy and Daisy, who both prove to be very good dancers, and Conrad spends a great deal of time with Pauline. Polly also spends some time talking with her friends again, then around nine o'clock, during a break, Ben goes to the stage.

"Before we continue ladies and gentlemen, I think we should introduce Polly and Daniel to their surprise."

The doors open and two trolleys are pushed in laden with gifts for Polly and Daniel. Both of them had no idea that this was going to happen and Polly is completely overcome. Daniel takes her hand and leads her to the stage.

"This is a most wonderful surprise and we thank you all very much. I'm sure Polly agrees, but for once she is speechless," he says, holding her tightly. They decide to leave the present opening until they return home and carry on with the dancing. The rest of the evening races by and soon it is time for some of the guests to depart. Daniel and Polly make sure they say goodbyes to everyone leaving, including a special thank you to his four colleagues who have watched over the proceedings, before settling down for a nightcap with Polly's family.

Then after enjoying a rapturous night together in a luxury suite, they join with Polly's parents for breakfast, before setting off for Kingston-on-Thames for a well-earned few days break.

*

On returning to their work, there will be much to do to ensure that all of their efforts over the year have not been for nothing. They have to be sure that the Soviet threat is suitably contained.

It will not go away, it will never go away, but they will continue to do everything in their power to stop it being significant. For the time being all is quiet, probably because the Soviets need to regroup and see out the adverse publicity of the Old Bailey trial.

Then, just before Christmas, Polly and Daniel receive news that they are to be honoured for their services, Polly to receive an MBE for outstanding service to her country and an example to others, and Daniel to receive a CBE for distinguished achievements for his country.

"This will be the best Christmas ever, Mummy, I just know it will," says Polly, as they arrive on Christmas Eve ready for the festivities.

And so it will prove to be just about the best Christmas the Spencer house has ever had. In the New Year, Polly and Daniel receive their awards and continue their fight against the Soviet menace. Polly especially will achieve high office in her fight, alongside Daniel, taking on the enemy in their very own backyard.

THE END

Made in the USA
Columbia, SC
17 January 2018